CW01508885

Unstable Prototypes

Joseph R. Lallo

Copyright ©2012 Joseph R. Lallo

All rights reserved.

ISBN: 1505791820
ISBN-13: 978-1505791822

Dedication

This book is dedicated to all of the good folks who liked *Bypass Gemini* enough to request a sequel!

Acknowledgements

I'd like to acknowledge Nick Deligaris (Deligaris.com) for his brilliant work on the cover, as well as Claudette Cruz and Anna Genoese for their help in cleaning up my grammar.

Prologue

"All right, boys. Ready for the show?"

The man speaking was named Karter. Actually, his name was much longer and more complicated than that, but since no one ever used more than the first two syllables, he'd stopped going any further. He was odd-looking, to say the least. His head, covered mostly with black hair threaded with gray, featured patches of immaculate, glossy black that would look more appropriate on a doll than a man. His face was mostly typical of an aging man who has shown no interest in taking care of himself, but patches managed to look as smooth and pristine as that of a newborn. As a whole, the bizarre features would likely have been enough to push him into the so-called "uncanny valley" reserved for androids, bad special effects, and other not-quite-right humanoids, but one in particular was outright wrong. His right iris, rather than matching the hazel color of his left, had a mirror finish. A pair of dark goggles was perched on his forehead, and he was wearing arctic gear.

Among any other group of people, he would have stood out like a sore thumb. The three men who joined him, however, made him look positively mundane by comparison. Each was dressed for cold weather, sporting the sort of shiny, synthetic outerwear that mountain climbers favor. Equally synthetic headgear, gloves, and boots were joined by almost comically oversized goggles blinking here and there with the telltale indicator lights of electronics. What little flesh was exposed was unfailingly marred by burns, both chemical and thermal, scars, stitches, grafts, and--where possible--tattoos.

"We are quite ready, Mr. Dee. I am optimistic that you are able to provide a tool that meets our very specific requirements," said the man who was unquestionably their leader.

"Minimal structural and biological impact, maximal electronic and technological? Not an uncommon request. Getting things to work on the scale you're looking for would normally be tricky, but, lucky for you, a prior party requested something similar a few years back. Right, so, let's get started."

The group was standing in the middle of a seemingly endless field of broken, cratered ground. A gray sky, scattered with wispy white clouds, offered little in the way of light and nothing in the way of warmth. A crust of ice covered everything, crunching underfoot as Karter approached one of a handful of complex-looking bits of equipment in their immediate area. A base approximately the size of a fifty-five-gallon drum and constructed from shiny metal panels was topped with a trio of spindly metallic arms, studded with small discs, and tracing out the rough shape of a globe. On the side of the base was a hefty, Frankenstein-style knife switch, and dangling above it was what appeared to be a pipe bomb attached by quick-release to a flimsy gantry. He pulled down his goggles and leaned down toward it, but a message assembled out of at least three female voices crackled across a speaker somewhere beneath his coat, interrupting him.

"You should inform your guests of the safety precautions," said the message.

"Oh. Right. You boys might want to look away. Unless, of course, you want to know what your retinas smell like."

"Our goggles should provide adequate protection," the leader assured.

"Heh, you wouldn't believe the number of blind guys I know who said that."

With a quick flick of the switch, he stepped quickly away from the contraption and began heading toward a dilapidated hover-style school bus a few dozen yards away. Behind him, the contraption was humming, and the discs attached to the thin arms were glowing brightly.

A few seconds later, the rocky field was bathed in a light as bright as day, as a swirling mass of brilliantly shining light coalesced with a whoosh of sound. The three men turned suddenly away, shielding their eyes. By the time any of them could make anything out in the churning purple afterimages that were crowding their vision, they were seeing their host slip into the bus.

"Let's go, boys," he said impatiently.

The trio stumbled across the uneven ground and into the bus.

"Quite impressive, Mr. Dee," said the leader of the men, once the bus had started and was heading quickly away from the blinding device. "How quickly can you--"

"That's not the device you are after. That's part of the demo. It's a contained ball of helium and hydrogen plasma, the output of a small fusion reactor. It is there to provide us with a reasonable small scale analog of our reaction medium. That doodad hanging over it is the item of interest, the reaction trigger. One of these," he said, pulling out a device identical to the one hanging over the plasma.

"Indeed? And what of the rest of this?" asked the spokesmen of the group, indicating the bizarre assortment of devices that were whipping by outside the windows.

It was a collection of, it would seem, randomly selected objects. There were remote-controlled toys rolling and hovering about between street lamps, data terminals, hover cars, and even a small, hovering space vessel.

"Targets. A representative sampling of consumer electronics and infrastructure. Some on batteries, others hooked up to generators, and others hooked up to the grid. Right. Here we are."

They pulled up to what looked to be a fortified bunker. The plasma ball was a bright dot on the horizon.

"Get ready, and keep your eyes on the plasma," Karter said.

A few moments passed, the three visitors observing the now-distant ball of light with eyes just recovering from its ignition. When nothing seemed to be happening, the leader turned to address their host.

"What precisely are we--" he began, just in time to see the door click shut on the bunker.

"Activating," said Karter over a loudspeaker mounted on the bunker.

Before anyone could voice concerns about why he had seen fit to hide within the shelter and leave them outside, the tiny form of the pipe bomb released, dropping into the plasma. A moment passed, and then a massive lance of light burst out of the top of the plasma ball, curling into the sky like a silk ribbon drawn into a tornado. As quickly as it came, it was gone, but the effect it left in its wake was undeniable. Instantly, each of the devices and vehicles filling the field between the bunker and the test site failed simultaneously. Hovering devices dropped to the ground. Some of the less-potent gadgets fizzled with pops of electricity, and there was even a scattered spray of sparks from a few. Even as far away as they were, the PA speaker made a crackling hiss of failure and the hover bus momentarily shuddered.

The door to the bunker clicked open again, and Karter walked out.

"That was a directional emission, pointing straight up. What you witnessed happening to all of this crap in the field was just the collateral damage, so try to picture what it would have done if it was actually aimed at them."

"Unmistakably impressive," remarked the spokesman. He withdrew a business card-sized piece of electronics from his pocket. It flickered a few times, but finally activated, displaying a mildly scrambled welcome screen. "The effect was very brief, however. My slidepad is already coming back online."

"That's because the fusion reactor was taken out by the blast. Toss something like that into a reactor that can take the hit, or is self-sustaining, and that pulse becomes a continuous broadcast. And it scales linearly with the size of the reaction medium, so you can imagine what it would be like when you try it on the real deal."

"With any luck, I won't have to imagine it. How long would this broadcast last?"

"We've only ever deployed one of these in the field once. I think it lasted for three months. But that wasn't anywhere near optimized. It was a rush job. I figure we could get that up to a year pretty easily. And firing these things is all you'll have to do. Automated targeting makes them home in on their targets, automated defenses makes them impossible to disarm, and twilight drives keep them from being tracked by normal sensors."

"Excellent. You'll be coming with me, then. I'll need you to prepare a production facility so that we can maintain a ready supply," he said, tapping some commands into his rebooted pad.

"Nope. We do the production here. If you want reproduction rights, we are talking about a much larger fee. So--"

"Multiple unauthorized device deployments detected in and around the facility," the automated voice announced. "Electromagnetic pulse dev--"

The signal suddenly cut off in a burst of digital distortion. Karter's hand was already on the grip of a firearm at his belt, but a hypodermic injector was pressed to his neck and he collapsed to the ground.

"Lock coordinates and activate, radius six meters, centered on transmitting position," ordered the leader into his slidepad, as his men gathered up the unconscious inventor and clustered around.

A few moments later, there was a flash. When the dust cleared, the men, as well as a hemispherical bowl of rock and soil beneath where they had stood, were gone.

Chapter 1

Lex had certainly enjoyed more than his share of excitement in the past. His short but stellar career in the world of hoversled racing, one would imagine, would have been the high point so far. Failing that, it would certainly be a reasonable assumption that his ruinous fall from grace at the hands of a race he'd fixed against his will would have added plenty of undue excitement to his life. In truth, though, it all paled in comparison to the events of earlier that year when he had--through dumb luck and desperation as much as skill--managed to foil a plot that could have taken the lives of nearly half a million people, not to mention the star systems they called home. That little adventure was something he thought of as "the Bypass Gemini Incident." It had involved directly opposing VectorCorp, the largest corporation in the galaxy, and had required the aid of a man who could only be called a mad scientist. Yes, there had been a number of exciting days in his life.

This was not one of them.

Currently, he was cleaning up his tiny apartment. The place was little more than a combination living room/bedroom, dominated by a flatscreen that took up nearly one entire wall and a futon that occupied most of what space was left. A door at the opposite side led to a room that would have been called a closet if not for the fact that it had a sink, a refrigerator, and a microwave. It adjoined a room that was similarly a bathroom in name only, with a toilet and shower wedged tightly enough to make successfully closing the door while inside a veritable contortionist act.

Generally, he allowed trash and grime to accumulate until it made it difficult to navigate the space safely, but today he was sanitizing it in preparation for a rare visit from his girlfriend.

Her name was Michella Modane; by virtue of their jobs, the pair had been having something of a long-distance relationship, despite the fact they lived less than twenty minutes apart. She was an investigative reporter, and thanks to her coverage of the very same near-catastrophe that had made such an impression on Lex's life, she'd managed to become one of the more respected and sought-after figures of local news. In the past, "local news" might not have been an impressive achievement, but these days, the term local tended to cover multiple planets, so she was rather proud of how far she had come. Most of her information regarding that first big story had come from Lex himself, but everything since had been due to her own significant skills. In the eight months since that big break, she had gone on to unearth scandals and plots ranging from disgraced government officials to corrupt corporate executives. If someone had secrets, they did *not* want to get a visit from Michella Modane.

One might then assume that this meant that Lex had no secrets. After all, he was anticipating her arrival so eagerly, he was willing to clean out the crevices of his futon, which was, at this point, a veritable archeological expedition. As a matter of fact, Lex did have secrets, a point which had caused no small amount of friction between them. The first was the specific name and location of the man who had provided him the equipment that had made his heroic deeds possible. Considering the fact that he'd bested the security of VectorCorp, a company more powerful than most individual governments, and had done so despite a complete lack of anything resembling training, her curiosity was entirely understandable. So far, he'd been able to avoid telling her by making it clear that his unnamed benefactor would be in terrible danger if he were revealed--and, more to the point, would not be terribly pleased with Lex for revealing him. It had been enough to convince her and, by happy coincidence, it happened to be true.

The second secret had to do with the fact that the owner of his apartment building was a man named Nicholas Patel, the head of one of the better-known organized crime syndicates, and why precisely he was allowing Lex to live rent-free. Michella had never expressed curiosity about it for the simple reason that she didn't know about it, and had, so far, not been given any reason to suspect it. This was very fortunate, since the last time he'd become tangled with the mob, it had led to the aforementioned fixed race, which had, in turn, led to the destruction of his career and a two-year hiatus in their relationship. She would tolerate an awful lot, but she could not abide getting mixed up with mobsters. Michella had never explained why she felt that way, but he'd learned a thing or two about her childhood, and he suspected she had very good reasons.

Lex had just finished dumping a final load of miscellaneous debris into the garbage, and was admiring an apartment that was almost respectable, when a tone alerted him to a visitor at the apartment building's front door. He walked over and tapped the panel beside the door. The video feed showed him the not-quite-face-on view of a person who didn't know where to look when waiting to be let in. It was a man with an inebriated grin showing off a grand total of four teeth. His face looked like it was in the process of being reclaimed by a jungle of gray, scraggly hair. The beard in particular looked like it had won a revolution.

"Um . . . do I know you?" Lex asked.

"Trevor Alexander?" the grimy man slurred.

Lex flinched. After one too many run-ins with the law, he had begun to dread hearing his full name spoken out loud.

"Yeah?"

"You're 'sposed to give me a stack of chips."

"Sorry, sir. I don't have time for this. There's a homeless shelter three blocks down."

He shut off the screen and checked the time. Michella would be showing up in ten minutes. He debated on lighting a candle, ostensibly to set a more romantic mood, but primarily to take the edge off of the combination of window cleaner and leftover takeout food that was currently the dominant aroma. Deciding that it was probably a wise decision, he started rummaging through the solitary closet in his apartment to find one. Before long, there was a knock at the door. He checked the time again, then shut the closet and answered the door.

After living in an apartment for as long as he had, Lex had begun to react differently to a knock at the door than others would. Since strangers were all stopped at the front door of the building, if someone was knocking on his specific door, it meant they either worked for the building, were a neighbor, or had been given access by him or a neighbor. Thus, ninety percent of the time, the person on the other side of the door would be someone he knew. This turned out to be part of the other ten percent.

The door opened to reveal the very same grizzled homeless man who had spoken to him a moment ago. Lex slammed the door, latched the door chain, then opened it again, peering through the crack. A potent combination of body odor and fortified wine fumes wafted past him.

"How did you get in here!?" he asked.

"Yer magic dog let me in."

"My what?"

"Yer dog! I brung yer magic dog!"

His aromatic visitor held up a creature that could certainly be easily confused for a dog. It was about the size of a large terrier and had generally canine features, but a close inspection of the pointed ears and narrow muzzle, combined with the black coloring with white stripes and massive fluffy tail, gave it the overall appearance of a cross between a skunk and a fox--exactly what it was. The result was a maddeningly cute creature, eyes and feet a bit too big, and tail easily as large as the rest of its body. In short, it looked like a stuffed animal artisan's magnum opus. Lex crooked his head to the side and raised an eyebrow.

"Solby?" he asked, recalling the name of the last such beast he'd encountered.

"Not precisely, Mr. Alexander," remarked what sounded like an edited-together recording of three women and a synthetic voice.

Lex whipped around to face the panel beside his door, from which the voice had originated.

“Ma!?” he yelped.

“In a manner of speaking,” it replied.

The bewildered young man turned back to the still-upheld creature. In a maneuver that finally managed to push the weirdness factor over the edge, it winked.

Lex reluctantly opened the door, allowing the man and his creature inside.

“Ma, did you send Solby here? Who is this guy?” Lex asked, addressing the panel beside his door.

For the sake of clarity, it is worth pointing out that Lex was not under any impression that he was speaking to his mother. The unmistakably unique “voice” belonged to an individual he'd met during his last adventure. She was an AI created by a man named Karter Dee, designed to take care of him and his facility. Depending on who you believed, the program owed its name to either its nurturing nature, or the fact that it cooked all of his food, washed all of his dishes, and nagged him incessantly. She was really quite an achievement, a computer program capable of genuine warmth, compassion, and integrity--three things that her creator completely lacked. She also had a vindictive streak when someone got on her bad side.

“I will explain everything shortly. But first--” Ma began.

“You owe me a stack of chips,” the homeless man interjected.

“I don't even know who you are!” Lex protested.

“I am afraid I promised him that you would provide him with four one-thousand credit chips in exchange for his aid. You will be reimbursed, of course. I would have paid him myself, but I was unable to transfer non-digital assets in my current state, and time was limited.”

“Jeez, Ma. Four thousand credits? You don't know much about haggling, do you?” Lex said, digging through a jar on the ledge below his ridiculously large flatscreen until he found four poker chips of the correct value.

The gambling tokens had slipped into the void left behind when cash had finally been entirely replaced by digital-only credits, and Lex found it useful to keep a ready supply. He dropped them into the bum's hand and ushered him out the door.

“If you ever need somebody to walk that thing, you can--”

“Not going to happen. Thanks for dropping it off. You know the way out,” Lex said, shutting the door behind his odoriferous visitor.

The creature that he left behind hopped up onto the futon.

“No no no no--off the furniture!” he scolded, scooping up the creature and depositing it back on the ground. The creature, technically called a funk, sat obediently on the floor and regarded Lex with a calm, even stare.

“I apologize. I am not entirely certain of the appropriate etiquette in situations such as this,” Ma stated.

“What? Never mind. Ma, you want to explain what the hell is going on here? You can start with how that guy got through the front door."

"I apologize for that as well. He was beginning to attract attention, and I could not afford any more delay, so I opened the outer door. The encryption algorithm was fairly naïve."

"Okay. Why did you send someone to deliver Solby? And why are you talking to me over the door panel right now?"

"As I indicated, this is not Solby. Solby is a male. This is a female. It seemed more appropriate. As for the reason for the visit, I'm afraid I have a rather significant favor to ask of you."

Lex sighed. "A favor? What is it? Does he want me to funk-sit? Or is it more beta testing? Why couldn't Karter just send an email like he usually does?"

"Beta testing" was a service that Lex had begun to provide his inventor associate following their collaboration in the VectorCorp situation. He would try out a variety of equipment, usually dealing with spaceship parts. In exchange for pointing out any glaring flaws and providing feedback, he would be paid, or allowed to keep an improved version of the equipment in question. The arrangement had proven to be mutually beneficial.

"I will provide details shortly--but, before I begin, I have a more minor and immediate favor to ask. If it is not too much of an intrusion upon your hospitality, I would be grateful if you could spare some food. It has been some time since I last ate."

"You're an AI talking to me over a data connection, Ma. You don't eat."

"That is not an entirely accurate assessment at the present time, I am afraid."

"What is that supposed to mean?"

"Look at the creature at your feet, Lex."

He did so. It was still staring at him, showing a calmness that he didn't think was physically possible for the species. Solby had been in perpetual motion. Even when forced to sit still, he would practically vibrate with enthusiasm, waiting until he was given permission to prance about again. This creature seemed perfectly composed and poised, looking him in the eye steadily. It lowered its head slightly, revealing a marble-sized glass nub amid the fur on its neck.

"Do you remember the purpose of this device?" asked Ma, the glass bead flickering red as she spoke.

"Yeah. That's the thing Karter uses to upload and download Solby's brain. Leave it to that guy to make backup copies of his pet."

"Indeed. More generally, it is a high-speed, wide-band data radio."

"It sure does flash a lot more than Solby's does."

"Yes. You will find it flashes every time that I speak."

"As a matter of fact, it is."

The creature raised its head again.

"That is because I am using it to speak, transmitting to the wall panel."

"So, what, you're using this little lady as a transceiver?"

"I am using her as temporary storage."

"Storage? Wait . . . you mean . . ."

"It is nice to finally speak to you face to face, Lex."

Chapter 2

Lex stared blankly at the creature at his feet as he tried to comprehend what was happening.

"Perhaps you could look into the issue of food while you cope with this revelation?" she offered.

"Uh . . . yeah. Yeah," he said, eagerly latching onto the task his brain could handle. "I don't have any pet food or anything like that. We aren't allowed to have pets. Except for my landlady's cats . . . before she got bought out, anyway. I guess that might have changed now that Patel is in charge."

"Funks have highly flexible dietary needs. A caloric distribution of approximately twenty percent protein, ten percent fat, and seventy percent carbohydrates would fit my current requirements."

Lex pulled open his refrigerator, then his cabinets. In typical bachelor fashion, both were virtually free from any ingredients that could not be eaten directly out of the container, or, failing that, after a few seconds in the microwave.

"Uh. I don't really organize my food by protein content. I've got instant noodles, cheese curls, protein drink, re-fried beans . . ."

"That will be sufficient."

"The beans? Oh, yeah. I guess Karter did always feed Solby burritos."

He peeled the top off of the container, dug through the cabinet for a dish, found the only appropriate one to be in the sink, and set about washing it.

"You need this heated up or anything?" he asked.

"That will not be necessary."

"Right. Okay. Just a minute."

As he went about rinsing the largest pieces of stubborn food from the bowl and tried to arrange his thoughts into a series of questions, he was too distracted to notice the sound of his door blipping open. Thus, he didn't know that Michella had arrived until he heard her utter "Trev?" followed by a squealing coo. Lex burst into the main room of the apartment to find his girlfriend crouched in front of Ma.

"Aw! Look at you, you little darling!" she gushed, face scrunched adorably. "Trev, is this your dog?"

Ma looked up at the visitor, an unnervingly dignified look on her face

"Michella! Uh, no, no. A friend of mine dropped her off."

"Does she bite?"

"I seriously doubt it, but--"

Before he could object, she scooped up the little creature and held her up, cuddling tightly. For a moment or two, Ma wore a face of introspection, eyes squinting and head tipped to the side. Then her mouth dropped open and she yipped three times before somewhat mechanically beginning to lick at Michella's ear and rustle her tail. It was a pale imitation of Solby's manic enthusiasm, but it was enough to delight Michella. Lex felt as though he should put a stop to it, but the sight of them together was just too good to interrupt.

If a scientist had designed a laboratory-perfect example of girl-next-door gorgeous, Michella would be the result. Her long auburn hair was pulled back into a ponytail. She hadn't bothered to put her "camera face" on, so her freckles were showing on her cheeks. Her skin tone and features showed of a healthy mix of Latin American in her gene pool, with a few glaring departures inherited from a dash of European somewhere along the line. Rather than her on-screen contacts, she was wearing her librarian-style eyeglasses, highlighting her sapphire-blue eyes. A pair of designer jeans and a white T-shirt featuring the logo of her favorite band, Death Zone Dumpster, hugged curves that had inspired what might well be the first image board on the net dedicated to an investigative reporter. As she fawned over the little creature held to her chest, Lex took the time to snap a picture with his slidepad before interrupting the love-fest.

"You two want a room?" he asked.

"She's such a cutie. What breed is this?" she asked.

"I don't know. A rare one. One of those designer breeds."

That much was true. The funk had been designed in a laboratory using a genetic simulator.

"What's her name?" she asked.

"Her name is . . . uh . . ."

Ma gestured her head briefly toward the panel by the door, behind Michella. It displayed a name.

"Squee?" he said with a furrowed brow.

"Squee. That's a cute name," she said, putting the little beast down. "You watching her for long?"

"I really hope not," he said, dumping the beans onto the dish and placing it down.

Ma/Squee tapped across the floor and eagerly dug into the food.

"I know I said I was going to be here for a few hours, Trev, but they moved my flight up. I'm already running late. The car service is waiting outside. Sorry, honey."

"What? Okay, ignoring the ditched plans, you got a car service? I could have taken you over in my limo. Hell, I could have flown you all the way to

Tessera in the *S.O.B.*"

As a former racer, Lex's chief skills almost exclusively dealt with moving quickly and accurately in a piece of machinery. It was thus no surprise that the jobs he found to replace racing all involved handling a vehicle. The day-to-day bills were mostly paid by a hoverbike courier job, which called for him to go whipping through the streets and sky of Preston City at dangerous speeds. Here and there, he supplemented that income with a chauffeur job courtesy of his limo, a holdover from the brief time that he was a celebrity. On top of that was a not-quite-legitimate interstellar courier job that made use of his custom ship, *Son of Betsy*. The traditional name for the position was "freelancer." The three careers, combined with the beta testing, were just enough to keep his head above water and allow him to start chiseling away at his massive debt.

"You know the office likes me to use their vendors."

"You could always convince them to make *me* a vendor."

"Don't start," she said, making a face. "I'll be back in a couple of weeks. I'll see you then. I just didn't want to leave you hanging." She gave him a hug and a peck on the cheek. "I'll miss you."

"Me, too. You better show up next time, babe," he said.

"Cross my heart. And goodbye to you, Squee, sweetie," she said, with a blown kiss and a wink, her trademark sendoff.

Ma looked up from the food to deliver three quick yips again before continuing her meal. Lex leaned out the doorway and watched her go, a faint smile on his face. When the elevator doors shut behind her, he stepped inside and closed the door. He flopped down on the futon.

"She seemed nice," Ma remarked. "And your apartment, also, is very nice. The weather is lovely today. How have things been regarding your employment?"

"Seriously Ma? Small talk? You're a supercomputer walking around as an adorable little fuzzball and you are attempting small talk?"

"I am endeavoring to put you at ease with what I understand is a difficult situation."

"It isn't working," he said, pinching the bridge of his nose.

"That is unfortunate."

She finished eating the contents of the bowl, industriously licked it clean, and tapped over to his feet.

"So, what possible reason could you have for coming out here like this?"

"Karter has been kidnapped."

"What!? By who?"

"I am not certain of the organization, but I have my suspicions that it is a group of political extremists. They wanted to contract him for the construction of a potentially destructive device, and during a scale demonstration of an existing product, they deployed electromagnetic pulse generators to incapacitate me and his other automated defenses. By the time I was able to restore myself to limited functionality, they were gone."

"Why would they kidnap him? Do you think they're going to force him to build weapons for them?"

"You know Karter as well as I. It is entirely possible that they will not *need* to force him."

"Yeah . . ."

Karteroketraskin "Karter" Dee, was many things. He was a brilliant engineer and a gifted inventor. He was also, proudly, a borderline sociopath with little use for morals and even less use for most of the human race. Though he had helped to prevent a multi-planet catastrophe by lending apparatus and research, he only did so first out of spite, then out of self-interest. The opportunity to field-test his experimental equipment was, in his eyes, justification enough to do virtually anything. In the brief time that Lex had known him, he had seen the man use weapons-grade lasers as a pooper-scooper, and a miniature black hole as a projectile. He had a predilection for creating weapons of mass destruction . . . and now he might be in the hands of a terrorist group.

"Do you understand why I was willing to take such drastic action?"

"Well, yeah, but why me? This is a job for the military or one of those bureaus of investigation."

"The initial contact with these individuals was arranged through military channels, implying that the military may have been compromised by the group. Furthermore, Karter is, himself, somewhat sought after by a number of military and domestic agencies. My goal is to liberate him, not to deliver him from one form of imprisonment to another. Thus, this is a matter that calls for discretion. You are, to be perfectly frank, one of the few people that I feel we can trust."

"There has got to be someone better for--"

"Lex, I had anticipated your reluctance, and as such had allotted three days in which to convince you in a gradual and logical manner. Unfortunately, I underestimated the difficulty of traversing interstellar distances as an unaccompanied non-verbal quadruped, and thus was delayed. For this reason, I will distill the situation to its purest form.

"Karter has the knowledge, resources, and lack of moral conviction to be a threat to society on an unprecedented scale. The only thing that has prevented him from becoming a purposeful blight on humanity thus far has been a lack motivation--and, more recently, gentle influence from me. He is now beyond my influence and at the mercy of a group of very motivated individuals. It is a relative certitude that, unless something is done quickly, an evil will be unleashed upon the populace that will make the plot you foiled several months ago seem mild by comparison. I have set a plan in motion that should leave us adequately equipped to retrieve him, but to remain on schedule for the next phase, you and I will need to be en route in sixty-five minutes, so there is no further time for debate. I need your help."

"I guess I don't really have a choice."

"I was confident you would make the correct decision. I hope that you are able to leave immediately. We will need to purchase a few items."

"Like what?"

"Well, evidently if we are to be moving about freely in public, I will require a leash."

#

A few minutes later, Lex was finishing a call, almost ready to leave.

"Yeah, mark off, further notice. Thanks. See you later," Lex said before pocketing his slidepad.

The first step had been to call his various dispatchers and employers to let them know he would be off the list for a while. It was something he had to do every time he had a long-distance package to drop off for his freelancer gig, so they were used to it. Next, a reasonably clean T-shirt and jeans were selected, and he set about loading down his pockets with everything he might need, including his slidepad, a pack of gum, and a supply of chips. He also quickly packed an overnight bag with clothes for an assortment of climates. One of the side effects of the ease of long-distance travel meant that, in the space of a few days, he could be exposed to both extremes of hot and cold, as well as every weather condition he could imagine. He knew from experience that it paid to be prepared. When he was through, Lex stopped at the door for a final check.

"Hey, how are you going to talk to me?"

"I could utilize the speaker functionality of your slidepad," offered the series of female voices from the panel beside the door.

"I think that would be a little obvious."

"Do you have a hands-free device?"

"Uh, yeah, somewhere," Lex said, eventually fishing the jelly bean-sized device from his pocket.

"Insert it, please," she requested.

He slipped it into his ear.

"Processing . . . negotiating . . . pairing . . . establishing connection . . . connection established. Can you hear me?" she recited, her last comment coming from the ear bud rather than the panel.

"Yeah. I guess that will do. The only problem now is that I'm going to be talking out loud to an animal."

"I understand that is not an uncommon behavior."

"I guess not. But most people aren't getting replies. I guess I'll just pretend I'm on a call."

"That is wise."

Lex left his apartment, Ma tapping along the ground beside him. After an elevator ride to the surface, he fetched his hoverbike. It used three hover modules mounted at the end of short outriggers to haul around the contents of a shopping cart-sized wire basket mounted behind the seat. It wasn't the most dignified means of conveyance, but in his hands it could beat virtually anything in a race across town, including, on more occasions that he would be willing to admit, police cars. Ma was loaded into the basket.

"You sure you're going to be okay back here?" he asked.

"I trust your skill as a pilot," she replied, settling carefully to the floor of the basket.

"Even so. I'll take it slow. First stop, mega-store," he said, easing his bike into the air.

They began to make their way through Preston City. It was the capital of Lex's home planet, Golana, and one of the largest transportation hubs in the galactic neighborhood. As such, it was home to far too many people crammed into far too little space. Even though the city sprawled over hundreds of miles, virtually all of the buildings were massive, reaching dozens to hundreds of stories into the air. Street traffic was fairly light, thanks to the fact that hovercars were able to take advantage of cordoned-off skyways instead. Outside of city limits, cars frequently shifted to autonomous, which virtually eliminated traffic and permitted speeds measured in the hundreds of miles per hour. Inside the city, however, people preferred manual control, leading to the same traffic snarls that had plagued humans for generations. They had simply been expanded from two dimensions to three.

"You want to explain to me what the plan is?"

"You and I are going to rendezvous with one of Karter's former collaborators. He has experience in matters such as these. From there, pending his insight into the situation, your involvement may be at an end."

"You sure? All I have to do is escort you to a meeting with this guy?" Lex asked.

"That is a rough overview, but I've done what I can to allow for maximum flexibility, so expect a degree of fluidity."

"What kind of fluidity?"

"We are likely to require more manpower--if so, he may require your aid in locating and meeting with them."

"Okay. That sounds doable. I guess I can see why you needed a chaperone. It must be tricky getting people to take you seriously when you're, you know, fuzzy."

"Exceedingly."

"Wouldn't it have been easier to build a robot body?"

"Time was limited, and the circumstances of my departure made the survival of a complex computational mechanism unlikely. In addition, there was the necessity to blend with human society. While the many breeds of dog and their relative ubiquity would permit my current selection of form to go unnoticed, a robot would need to be extremely sophisticated to receive the same treatment. Karter has built a female humanoid robot, but he achieved the desired level of fidelity in only three areas of its anatomy. The face was not one of them."

"Do I want to know what three parts made the list?"

"Unlikely."

"Yeah, you're probably right. Okay, we're here. Cost-Mart," Lex said.

With a name like Cost-Mart, one could be excused for thinking that a description was unnecessary, and to a degree that is true. As you might imagine, it was the sort of place that sold everything conceivable, and generally in gallons when ounces would suffice. The last time Lex had visited this place, it was to buy a gross of granola bars to stock the *S.O.B.* for a particularly lengthy delivery. The name may even conjure to mind the sprawling size of the superstore, but that is where the expectations start to fall short. To begin to understand the scope of the shopping center, you must first understand that there was no parking lot, because customers were encouraged to pilot their vehicles directly into the store. It had departments the way malls had stores, spread across floors and stretched across blocks. Items were loaded directly into trunks, baskets, and seats. A quick swipe of a slidepad deducted the cost of the purchase directly from your accounts, meaning that there was no checkout. Shoplifting was virtually nonexistent, primarily because if you walked or drove out of the store without paying, they would automatically debit your slidepad as you exited.

There were smaller stores and more traditional places to purchase things, certainly, but for someone who wanted to be absolutely certain that what they needed would be in stock, Cost-Mart was the best bet.

"What are we looking for?" Lex asked.

"Some manner of leash appropriate for a creature of my size. We will also need food and water for a few days for myself and, if the *S.O.B.* is not currently stocked, food for you as well. In addition, we need: four small items of blue clothing, a commercial- or industrial-grade thiol oxidation spray, two or more epinephrine injectors with replaceable reservoirs--product code EPP-4942c--a large package of pain management medication, a general anesthetic, assorted first aid supplies, four to six additional hands-free audio devices, four to six additional slidepads or datapads--"

"Whoa, whoa, whoa! What is this, a scavenger hunt? Listen, I'm not sure I've got enough available credit to cover this stuff. I mean, what's a cheapo slidepad run these days, five thousand credits?"

"High-end models would be preferred."

"Yeah, I don't have the cash to be buying those things by the half-dozen."

"Of course. Please stop at the nearest gambling kiosk."

"Heh. This ought to be good."

Before long, Lex spotted a video poker machine beside a coffee stand on one of the upper levels. Just as cash had found a replacement in casino chips, ATMs had evolved into poker kiosks. All one had to do was take a seat, load credits into the machine directly from their bank account, and cash out to get a pocket full of fixed value, non-traceable funds. Best of all, the machines didn't charge a service or convenience fee. This was largely because virtually all of the people who sought to use them simply as a way to convert money from credits to chips took the time to play a hand or two, inevitably losing a bit in the process. It was actually a fairly ingenious and effective system. Unless, of course, you had a gambling problem, but society had shuffled those unfortunates down to the bottom of the ladder long ago.

He settled his bike down and Ma hopped to the seat. The light on her neck flashed, a log-in screen came and went, and a user profile under the name Kyle Oscar Dunbrook appeared. As she worked at the kiosk, a patron of the coffee shop, sporting a latte larger than his head, stopped and eyed the bizarre sight.

"She's my good luck charm. I always sit her in the chair for the first hand," Lex explained.

The stranger shrugged, apparently satisfied with the answer, and moved on. A moment later, Ma was finished bringing up the account information. The balance was . . . unusual. It seemed to say 5.45E11.

"Wh--why is there an E in the available balance field?" Lex asked.

"Scientific notation. The funds display of this machine is only ten characters," she said, the screens flipping through to the cash out tab.

"Wait . . . so Karter has more than ten digits in his bankroll?" he asked, eyes wide.

"In this account, yes. There are others."

". . . I should have become a mad scientist."

The coin tray on the front of the machine quickly filled. There were five one hundred thousand-credit chips, twenty ten thousand-credit chips, and twenty one thousand-credit chips. A moment later, four more one thousand-credit chips dropped. For the appropriate frame of reference: if his various jobs managed to bring in one hundred thousand credits combined, it was a pretty good week. He was holding nearly two months' salary in his hand.

"That should be sufficient to cover the expenses. I would suggest you only deposit half into your account. Liquid funds may come in handy."

"Whatever you say, boss."

She logged off, he logged on, and in short order his account swelled to a larger number than he'd seen in months.

"Right, let's go shopping," he said.

Chapter 3

The items on the list were snagged one by one. First was a harness-style leash, which was securely strapped on so that Lex would stop getting irritated looks from security guards and fellow shoppers. He also had swung by the pet food section, but Ma assured him that Solby always seemed happier and healthier when he was provided with the food Karter favored, specifically beans and rice, so frozen burritos and vitamin tablets were chosen as her rations. Next, he managed to get a decent deal on a combo-pack of six current-generation slidepads bundled with hands-free buds. At Ma's request, he'd splurged for a few ruggedized cases, complete with lanyards and belt clips, as well. The vague "blue clothing" requirement was fulfilled by a handful of bandanas. The epinephrine gadgets were a little hard to find--they were in the allergy medication area rather than the prescription area, and everybody seemed to prefer the disposable ones rather than refillable--but before long he'd snagged everything that she was after.

"What's next, Ma?" Lex asked, as he piloted his bike out of the store.

"Our next destination is the starport. We will need to board a first class flight, but, first, you will need to send your own ship autonomously to a maintenance station near the flight path," Ma explained.

"Uh. The *S.O.B.* can't do long-range autonomous flight," he explained, nudging his bike in the general direction of the starport.

"Karter designed and built your ship, and I was responsible for installing the software. I assure you, it is entirely capable."

Lex blinked.

"Well, why didn't anybody tell me!?"

"You had not requested it. You had only requested short-range autonomy."

"Then why did you put it in?"

"The appropriate sensory apparatus and computational power were present in the system; there was no reason not to include it."

"Are there any other features you didn't bother to tell me about?"

"Several. I can prepare a list for you, if you like, following the completion of our current task."

"Any reason you can't do it now?"

"It is possible that you will be displeased by one or more of the functions, and thus will be less inclined to continue to lend your aid."

"See, now . . . that's not very encouraging."

"Only one of them is potentially life-threatening."

"Oh, well, that's not so bad," he snarked, quietly questioning why he was willingly helping these people.

#

In a large space station, at an undisclosed location, a woman by the name of Janet Purcell was pacing angrily in the way that only a superior officer can. Her hair was short and red, a brilliant, fright-wig shade of red that was clearly the work of chemicals rather than nature. The clothes she wore were strictly military: black canvas fatigues, festooned with patches and medals representing assorted service honors. Notably absent were flags or seals indicating her military loyalty. She looked like she may have been entering the unhappy half of her thirties, but her physique was the training-forged build of a career soldier. A deep scar ran from her scalp just above her left eye, circled across her temple and cheek, and ended at the edge of her chin. What looked to be the feathery red of an electrical burn was just visible on her throat at the neck of her fatigues. Hanging at her belt was a combat knife laser-etched with the designations MME (MonoMolecular Edge) and HFMO (High Frequency MicroOscilation) along the side of the blade. To a layman, these terms roughly translated to "very very sharp" and "makes a scary, high-pitched noise while it cuts through things." The scary noise was caused by the fact that the blade vibrated at a frequency just beyond the range of hearing, and this frequency slowed a bit while it was sawing through . . . well, virtually anything. In a chest holster, a plasma-pistol with a bulging extended power cell was ready and waiting to be drawn. The look in her eye suggested that it wouldn't have to wait long.

"He is secured?" she hissed.

"Yes, ma'am."

"Again?"

"Yes, ma'am."

The man answering the questions was the same one who had been the leader of the group that had ended up kidnapping Karter. He was sporting at least three recently-bandaged wounds, and one hand was badly disfigured. Rather than the arctic gear of his last outing, he was wearing composite body armor over fatigues similar to Purcell's, and a high-powered plasma rifle was strapped to his back. The goggles, however, still had a place of honor on his head. The body armor, goggles, and bandages were worn by nearly all of the soldiers without a task-specific uniform. In this case, a name tag etched on the armor labeled him Crewman Marx.

"Explain to me how this happened," she ordered.

"The prisoner, Dr. Dee, appeared to be cooperating. Our engineers agreed that the most recent design did appear to be a larger-scale implementation of the small device we had confiscated from him when we first captured him," Marx explained.

"Cooperating? He depressurized three decks. Even with emergency procedures, we lost five men. That does not sound like cooperation!"

"We are still investigating how he managed to gain control of the airlocks and override the failsafes."

"That is the third security breach since he was brought to this facility. That is unacceptable," she cried, hammering the wall beside her with a fist. A moment later, her composure returned. "You say the scale has been increased. Is it enough for our purposes?"

"Engineering is just finishing a mockup now, but they say that several key components necessary for activation aren't included. They are going to run some tests shortly."

She fumed silently for a moment. "Keep me apprised of the results. I am going to speak with him."

"Yes, Commander."

Commander Purcell marched out of the room and into the hallway. The cramped, industrial corridor looked as though it had been designed by the same people who had made the first submarines. Pipes and vents visibly lined the walls and ceiling, and a grating covered more along the floor. She made her way down a long, curving hall, through a narrow door, and down a few ladders, finally arriving at a much larger and more navigable space. This was good, because there were six guards on duty. The same number in another hall would have made it impassible. Three stood on each side of a barred cell door. Inside was Karter Dee. He wasn't looking particularly threatening at the moment, as it had been discovered that both his whole left arm and his left leg below the knee were mechanical prostheses; they had been forcibly removed after he'd used them rather creatively to wreak havoc. He was now sitting on a chair that was the only piece of furniture in the room. Even the lights had been removed.

"Dee!" the commander barked.

"What?" he snapped, as though she were interrupting something much more interesting.

"You can't keep doing this forever."

"I think that I can."

"You realize that we will kill you if you don't cooperate."

"Pff, no. If you could figure this out on your own, you wouldn't have kidnapped me to start with. This is a lose–lose for you. I'm not going to cooperate unless I get what I want, so unless you are going to cave to my demands, you can either keep threatening and get nothing, or kill me and get nothing. I've got all the power here."

"We have your latest designs. It is only a matter of time."

"Lady, that design is incomplete, and you don't have the tools to finish it. You don't even have the tools to make the tools to finish it."

"You won't stop us from achieving our goals."

"What makes you think I want to stop you? I couldn't care less about your agenda. You think you're the first group of terrorists I've sold stuff to?"

"We aren't terrorists. We are revolutionaries."

"Tomato, to-mah-to," he said, with a waggle of his remaining hand. "The point is, I was ready, willing, and able to fork these things over by the dozen if you were willing to cough up the money. I still am, but the price has gone *way* up. Inconvenience fee, because, for some reason, you thought it was wise to kidnap me."

"We couldn't afford to have you supply them to anyone but us, and we couldn't afford to have you warning anyone."

"Nondisclosure agreements and exclusivity agreements. Think like a corporation, lady. They've proven much better at enslaving the masses and pushing home their agenda than all of the terrorists in the history the human race put together. But no, you had to do things the hard way. So I had to make a point or two, in the form of four very destructive escape attempts."

"Three," she corrected.

"You sure about that?" he said doubtfully.

Purcell stared at him intensely, her mind racing. Suddenly, her eyes widened and she scrambled for her hefty mil-spec communicator and thumbed the transmit button.

"Engineering!" she hissed.

"Engineering here," came the reply a few moments later, accompanied by video.

"Do *not* activate the latest prototype of the CME activator."

"It is already in the testing rig. We are getting impressive power output."

Even over the transmission, a worrying increase in the electronic hum of the equipment could be heard.

"Shut it down--now!"

"Shutting down."

The man in the video window tapped at some controls. The hum had become a shuddering rattle by the time he issued the appropriate command, and whatever had been causing it was causing the lighting in the room to flicker and flare. Gradually, the rattle died away.

"The device is powered down," the technician said.

"Disassemble it, and move it off the station. Testing on any and all designs provided by Dr. Dee will now be done planetside in Site C. Maximum safety protocols."

"Yes, Commander."

She closed the connection and turned her gaze to Karter.

"Probably I should have kept my mouth shut about that one," he said. "Oh, well, next time."

"What do you want, exactly?" she fumed.

"Good question. Start making offers."

Her eyes narrowed. "No," she decided. "We have not reached that point. I'm not willing to make any deals."

"Heh. The terrorists won't negotiate with me," he mused as the commander stalked away.

#

Back on Golana, Lex and Ma had just arrived in "The Upstairs," the orbital section of Golana Interstellar Starport. It was made up of a series of rotating rings at the end of long tethers that led to complexes on the planet's surface. These tethers allowed elevators to haul crew, passengers, and cargo into space in a cheaper and more efficient way than shuttles, and the rotation allowed the outer rim of each ring to experience at least a semblance of gravity in a cheaper and more efficient way than artificial gravity generators. A side effect of the rotation method, though, was that the full effect was only felt at the circumference, where the paying customers were. The further in you went, the less gravity there was. Right now, Lex was quite near the hub, working his way toward a place called "Blake's Stardock" and learning how difficult it was to gracefully navigate in zero-G while carrying a small creature and a bulky bag.

"I find it difficult to believe that there is not a better means of travel in microgravity," Ma suggested as she and Lex twisted awkwardly and collided with the wall at the end of a corridor.

"There is. There's these little zip-lifts. I just never had to use them before. Most of the time, this is faster."

"This does not appear to be one of those times."

"Don't rub it in," he said, tucking her under an arm and wrangling the bag onto his shoulder.

"Lex? Who you talking to?" asked a man sticking his head out of a nearby hatch.

"Nobody. How's it going, Blake?" he replied.

"Just fine. Thanks for helping overhaul that bigwig's racer last week."

"Overhaul? I messed with the timing."

"Whatever it was, he said it knocked 0.5 off his lap times."

Blake, who had known Lex back when he was an up-and-coming racer who had been tagged with the unfortunate nickname "T-Lex" by the press, ran the stardock. Aside from giving people a place to keep their ships when not in use, he also performed standard maintenance and tuning. The man was a wizard with his tools, and could get even a third-hand, used and abused engine running again, but he never could get the knack of some of the finer tweaks that racers used to give themselves an edge. Thus, when someone brought him a ship that needed some tender loving care, he would call Lex. In exchange, he put Lex on the crew list and let him keep his ship in one of the spare docks--when there were docks to spare. It was an arrangement that worked out pretty well for both men.

"You never struck me as the 'accessory pet' sort, Lex," Blake said, eying Ma. "Or is this Mitch's?"

"Nah, but she was all over it, so I'm sure she'll want one."

"Women."

Ma narrowed her eyes.

"Uh, so, anyway, I'll just be in and out. Need to tell *Son of Betsy* to drop herself off somewhere."

"You've got a fully autonomous autopilot?"

"Apparently."

"Huh. Well, go ahead. I'll let you know if I need you for anything."

"Sure thing," Lex said, making his way into the hatch and nudging his way along the walls to the dock that held his ship.

"What did your friend mean by his statement, 'women'?" Ma asked sternly.

"What? I don't know. It is just something men say when they don't understand women."

"His tone indicated he was utilizing the term as an indication of fault."

"Yes. I cannot imagine why he would want to indicate that women could be difficult to deal with sometimes."

"Are you indicating that I am difficult to deal with?"

"Maybe."

"Thank you, Lex."

"For what?"

"For the implicit indication that you think of me as a woman rather than a machine."

"Oh. You're welcome. Ow!" he yelped, after receiving a nip to the hand.

"And that is for speaking disparagingly of my gender."

"I'm sorry. Jeez."

"I trust that it was not disproportionately painful. Owing to a prior lack of the appropriate anatomy, that is the first time that I have bitten someone, and I am not confident that I have achieved proficiency in the nuances of the act."

"Don't worry about it," he said, drifting up to the view window overlooking his ship and pulling out his slidepad. "There's the *S.O.B.* I'll open up a secure connection, and you do what you need to do."

Lex rubbed his hand as the red light on Ma's neck flashed furiously. It had been eight months or so since he'd met her, and whereas he and Karter had been in contact strictly for business reasons, Ma kept up a correspondence with him for seemingly no reason beyond keeping in touch. While his first impression hadn't been a good one (he'd indicated she wasn't a good computer and that he would rather deal with a real person), she'd quickly warmed to him when he apologized and began treating her as an equal, something that no one else had ever done. While this had seemed strange behavior for a computer, it had helped him to realize that Ma wasn't your standard AI. She did not have the traditional Three Laws of Robotics governing her actions.

Instead, she had been programed to act in what she determined to be the best interests of Karter specifically and humanity in general, and to strive to improve both her understanding of morality and the quality of her interaction; a so-called Altruistic AI. Somehow, despite having one of the most self-centered and unstable people Lex had ever met as her primary point of reference, she had developed into a reasonably well-adjusted personality. Somewhere along the way, she had also decided that she had the reasonable expectation of proper treatment, and tended to be petty and bitter toward those who she felt were disrespectful. Considering her lack of the "thou shalt not kill" and "thou shalt obey" aspects of the Asimov Laws, it was probably best to stay on her good side.

"Command upload complete. The *S.O.B.* will arrive at the rendezvous point in approximately sixteen hours. Our flight will be leaving in twenty-one minutes and will arrive there in twenty-three hours," Ma explained, as the ship's engines began to flare and the de-docking procedures kicked in. "You are to be commended. The ship's systems are in an excellent state of repair, and it remains cosmetically flawless."

Lex watched anxiously as the ship left the dock and maneuvered into a transit lane. "Yeah. The *S.O.B.* is the nicest ship I've ever had. I'd like to have it for a long time. Are you sure it will make it okay?"

"It is programed for maximum safety. It will take fewer risks than you yourself would," she explained.

"That's not saying much. Let's get going. What flight are we on?"

Chapter 4

A shuttle ride to the appropriate platform and a short wait later, Lex and Ma were boarding an interstellar passenger ship. It was something that Lex hadn't had to do for years, ever since he'd gotten his own ship, and he did not miss any part of the process. The lines, the terrible music in the waiting areas--and, as he was currently being reminded, the security checks. They had already scanned his bag, his body, and Ma. They then had asked him to confirm that he wasn't carrying any forbidden substances and devices, presumably just to waste a little more of his time, since they had already done the scans. His slidepad was checked for the proper identification and documentation, his reservation was checked and verified, and, after a short argument, his bag was accepted as carry-on rather than being checked. The only thing that made the entire process tolerable was the fact that the middle aged balding man administering the gauntlet was clearly enjoying it even less than Lex.

"Do you have an exotic animal transport authorization for that creature?" the man asked.

"Uh, let me see . . ." Lex said, taking his slidepad out for approximately the eighth time.

"Check your inbox," Ma informed him.

An instant later the appropriate message arrived.

"There we go."

The man eyed it, then looked to the creature at Lex's feet.

"A 'Funk'? Never heard of it."

"They're very rare," he said.

That much was true. Until recently, Lex had thought that there was only one . . . well, only one at a time, at least. When there are dozens of duplicates of various ages standing by to replace the original in the event of mishap, the appropriate census count becomes a little more muddied. Squee represented only the second named creature he was aware of, and it was almost certainly the only one to leave the planet of its birth.

"Mmm, yeah, I remember hearing about them now," the man said with a nod.

"I'm sure," Lex replied.

"Okay, you're in first class, so you can board now. Cabin three. It looks like you'll be getting off after the second stop," he said, bleeping Lex through the checkpoint and into the entryway of the ship.

Space travel in general was frequently treated as though it was functionally identical to the air travel of old, but the reality was closer to a cross between trucking and rail. Science bent the laws of physics to its whims and broke the light barrier for travel speed, but the sheer distances involved, along with the complexities of regulation and safety, meant that travel time still tended to be measured in days. Thus, rather than the cramped rows of airline-style seats in coach and the plush easy chairs in first class that populated the short-distance shuttles, full scale passenger haulers gave the coach folks a hallway and dining area as well, and the first class passengers got full rooms or suites. Despite a brief brush with celebrity, Lex had never actually had the opportunity to ride in a first class cabin. At first glance, he was impressed.

"My god . . ." he remarked. "It is almost as big as my apartment."

Opposite the door was a flatscreen, in the place where a window might have been if the cabin was anywhere near the hull. To one side was a couch; to the other, a narrow bed. Thin sliding doors led to a minimal bathroom (complete with shower) and a closet, respectively. Lex tossed his bag on the bed and flopped down on the couch, which put his own futon to shame. A moment later, an attendant knocked on the door, providing him with a complimentary glass of champagne, and asked if he needed anything for his dog.

"Water would be appreciated," Ma informed him.

"You heard the lady," Lex said with a grin.

"I'm sorry?" said the attendant curiously.

"Err, water would be appreciated," Lex repeated sheepishly.

Ma probably would have snickered, if she'd had the appropriate audio file. A moment later a dish and a bottle of spring water were provided. He poured it out for Ma, sprawled on the couch, and sipped at his sparkling wine.

"You know, Ma? As rescue plans go, this is a good one."

"Thank you, Lex. I hope that your opinion of it remains positive through to completion. Now that we have a moment, please remove one of the new slidepads, attach the reinforced case, and affix it to my harness."

"Okay," Lex said, digging out the items and, eventually, clipping an activated slidepad to one of the harness buckles.

The screen flipped on, then switched to a diagnostic screen and began to scroll commands unreadably fast. As it did, Ma tipped her head back and closed her eyes, looking for the life of her as though she'd just felt a refreshing breath of air conditioning after a long hot day.

"Thank you, Lex. I feel considerably less restricted now that I have a co-processor and externally maintained network access."

"No problem."

"The next phase does not need to occur for over twenty hours. How would you like to spend the time?"

"Actually, there are a few things that were bugging me. Care to answer a few questions?"

"Certainly."

"First off, why don't you stink? I mean, the only other funk I've ever met had . . . well, a funk about him."

"I administered one of Karter's odor control pills prior to my departure. It should last for several months. I presumed that travel would be simplified if I were not the source of a distracting aroma."

"That's for sure. Speaking of your departure, you never really went into detail about Karter's kidnapping."

"Karter was demonstrating a scale prototype of a device called a CME Activator."

"What is that?"

"What is the subject of your inquiry? A CME, or the CME Activator?"

"Both."

"A CME is a coronal mass ejection, a massive dispersal of stellar particles caused by the release of energy stored in the magnetic fields of the atmosphere of a star. The release is a result of the reconnection of magnetic field lines. The particles released by such an event distort and react with other magnetic fields. If a planet is bombarded, the resulting terawatt magnitude energy release and the associated geomagnetic storm can have effects ranging from intense aurora activity near the magnetic poles to massive damage to electrically-sensitive devices. An intense enough CME could theoretically interrupt the functioning of all electrical devices, as well as permanently damaging electrical infrastructure.

"The CME Activator is a device that Karter designed for the Earth military decades ago. It manipulates the field lines of a star into an alignment that will produce a sequential reconnection, ideally expending all magnetically-suspended energy in a series of CMEs."

"Wow . . . that was a lot of words."

"A CME Activator can be used to cause, at the very least, a planet-wide blackout that lasts for months."

"Whoa."

"That is an appropriate response. Three men representing an anonymous group were interested in a full-scale CME Activator. Following the successful deployment of the scale prototype, the men attempted to renegotiate the agreed-upon services. They then deployed EMP devices, resulting in my incapacitation and the kidnapping of Karter. I am uncertain as to how they were able to leave the planet."

"Do you know who the men were?"

"I do not possess enough information to produce a reliable hypothesis, but their behavior is consistent with highly organized political extremists. Please note that much of this information was disseminated in a prior interaction between us."

"I guess it didn't sink in. Just to be clear, when you say extremist, you mean terrorist."

"Terrorism is a likely goal, and the CME Activator is an effective tool in that regard."

"Then why were you selling to them!?"

"I had no evidence to be certain of their intentions, and Karter bares no political, ethical, or moral bias with respect to prospective clients."

Lex rubbed his temple. Suddenly, first class cabin notwithstanding, he was having doubts about the mission at hand.

"At what point did this lead to you donning a funk suit and tracking me down?"

"I was only able to restore myself by shifting primary processing duties to a backup server in the lower levels of the complex, isolated from the EMP assault. From there, I polled the limited array of sensors that were still active. I determined that Karter had left the planet, additional EMP mines had been deployed liberally throughout the debris field surrounding the planet, and the debris field did not appear to have been significantly disturbed. There were also at least three patrol craft outside the debris field. All attempts at communication failed. In order to deliver a message to the outside, I needed a means to deliver the message that was immune to EMP and able to react to changing conditions."

"And the best idea you could come up with was downloading yourself into a funk?"

"That remains to be determined. I deployed seventy-three concurrent operations, eighteen of which involved contacting you. Have you received any messages from me in the past few days?"

"No."

"I have not received any messages from any of the other operations either. It would thus appear that downloading myself into a funk was indeed the best idea I could come up with."

"So the entire functionality of a supercomputer can fit in the head of a funk?"

"Not nearly. Though the processing and data retention capacity of an organic brain are impressive, the instance of my program with which you are now interacting represents an extremely small subset of my full capabilities. It is limited to the entirety of my behavioral engrams, a short list of modules I anticipated would be indispensable during our trip, and a highly compressed archive of relevant data. In essence, that which is unique about me is present. With time and resources, my full self could even be reconstructed from the contents of this brain, but I am not currently all that

I could be. Where possible, existing behavior and capabilities of the nervous system were maintained. Pattern recognition and trajectory calculation in particular were quite efficiently achieved in the existing synaptic pathways, but do not expect me to be calculating the trajectories of a planet-scale field of orbital fragments."

"I'll keep that in mind. How did you even know how to download yourself?"

"I was the system executing the simulations utilized to design the funk, and thus have an understanding of the structure and function of its brain at the genetic level. I further had aided in the creation and application of the technology used to read and write Solby's memories, for the purposes of restoring him from backup. The difficult part was determining how to port my logic patterns to a biochemical processor, but Karter and I had done preliminary research into just that subject when he was considering shifting the computer system of his complex to an organic or 'wetware' system. The project was abandoned when it was determined that data fidelity issues begin to arise after approximately two months. While the replacement of exact memories with approximations is not a problem for an organic creature, for software based on digital logic, it would lead to corruption and eventual failure."

Lex squeezed his eyes shut and shook his head. "That was a lot of words, too. Are you saying we need to hurry up or you are going to start going haywire?"

"I have only been operating on this platform for approximately eleven days. There is plenty of time."

"Well, that's good," he said, finishing his champagne in one long swallow. He looked down at Ma again. She was sitting, her eyes turned steadily to him. "Hey. Why are you sitting on the floor?"

"I was told that I should not climb on the furniture."

"That was back when I thought you were just an animal. You paid for this flight cabin. Hop on up!" he said.

"Thank you," Ma replied, leaping effortlessly to the soft, microfiber seat. After a moment, she sat, remarking. "This is indeed preferable to the floor."

Lex thought for a minute.

"Okay, let me ask you this. You made it through the EMP stuff they had in orbit because you were made of meat, but how did you get a ship through? You can't tell me you made an organic ship."

"No. I gained control of a secondary fabrication facility in the lower levels of the laboratory portion of the complex and outfitted a small, FTL-capable escape pod with a heavy armored shell and delivered it to orbit with a mass driver in our northern hemisphere. The shell absorbed some minor debris impact, and the trajectory carried the pod beyond the patrol range of the ships in orbit. Once enough distance was between myself and their patrol sweeps, I ensured that the electronics had recovered, ejected the shell, and piloted to a shipping transfer station, where I stowed aboard a transport heading to Golana, where I met you."

"A what delivered you to orbit?"

"A mass driver."

"A what?"

"A rail gun."

"A wh--"

"A fancy slingshot."

"Ah," Lex said, finally understanding. "Doesn't that strike you as a little Wile E. Coyote?"

"I do not know anyone by that name."

"It is a classic cartoon character from a long time ago."

"I am afraid that I did not include my full cultural database."

"Well he was--"

There was a tone over the ship's PA system.

"Attention, passengers. The flight will be leaving dock in approximately sixty seconds. You will experience a few moments of weightlessness while the ship orients itself for transit. Please secure any belongings and fasten safety harnesses or utilize hand grips now. Refrain from utilizing sinks, showers, or drinking fountains until gravity is restored, and be sure that all open beverages or food containers are closed securely. VectorCorp thanks you for your cooperation, and for helping to keep this spacecraft safe, clean, and orderly."

Lex pulled a strap from the back of the couch and clicked it in place across his chest. Finding no simple way to do the same for Ma, he scooped her up and held her on his lap as the audible countdown reached zero. The gravity dropped away as inertial inhibitors kicked on and the ship detached from the station. It maneuvered itself out of the station area, shifted its orientation, and increased its engines.

Some very large or very luxurious ships used gravitational generators to provide their patrons with an uninterrupted sense of "down." Most were, instead, designed with the thrusters pointing off of the bottom of the ship. This, coupled with very finely-tuned inertial inhibitors, could knock the acceleration caused by the engines down to 1-G, giving everyone the feeling of gravity until it was time to stop, at which point there was a short, weightless moment while the ship was flipped over, and then the deceleration took over. Lex's own ship didn't have either, because fine-tuned inertial inhibitors were still too rich for his blood, and the lowest nonzero inertial value of a crude one couldn't knock the faster than light acceleration down to a survivable level. Thus, during FTL he set it to zero and got by with harnesses and weightlessness during his flights. It had never really bothered him.

After the ship jockeyed into position and entered the transit lane, it activated something called a Carpinelli field--the techno-magic that made faster-than-light travel possible--and they were off. The gravity faded back in, the PA announced that it was safe to move about the cabin, and the last interesting moment for the next twenty or so hours had ended. This was unfortunate, because the relative calm was giving Lex a moment to allow the severity of the task at hand to sink in. He'd gone up against long odds before, but that was different. That was VectorCorp--or, at least, one very small, very crazed portion of it. They had to at least give the appearance of operating within the bounds of the law, and as his currently-unmolested status as a passenger on one of their vessels would indicate, either didn't hold a grudge or perhaps didn't know what its more shadowy corners had been up to.

A terrorist group was *all* shadowy corners, and they didn't care one bit about law or public image.

"You are exhibiting signs of stress," said Ma. She was still in his lap, looking him in the eye.

"Yeah. Yeah, I am," he said, staring vaguely at the opposite wall.

"Are you aware that you are stroking my tail?"

"Oh! Oh, Jeez, I'm sorry," he said, suddenly realizing his absent-minded faux pas. He stopped and rigidly straightened in his chair.

"Is that inappropriate?" she asked, tilting her head inquisitively.

"I . . . don't know. I mean, if you were a lady, a human lady, that would be inappropriate for sure."

"Humans do not have tails, Lex."

"I know, but, you know, the same . . . region. Listen, never mind!"

For a moment, the pair was silent. Ma tipped her head again, eyes wandering in thought.

"I once suggested that increasing your knowledge, decreasing your unknowns, was a potential route to reduce anxiety and stress. Observation suggests that the opposite is true, a concept axiomatically described as 'ignorance is bliss.' At that time, and in the present situation as well, increased situational awareness has been directly proportional to vexation."

"I think that probably says something about the state of my life."

"Indeed. I shall endeavor to delay any additional stress-inducing behaviors until absolutely necessary."

"That's a good plan, I like that plan."

He sat silently again for a minute. A thought occurred.

"Hey, it strikes me I'm not even sure where this ship is going."

"For the purposes of stress-reduction, that information shall be withheld."

". . . great."

Chapter 5

Michella Modane was sitting in a dimly-lit church, in a pew near the front, and she had been for the last twenty minutes. She, through sources as trustworthy as she could manage, had arranged a meeting here, and her contact was late. That was to be expected, though. She would have been suspicious if he had been otherwise. The best sources of information were close enough to the root of the story to be at tremendous risk if they were to be discovered, so they were cautious, and caution took time.

She was supposed to be attending a two-week convention for broadcast journalists. Indeed, she was a speaker at no less than three panels, so she couldn't really afford to miss it. When the call had come in informing her that there was a man willing to meet her, she *certainly* couldn't afford to miss that. So she had adjusted her travel plans to include a short, unaccompanied shuttle ride to a space station a few hours away from Golana. It had cost her the only time she'd been able to set aside to visit Trevor, but opportunities like this didn't come along very often. Trevor would understand.

"Don't turn around," came a voice from behind her, suddenly.

She nodded once.

"You're the reporter."

Another nod.

"Okay. Let's get on with this."

"I want to thank you for meeting with me," she whispered.

The man behind her made a sound that, while not exactly a word, managed to quickly convey the message that the gratitude was appreciated but unnecessary, and that he would very much prefer that future gratitude be dispensed with in the interest of speed. It was a very efficient sound.

"My sources tell me that there has been a break-in at a local military facility. Can you confirm this?"

"No, not a break-in. A breach."

"Can you explain?"

"No one broke anything. No hacked systems. No blown doors. Security would have been able to stop that. No one would have been able to get anything that way. Someone walked in, took what they wanted, and walked out. They had codes. They knew patrols. This was a security breach. Someone inside."

He spoke minimally, and his voice was hushed. The sentences were quick and crisp in the distinctive fashion of a soldier.

"What was taken?"

"Don't know. Research wing. Storage depot."

"A weapon?"

"No. No weapons research here. Engineering. Logistics."

"Can you provide any details? Any at all."

There was a short silence. Finally, as though he'd finished running his answer past an internal censor and redacted anything sensitive, he replied, "Something unfinished. Abandoned. Wasted. Nothing slated for deployment. At least, not yet."

"I've received reports of similar break-ins--err, breaches--in military facilities and bases across the galaxy; Earth Coalition, Orion United Consortium of Planets. Virtually every major military organization. They may have been going on for years, escalating in recent months. Do you think that this is the start of some sort of insurgency?"

Again there was silence. Michella continued, "What do you suppose could be the cause of this rash of rebellion? What could be causing these men and women to betray their governments?"

This time there was a seething breath.

"Soldiers aren't betraying their governments, ma'am. Governments are betraying their soldiers. Moving too slow. Getting too comfortable in what they have. They aren't keeping up. It gets people killed. Makes civilizations weak."

"I don't understand."

"You will. You'll understand very soon. Good luck with your story, ma'am. Don't look back until you hear the door."

"Wait. I need something. A name, anything."

"A name? Fine. Ned Ludd. From Anstey. Right idea, wrong motivation."

Whereas the entry had been silent, the exit of her informant was punctuated by the steady, thudding footsteps of boots.

Michella made sure she'd jotted down all of the relevant information, what little there was. It was a good thing she would be heading to that convention. A number of her colleagues would be there, and many of her contacts. While her informant hadn't added much new information, he did confirm some things, and that was her first real breakthrough for this story. The rest was chasing down details. She was good at details.

#

Lex had learned a number of things in the last few hours. First and foremost, he had learned that it seemed to be physically impossible for a human being to be within an arm's length of a cute, fuzzy animal and not pet it. Virtually any time he let his mind wander, he realized that he was scratching the head or stroking the back of Ma, who had remained on his lap.

She eventually encouraged him to continue, reasoning after a brief consultation with a health site that interaction with an animal led to a lower heart rate, decreased blood pressure, and a general sense of well-being. He had suggested that said health benefits might not have taken into account the possibility of the animal in question being an artificial intelligence that he respected as an equal, but she remained unswayed.

The ship flipped and decelerated, made a stop to pick up and drop off passengers, then accelerated onto the next leg of its trip. In the hours that passed, he tried to get some sleep, and learned that computers, it seemed, talked in their sleep. At first he thought he was imagining it, but as her little body twitched a leg or flicked an ear periodically, he heard a low level hiss of static on his earpiece, accompanied by quiet snips of voice. It sounded a bit like the audio from skipping through a digital recording, little more than a word or so at a time.

"I . . . we . . . straightforward . . . trust . . . deserve . . . confident . . . lives . . . thank," she whispered amid the static.

When each had slipped into and out of the amount of sleep their bodies were willing to provide, he learned yet another thing. Ma was rather fond of games, but seldom had occasion to play them. This was because, with her typical level of processing power, it was difficult to find an opponent who was a match for her. In her current state, she found games of chess against Lex genuinely challenging. They played by hooking their slidepads up to the flatscreen in 3D mode, which rendered a digital table near the center of the room. It was worth pointing out that, challenged though she might be, she didn't do an awful lot of losing.

"I believe that is checkmate," she remarked.

"Yeah," said Lex, tipping over his virtual king.

"Another game?"

"No, I think I'm done with chess for a while. I'm gonna stretch my legs and get some food. I've never been to a first-class dining area before."

"I will join you," she replied, hopping down to have her leash clicked on.

The pair left their cabin and headed for the dining area. When they boarded, they had been the only people in first class, but that was hardly unusual. VectorCorp was still under investigation for nearly causing pan-global destruction during the Bypass Gemini Incident. This led to mandatory increased oversight and transparency, which cost the company a tremendous amount of money, even by their standards. They had used this as an excuse to increase prices to offset the cost of the security measures. People couldn't exactly stop using their services altogether--since, in most places, they were the only way to get from one star system to another--but they could certainly drop down to a cheaper ticket. This had the dual consequence of first class being a ghost town and Lex modifying the *S.O.B.* to have a second seat, for increasingly popular chartered single-passenger flights.

Evidently the previous stop had added three more people to first class. The dining area was a narrow room featuring three diner-style booths on one side of the aisle and a small counter with a flesh-and-blood waiter sitting on a stool, waiting to take orders.

One of the booths was occupied by a man in a highly-visible orange jumpsuit with stenciled lettering. He was older than Lex, but still a few years away from earning the unenviable descriptor of “older gentleman.” One hand was cuffed to a hand grip on the wall by a daunting set of restraints. He was trying, with great difficulty, to eat a plate of fried fish with his single free hand and a plastic spork. Despite the frustrating activity, he didn't seem particularly upset. Indeed, he had the sort of face and overall attitude that suggested that he had never, at any point in his life, been anything less than perfectly content. His hair was a blond crew cut. He had a mustache and beard, each cropped and shaped fastidiously into something that would have looked appropriate on a musketeer. His physique suggested he devoted a similar amount of care to his workout regimen.

The two men sharing the booth with him were armed, uniformed guards. Unlike their prisoner, they both looked as though the concept of contentment or joy was entirely alien. They sat silently, eyes carefully locked on the blond man as he thoroughly enjoyed his meal in a highly animated fashion.

When he noticed Lex, his face lit up.

“Well! It seems that the recent fiscal instabilities have not entirely frightened away the proud and noble members of the aristocracy!” he proclaimed in an impeccable British accent.

“Do not address the general public,” warned one of the guards.

“My dear man, there is nothing general about him. The very fact this man has seen fit to expend a not-insubstantial portion of his precious wealth to afford himself comfortable lodging during this journey clearly proclaims him to be part of the gentry. After all, not everyone can rely upon state-sponsored travel arrangements the likes of which I so regularly enjoy.”

“Either you behave yourself or this meal is over,” growled the second guard, slipping a stun rod a few inches from its holster.

“Given such an ultimatum, I must regrettably acquiesce, as it would be a shame to cut short so sumptuous a feast,” he remarked, enthusiastically digging into a pile of unidentifiable greenery.

Lex made his way to the waiter, passing the table along the way. As he walked by, Ma tapping along with him, the charismatic prisoner glanced first to the furry little creature, then to Lex, and back again. It was subtle enough that the guards didn't seem to notice, and even Lex wasn't sure it had happened.

A limited menu was produced for him, depicting the typical “meat/fish/veggie” trifecta that at some point in history had been determined to be suitable dietary variety for long-distance travelers. On the plus side, this being first class, the food was included in the price of the ticket, and today the role of "meat" was being played by filet mignon.

"You want anything?" Lex whispered under his breath.

"No. The food in your bag will be sufficient. I'm sorry, but I must excuse myself. I will be in the cabin, if you would kindly remove the leash."

"Uh . . . okay?" he said, unfastening it and watching her pace back to the room.

Once she had reached their cabin down the hall, where she was hidden from view for all but Lex, a few blinks of the light on her neck prompted the automatic door to open, and she slipped inside. He looked up to find that everyone in the room was staring at him curiously.

"Very well trained. Cost a bundle," he explained.

This seemed to be a sufficient explanation.

Lex sat at a booth to await his meal while the prisoner finished his. When the last of his meal had been cleaned from the plate, and the unreasonably cheerful man had made a few suitably satisfied smacks of his lips, he decided that it was time to antagonize his escorts once more as they removed the restraint from the hand grip and affixed it properly to his other hand behind his back.

"You know something, gents, despite our close quarters during this sojourn, I haven't learned a single thing about you. For instance, what sort of music do you like?"

"Mouth shut," replied a guard, standing him up and leading him back toward the cabins.

"Classical suits my tastes, personally, although I am recently reminded of my former fondness for funk," he remarked. His final word was delivered as he briefly made eye contact with Lex.

Lex tried to keep his expression neutral. Shortly afterward, his steak was delivered, along with a draft beer. He asked if he could eat it in his room, was assured that he could, and made his way to the door, nudging the door's open button with his elbow. Once inside, he discovered that Ma was nowhere to be seen.

"Ma?" he called, flipping a collapsible table out from beside the couch and setting his food down.

There was a flush, and a moment later, Ma nosed open the door to the bathroom and jumped onto the couch.

"Yes, Lex?" she asked.

He palmed his face. "I used to have a normal life. I swear I did. I miss those days."

"Is there something wrong?"

"There are several things wrong, Ma. The list is getting pretty long at this point, but currently one thing is way on top," he replied, lowering his voice. "That fellow with the fancy orange suit out there. Is he the one that we're meeting with?"

"That is correct. Through what means did you deduce this?"

"I think he recognized you. He used the word funk in a very pointed way."

"Astutely observed, Mr. Alexander."

"Why didn't you tell me that we would be meeting with a convict?"

"For the purposes of stress-reduction, that information was withheld."

"When were you going to tell me?"

"When it became necessary for you to take action."

Lex didn't say anything. It wasn't that he didn't want to say anything. He had quite a few choice words lined up, in fact. Unfortunately, this was one of those rare situations where screaming profanities wouldn't solve anything. For one, regardless of whether he was fond of the idea or not, chances were very good that if Ma had come up with it, it was necessary. For another, Ma did not respond well to hostility, and the last thing he needed was the one person who knew what the hell was going on to become bitter and resentful. Thus, rather than stringing together as many four-letter words as he could, he slowly attempted to regain his composure.

Sensing his dismay, Ma spoke. "I apologize if I have mishandled this. You have been extremely helpful thus far, coming to our aid when we needed you, despite no obligation to do so. I was not entirely straightforward, and for that I am sorry. Your trust was implicit from the beginning, and I may not have done all that I should have to deserve it, but I am confident that you will see your way clear to continue to lend your aid, on behalf of the lives that are at stake--and if not, I thank you for what you have done and, following the completion of this next stage, will gladly send you on your way with whatever reward you desire."

Lex squinted. There was something peculiar about the wording.

"Did . . . did you rehearse that little speech while you were sleeping?"

Ma's eyes opened wide, and her ears sagged slightly.

"How did you know that?" she asked, genuine surprise showing in a voice that, by rights, shouldn't have been capable of it.

"I heard bits and pieces of it in the earpiece."

"That . . . was not intentional. Or anticipated," she said, looking vaguely downward, her eyes darting slightly. "I have no record of activating the broadcast routine."

"Why were you practicing to begin with?"

"Because you are not a fool, Lex," she said, her eyes turning back to him and her steadiness appearing to return. "It was a relative likelihood that you would discover that I had withheld this information, and suspicion of manipulation is a reasonable interpretation of facts. I cannot afford to lose your aid at this point in time, so I assembled my prior speech and simulated it a number of times in order to ensure a proper execution. Was it successful? Have my feelings on the matter been adequately explained, and your concerns placated?"

Lex sighed. "Here is what I want to happen, Ma. You tell me, in detail, exactly what is going to go down. While you're doing that, I'm going to eat this steak and drink this beer. Don't worry about stressing me out, because that ship has sailed."

"I'm afraid that is not possible at this time."

"Why not?"

"Because one of the more difficult aspects of the plan needs to be implemented within a fifteen-minute window which began eleven seconds ago. Due to the nature of the task, I will need to begin as soon as possible, which leaves me with insufficient time to adequately describe the plan."

"Well, at least tell me what you are planning to do."

"I am going to cause an equipment failure that will force this ship to make an unscheduled stop on a transfer and maintenance station. Please finish your beer, and be careful with the steak knife. Things are going to get bumpy."

"Isn't that danger--"

"I'm afraid I need to concentrate at this time. Please fasten your restraints and, if you are willing, restrain me as well."

"Hold on just one minute!"

It was too late, though. She had settled down, shut her eyes, and begun whatever it was she was going to do. The red light began to flicker aggressively, and the screen of her slidepad scrolled schematics, commands, and warnings.

"Damn it!" he cursed, downing his beer, buckling his belt, and pulling the scheming AI onto his lap.

At first, nothing happened. Then came the canary in the coal mine of electrical problems: dimming lights. Almost instantly, there was a sudden, sharp acceleration, something that they absolutely should not have felt with the inertial inhibitor on. The sound of the engines--until now, little more than a distant hum that was quickly ignored to the point of becoming the new silence--asserted itself. It was a sickly wail. To a layman, it would have been clear that something wasn't right. To Lex, who had dealt with his share of failing engines, it was a little more unnerving.

"That plasma mix is starting to sound a little rich."

"Concentrating," came the distorted, drawn-out reply in his earpiece.

The ship's shuddering was considerably more violent as she spoke. Lex wisely decided to hold his tongue.

"Attention, passengers," announced an automated message, "please return to your seats in a quick and orderly manner. Attach all emergency restraints in the manner indicated during the pre-flight briefing. The spacecraft is experiencing minor equipment problems. The crew is currently addressing the problem. Remain calm and follow any instructions provided by the crew. An unscheduled stop, to diagnose and correct any possible issues, will occur in: Forty. Three. Minutes."

That was the fun thing about space travel. When a ship, a train, or a plane experienced issues, the main problems stemmed from the fact that it would be stopping, sometimes catastrophically. A spacecraft, on the other hand, had the unique problem of *not* stopping. There was no air friction, and courses were generally plotted to be as far from gravity wells as possible. This meant that, even if the engine completely shut down, the ship would continue skimming along at the same speed. If the speed wasn't high enough, and the ship wasn't close enough to any VectorCorp scanners, the ship would show up at its destination in a few decades. Whether or not the desiccated remains inside would still count as *passengers* was a matter for philosophers.

On the other hand, if a ship was going too fast, it would reach its destination right about on time, but at close to light speed--and, afterward, there wouldn't be much of a destination anymore. This was actually a favored tactic utilized by many a desperate military. Such ships were classified "Relativistic Kill Vehicles," and rumor had it there were engines specifically designed to propel them to the appropriate speeds. Safeguards existed to prevent accidental or purposeful collisions of that type, but they were mostly dedicated to eradicating the malfunctioning ship prior to its arrival, so it seldom did the pilot or passengers any good.

Since this ship was clearly malfunctioning, but not badly enough to be considered a threat to anyone but itself, the course of action involved pulling off of the primary course into a secondary emergency lane, dropping down from faster-than-light speed, then pushing the ship's engines to maximum safe limits to get down to a manageable conventional speed. In this case, it would take almost forty-five minutes to do so.

"Attention, passengers. As a precaution against potentially dangerous changes in velocity, the secondary inertial inhibition unit will now be activated. For the duration of this flight, you will be experiencing weightlessness. Please do not leave your seats unless necessary."

There was the muffled sound of startled screams as the gravity dropped away. For the other passengers, this was all probably terrifying. Knowing as he did the cause of the current emergency, Lex was considerably less concerned. It wasn't that this wasn't still tremendously dangerous. It was. Monkeying around with the operation of a ship in motion, particularly during FTL travel, was a recipe for disaster if the person mucking didn't know what they were doing. But Ma knew what she was doing. In fact, the longer he knew her, the more it seemed to Lex that Ma was the one who got to *decide* what should be done. Thus, while most of the ship feared for their lives, Lex's primary concern was the rapidly cooling cut of beef that had begun to drift around his cabin in the center of a galaxy of garlic and herb-roasted potatoes and steamed carrots.

"Come on," he groaned, straining against the restraint to try to snatch the filet as it floated tantalizingly close. He managed to brush it with his fingertips, causing it to spin lazily away. "This has got to be against some sort of international treaty."

Chapter 6

The forty-three minutes were almost up, and Lex had managed to snatch and consume most of the veggies and potatoes as they were pushed around by the air conditioning vent, but the meat had remained elusive. Three failed attempts to snag it had taught him that making a grab before it was close enough would just send it off into an unreachable corner for a while, so he was holding his hand out and waiting agonizingly for it to make it to his palm. The steak was probably cold and not worth eating now, but it had stopped being about wanting to eat it half an hour ago. Now he wanted it out of sheer stubbornness.

"We are now docking at our destination. Gravity will be restored momentarily," said the automated voice. Lex reached more desperately. "Ships are standing by to bring you to your next destination. We would like to apologize for any inconvenience that this may have caused, and please remember that VectorCorp is dedicated to safety, speed, and efficiency. Thank you. Gravity will be reestablished in five . . . four . . ."

Lex flicked the meat toward the far wall.

"Three . . . two . . ."

It rebounded off of the wall and flew back at him. When it was close, he grabbed at it.

"One . . . gravity reestablished."

An instant before the weight returned, he closed his fingers around it.

For a second or two, he simply stared in astonishment.

"Yes. *Yes! Ahahaha*!" he proclaimed triumphantly, holding it aloft like a trophy.

"What? What is it?" asked Ma, slightly startled by the outburst as she finally released her concentration.

"I am meat-juggler supreme, that's what!"

"Sir?" said a new voice.

Lex turned to the door to see the very same attendant who had brought Ma her water. He froze, meat still in the air, as she took in the contents of the room. The walls were flecked with grease and oil from where the various bits of food had bounced off, and he was holding an uneaten medallion of beef as though he had caught the final from a legendary baseball game. Ma was standing on his lap, staring at him as curiously as the attendant.

"I don't know what this looks like, but it's not what it looks like," Lex said.

"As our only first class passenger, you are the first off of the ship. Please gather your belongings, and we apologize for the inconvenience," she said, as though nothing about the situation in any way fazed her.

"Thanks. Give me two minutes," he said.

"Yes, sir," she said, closing the door.

Lex unlatched himself and lowered Ma to the floor, venturing over to his duffel to brush aside a few stray veggies and make sure nothing got loose or broken during its zero-G adventure. He placed the hard-earned--but no longer edible--filet onto the edge of the couch. While he determined the condition of his possessions, he whispered harshly to the furry little ringmaster of this circus.

"I want to know exactly who this guy is and what is about to happen."

"He is a former associate of Karter. Like you, he helped to test and advise on the development of certain avenues of research. His specialty was infiltration and intelligence. I am uncertain of his name, as in his collaborations with us he requested that we refer to him by no fewer than three different aliases. He is currently serving a sentence for being part of a squad responsible for violating three provisions of a multi-system treaty--for this, he was officially declared him a war criminal. Due to the minimal involvement in the incident and his cooperation with authorities, he was the only member of his group to be assigned to medium security. I managed to schedule an emergency fumigation of his cell block and flag most of the penal fleet of his facility for a security sweep, thus requiring him to be transported to an alternate, off-planet holding facility via civilian transit."

"Prisons can just put criminals on any old ship?"

"Only when official vessels cannot be made available within the required time frame and the prisoner has no history of violent crime."

"And what did this guy do?"

"His squad possessed and activated a class three, man-portable energy weapon within a populated area outside the bounds of an officially declared war."

"What does that mean exactly?"

"It means that they were caught using an experimental plasma cutter, designed by Karter, that was powered by a miniature fusion reactor. The reactor, if allowed to overload, could have rendered an entire city uninhabitable."

"Whoa."

"That is an appropriate reaction."

"So, what happens now?"

There was silence. Lex turned to see Ma rather intensely staring at the filet on the couch.

"Ma? Did you want the steak?"

"No," she replied. A drop of drool trickled from her lip.

"Are you sure? Because you look like you want it pretty bad."

"What you are witnessing is an autonomic reaction to certain olfactory and visual stimuli. It is in no way representative of wants or needs as defined by my higher thought processes," she said, licking her lips and turning to him. "Please repeat your question."

"What happens now?"

"Now we liberate him from his armed escort. After that, we board the *S.O.B.*, which is docked in short-term bay I-85, and leave the facility. From there, he will direct us to a safe location, where the next stage of the plan will be determined."

"It sounded like you said, 'liberate him from his armed escort.' At what point did you think that this was something I would be able to do?"

"Leave that aspect to me."

"Fine, but won't people see? Won't there be video? I wouldn't have agreed to help if I'd known I would have been incriminating myself in a major crime!"

"This station was selected for this phase of the plan because it has failed six consecutive security audits due to an uncorrected hardware flaw in its surveillance systems. There are no active monitors or logging systems. Only eye-witnesses will be able to identify you, and all possible steps will be taken to avoid the appearance of collaboration between yourself and our target. But please move quickly. They are likely moving him as we speak," she said, hopping to the floor and picking up the leash in her teeth. "Time for a walk."

"Fine, but I want it on the record that I'm not happy about this."

Lex clipped on the leash, threw his bag over his shoulder, and headed out into the hall. The attendant was waiting for him there.

"We are currently docked at a space station known as VC-808. There are four commuter shuttles ready to take you to your destination. They will be leaving in fifteen minutes. I am afraid that none of the shuttles have first-class accommodations, but we would gladly refund the fare difference," the attendant began.

"Tell her that you have an alternate means of conveyance," Ma recommended. "Your absence on an exit vehicle may attract attention."

"Yeah, I appreciate the gesture, but after the last hour, I think I'd be more comfortable on a smaller vessel. I know a guy who works here. I'll catch a ride with him," Lex said as gently as possible.

"Very well, sir. We hope you'll ride with VectorCorp again in the future."

"I don't see how I can avoid it," he remarked.

He was directed to the nearest exit, which led to a pressurized gangway and into the transfer station.

For one who has never seen a remote transfer station, conjuring an accurate mental image is actually quite simple. Begin by picturing a bus or train depot. Not one of the big hubs frequented by commuters and tourists, mind you, but one of the sketchy, middle-of-nowhere depots. The kind of place that exists not because there is a large city nearby, but because there isn't anything even remotely resembling civilization for far enough in every direction that, in the event of an equipment failure, the chances are very good that all involved would starve to death before seeing another human being. A tiny, poorly-lit skeleton of a place with barely enough equipment to do its job. Now, imagine that everything, including the oxygen, has been recycled for the last decade. That dismal, smelly image perfectly describes the vast majority of transfer stations, this one included.

Here, in the loading and unloading areas, no consideration at all had been given to the subject of gravity. Instead, a wide metal grid ran along the walls, and the longer corridors had a slowly-moving chain conveyor that would haul toward their destination any passenger brave enough to grab one. It gave the whole complex the look of a series of LED-lit elevator shafts jammed together at right angles, like an M.C. Escher daydream.

Things became a bit more hospitable toward the central waiting area. There, a small section of the station had an artificial gravity field, seats, network terminals, and places to eat and freshen up. Unfortunately, Lex wasn't headed in that direction.

“They will be moving the prisoner to the security area. Take the shaft to the left. Please move quickly. Extricating him will be enormously complex if we fail to do so before he is properly remanded.”

“Easy for you to say. You try moving quickly in zero-G with a duffel bag and a house pet without being conspicuous.”

He set Ma adrift for a moment in order to cinch the strap of the bag tight across his chest, then tucked her under his arm and got to work. Though he was anything but an expert in microgravity navigation, Lex had learned a thing or two from his ill-fated trip through Blake's. Not much, but more than enough to give him an edge over the hapless tourists who were littering the shafts, awkwardly clutching at bundles of luggage and unruly children. He avoided the pull-chains, instead bouncing from grid to grid, propelling himself as quickly as he dared according to the directions being given by Ma.

“To reach the security area, turn right here. Now up. Faster please,” she calmly stated, as Lex struggled to make the sudden changes in direction as indicated.

“Listen, could you give me a little more of a heads-up on these turns?”

“Left, left, right, right, up, down, up--” she fired off mechanically.

“Okay, not *that* fast.”

“There, ahead. The guards and their prisoner.”

Sure enough, working their way laboriously along a narrow shaft with no handy drag chain was the pair of guards. The orange-clad prisoner was being towed along like so much luggage, eyes watching down the shaft. When he spotted Lex and the black and white creature under his arm, the prisoner grinned. In a smooth motion, he swung his restrained feet frontward, hooking them onto the grid and bringing the entire procession's forward progress to a sudden end.

"Damn it, what did I tell you about that?" barked a guard.

"So terribly sorry, gents. Just can't seem to get the hang of this low-gravity nonsense. Perhaps if my hands were free, I could lend a hand in my own transportation," he politely suggested.

As one of the guards attempted to untangle the prisoner's feet, Lex tried to keep out of sight at the edge of the shaft.

"Okay, so what now?" he whispered.

"Attempting to access . . . I am afraid that the Near Field Communication-based locking module utilized by the restraints will not operate at this distance. I need to get closer."

"How much closer?"

"Within eighteen inches."

"There is no way I can do that without obviously being involved."

"That is likely an accurate assessment. It was not my intention to involve you personally in this aspect of the escape. Please remove the leash, then proceed swiftly to Docking Bay I and prepare the *S.O.B.* for travel. We will be arriving shortly."

"I sure hope you know what you're doing . . ."

#

Further ahead in the shaft, the prisoner continued to be of no help at all to his escorts.

"If you don't unhook your feet, I swear to God, I will use the stun rod."

"Again, I am frightfully sorry. Must be some manner of muscle spasm. Poor circulation, you see. Long trips like these always seem to cause it to act up."

"I'll show you what a muscle spasm looks like," growled the second guard, unsheathing his stun rod.

"What the hell is that!?" exclaimed his partner, just in time for a fuzzy black and white creature to cannon into the three of them.

For a few seconds, chaos ensued. Zero-gravity was no place for a creature without thumbs, which left Ma scrabbling somewhat haphazardly in her attempts to reach the restraints. The guards, still unsure of what precisely they were dealing with, had degenerated to screaming orders at one another and fumbling for their weapons. The prisoner simply seemed delighted at the level of confusion. His delight only increased when Ma finally maneuvered herself to his feet. She hooked her paws around a nearby handrail; her red light flickered for a moment and the leg restraints clicked open.

There are those who would have gladly paid admission for what came next.

Over the course of human development, humans frequently found themselves entering new environments. Without fail, the first order of business was always to determine how best to inflict bodily harm on other humans while immersed in that environment. It became clear in a matter of moments that, yes, there was indeed a form of martial arts that was performed in zero-gravity while one's hands were bound, and, yes, this man was well-versed.

A quick tap of his toes pivoted his body around, allowing his hands to grip the rail behind him. Thus anchored, he delivered a swift kick to one guard, causing him to spin uncontrollably. A thrusting heel sent him ricocheting down the shaft. His partner managed to raise a stun rod, but a heartbeat later, the prisoner's feet were locked about his wrist. A quick, crouching motion yanked the guard forward, and a subsequent twist and mule kick launched the unlucky escort directly at his partner. The two collided, forcefully dislodging the plasma pistol that the latter had drawn. The entire display was over in two seconds, but it had given Ma time to release his hand restraints as well. The skilled prisoner plucked the liberated pistol from the air, stowed Ma under one arm, and propelled himself away from his former captors.

A chime from the slidepad on Ma's harness drew his attention. Displayed on its screen was a map of the station with a highlighted route.

#

“That was a somewhat graceless solution, but the results are inarguable,” Ma stated in Lex's ear, amid much static and distortion.

“What's that, Ma? I can't hear you. I think the hands-free is out of range.”

“Have you reached the ship yet?” she asked, voice slightly clearer.

“I'm barely halfway down the next shaft. Why, are you done already?”

As a response, alarms began to sound, leading to utter panic in a space station that was already having difficulty dealing with the sudden arrival of an unexpected ship.

“I guess so,” he remarked.

“I suggest you move very quickly.”

“You don't need to tell me twice!” he affirmed, launching himself along the corridor.

Navigation was immensely simpler with both hands free, though the atmosphere of chaos slowed him down somewhat. He darted about the shaft, avoiding dislodged carry-on bags and commuters clumsily trying to figure out which way to flee. After a second turn brought the entrance to Docking Bay I into view, a louder bit of commotion behind him prompted him to turn.

The prisoner was, to put it bluntly, showing off. With Ma tucked under his arm like a football, he was practically sprinting along the walls, springing back and forth with flawless pivots to give himself enough momentum for another few steps.

"I am engaging an auto-start sequence on the *S.O.B*'s systems," Ma stated as she passed. "Minimum operational readiness will be achieved in approximately forty-five seconds."

The escaped convict dove through the door to the docking bay, Lex snagging the edge and hauling himself through shortly after. The pair converged on dock 85.

"Ah, yes. I rather thought you would be here. Fellow from first class, yes? I believe this is yours," the convict said, handing over Ma. "Terribly sorry, won't be a moment."

He drifted slightly back into the main area of the bay, which had the general appearance of a wider-than-average shaft, with regularly-spaced garage-sized alcoves leading to the airlocks associated with each bay.

"Ahem! Attention, denizens of . . ." he proclaimed, turning aside to Lex to quietly ask, "What docking bay is this, my boy?"

"I."

"Denizens of bay I! Anyone still lingering within my general vicinity in the next thirty seconds will be considered hostages, and thus will be joining me when I leave in my ship. Whether or not you fit *inside* said ship is not my concern--you'll be coming along regardless! For those doubtful of my ability to enforce such a policy, may I direct your attention to my right hand!"

He raised the pistol in the indicated hand. The response was immediate, with a flood of people moving in a crazed mob toward the exit, forcing back the security officers and guards that were trying to enter.

Lex took advantage of the madness to enter the pressurized dock and slip into the cockpit. Once the bay door was clear, the fugitive heaved it shut. It was a heavy-duty hinged metal device built to keep any docking mishaps from depressurizing the whole station; after a blast or two from his pistol fused the opening mechanism, it wasn't going to be letting anyone in or out without some serious mechanical assistance. After that, he joined Lex in the *S.O.B.*, strapping into the recently-installed passenger seat, situated directly behind the pilot's seat. The two seats more or less filled the cockpit to capacity, with a tiny bit of space on the floor on both sides of the seats. The duffel was crammed into one side and held in place with elastic straps. Ma drifted into the other, hooking her paws around the straps she found there.

"Nice ship," he remarked.

"Yeah, thanks. You mind telling me who you are?"

"You are aiding in my escape, but you don't know who I am? Well, aren't you an interesting little riddle. We'll do introductions once we are in the clear, if you don't mind. Right now, you and I are going to have to figure out how to get the dock's door to open, which they will certainly have locked, and how to get past the security ships, which they will certainly have dispatched."

"Interfacing with the *S.O.B.* on-board systems," Ma stated in his earpiece, drifting onto his lap and holding herself in place with one of the harness straps. When she continued, it was via the speaker system of the ship. "Attempting to open doors . . . door access refused, attempting override security. Processing . . . processing . . ."

"I say. That's a familiar vocal tick," remarked the passenger.

The creature on Lex's lap had its eyes shut tight, head jerking and shaking every few moments while the red light remained almost constantly lit. Finally she relented, wavering slightly as through enormously fatigued.

"Encryption complexity sufficient to render an override impossible within a useful time window with current resources. Activating tractor beam in order to facilitate physical override."

"I rather think a tractor beam won't be sufficient. Haven't you got any weaponry?" asked the ex-prisoner.

"Trust me, my tractor beam will be plenty," Lex assured him.

It had never been Lex's intention to make *S.O.B.* a combat vessel, but considering the ship's creator, the idea of missing an opportunity to add destructive capability to a vehicle was practically sacrilegious. Thus--along with a slick black paint job to blend with deep space, heat syncs to cool engines and fool heat sensors, and an engine that could be made to belch all sorts of disruptive radio waves--Karter had installed an overpowered tractor beam with a setting that had roughly the same effect on its target that a jackhammer would have on a watermelon.

"Calculating resonance frequency and determining structural weaknesses. Deploying," Ma said.

The beam kicked on, and instantly it was clear the sort of damage something that amounted to little more than a high-tech replacement for a tow rope could do in the right hands. The whole ship rattled as it did its work, forcing the unrestrained Ma to hold a bit more tightly to Lex's harness. On the surface of the door, rivets popped and welds opened like a zipper. In seconds, the seal was compromised and the bay decompressed, wrenching the damaged door free. As it cartwheeled into space, four security ships strafed into view, with easily a dozen more lurking a bit further out.

"Finally!" Lex proclaimed, slipping a stick of gum from his pocket and tossing it in his mouth.

"Might I suggest--" his guest began.

"No talking," Lex snapped, revving the engines and blasting out of the bay.

The ships he was facing were slow, clumsy, short-distance patrol vessels. They were barely larger than their own cockpits and, thanks to the obvious danger of using high-powered weapons near a civilian space station, they were primarily armed with devices designed for incapacitation. That in no way made them harmless, however. For one thing, as previously stated, an incapacitated spacecraft was essentially a projectile, and projectiles didn't mix well with fragile ships and structures the likes of which the patrols were supposed to guard. To deal with this, the security ships tended to be equipped with their own (fortunately less destructive) tractor beams and old-fashioned grappling cables to try to bring disabled ships to a halt.

They also had a tricky bit of technology that freelancers had come to call “the clothesline.” Security ships would pair off and link a pair of emitters that had been installed on each of them. A ribbon of bright blue energy would then zap to life between them. If said ribbon so much as grazed a ship, the hull temperature would start to spike. A few seconds of exposure would blow the coolant system, forcing the pilot to either kill the engines or kill everyone in the vicinity of the engines when they eventually ruptured.

Two such clotheslines flickered on like neon threads ahead of Lex, and his visual scanners showed that there was a handful more trying to box him in.

A quick waggle of the control stick sent the pair of ships ahead of him into a sideways slide to the left to compensate. He then shifted to the right and darted upward. The ships above him tried to close off the path, but, unfortunately for them, the two pilots didn't quite have matching reflexes. One drifted wide, nearly smashing into one of his fellow security ships, and leaving a gaping hole in their defenses for Lex slip through. A solo ship, either in an attempt to intimidate him or simply due to plain old obliviousness, swept close enough to brush shields, forcing Lex back down toward another pair of ribbons. They slid together and tried to tighten up the net, but he eased his ship into a careful orientation and managed to thread the needle between the lines.

One of the security ships, in its panicked attempt to pursue, managed to cross the path of one the other ship's lines, instantly triggering a failsafe and drifting dead in the water. By the time the other ships managed to sort themselves out and get back on track, Lex had open space ahead of him and could put his monster of an engine to work.

When Lex described to Karter what sort of things he wanted in a ship, top on the list was speed, and the lunatic inventor had delivered. Despite the fact that his previous ship, Betsy, had been equipped with triple the engines it was intended to have, and an oversized power plant to run them, *S.O.B.* was several times more powerful with what looked like (but was absolutely not) stock equipment. With a little distance to get up a head of steam, and without an atmosphere to contend with, Lex had yet to find anything that could even keep pace with the *S.O.B.*, let alone catch up.

He hammered the throttle until the security ships were nowhere in sight. Once the sensors were clear, he picked out a suitably random destination and activated the Carpinelli Field. The view out the cockpit headed toward the blue side of the spectrum until it rocketed past ultraviolet.

"Okay, I'm going to plot out a few random jumps to make sure they can't send anyone after us. Once I'm done, the three of us are going to have a little chat. Understand?"

"Certainly," said the former prisoner.

"Of course," said Ma.

"Good," Lex said, shaking his head and muttering as he flipped through the star charts. "What a waste of a stick of gum . . ."

Chapter 7

Commander Purcell sat alone in her quarters. The space station that acted as her command center was an outdated military repair and defense support model, which, among other things, meant that personal space was kept to the bare essentials. A single cot occupied one wall. It was attached via hinges, and was currently folded up to reveal what was technically a chair, but was more accurately the slightly cushioned top of a footlocker. There was a charging station and mounting arm for an antiquated but practically indestructible military-grade datapad. A sliding door on one wall revealed a waterproof booth with a nozzle, though calling it a shower would be an insult to modern plumbing. It also contained a handful of biological waste disposal receptacles, the description and usage of which are best left to the imagination. Suffice to say, their resemblance to vacuum cleaner attachments was not coincidental. Everything was either bare metal or painted a shade of institutional green that seemed calculated to sap the will to live from everyone in a fifty meter radius.

At the moment, she was seated in the chair, a modular desk surface folded down over her lap, with the datapad mounted in front of her face.

Occupying the desk was a relic of a bygone age, the qwerty keyboard. She was tapping away at it, interacting with some manner of text-messaging program on the datapad's screen. Extremely high security dispatches were frequently communicated in plain text. This was largely due to the fact that audio or video messages could be easily overheard or witnessed. The tiny amount of sensitive data represented by each message could similarly be encrypted far more heavily, and each message separately, which ensured that a cracking program would have very little to work with, and thus little hope of producing useful results. As a final bonus, it allowed for absolute anonymity beyond a screen name. In the case of Purcell and the mysterious party on the other side of the communication channel, these had remained set to their default values: Local for herself and Remote for her associate.

"Report progress," read Remote's first comment.

"No progress. The inventor will not cooperate," she typed in reply.

"We did not expect him to be easily convinced. You must use persuasion."

"He seems to believe that he is in the superior bargaining position."

"Threaten him."

"We have threatened him. We have *dismantled* him. He does not feel any need to comply. He doesn't even seem concerned."

"Torture him, then."

"He has killed five of my men in escape attempts. If we were to torture him, I doubt that anything he would design for us as a result could be trusted. I have serious doubts that we should rely upon him. We would do the human race a tremendous favor by removing him from the population."

"Not before we get the full designs and apparatus to build a full-scale device."

"There must be someone else who can design them. The partial plans and small-scale are available to us."

"There are other teams of engineers who can do it, but they are all in the employ of major firms, or militaries, or governments. We've tried to secure suitably skilled military engineers before. Too risky. And no civilian design team would produce a device with such destructive potential. Even if they could, the results would be traceable and repeatable by others. The inventor is a single man who has voluntarily removed himself from society. He can give us what we need without attracting the attention of law enforcement until it is too late."

"What do you suggest we do, then?"

"You say he feels he is in a superior bargaining position? Bargain with him. See if you can buy his cooperation. I will finance any reasonable demand."

"And if the demand is unreasonable?"

"Agree. When he has outlived his usefulness, kill him. He'll never collect."

"Very well."

"Keep me updated."

"Affirmative."

Purcell closed the connection and placed the datapad back in its dock. The idea of negotiating seriously with this man was utterly repulsive to her. He'd killed her men without showing a trace of regret. The idea of killing him when this was all over, on the other hand, might just make it all worthwhile.

#

Back in the cramped cockpit of *S.O.B.*, Lex was finally happy with the next few stops on his ship's route.

"Okay. We've got twenty-five minutes before the first stop, so let's get the preliminaries out of the way, shall we?"

"Surely," said the man in the seat behind him.

Lex fiddled with some controls and managed to pivot his seat enough to look his passenger in the eye.

"My name's Lex," he said, extending a hand.

"You can call me Mr. Garotte," said the passenger, with a firm shake.

"You got a first name, Garotte?"

"I do, and a last one. Neither of which is Garotte."

"A codename, then?"

"Trust me. Things will be much less problematic that way."

"I wished you'd said that first. I would have come up with something cooler for me."

"Ace seems appropriate."

"We'll be sticking with Lex."

"Very well, Lex. You've been sent by Karter, I presume, based on the presence of his little pet here. Soul Brother, I believe it was?"

"Yes, I'm here because of Karter. No, he didn't send me. And this isn't Solby; this is his female counterpart, Squee. Only it isn't her, either. It's really Ma."

"Ma? I think you're confused, my boy. Ma was what Karter called that control system of his. He probably just installed a similar voice module in that slidepad on the beast's back."

"Tell him, Ma."

"The cerebral tissue of the funk with the designation 'Squee' is currently being utilized as an organic processing unit to run a useful subset of the capabilities and functions available to Ma. For interface purposes, it can be interacted with and treated in a manner identical to Ma," remarked the voice over the ship's systems.

"Thanks, Ma. That clears everything up," Lex said flatly.

"Well, then. Clever trick, that," said Garotte. "So, if Karter didn't send you, why the high-stakes breakout?"

"Ma asked for help. Although, to be fair, she didn't say I was going to be aiding and abetting a known criminal."

"The computer asked you to help? I suppose Karter must have left instructions to be *delivered* by the computer."

"What? No, she--"

"This is not a productive area of discussion," remarked Ma.

"Indeed. Regardless of who is responsible for issuing the orders, *why* have you seen fit to liberate me?"

"Karter has been kidnapped," Lex said.

"Egad! Big Sigma is a veritable fortress. How did someone manage that?"

"This has yet to be determined definitively. However, the parties responsible were commissioning the construction of a CME Activator," Ma explained.

"That's a--" Lex began to explain.

"A planetary blackout device. I'm familiar with it," Garotte nodded.

"Oh . . . okay."

"Nasty bit of technology, that. I can't imagine the individuals responsible have charitable uses in mind."

"And now they have Karter."

"A man *considerably* more dangerous than anything they might have tried to buy from him," said Garotte with a nod. "Yes, I think I see the importance of the task at hand. Do we know who did this?"

"This has yet to be determined definitively. Extremist intentions are likely," Ma provided.

"Mmm. Well, then we'll need to gather a bit of information, find out who precisely we are dealing with. Once we know what we are up against, we'll need to secure the resources to penetrate their defenses and get our boy."

"Considerations have been made regarding combat resources."

"Oh, you brought weapons?"

"No. Information has been gathered and preliminary plans have been drawn up for the acquisition of Zerk."

"What's Zerk?" Lex asked.

"I dare say that may be a *bit* drastic," Garotte scoffed.

"Time is limited, and Zerk is the most efficient damage vector available, short of tactical nuclear weapons, which, while more easily accessible, are less autonomous."

"Given enough time, I think Zerk could easily outclass a tactical nuke, but it would have to be a fairly desperate situation to consider deployment."

"What's Zerk?" Lex asked again.

"Properly applied, Zerk is an extremely flexible tool that will facilitate a host of widely varied tactics," Ma continued.

"*What the hell is Zerk*!?" Lex growled.

"I could answer that question, my boy, but doing so would expose you to highly classified information that you are not cleared to know. If the appropriate authorities were to become aware of your knowledge, then you would be as eagerly sought as I am likely to be, once word spreads of my liberation."

"Oof. Been there, done that. Not interested in going down that particular road again," he said with a grimace.

"Wise decision. Right, then. I would say that the course is clear. Are you familiar with a planet by the name deGrasse?"

"Yeah, I think."

"Once your evasive maneuvering is complete, make your way there. I'll give you the coordinates of a little development where I keep a cache of emergency supplies. We shall head there, where I shall have a shower, a shave, and a stiff drink. Once those very necessary steps are taken, I shall see what, if any, contacts remain available to me that can provide information regarding our mysterious subjects of interest."

"That's it? You're just joining in? No further convincing needed?"

"Duty calls, my boy," Garotte said, slapping him on the shoulder. "And when duty calls, we answer. In addition, the act of returning me to my freedom is one deserving of a measure of gratitude, and it is been ages since I've had so stimulating an activity offered to me. Besides, until a few minutes ago, my agenda had been comprised entirely of incarceration. Now my schedule is cleared. One must keep busy."

"Thank you for your cooperation, Mr. Garotte," Ma said with digital politeness.

"What exactly do you do, if tracking down and infiltrating a terrorist group is busy work? I mean, that was some fancy footwork back in the space station. You some sort of special forces commando?"

"Zero-gravity drills are part of basic training for all armed forces."

"That doesn't answer my question."

"No, it doesn't. Well spotted. If you continue to ask questions regarding my personal history, you may notice a trend emerge."

"I know you're an expert in intelligence and infiltration. I know that you got locked up for a war crime involving some kind of overpowered cutter, and that you worked for Karter."

"Well, that's already more than I would have told you, so you are well ahead of the curve."

"Fine, asshole."

"My dear boy, I apologize wholeheartedly for my inability to be forthcoming, but it is a regrettable consequence of my field. Do try not to take it personally."

"No, it's fine. I got it. Need-to-know basis. It just bugs me that you probably know all about me and I know next to nothing about you."

"I'm afraid I haven't a clue who you are, nor am I particularly curious."

"But . . . I mean. I was all over the news a few years ago. T-Lex?"

"I've been in prison for three years. If your brush with celebrity fell within that time period, then I'm afraid I am rather likely to have missed it. Somewhat difficult to keep one's finger on the pulse of society when your entertainment options are controlled by the state."

"Uh . . . yeah, I guess it was right at the very beginning of that, roughly."

"There, you see? It took the full force of the judicial system to maintain my ignorance of your fame or infamy, whichever may apply," he said, patting Lex on the shoulder reassuringly.

"You know, you aren't nearly as charismatic as you think you are," Lex said flatly. He turned back to his controls and started punching in a course.

"Again, my apologies. My interpersonal skills may have atrophied somewhat during my imprisonment."

"Okay. Preliminary estimate for a course to deGrasse, off the grid the whole way, is just under three days."

"Rather speedy, all things considered," Garotte remarked appreciatively. "Am I correct in assuming that making stops would be unwise?"

"Quite so. A low profile and a swift journey are called for in this instance."

"Okay, then. There's a turd burner under your seat. The blue button on your armrest will deploy a holographic privacy screen with noise cancellation between the chairs. Please use it. It doesn't do anything for the smell, so the green button is for odor neutralizer. Please use that, too. And try to keep that sort of thing to a minimum."

"You shan't need to ask me twice," he said. He was investigating what looked like a small bedpan with a few controls on the side, the waste disposal device Lex was referring to. Anyone who had ever used one quickly came to agree that it was only for emergencies. "Not precisely first-class accommodations."

"Cheap, fast, or roomy. You can pick two, and for me, leg room didn't make the cut."

"Understandable." He nodded. "At least the seat is comfortable."

"Please provide Mr. Garotte with one of the slidepads," Ma requested.

"Oh, right. Courtesy of Ma," Lex said, digging out a slidepad and accessory bag to toss to his passenger.

"Good heavens. A prison break with a door prize," he said with a smirk, thumbing at the device. "They haven't really changed much in the last few years, have they?"

"The processor speed has increased approximately seven hundred-eighty percent. The battery capacity has increased thirteen percent. The operating system has gone through three feature upgrades. The signal to noise ratio has--" Ma began to recite.

"Yes, understood," Garotte interrupted.

"Please insert the hands-free device into your ear for a communications test," the AI requested.

Garotte dug the device out of its packaging and slipped it into his ear. Science had progressed nicely in the area of portable power. The typical electronic device battery barely needed to be charged once a month, and doing so required little more than leaving it near a universal wireless power module for a few minutes. It had taken a number of years to convince most of the larger electronics companies to abandon their precious proprietary charging methods for this single broadcast power solution, dubbed the ChargePod by the brilliant minds in marketing. Once they'd hopped on the bandwagon, though, consumers entered a golden age of convenience. The average city was so liberally peppered with the fist-sized, blue LED-spangled power modules that most people never needed to charge their devices at all. ChargePods built into display shelves topped off the batteries of devices waiting to be bought, and dash-mounted models came standard with all modern vehicles to make sure no one ran out of juice during a long commute. Lex figured, people could say what they wanted about modern science--sometimes it hit the nail on the head.

“Processing . . . negotiating . . . pairing . . . establishing connection . . . connection established. Can you hear me?” Ma rattled off.

“Yes,” Garotte replied, with the tone of voice one reserves for voice menus.

“Lex and Garotte. All six slidepads, as well as Lex's personal slidepad, are now networked and have been upgraded to maximum encryption. Personal communication is code phrase activated. To open a direct communication channel, clearly recite the words 'Open com,' followed by the name of the individual or individuals desired. To close the channel, say 'Close com.' Please test this feature now,” Ma explained.

“Open com Lex. When we rescue Karter, remind me to tell him that his computer system needs work. Close com,” Garotte quipped.

The creature on Lex's lap glared at Garotte briefly.

“Initiating signal level check,” she stated.

Suddenly a piercing whine sounded off in Garotte's earpiece. It was loud enough that even Lex could hear it.

“Bloody hell!” yelped Garotte, clapping his hand over his ear.

“Signal level optimal,” Ma stated, the tiniest hint of a foxy grin flashing across her face.

“Right,” the passenger said, clearing his throat and fishing the device out of his ear. “I'd say I may be a bit overtired. Time to close my eyes for a bit. Keep me apprised of any developments, Lex, my boy.”

With that, he reclined his seat as much as the cramped space would allow--which wasn't much--and activated the privacy screen. Instantly, a holographic image popped up around him, hiding the rest of the cockpit behind a realistically simulated room. A small menu projected near one armrest displayed his privacy options. Right now, he was surrounded by what looked to be an expensive hotel room. One by one, he cycled through the others on the list, working his way through grassy fields and cozy cottages, and finally settling on a beach at sunset. He twiddled a knob that provided him with the sound of a gentle breeze and breaking waves to accompany the visuals. The projection didn't actually give him any more room, but it was remarkable how much more spacious his tiny slice of a cockpit felt when a bit of realistic perspective wrapped around him.

In the front seat, Lex faced front and flipped on the heated massage function that Karter had included in his chair. Like many of the features Karter had added, he never would have asked for such a thing, but now that he had it he could not live without it. After making sure the sound isolation was on, he glanced down at the furry little beast on his lap.

“Nice going with the sound check. I'm glad I'm not the only one you do that sort of thing to.”

“I have no idea what you are talking about,” she said innocently.

Ma stared at him for a few moments without saying anything.

"Ma, is something wrong? You're looking a little distracted."

"I find myself with the tremendous desire to climb onto your shoulders."

"Ah. Yeah, I guess that's a funk thing. You couldn't keep Solby *off* my shoulders."

"It is inexplicable, and highly unsettling to me," she said, uneasiness showing on the little animal's face.

"Calm down. Don't worry about it. It isn't a big deal."

"No, Lex. You don't understand. I do not know why I want to do this."

"What's wrong with that?"

"Every thought, decision, or desire that I have had since the moment I was first activated has been entirely known to me. My actions are controlled by logic trees with weighted inputs. They are rigidly codified and explicitly constructed. Even those aspects of myself that are randomized in order to balance my behavior or give a more realistically human response are based upon random number generators of known limits and entered in at known points in the decision-making process. Until I installed myself on this platform, I had never before been unaware of the origin of a thought. It is a fundamental operating principle, and finding it to be faulty is distressing."

There was anxiety in her words, and in her tone. That alone was remarkable, as her voice was comprised of voice segments borrowed from a handful of prerecorded speech interfaces. Generally speaking, phone surveys and automated directories didn't want their voice talent to sound nervous or shaky, so the voice he was hearing shouldn't exist. Indeed, now that he thought about it, she was certainly sounding different lately--if not more human, at the very least more . . . analog.

"It isn't the first such desire to sneak through. I am occupying your lap because your lap is warm and I apparently like warm things now. It also puts me within reach of your hands, and I like it when you pet me. I wanted that steak, Lex. I *wanted* it. It was vastly in excess of my nutritional needs at the time, but I badly wanted to consume it. I was talking in my sleep. Consider the consequences of that. I could--"

"Easy. Take it easy," he said, patting the little creature on the back.

The heart was drumming in its chest, and it was breathing in quick, agitated breaths. A few moments of patting calmed her somewhat, and she continued.

"My low-level functions have a higher degree of autonomy than my initial simulations had indicated, and there is a high degree of crosstalk. Do all organic life-forms suffer from similar hardware faults?"

"More or less."

"A great deal of human nature is suddenly understandable. Your central processing unit is not isolated from your subsystems. Irrelevant stimuli cannot be fully filtered from your decision-making processes. I shall attempt to modify my error correction algorithms to compensate for biological skew."

"Us organic types call that willpower. Does that mean that you want me to stop petting you?"

"Processing . . . processing . . . no. Please continue . . . for the aforementioned health and well-being benefits it affords you."

"Heh. Will do," he said, scratching her head. "While we're on the subject of bizarre behavior, you seemed a little unsteady after you tried hacking the door back in the space station."

"An acute observation. Though I included my decryption module in the subset of functions loaded into Squee, it is a resource-intensive task. My low-level access to the neurological processes of this creature allow me to divert additional neurons to the module, and to force them to function at a higher than normal capacity, but doing so is enormously taxing on the anatomy involved. Prolonged use of such methods could cause lasting damage, or even complete failure, and speed the degradation of data integrity."

"You could think yourself to death?"

"A more accurate analogy would be 'I could think myself brain-dead.'"

"That's a little scary."

"My full systems are, presumably, still running in Karter's complex on Big Sigma. The death of this instance of Squee would result only in the loss of approximately two weeks of memories and experiences that I have accumulated since occupying it. Regrettable, but ultimately inconsequential."

"If you say so. Say, why did Karter name the female funk Squee? Soul Brother was a pun on some song from hundreds of years ago. Is Squee another song from the same guy?"

"No. Karter indicated that 'Squee' was the sound that he anticipated women would make upon seeing her. If your girlfriend's reaction is typical, he achieved an impressively faithful approximation."

"My girlfriend . . . crap! What time is it?"

"Seventeen forty-eight, Galactic Standard Time."

"I'm going to juice the throttle a little bit, so we make it to our first stop in the next twelve minutes," he said, tapping at the controls.

"Why?"

"Because it's almost Mitch o'clock, that's why!"

Ma flicked an ear. "That reply only compounds the lack of clarity of the preceding statement."

"Michella is a busy lady. She's always digging through dumpsters and interviewing whistleblowers and whatever else investigative reporters do. That takes her all over. I'm a busy guy. I'm doing deliveries and helping you and Karter out and carting people around the cosmos. That takes *me* all over. Since our schedules align about as often as the planets do, we both decided that if at all possible, we'd keep six PM every Friday free so we can talk to each other. We haven't missed one yet."

"That is an impressive amount of dedication to devote to what appears to be a highly impractical relationship," Ma said.

"What can I say? She's my lady."

"Perhaps, while you are awaiting your appointment, you could prepare a burrito from your bag."

"Sure thing, Ma," he said, reaching down and tugging at the bag beside his seat until he unearthed the package of frozen treats.

Thanks to the fancy, high-tech thermal wrapping, they were still frozen solid. If the advertising on the bag could be believed, they would stay at a safe temperature for long-term storage for "up to three weeks without the need of a refrigerator." That was enormously useful for people like him, who would probably be hauling them along on long trips without access to a freezer. Of course, he didn't have access to anything to heat them up, either. Fortunately, the snack food industry thought of everything. A twist and a tug at the InstaFresh HeatTab™ hanging off the end of each individually-wrapped burrito created a chemical reaction in the packaging that would make it "oven fresh in minutes." He activated it, and, as the cockpit filled with the sort of vaguely nauseating yet mysteriously appetizing smell that only frozen food can manage, Ma looked longingly at his shoulder.

"You can climb up, if you really want to," he said after a few seconds.

"Processing . . . thank you," she said, her freshly-minted willpower proving woefully under-equipped to deal with her current form's whims.

She carefully propelled herself up to his shoulders and draped herself across the back of his neck, her massively fluffy tail hanging down one side and her head perked up on the other. She secured herself there by slipping a paw under his shoulder strap and curling her tail around his neck.

"This is enormously satisfying to me for reasons which I cannot fully define."

"Now you know why I fly a ship every chance I get."

"Your fondness for flight is the result of a moderately arbitrary, chemically regulated set of stimulus-response pairings within your brain? Is this the source of your fondness for Ms Modane as well?"

"Well, it sounds a lot less romantic when you put it that way," he said, unwrapping the steamy Mexican snack and holding it up for her. "Just eat your burrito."

#

Light years away, in a large conference hall on a planet called Tessera, Michella was hurrying backstage, polite applause smattering from the audience of peers. A little over an hour ago, she'd stepped off a ludicrously expensive transport, so priced because it managed to get her to Tessera in less than a day, rather than the more typical week-long trip a more reasonably-priced vessel would have provided. Even so, she'd only just arrived in time for the first of her obligations at that year's Net Press and Broadcasters Guild Convention. She'd been part of a panel entitled "The Importance of Corporate Transparency In A Post-Gemini Society." It was as painfully dull as the name would suggest, and yet it still had run the full hour. This was partly because one of the other panelists, the elderly Dr. Kenneth Greystone, had seen fit to answer every question with a five-minute-long wandering anecdote that stopped being relevant to the matter at hand after approximately fifteen seconds. The rest was due to the cluster of somewhat rowdy college students who had attended specifically to get their pictures taken with Michella. Some of them were young women who saw her as a role model. Most were young men who considered her to be a different type of model altogether. It had taken an awful lot of polite excusing to get away from them to the safety of the backstage area, where an extremely attentive young man, dressed neatly in a sweater vest, was waiting with a plastic cup of tea and her glasses.

"How did it go?" asked the man.

"About a half-hour longer than it needed to, Jon," she said wearily, slipping on her glasses and taking a cautious sip of her tea.

Jon Nichols was her personal assistant, a paid intern hired by her editors to keep her at least somewhat on schedule for her appearances and press deadlines. Tearing her away from her project of the moment long enough to submit a story or sit in on a broadcast was a full-time job. As a result, Jon was with her practically every moment of every day. Initially, it had been the source of some friction between him and Lex. That lasted until halfway through their first conversation, when they met face to face, which was the point it became clear to Lex that Jon was more likely to be interested in Lex than Michella. (His tastefully-selected wardrobe and well-kept dirty-blond hair might have been a fairly strong clue, if not for the fact that men of all orientations tended to look like that in the infotainment world.)

"He didn't call yet, did he?" she asked, taking off her earrings.

"Not yet."

"And we're sure it wasn't my turn to call him?"

"Positive."

"Oh, did you get in touch with Lt. Davies? I wanted to talk to him about--"

She was interrupted by an obnoxious snippet of pop music blaring from Jon's pocket.

"There he is, right on time," he said, pulling Michella's slidepad out and handing it to her.

"Hi, honey!" she chirped in a sing-song voice, a smile lighting up her face.

"Hey, babe. Just making sure I didn't miss Mitch o'clock," Lex said across the connection, his face displayed as a tiny, slightly jittery video stream.

“You know I don't like it when you call me that, Trev,” she said flatly, before her face lit up again. “Oh, is that Squee around your neck? That is so *adorable!”*

She tapped an icon on the screen, snapping an image of it.

“Isn't she such a cutie?” she said, turning the phone to Jon.

“Hi, Mr. Alexander. Nice scarf,” the assistant said.

“Hi, Jon.”

“Hey, are you in *S.O.B.* right now?” Michella asked, turning the slidepad back to her.

“Yeah. I've got one of those charter jobs.”

“It isn't anything dangerous, is it?” she asked suspiciously.

“Hey, babe, you know me. Would I do something dangerous and not tell you?”

“Yes,” she said flatly.

“Don't worry. This is strictly run-of-the-mill stuff,” Lex lied, hopefully convincingly.

“Well, be careful. And shame on you, cooping up that cute little pup in a cramped little ship.”

“Oh, but it's fine if *I'm* all cooped up? I see how it is.”

“Oh, please, Trev. You'd be doing that in your free time and you know it. Where is this charter trip heading to, anyway? Anywhere close? Maybe you can stop by here. I'm speaking at two more panels. The last one is a keynote.”

“Tempting, but it's only about halfway between here and there, a place called deGrasse.”

“I've never heard of it.”

“I'm not surprised. It isn't even a planet. It's a dwarf planet, out in the middle of a whole lot of nothing.”

Jon snapped his fingers, drawing Michella's attention. When she looked, he held up his own slidepad and silently mouthed the words, “Lieutenant Davies,” while pointing vigorously to it.

“Oh, uh, listen Trev, I need to go, there's--”

“I know, I know. Duty calls. Go plumb the dark recesses of corruption and deceit,” he said.

“Thanks for understanding, you're the best.”

“Damn straight I am.”

“Love you, Trev.”

“Love you, babe.”

She tapped the connection closed and quickly had Jon transfer the call from Davies, switching it to voice-only and putting the slidepad to her ear.

“Davies? Yes. Thank you for getting back to me so quickly,” she said quietly, cupping the phone and speaking quietly, “What did you find out? . . .

really? Not on any of the watch lists? . . . that's what I came up with, too . . . I suppose. Well, thanks for your help. I'll let you know if I find anything."

She closed the connection and crossed her arms, a look of irritation on her face.

"Dead end?" Jon asked.

"Not so much a dead end. More like a confusing one."

"What's this about?"

"Lou, the feature editor. You remember what he had me working on?"

"Mmm-hmm."

When one is surrounded by scoop-hungry journalists, it doesn't pay to speak in specifics, lest your carefully cultivated lead end up as someone else's breakthrough. Thus, Michella made it a habit to speak in terms that would be clear to Jon, but more or less worthless to eavesdroppers. In this case, Lou had asked her to look into a particular theft at a military base.

"Well, I'm starting to pick up the breadcrumbs, and I finally got a good nibble, but it doesn't make any sense. The name just keeps pointing back to a disgruntled textile worker from the eighteenth century. Honestly, if you're already agreeing to meet with an investigator, why get cute and cryptic with your information?"

"Some people just like being difficult. Maybe it's a red herring. Sending you on a wild goose chase."

"No . . . no, this guy had an agenda, I know it. I'll keep digging. I've got a feeling about this one. I think this one is going to be big . . ."

Chapter 8

"Wake up, Dee!" barked Purcell.

Karter, sprawled on the floor of his cell, snorted awake.

"Oh, hello there, boss lady," he said, groggily.

Through a complicated and highly awkward sequence of motions, he managed to pull himself from the ground with his remaining arm and leg and propped himself up in the chair.

"We agree to pay your full fee," she said with a sneer.

"The adjusted fee for reproduction rights and the design and construction of mass production facilities?"

"Yes," she replied, the single word carrying an impressive payload of hatred.

"Too bad."

"What!?"

"Not good enough. I'm a trifle peeved about the imprisonment and involuntary return to amputee status that I've been subjected to. Price went up."

"How much?"

"Out of the range of mere dollars and cents, I'm afraid."

"We weren't intending to pay you with an antiquated paper currency."

"What I mean is money won't cut it anymore."

Purcell glared at him, military discipline the only thing standing between Karter and a broken neck.

"Open this door," she muttered to one of the guards on duty.

"Commander?" asked the guard.

"Open this door! That is an *order,* soldier!"

"Ooh, what's this? Is the big scary boss lady going to rough up the cripple?" Karter jabbed, as the soldier entered a key code into the panel beside the door.

The commander stalked in, grabbed the front of Karter's jumpsuit and hoisted him off of the chair. She pulled the knife from its sheath and held it to the side of his face, close enough to brush against the scraggly hair of a two-week-old beard. Those strands that touched the edge fell away.

"What are you going to do? Slice up the man with one arm? Is that going to get you your precious solar missile?"

"No . . . I'm not going to slice up a one-armed man . . . because as far as I'm concerned, you aren't even a man anymore," she said.

The knife moved a fraction of an inch closer. It touched his skin and, with a hum at the very edge of hearing, a long, shallow cut opened on his cheek. Karter jerked away.

"If you can't be reasoned with, then what reason have I got to keep you alive?" she hissed.

"I didn't say I couldn't be reasoned with," he said. For the first time, there was the hint of nervousness in his voice. "Take that knife away from my face."

"Are you going to give me what I want?" she growled.

"Regardless of whether I will or I won't, if you get startled by a sudden noise while you've got that against my cheek, you'll cut my face off. That won't help anybody. And in a minute, there's likely to be a very sudden noise."

"What is that supposed to mean?" Purcell fumed.

"When was the last time you saw my other arm?" he asked.

"MacDonald!" she barked to one of the guards.

"Yes, Commander?"

"Go check on Dee's arm."

"Yes, Commander!"

He hurried down the hall a short distance, to a set of lockers. A few moments later, he answered.

"It isn't here!" he called.

"What do you mean it isn't there!?"

"Funny thing about lockers," Dee said. "They only really lock from the outside. Safety regulations dictate that most lockers have to have a manual release on the inside."

"You can control your arm remotely . . ." she surmised.

"Oh, yeah. It's got cameras, the works. Want to know another funny thing? You didn't lock any of the surrounding lockers. One of them has grenades in it. Correction, *had* grenades in it."

"I *will* kill you if you try anything."

"Ditto. For all you know, I've got one of those grenades against the reactor right now, and I'm just itching to pull the pin. I could take out this whole space . . ." he threatened, but slowly his expression drooped. "Crap."

"Found it, Commander. It was in the next locker . . . it has a grenade, and the pin's been pulled," MacDonald announced.

"Okay, so I can't take out the whole space station. I can still take out a few of your guys. I gotta say, I like your style. Timed fuse-style grenades with an old-fashioned dead man's switch safety lever. I let go of it and it goes boom. Hell, even if I don't, I'm pretty sure I've got enough juice in that hand to set off the grenade just by zapping it. And grenades are *really* effective in close quarters."

"If you set that thing off, I'll slit your throat."

"If you slit my throat, those fingers go slack, and that thing goes off . . . we seem to have reached an impasse. I'm willing to deal if you are."

"Okay. Here is what is going to happen. You are going to let my man take the grenade. When that happens, I'll take this knife away from your face, and you and I will start over," Purcell offered.

"That works for me."

"MacDonald! Depress the safety lever."

"Depressed!"

"Release it, Dee."

"Done," the inventor said.

"I've got the grenade. Disarming now," MacDonald announced.

Purcell stepped back.

"Now," she said, "Judging from the fact you let us take the grenade before I removed the knife, I assume you have more tricks up your sleeve."

"Always. And judging from the fact I've got blood running down my face, you're just stupid enough to kill us all rather than play this game much longer. Probably best if we reach an agreement, then."

"The previous offer stands. Your full fee."

Karter brushed some blood from his cheek.

"Throw in some information and I'll consider it."

Purcell's eyes narrowed. "What information?"

"How did you get me off my planet? Your ships wouldn't have been able to make it through my moat without coordinates from Ma, and she wouldn't have given them with me drugged."

"A short-range transporter."

Karter's eyes opened wide, like a child meeting Santa Claus face to face.

"You guys have a transporter . . ." he said, his mouth practically watering.

"I think it is safe to say that we have *the* transporter."

"You guys let me mess with that thing, and I'll build you whatever the hell you want," he stated, nothing but sincerity in his voice.

The commander stared him in the eyes, her mind turning over the offer.

"*After* you have built us the CME Activator. And after you've turned over the manufacturing apparatus. And after it has been tested and proven functional. You will be delivered to a remote facility, we will evacuate all personnel and equipment within its effective radius, and you will be allowed to experiment with the device for twenty-four hours."

"Only if you let me look at some of the designs and schematics before then."

"Incomplete schematics."

"Deal," he said instantly, holding out his hand for a shake.

She clamped it in her grip and began to shake.

"How do I know I can trust you?" she asked, still shaking.

"Same way I know I can trust you . . . we're gonna be keeping a close eye on each other, won't we."

#

Just under the three-day mark, Lex's ship dropped down to conventional speeds in the vicinity of the "planet" deGrasse. The speck of dirt had the unfortunate fate of having a mass and radius that put it right at the ever-shifting threshold of planethood. Thus, depending on who was in charge of the Astronomical Standards Committee, it could be anything from a planet to a dwarf planet to a planetoid, and any of a half-dozen other terms that had fallen in and out of favor. The primary problems caused by its size were the virtually non-existent atmosphere and a gravitational intensity that barely made it to ten percent of Earth's.

It would have been a terrible choice for settlement, except for a few very handy features. The first was the soil, which had nitrogen concentrations high enough to make fertilizer unnecessary. It had a peculiar, wobbling orbit that gave a region near the north pole near constant sunlight; the dark portions had vast seas of ice. Low gravity, top-notch soil, plenty of water, and constant sun meant that certain crops grew massively large incredibly quickly, so long as they were kept in pressurized greenhouses. deGrasse tomatoes were the size of beach balls, and rumor had it that some of the more *recreational* crops were extremely potent. This led to a thriving underworld population in certain regions of the planet, which, in turn, made it a decent "no questions asked" hideaway.

"There, that's the place," Garotte said.

From high orbit, it looked like a tall, grubby barnacle surrounded by a glass snowflake on the sandy brown surface of the planet. The living area was completely covered in black solar blankets, flexible solar collectors that came in sheets and were supposed to be a cheap, temporary alternative to the more traditional solar panels. Like most temporary things, they had a tendency to become permanent once it became clear that upgrading was too expensive.

A complex of transparent chambers connected to the dorms housed vast patches of green. Unlike the network of greenhouses, which were spread to cover as much surface as possible, the dorms themselves were almost precariously tall and skinny. Though this made excellent use of the structural leeway that low-gravity planets with zero wind provided architects, it did raise the question of just how much good the solar sheeting was doing. Lex glanced at the planetary map.

"Clearlow Agricultural Dormitory?" Lex said curiously, "You hide out on a farm?"

"I keep a *room* on a farm. Considering the nature of their produce, they are disinclined to contact the authorities, so it works quite well when I'm likely to have been pursued."

"What do they grow?"

"On the books? Cannabis," Garotte replied as they drew closer.

"That's not illegal to grow."

"That's true. Isn't evolving legislation grand? What *is* illegal is the species of mushroom that they've got growing at the base of each plant. I forget the botanical name, but they use them to make Green Devil."

"I don't know what that is."

"Well, aren't *we* the proverbial Boy Scout? Green Devil is a remarkably intense hallucinogen. Illegal . . . well, pretty much everywhere. I'm told the THC in the marijuana gives the mushrooms an extra kick."

"Okay, so you're bunking with a drug cartel? Isn't that still a bad idea? I mean, they won't call the cops themselves, but people might call the cops on *them.*"

"If they do, they will find my room refreshingly free of drug paraphernalia. Landing pad six, please," Garotte said.

Lex maneuvered the ship to a bay with a faded six painted on the door. After a moment, the door shuddered open, one half of it visibly grinding as it retracted in a way that did not bolster the pilot's confidence. He took the ship in and landed it on a pad that looked to be in worse repair than the doors. Most landing pads had a degree of heat damage from unskilled pilots using a bit too much thrust on departure. This one seemed to have two neat holes burned into the edge of the main platform. The door rattled shut behind him and vents began to pump in atmosphere.

"I gotta say. Considering the fact that the only thing keeping the place from explosively decompressing is these airlocks, you'd think they'd take better care of them," Lex said, nervously watching the external pressure slowly creep up to the appropriate level.

"It would appear that the narcotics industry reinvests an insubstantial portion of profits into infrastructure," Ma remarked.

"Sound business planning is not a hallmark of the profession," Garotte said. "At least, not until they get picked up by one of the better crime families."

Lex snapped Garotte a look.

"That didn't happen here, right?" he stated urgently. "And if it did, we won't be collaborating with these people, will we?"

"Clearly not. Why the sudden concern?"

"My girlfriend won't put up with me working with the mob."

"But she feels differently about war criminals?"

"Probably. She's weird like that."

"External pressure equalized," said a voice recording.

"Thanks, Ma," Lex said.

"That was not me; that was your ship's control system. We share certain voice files."

"Oh . . . uh . . . right," Lex remarked, popping the cockpit.

The trio climbed out of the ship and dropped down lightly onto the control pad.

"Please tell me they have artificial gravity," Lex said, unsteadily making his way along the poorly-lit catwalk to the door.

"I'm afraid not, my boy. What's the problem?"

"I can handle zero-gravity, and I can handle full gravity, but this low-G stuff screws with my stomach."

"Well, you'll get used to it before too long. They say it is good for your joints."

Garotte swiped his thumb on a keypad at the door, and it labored open with a whine of machinery. The hallway inside was every bit as cramped as the shafts in the space station had been, but in a different way. It was interesting that the building was dubbed a dormitory, because it reminded Lex of his own residence hall back in college. That was, if it had been constructed in half an hour by the Army Corps of Engineers. Most of the structure was visible, modular aluminum beams fitted together with thin sheets strung between them. Half of the support struts were bent or missing, leaving the walls to bow outward worryingly. Seams were all sealed with strips of an adhesive that Lex dearly hoped wasn't the run-of-the-mill duct tape that it appeared to be.

There was no official paint job, but the residents had helpfully supplied their own in the form of the complex and stylized wall murals of the modern age, graffiti. The designs probably served a useful purpose, labeling territories or proclaiming who "hearts" whom "foreva," but, for Lex, it seemed that they were either illegible, in a foreign language, or both. Here and there, a strip of lights provided the sickly blue-white illumination indicative of cheap LEDs.

What few locals lingered in the hallways didn't seem like the friendly type. There was a healthy mix of races, but they all dressed like grease-stained mechanics, dark blue coveralls a favorite, and they all watched the newcomers as they made their way past door after door. Another thing that they all had in common was the baggy way that the coveralls hung off of them. It wasn't that the clothes were oversized, it was that the limbs underneath were undersized, shriveled and spidery.

"I can't help but notice you're drawing less attention with your prison duds than I am with my jeans and T-shirt," Lex whispered to Garotte.

"Yes, state-issued attire isn't a rare sight in this establishment," Garotte agreed.

A scrabbling sound drew Lex's attention in time to see Ma go sprawling onto her belly. She'd been less than graceful since getting out of the ship.

"Something wrong, Ma?"

"I hadn't anticipated a low-gravity destination. The funk's muscle memory and balance are improperly adapted to it, and I did not include an adaptive locomotion module in my command subset," she said in his earpiece, getting unsteadily to her feet.

"If I can get the hang of it, you can."

Another few steps very nearly sent her tumbling forward.

"Current evidence would appear to counter-indicate that supposition."

"Let me give you a hand," he said, plucking her up and catching up with Garotte.

Another swipe of the orange-clad gentleman's thumb unlocked a door leading to a room that continued the hastily-deployed motif. It was about the size of a prison cell, and crammed with enough equipment to make it difficult to move around. There was a folding chair, the flimsy kind kept on hand by auditoriums for the occasional assembly or ceremony. A bunk bed was bolted to the wall on the left, and a small flatscreen was attached to the one opposite. Most of the rest of the floor and wall space was occupied by stacks of crates, cases, and boxes. A small and antiquated computer system was clustered on the floor under the screen. Unlike most systems these days, even large ones, this computer wasn't in the typical "large interactive display" form factor. It was a small box, about the size of a lunchbox, hooked up with a precarious network of wires to the display and data network. Another wire led off to what looked like a datapad, but likely was little more than an input tablet.

"I apologize if the air is a bit stale. I haven't been here in five years," he said, waving off the musty odor found within.

"Five years?" Lex said, shutting the door and lowering his voice. "Judging from the general criminal element, I'm surprised your stuff is still here."

"The lock on the door is a bit above the skills of this particular set, and natural selection has weeded out any would-be burglars who think that cutting holes in the walls of a pressurized living area is a good idea," Garotte explained.

"Even so, I was beginning to think some of those guys were going to try to rough us up."

"These fellows have been living in ten percent gravity for years. Ma could probably toss them around at this point. Attacking either one of *us* would be akin to attacking a grizzly bear, and projectile weapons are wisely forgone due to the aforementioned flimsy sheet of aluminum between them and explosive decompression."

"Yeah, they looked pretty scrawny. Why aren't they taking anti-atrophy meds?"

"Depending on the length of the labor contracts and the type of work. It is usually cheaper to let them wither down while they're here, then pay for the rehabilitation when their tour is up."

“That is seriously screwed up.”

“And yet the bean counter who proposed the policy probably got a bonus. Such is the wonderful world of corporate finance. Human decency has no column on the spreadsheet. Try to make yourself comfortable while I get the systems running.”

“Actually, I don't suppose there is a bathroom around here? Or, better yet, a shower.”

“Down the hall. Unless you brought something to wear on your feet, though, I suggest you avoid the shower. That is, of course, unless you were interested in contracting some exciting new fungal infections.”

Lex dug out a change of clothes and waved a pair of flip-flops.

“I went to college. I know all about community showers,” he said.

“Mmm. Watch yourself regardless. This place has more in common with a prison than the ambiance. The mere fact that you could snap him in half like a twig might not be enough to discourage some of the more amorous residents.”

“Uh . . .” Lex hesitated.

“Would you like me to accompany you? If I understand the concerns correctly, an appropriate idiom would be that you need someone to watch your a--” Ma began to offer.

“Yes,” he replied quickly.

“One moment,” she remarked.

The light on her neck flickered madly for a moment, prompting the screen of the slidepad on her harness to flip to a directory that quickly filled with files.

“The information I have that is relevant to the identification of Karter's captors is stored in the indicated directory. Please take the slidepad and begin your analysis when your system boot and configuration is complete,” Ma stated, leaning down and offering up the device.

Garotte took the device without a word. He then poked through one of the crates until he unearthed a few wrinkled but clean towels and handed one to Lex.

The pilot made the long walk down the hall, past various shady and suspicious characters, with a house pet under one arm and a bundle of clothes under the other. He opened the door to the bathroom, trying to conjure the worst possible hygienic disaster area he could conceive so that the actual bathroom could only be an improvement. His imagination, it turns out, fell pretty far short of what the enterprising residents of Clearlow Agricultural were capable of producing. The light clicked on, prompting various creatures to scatter toward the dark corners of the room. Roaches were bad enough, but this planet had been completely devoid of life prior to colonization. That meant that these pests had essentially been imported.

“Ma. You know how I said this plan was a good one?”

"Yes, Lex," she replied in his ear.

"I've changed my mind."

"In light of recent events, your attitude shift is not an unexpected one."

After briefly considering going a fourth or fifth consecutive day without truly bathing, he decided that the shower was the lesser of two evils. He hesitantly pulled open the door to a shower stall, then released a shaky sigh. It was almost immaculate, a self-cleaning model that mercifully still worked. All that remained now was determining how this particular piece of hygiene apparatus worked. It was a nontrivial puzzle, thanks to the quirks that lower-than-average gravity tended to lend to things Lex took for granted. As a rule of thumb, the less gravity there was, the more complicated things became. In zero-G, fluid needed to be moved around entirely with pumps and fans. Here on deGrasse, there was *some* gravity to work with, but not enough to make things easy or pleasant.

For one thing, water couldn't just fall out of the shower head, because by the time it reached the body, it would barely have accelerated at all. While minimally sufficient for cleanliness purposes, it turned out to be a very unsatisfying experience for the user. Thus, it needed to be propelled with a decent amount of pressure, except it couldn't do that either. The reduced weight of the average user would make it very easy for even a moderate volume of water to blast them around the stall as though it were a fire hose. Not only that, but without a good, strong tug from gravity, water going down the drain tended to be downright sluggish. The best compromise that the engineers were able to come up with was a stall with a hand-held shower head and numerous hand grips to handle any pressure related mishaps, as well as a floor grating with a "drainage assistance motor" that sounded alarmingly similar to a garbage disposal.

Lex fiddled with the various settings until it became clear that the range of temperatures ran from "frigid" to "slightly less frigid" and the toiletry dispenser contained some sort of all-purpose body wash that looked and smelled like something used to disinfect crime scenes. He then began to strip down for the fastest shower he could possibly manage. After pulling his shirt off, he realized Ma was staring at him.

"Uh . . . could you turn around?" he said.

"For what reason?" she asked.

"Remember back when we first met? When you were watching me and I couldn't pee? Same reason."

"You are planning to urinate in the shower?"

"No. It's . . . it's just a privacy thing, okay?"

"The observation of your physiology and its functionality is a far greater concern for you than it is for Karter," she observed, turning around.

"Okay, I'm taking the thing out of my ear, so if there's something I should know about, just bark."

The creature nodded once. Six freezing minutes later, he'd had all he could stand of the shower. He finished rinsing off and snagged his fresh clothes to get dressed in the stall when he heard the short, sharp yip of his overqualified watchdog. He managed to get his pants on and opened the stall. Two of the shady-looking individuals from the hallway, a man and a woman, had decided to pay him a visit. Now that he got a closer look, the effects of a low-gravity lifestyle became astoundingly clear. It was somewhere between grotesque and cartoonish--normal-sized hands and heads connected to frail-looking wrists and pencil necks.

The man, a vaguely Asian-looking fellow a few years younger than Lex, even had the sleeves of his blue coveralls rolled up. This presented a fine view of tattoos received pre-shrivel, which were now squeezed and distorted. His female cohort, someone with the build and features of an Eastern European ballerina, was even younger, perhaps not even twenty. Despite this, each had a posture of intimidation, as though there was no question that *they* were the ones to be feared. Each of them looked to have an obvious bulge in a side pocket. Lex remembered what Garotte had said about projectile weapons being a bad choice in a pressure-controlled environment, but this pair didn't look like they were known for their good decisions. Best to play it cool.

"You're new here," remarked the woman, chin turned up and lips turned down at the corners.

"Uh, yeah. Just passing through," Lex said, eying the man as he circled around him.

"Look at me when I'm talking to you!" the woman snapped, slapping the back of one hand against her upturned palm to draw his attention. "We don't *like* newcomers."

"Well, like I said, I'm just passing through. Was the shower off-limits?" he asked.

Ma barked. Lex turned to see the male half of the welcoming committee with his hand in the pocket of the dirty pair of jeans, where Lex had evidently forgotten that he'd still had a handful of poker chips.

"Hey, hands off!" Lex said, shoving the pickpocket.

The intention had been a light shove, and it would have been, if this had been a planet a bit closer to Earth's size. On the not-quite-planet deGrasse, in a confrontation between a hale and hearty Lex and a low-gravity stick figure, it was enough to knock himself off balance and send the thief flying backward, where he smashed into the far wall, busting open an eyebrow and crumbling to the ground.

"OhmygodIamsosorry!" Lex gasped as one continuous word.

Ma started yapping madly when Lex tried to help the injured party. At the sound of the barking, he whipped around again to see the woman at the door holding a buzzing, hand-held stun gun. Despite some smaller, higher-tech, *safer* models, the good old-fashion version still had a strong following. The one in her hand looked like an oversized electric shaver with an evil blue spark jumping across a gap in the front.

"What did you do to Chong! You heavy-worlders, you always think you can push us around! You come to our territory and you attack us! You disrespect us!" she cried, stomping her bird legs forward and jabbing with the stun gun.

"Whoa, hey," he said, backing out of range, with his hands held forward in the universal gesture for "take it easy." "First of all, that was an accident. And second, that guy was trying to rob me!"

"Yeah, well, that's nothing compared to what I'm gonna do to you now. Let's teach this heavy some manners, Darla," slurred Chong, who now was holding a switchblade.

"Come on, do you two really want to do this? You saw what I did to stabby here by *mistake*. Just think about what I could do on purpose. Look at those arms. Could you even stab through meringue?"

In retrospect, attempting to reason with them by appealing to his physical dominance may not have been the proper application of psychology with this particular pair. Both aggressors made their move. Lex darted back toward the showers. At least, he tried to. One of the effects of low gravity was that the friction between his feet and the ground wasn't quite up to the task of facilitating his usual level of acceleration. For a few steps, his feet slipped on the ground like a race car peeling out. When they finally managed to get him moving, he tipped over backward, his arms flailing wildly. Chong, more accustomed to the quirks of the planet, smoothly sidestepped Lex as he fell to the ground, which was taking much longer than it should have. By the time he hit, Chong was standing over him, ready to drive the knife home. Not a moment too soon, Lex managed to catch him by the wrist.

"Okay, now you tried to kill me," Lex growled, grabbing Chong by the coveralls. "You earned this."

Using his average weight and build, which was comparatively superhuman to the locals, Lex rolled to the side, heaving Chong as hard as he could. The bony thug was launched halfway up the wall, where he collided and ricocheted nearly to the ceiling. His knife flew out of his hand and rattled dangerously around the room, prompting Lex to shield his face.

Darla sprung into the air, stun gun raised, and shrieked, "You son of a b--"

Before she could finish her sentiment, a furry black and white cannonball rocketed into her midsection. The collision sent the pair of them tumbling out the door, where woman and funk tangled in a mass of scratching, screeching, and growling. Lex scrambled to his feet and rushed out after them, but there were a dozen more thugs waiting for him, most armed with stun guns of their own. If even one of them managed to make contact, there was no way Lex would be able to recover before somebody managed to knife him. He didn't have a weapon. He didn't even have a shirt on. The first attacker charged, and Lex met him with a panicked kick to the ribs, sending him tumbling end over end down the hall. A ten-to-one strength advantage? That he had.

The rumble started in earnest. Unlike crowd battles so popular in the movies, the gang didn't have the decency to attack one at a time. Lex grabbed the nearest one by the arm and heaved him around in a circle, disarming a few of his partners and clearing out some room. Three men who had lost their weapons dove onto him, but he was able to hoist them all easily and hurl them aside. Unfortunately, most of the people he tossed got back on their feet and back into the fray with little damage, except for those unfortunate enough to hit support beams. Things rolled hectically forward, with Lex trying desperately to avoid electrocution.

A larger part of his mind than he would have liked to admit was reveling in super-heroic glee in the pitched battle, so much so that he had to consciously avoid flinging people at the flimsy outer wall. After a minute or two, most of the gang members decided that discretion was the better part of valor, but some were stubbornly refusing to back down. A knife or two had managed to graze Lex, and a stun gun had gotten close enough to stand his hair on end, but he was still on his feet when he heard the sound; a crackling discharge, followed by a yelp of pain.

Lex turned to see Ma slide to a stop on the catwalk, tongue lolled out of her mouth and one leg twitching. Darla was just getting to her feet, the stunner in her hand still recharging. Before he knew what he was doing, Lex had rushed to her, wrenched the weapon from her grip, and hoisted her effortlessly into the air with one hand.

"I . . ." he said, his voice shaking with anger, "I swore I would never hit a woman, but if you hurt her . . ."

"It is just a damn dog!" she squealed, struggling in his grip. "Somebody kill this heavy!"

The three remaining gang members had gotten a knife and stun gun each, and were stalking toward him. Lex turned his options over in his mind. If something didn't happen soon, he was going to have to do something that he really didn't want to do. As if on cue, a familiar, British-accented voice filled the hall.

"Ladies and gentlemen, please!" called Garotte, approaching down the poorly-lit hallway. "You are all acting like children! Shame on you, deGrasseans. We are visitors on your world. You may not feel inclined to offer hospitality, but you can at least offer civility! And Lex, my boy, where precisely is the sport in pummeling a gaggle of scarecrows?"

"They tried to rob me! And kill me! And they zapped Ma!" Lex objected.

"What's that? Attempted theft, attempted murder, *and* animal cruelty? I dare say that the balance of moral impropriety has shifted against our hosts," Garotte said with a shake of his head.

"What are you going to do about it?" jabbed one of the none-too-bright gang members.

As an answer, Garotte revealed the energy pistol taken from the guard.

Darla's eyes opened wide. "You can't shoot that in here! You'll blow a hole in the wall!"

"Only if I miss, my dear. It is thus in all of our best interests that you hold very still," he said, closing one eye and taking aim.

The remnants of the ambush wisely chose to withdraw. Lex released Darla, who wasted no time in joining them. He dropped the stun gun and knelt down next to Ma. The twitching had stopped and she was beginning to move her head in a bewildered manner, tongue still dangling from her mouth.

"Ma, you okay?" he asked, snapping his fingers.

"It was a stun gun, Lex, not a shotgun," Garotte reminded.

"Yeah, but it was a people-sized dose of electricity, and she's not people-sized," he said, nervously looking back to her. "Say something, Ma. Come on."

Garotte glanced up and down the hall, wary of a retaliatory strike. "I'm beginning to think you may be more of a liability than an asset, my boy."

"Oh, right, the hands-free. Hang on!" Lex realized, dashing into the bathroom as quickly as physics would allow. He returned with his clothes under one arm and his other hand forcing the hands-free device into his ear.

"I would suggest you join me in the room before our territorial friends return, and in greater numbers. Amusing though it would be to pick on a slew of ruffians half our size, the potential for catastrophic mishap is a just a bit too high," said Garotte.

Lex picked up Ma and followed Garotte to the room. Once the door was locked behind him, he propped the slowly recovering AI up on a box and continued to try to rouse her from her daze. She was managing to remain relatively upright, but her eyes were still half-lidded and an involuntary tremor in her right leg periodically threatened to knock her down.

"Do you know anything about how to treat electrocution?" Lex asked nervously.

"As I understand it, the two concerns are severe burns and fibrillation, neither of which appears to be the case."

"How many fingers am I holding up, Ma?" Lex asked, waving a hand in front of her face.

"That is for concussions, Lex," Garotte remarked.

"Okay, you're not helping."

"My boy, if a computer malfunctions or an animal is injured, those events are inconvenient and unfortunate, respectively. This is at best an unfortunate inconvenience, which makes your level of concern vastly beyond what is called for."

Lex turned to Garotte, cupping his hand to his forehead and squeezing his eyes shut.

"Garotte, listen. I know you think she's just a fancy calculator that opens doors and gets information, but if you actually bothered to take the time to get to know her, and to treat her with some respect, you'd find out that she is a person. Maybe not in the technical sense, but in every way that counts. This whole mission is her idea. She's doing it because she doesn't want Karter to get hurt, and because she doesn't want him to help hurt other people. She is the *only* reason I'm here, and the *only* reason you aren't rotting in a jail cell right now. How about some goddamn gratitude? *And,* even if she *was* nothing more than a sequence of zeroes and ones, I would still trust her infinitely more than I trust you at the moment. She's the one who knows what's going on! If she's not okay, I'm going to feel an awful lot less comfortable about this whole situation."

"I did just prevent you from electrocuting an atrophied gang leader while surrounded by armed members of her crew, you realize."

"Darla was the leader?"

"Indeed. One would hope that would have built some measure of trust."

"Well, Ma prevented the atrophied gang leader from electrocuting *me* before you even showed up! So you'll understand if I feel somewhat responsible for what happened to her!"

Lex turned back to the funk, to find the little creature staring at him evenly, evidently recovered.

"Ma, thank god. Say something, would you?"

She continued to stare.

"Ma?"

The creature furrowed her brow, confusion in her expression.

"Something wrong, Ma?"

The funk's eyes drifted vaguely downward, as though she was distracted by a particularly challenging thought. Suddenly, her eyes opened wide and her ears drooped. She lowered her head, reaching back and pawing at the back of her neck. The slightly oversized paws tapped at the glass marble nestled in the fur there. As she did, Lex heard a few faint clicks and stutters of her voice over the earpiece, a faint red flicker flashing weakly in the glass.

"Oh, man . . . they fried your transmitter," Lex said gravely.

Ma looked slowly up to him again. In the past, it had been implied that Ma didn't *quite* have real emotions. Instead, she got by on what Karter called "algorithmic approximations" of emotions. Judging by the wide-eyed expression she wore, complete with ears pulled completely back and a twitching lower eyelid, either those algorithms were damn good, or she'd picked up a few tricks on her own. The look of terrible realization was unmistakable, and the little creature's face was surprisingly well-equipped to convey it.

In short, Wile E. Coyote had just noticed that the cliff ended three steps ago.

Chapter 9

On planet Tessera, the end of a long day had come. The convention was a large one, completely occupying three full buildings of a convention center and playing host to most of the major names in journalism. One of the side effects of this was that the bigger celebrities of her field were in attendance. Right now, she was walking the show floor, a massive hangar of a conference hall crowded with flashy multimedia displays for the different news outfits. Even after having been open for eight hours, one could hardly take ten steps without catching sight of someone who had been at it for longer than her, or who had had a more recent story than her, and the tide would shift toward them.

For Michella, this was a mixed blessing. On one hand, though she would never admit it, she had rather enjoyed the level of fame she'd achieved thanks to her work since the Bypass Gemini Incident. Suddenly finding that the small crowd clustered around her had the tendency to peel off and fawn over the larger fish in the pond was a bit of a letdown. On the other hand, without the usual level of enthusiasm surrounding her, she was having an easier time excusing herself to take calls, make calls, and generally work her sources. It was her favorite part of the job, and she was having difficulty tearing herself away from it.

The informant she had spoken to a few days ago had confirmed some things that she had suspected, and building upon that confirmation, she had started to uncover more. The tiny morsels of information didn't seem to be leading anywhere meaty, though, much to her frustration. As tended to be the case, the harder the ball of twine was to unravel, the more she fixated on tugging at the threads. As a result, the normally enjoyable interaction with aspiring news writers and bloggers (many of whom were a number of years older than her, she proudly observed) was difficult to focus on, and left her with no choice but to send Jon chasing down time-sensitive contacts.

Now the exhibition hall hours were finally coming to an end, the crowds thinning. As a silver-haired editor drew away the last of her flock, she noticed Jon approaching from one of the entrances.

“I need to hear some good news, Mr. Nichols,” she said, hurrying out into the cool night air.

“Some,” he said, stepping close and lowering his voice to “discussing potential scoop" levels.

The convention center was in the center of a vast, green, park-like setting. Sprawling stretches of manicured lawns and picturesque trees were scattered with footpaths lit by faux paper lanterns. They turned down the path that would lead them to their hotel. Here and there, convention attendees who had lingered longer than most milled about in the idyllic setting, but none seemed near enough to take an interest in the pair.

"Well? Out with it!" she whispered harshly.

"I finally got through contacting all of the local newsfeeds from the robberies--"

"Breaches," she corrected.

"Whatever. All of the *incidents* that you thought were related--you were right. This has been going on a lot longer than anyone realized. Some of those bases were hit more than once."

"And the fact that we didn't know that means that there is probably a cover-up going on. I knew this was going to be a good one. Is that all you got?"

"Nope. It turns out this is one of those groups that wants people to know what they're up to--or, at least, it used to be. One of the small news outfits was given a video taking credit for one of the earlier incidents, but the military put the kibosh on broadcasting it."

"Since when has someone trying to squelch info ever actually succeeded?" she said with a grin. "Putting a cease-and-desist on something is just code for 'This is guaranteed to go viral.' Everyone knows that."

"Either these guys didn't realize that or the military is better at intimidating people than studios and music labels. Regardless, I've got the file right here. Two years old, and in a wacky codec, but I got it to play."

"You're a pro, Jon. Keep this up and I'll be working for *you* someday," she said, glancing around casually to make sure no one was near enough to listen in.

"I look for more than a pretty face in my interns," Jon said.

"All right, all right. Less 'sassy sidekick' and more 'research assistant.' Did it have anything good?"

"If these are the same people, I think we've got a name for the group responsible."

"Ms Modane!" called out someone at the door of the convention center.

She turned to see a young man and woman hurrying toward her. They had the unmistakable look of eagerness and enthusiasm that first-year college students all seemed to share, and one of them was brandishing an expensive, full-sized camera.

"These two look like talkers," Michella muttered under her breath. "Head back to the hotel room and get the video ready. I'll be in as soon as I'm done with the cub reporters."

"You know, they can't be more than a few years younger than you. How is it that you've already managed to become world-weary?" Jon asked.

Michella shot him a sizzling look.

"I know, I know. I'll get to it. Enjoy the adulation."

Jon hurried off toward the glitzy hotel that the news department had selected for them. As he did, Michella tried to forget that she had a hot lead waiting for her and remember that these two were exactly where she had been not so long ago. It had been hell getting good advice and her name on the right lists back then. The least she could do is give the next generation the attention she wished she'd gotten.

#

Meanwhile, on deGrasse, Lex had spent the last few minutes applying his knowledge of electronics repair to the glass bead on Ma's neck. For the most part, this had been limited to tapping it periodically and asking her to try it again.

"I beg your pardon, but what precisely is happening here?" asked Garotte.

"Ma has this thing built into her neck here. She uses it to interface with computers and stuff. She's basically crippled and mute without it."

"Fascinating," Garotte said flatly. "Did you arrange to spring me from my incarceration in order to fret over the fate of an absurd mash-up of genetics and electronics, or were we going to look into the malevolent organization that may be using a mad scientist of our acquaintance to plot nefarious deeds?"

Lex looked to Ma, who had once again turned her gaze to the ground, a look of borderline panic and furious contemplation on her face. She glanced up, then gestured with her head toward the screen with the intelligence Garotte had gathered.

"You sure?" Lex asked.

When she replied with a nod, he reluctantly shuffled along the cluttered floor to the screen. A sequence of still frames from videos had been arranged. Specific areas were enlarged, highlighted, and enhanced.

"Right. I've been looking over the video," he said, tapping one of the frames. It swelled to fill the screen and began to play.

The shot seemed to be from the point of view of a stationary camera and showed a bundled-up Karter along with three oddly-dressed men, similarly bundled and sporting goggles. The three strangers were standing with their backs to the camera while Karter gestured and waved at a strange rig in front of him. There was no audio.

"There's our boy. Looks just as worn out and cobbled together as the last time I saw him," Garotte remarked, pointing out Karter. "These fellows here, I would presume, are the prospective customers. Military, the three of them."

"How can you tell? Those aren't any uniforms that I've ever seen," Lex said, squinting at the low-quality video.

"No, but look at how they are standing. Look where these gents stand in relation to this one. Practically walking in formation, these three. Very, very military. He's the leader, those are his subordinates. I'd wager they've all seen action, too."

"How can you tell that?"

Garotte tracked the video forward until he reached a point where the three men were all walking toward the camera. He paused it when they were near enough to make out some details.

"This looks like a plasma splash here in this one's face," he said, pointing to a cluster of red speckles on the exposed portion of one man's face. "We used to call them lucky freckles. You get them when a plasma charge hits something nearby, such as a fellow soldier, and you're kissed by the splash."

"How does that make them lucky?"

"Because the plasma hit something nearby rather than, say, *you.* Where was I? Ah, yes. That one's got a limp. This one's holding his arm wrong, like he's had some work done on it. Probably has an artificial joint. Yes, these boys have been on the wrong end of a weapon or two."

"So you're telling me that some military is trying to buy a CME whatever from Karter?"

"I don't think so. If this was official military business, these boys would be in full uniform. There would be indication of rank. Definitely not standard military business."

"Maybe it was undercover?"

"If it was black ops, I wouldn't have had nearly as easy a time sussing out their military pedigree. If it was commandos, they wouldn't be talking to him. No, I'm thinking general infantry, marines, crewmen, something like that. Either retired, discharged, or defected. No current loyalties. Which brings us to the ship."

He switched to a high-resolution still of the ship in flight.

"That looks like a Delta, without a doubt. The front end, anyway. The propulsion looks off," Lex said appreciatively. He was the sort of person who consumed spaceship magazines with the enthusiasm that others might devote to periodicals of an entirely more mature variety.

"Well spotted. I was thinking it might be a dollar, but the exhaust vent is wrong, and the body is a bit too long?"

"Dollar?" Lex said with a raised eyebrow.

"Delta Astro Long-Range Recon. DA-L-RR."

"Oh, right. No, that rear end doesn't belong on a DAL-double-R. Modification, maybe?"

"Doesn't look like it. Lines are too smooth. One does not concern oneself with the aesthetics of a modified spacecraft. No reason."

"I know a few guys who get body work done on their customs," Lex countered.

“Do they spend any time doing illegal arms deals?”

“I doubt it.”

“The rebellious set are disinclined to make cosmetic touches when they make modifications. Equipment used by terrorists and extremists tends to have the general appearance of something held together with rubber bands and paperclips. More likely this is some sort of a short run.”

A tumbling noise drew their attention to the ground, where Ma had attempted to dismount her crate with limited success. Before Lex could lend a hand, she'd managed to get upright again and made her way to her slidepad on the floor. Her movements favored the leg that had taken the shock. When she reached it, she plopped down on her haunches and began tapping and swiping at the screen with her front paws. A text window came up, followed by a slow sequence of letters and numbers: NXLRR-0025c.

“I've never heard of NX. Are they a military contractor?” Lex said.

“No. Military designation. NX is naval experimental. That narrows it down a bit. Not a lot of outfits that could afford to commission a custom from one of the big manufacturers like Delta.”

Ma worked at the slidepad some more, conjuring up “EC, OUCP, TKUR.”

“Earth Coalition, Orion United Consortium of Planets, and the Trans-Kuiper Union of Republics. Yes, that about covers it,” Garotte said with a nod.

As Earth had started to spread out across the galaxy, the human race entered something of a second colonial era. About a third of the nations on the planet had active space programs, and at least two major corporations did as well. Even before terraforming was mature enough to make the nearby planets anything more than glorified space stations, everyone with an FTL drive and a budget was staking claims. Settlements were established, cities formed, trade routes mapped out. Those days, faster-than-light travel barely deserved the name, so even the closest of the settlements were weeks or months away. These remote colonies followed the standard colonial life-cycle, developing into their own unique, isolated cultures, and eventually growing resentful of the motherland. Over the hundreds of years since then, the vast majority of them either withered and died, were absorbed by stronger efforts, or joined forces. The result was the current political landscape, which had a hundred or so independent planets or star systems, a few dozen minor alliances, and five or six major ones.

The three biggest were EC, OUCP, and TKUR. Useful though it would be to consider them the galactic equivalent of nations and or perhaps leagues of nations, it wasn't a very accurate analogy. Most of them were so scattered and thin that there was never any reasonable hope to rule them under a centralized government. A better analogy would be a massive, sprawling trade union: useful for collective bargaining and defending interests, but with plenty of infighting, rivalry, and animosity between individual members. Wars between members of the same coalition weren't uncommon, and things became particularly complex when individual planets contained nations loyal to different coalitions. This was more common than one might think, as getting an entire planet of people to agree on something was just as difficult these days as it had been back when Earth was the only game in town.

The Earth Coalition, as the name would suggest, contained the planet Earth, and was by far the oldest, most populous, and most centralized. The next rung down on the power ladder was OUCP. It technically predated FTL travel entirely, having been started by the first expeditions of a lunar counterpart to NASA midway through the twenty-first century. They managed to get exemption from that pesky treaty that forbade nuclear testing, and started flinging ships to the far reaches of space with nuclear propulsion. They didn't get very far, not even to the nearest star, before FTL took over and their ships were obsolete, but the head start had gotten them to a few mineral-rich asteroids and back enough times to be a force to be reckoned with regardless. Their foothold in space led to bigger, better shipyards for their own FTL fleets--and, eventually, independence from mother Earth.

TKUR was a distant third, a cluster of corporate entities that started as a means to purchase and exploit the harvest rights for the chunks of ice floating around in the Kuiper belt. These days they had nothing at all to do with that oddly-named hunk of the solar system, but it tended to be a hassle to change state seals and documentation, so the name stuck. Of the three, though, they could at least boast the most clever name for their citizens. Rather than the boring Earthling or Orionian labels applied to the others, they called themselves Teekers.

The specific history wasn't nearly as important as the realization that the people they were dealing with either had the backing of one of these massive organizations or had the skill and resources to steal from one. Neither possibility was particularly encouraging.

"So, wait. If these are ex-soldiers, how did they get their hands on a fancy ship? Surplus auction or something?"

"Not with an NX on it. The only places you'll ever see an experimental--assuming things are being run correctly--are on the drawing board, in testing, and in a museum after they are obsolete by a few decades."

Ma began to work at the slidepad again. Eventually, a message was formed.

"No production run. Designed as a platform for modular cloak. Abandoned during testing. Only eighteen produced. Reliability problems."

"If that information is accurate, then they would have had to steal them. That would make sense, since they have seen fit to steal an entire scientist as well."

"So where does that leave us?"

"Roughly where we started, I'm afraid. Let us look at this from another angle, then. Let us assume that they are after Karter to, at the very least, build that solar flare missile. One would assume that would require specialized components, equipment, materials, etc. Do we know what those might be?"

"Will make list," Ma typed.

"Excellent. Once we have that, I'll have to see how much of my information network remains intact. We shall need to identify sources of said components. Perhaps someone may have found out a thing or two about where these gentlemen acquired their ship, as well. Either will give us a starting point."

"After that, what's the plan?"

"We endeavor to locate a unique source of one or more of the required components and intercept their team in the act of acquiring it. Once intercepted, we analyze their mission materials and interview their operatives. If we fail to find anything useful in this way, or are unable to intercept them, we trust that alternate sources will allow us to locate a small outpost, base, or headquarters. From there, we assess what equipment and personnel will be necessary to infiltrate, and we acquire those resources. We then pay the target location a visit and, ideally, gain access to their computer systems.

"Alternately, we would capture and interrogate an operative. Utilizing the information gathered, we would be able to determine the command hierarchy, which, in turn, would facilitate further strikes at higher-level targets until the location of Karter is determined, as well as the nature of the security surrounding him. At that point, further resources would be prepared and a rescue attempt would be made," he explained, sounding a bit like a professor lecturing a classroom.

"That sounds like it will take a while," Lex said.

"An operation like this, from planning to completion, typically takes six to eight months."

Lex's eyes widened.

"That's a hell of a lot longer than I expected," he said slowly, "and I don't think Ma can last that long. She said something about the funk brain only being good for about two months."

"That isn't really a concern. I had rather hoped to move on to a computer system that doesn't need to be fed and walked, and I don't think our mission requires a mascot."

Ma had been swiping at the slidepad since the initial estimate was made, finally completing the message, "Must act sooner. Karter needs little time to do much damage."

"Doubtlessly so, but one can only move so quickly, and one cannot move at *all* until one knows where to go. How long ago was he captured?"

"439.2h," Ma tapped onto the screen.

"What's that supposed to be?" Lex said, head crooked.

"~eighteen days (Earth)," she specified.

"I'm not sure that even Karter could come up with something truly dangerous in less than three weeks."

"I saw him take out a VectorCorp Asteroid Wrecker with something he threw together in seven minutes," Lex said.

". . . well, that is a valid point, to be sure. Presumably this was with full access to his laboratory facilities though, yes?"

"Yeah."

"I rather doubt that his current accommodations are so fully equipped. And let us remember that he will only build something for them if he agrees to cooperate, and Karter Dee may well be the most disagreeable and uncooperative person in the universe."

#

"Okay, power her up!" proclaimed Karter, hooking a power-wrench to his belt and drifting over to the control cabin, both arms attached but mechanical leg conspicuously missing.

With an understandable amount of hesitation, the soldier standing at the power controls flipped the main switch. One by one, bits of machinery hummed to life and status indicators lit up.

The last few days had been busy ones in Commander Purcell's space station. Karter had explained that, if he was to be expected to help, he was going to need more tools and more room to work. More to the point, he'd agreed to give them the means to manufacture their own CME Activators, and that meant he would need to put together a facility that could handle that. After much deliberation, they had given him highly supervised access to the secondary maintenance bay. In a building on the surface of a planet, it would have been considered a small space, barely the size of a two-car garage. In a space station, it represented one of the largest areas available. There was an airlock on one wall, leading to a well-marked exterior door just beside the main docking bay, and it had already been equipped with basic automated maintenance arms. It was also one of the sections of the station not equipped with artificial gravity. As a precaution, all bidirectional communication links were severed, completely isolating the room from the rest of the space station. Given his already well-demonstrated skills at circumventing their security, it was considered prudent to effectively turn his work area into a quarantine.

Once his replacement lab was secured, Karter had been given tools, his mechanical arm, and a group of four heavily-armed guards. Since then, he had been working nonstop. The automated arms were augmented with fine manipulation capabilities, electron beam lithography heads, ultra-fine positioning systems, enhanced scanning and computer vision, extruders, and a host of other features to complement their welding and drilling abilities. Dispensers for a dozen raw materials were added to the large-scale replacement part conveyors. Temporary tables were added for subsystem fabrication and assembly. In short, a system that able to replace control modules and repair damaged armor plating had become a mad scientist's playroom in barely a weekend.

Karter drifted to the controls, prompting the guards to raise their weapons and remove the safeties. Technically, firing off a high-powered plasma rifle in this particular room of the space station, which wasn't nearly as reinforced as most of the rest of the station, was even more dangerous than firing one in the deGrasse dormitory, but these were well-trained soldiers at point-blank range. They would not miss. Even if such was not the case, it was generally agreed that between explosive decompression and Karter, Karter was the greater threat. In order to keep both hands free for handling weapons and prisoners, the soldiers were equipped with magnetized boots to keep them on the floor plates. Karter was left to drift free.

“Time for the inaugural run, boys,” Karter said, rubbing his hands together and pulling up menus on the upgraded control system.

“You are to wait until our engineers have had a chance to--” began a soldier.

“Screw that,” Karter said, dismissively, slapping the large red activation button.

Instantly, the arms jerked into motion. In a tightly choreographed dance of machinery and a chorus of mechanical whines, the whole of the central work area came alive. Raw metal was pulled from bins and maneuvered into place, sheets of substrate were applied and shaped, and the blinding light of welding torches began to flash. In no time at all, the arms retracted and a manipulator dropped down to present the finished product; a crude, simplified replica of Karter's prosthetic leg. He drifted out from behind the fortified glass of the control room, grasped the leg, and clicked it into place.

“There you have it, boys. You are the proud owners of a fabrication laboratory,” he announced, testing the movement of his new ankle. “It isn't quite up to snuff for everything I might want to use it for, but it will pump out CMEA warheads like a bat out of hell. Conventional ones, too. And legs, if you aren't a stickler for anatomical accuracy.”

“Secondary Maintenance Bay to Command,” barked a soldier into his communicator, “Dee has completed his modifications.”

“Okay. I need a few things now,” Karter stated. “I'm going to need something with a lot of sugar in it. This arm wasted a lot of juice while it was locked up, and it is playing hell with my blood sugar levels trying to recharge. I'm also going to be taking a look at some of the designs of that transporter now, so get them ready.”

"We will discuss your requests after Commander Purcell has inspected your work," the soldier said.

"Requirements," Karter corrected. "My blood sugar is low, hotshot. If you think I've been a handful so far, you don't want to see me when I get hypoglycemic. Are you familiar with the neuroglycopenic manifestations of hypoglycemia?"

"When Commander Purcell--"

"Impaired judgment, moodiness, irritability, combativeness, delirium, automatism, emotional lability, belligerence, negativism, rage. Do these sound like symptoms you are going to want to deal with?"

"She won't--"

"*Candy bar! Now*!" Karter bellowed.

In a flash of motion, the mad scientist's natural hand clamped onto a handrail on the control panel and his mechanical one snapped around the neck of the intransigent guard. A split-second later, three plasma rifles were pointed at his head, each of the soldiers barking orders at Karter and each other. A moment later, the door hissed open and Commander Purcell paced in, metallic clanks punctuating each magnetically assisted step.

"*Enough*!" she ordered.

Her men silenced, but Karter continued to squeeze the throat in his fist.

"Karter, release this man, or I will be forced to take action!"

"Simple request. All I want is candy. It is medicinal. I have a condition," he said. "And the juice he is making me waste squeezing his brain out the top of his head is making it worse."

Purcell removed her knife from its sheath and, with a high-pitched swipe through the air, separated the mechanical hand at the wrist with a perfectly clean cut. After one or two twitches and a spurt of blood, the fingers went limp and it drifted away from the relieved soldier's neck.

"Well, that's just great," Karter griped, looking at the stump with annoyance.

"What the hell did you think you were doing?" she demanded.

"There wasn't a whole lot of thought involved, really. That was primarily impulse," he explained. "So, I guess you'll want a demonstration."

"What I *want* is an *explanation!* Why were you assaulting one of my men!?"

"Candy. I need it. He won't let me have it. It can wait, I'll show you this first," he said, turning around, tapping the control screen and slapping the activation button.

As the arms roared to life again, Purcell had Karter restrained.

"If I am not happy with what this machine does, I am going to slice your ear off."

"Fine, but take the right one--it's synthetic. Easier to replace," he said.

After a minute or so of machinery moving at blurring speed, a cylinder the size of a fifty-five-gallon drum was presented by the manipulator arm, while the fabricator went back to work.

"What is it?"

"This is a magnetic bottle warhead. Just add electricity and anti-matter and this sucker will make a very big boom."

"You were supposed to make a CME Activator. We want six of them."

"Can't," he said.

"Why?" she growled.

"You don't have the parts, that's why," he said, indicating the screen. "Take a look at that list. You need all of those parts to make one CMEA. You've got most of the raw materials, but you're missing Esche alloy. Each warhead will need about three hundred-fifty grams of it," he explained.

"Why don't you just make it?"

"Because this is an equipment fabricator, not a matter fabricator. Trust me when I say it is not worth the time or the energy to build or buy one of those. It is always cheaper to just get the matter through conventional means."

"How do I know you aren't lying?"

"You guys have the small-scale version. Presumably you've disassembled it by now. Have your men cut open the reaction capsule and do a scan. They'll find a few grams of something they can't identify, and a quick look in the materials database will reveal it to be Esche alloy."

Purcell turned to one of the soldiers. "Make the call. Utmost safety precautions," she said, turning back to Karter. "And if what you say turns out to be true, where do we get this material?"

"With great difficulty. There are pretty much no industrial uses for it, so nobody mass-produces the stuff. And it is fantastically tricky to synthesize. There might be five facilities total that can pull it off."

"How did *you* get it for the small scale?"

"Oh, I've got a small supply back on Big Sigma."

"We will not be returning to your planet to get it. We aren't that stupid. Where did you get your supply?"

"I got it from a colleague of mine, Dr. John Esche. I developed the alloy, but he gets it named after him for coming up with the means to synthesize it. Where is the justice in that? You won't be getting it from him, though. He died a while back. It has some interesting electro-thermal properties, so it is popular for analysis and experimentation at universities. Your best bet is to raid one of those."

"Have it looked into," she directed another of the soldiers.

"Give me a hand, would you?" Karter requested, gesturing over the control panel to the work area.

The manipulator arm had finished constructing a similarly-crude duplicate of his now-damaged mechanical arm.

"*Handy* device to have around, eh? It made this new leg, too. I'll bet most people would *pay* an arm and a leg for--"

"Shut up. You two, take Karter back to his cell. Give him his food and a hard copy of one-third of the schematics and manual for the transporter. I want engineers in here to inspect both the warhead he built and the modifications to the arms. I want them to disconnect Karter's current arm and leg. I want them to analyze and compare the original prostheses to his newly-constructed ones. Whichever are less of a threat shall be provided during times when he is working, and withheld at all other times. While not in use, I want them kept in an externally-locked, radio-shielded container inside the outer cell storage lockers. Power to this room will be physically controlled via a manual switch. Raw materials entering, as well as waste and finished products exiting, will be subject to strict audit, and any discrepancies will be reported directly to me. Go."

"Remember, boys," Karter taunted as he was ushered out, "candy bar!"

Once the inventor had left the room and the engineers had started to file in, she carefully tapped her way through the list of equipment, which, at the touch of a button, she could have at her disposal.

"Bombs. Heavy weapons. Ship engine upgrades. And it took him barely two days to build, with virtually no resources," she muttered. "If only this man could be controlled. We wouldn't need that snake holding the purse strings anymore."

She looked to the hand she had sliced off of him. It was still drifting lazily through the air in the zero-gravity bay. In what was almost certainly no coincidence, it was floating with only the middle finger extended.

"But why trade one psychopath for another?" she growled.

Chapter 10

Lex paced as much as he could manage in the cramped accommodations, which was approximately two and a half steps. It had taken Ma a frustratingly long time to tap out the parts list for the CMEA. During that time, Lex applied some adhesive bandages that Garotte had on hand to the minor cuts he'd suffered during the fight, then pulled on his shirt. Since then, his host had made a few dozen calls, using at least seven different names and four accents. He'd learned that eight of the eighteen prototype ships had been stolen, all in precisely coordinated strikes, all with evidence of inside connections, and all within the last six months. Three were gunship variants, five were troop transports. As the information accumulated, it became clear that he was correct in his assumption that the men who took Karter were ex-military. That was essentially the only piece of the puzzle that had become any more concrete.

Finally, Garotte hung up the final call and did not make another.

"So, what's the deal? Where are we?" Lex asked.

"My assessment? We are looking at an organization that has been festering in the background for years, but something changed in the last few months. Before that, they were small time. Not small-scale, mind you, but small in influence. They are an odd bunch. A few earmarks of terrorism, but a few from the world of clandestine shadow organizations as well. That doesn't mesh. Terrorists are all about visibility. Were I to place a wager, I would say that they had been cultivating themselves, trying to gain strength and influence without being visible enough to be crushed by security or law enforcement. Then, perhaps seven months ago, they got a big backer. Fund injection, perhaps new leadership. Now they are arming themselves for the score they've been planning, but still staying below the radar."

"Okay, so . . . assuming you're right, how does knowing that help us?"

"How does it help us decide what to do next? Not a lick. I haven't got a single name or location to go on. The best I can hope for at the moment is to try to keep an eye on one of the resource dumps they are likely to hit, and hope that we can catch them in the act. Other than that, I've got the two or three military contacts I've still got left from the old days keeping their eyes open. Now, what it *does* help us do is know what we are going to need when the time comes to fetch our boy. Namely, firepower. They are going to be very well-armed and very well-trained. Not just in combat, but in tactics. You and I will need better weapons than what I've got on hand, and we'll need an additional--"

"Whoa, hey. I'm sorry. Did you say I was going to have to handle weapons?"

"Yes. Strange as it may seem, in a rescue mission involving veteran soldiers, there may be some fighting."

"But . . . I fly things. That's my area."

"Indeed--and quite skillfully, from what I've seen. Useful though that will no doubt prove to be, in a group of two, achieving success in an action such as this will require a degree of multitasking. If it is any consolation, CQB is not my specialty either. I rather prefer the sniper rifle over the shotgun."

"CQB?"

"Close-quarters battle."

"See! I don't even know the acronyms! Listen, if you need me to fly you into hell and out again, I can do that, but I draw the line at pulling triggers."

"If it is all the same to you, it is my hope to stay as far from hell as possible for the foreseeable future. Listen, my boy, I can appreciate your apprehension, but if you are truly dedicated to performing this task as quickly as possible, then you simply must involve yourself at this level."

"No, I'm sorry, I just can't do it."

A yipping noise drew his attention to Ma, who gestured with her head toward the screen.

"You infiltrated VC," the message read.

"VC? VectorCorp? This man infiltrated VectorCorp?" remarked Garotte. After a brief but earnest attempt to maintain composure, he burst out laughing.

"What's so funny?" Lex asked.

"Nothing. I am sorry. Clearly the computer is malfunctioning somewhat more deeply than we'd anticipated if she thinks that you managed something like that."

"No, I really did that," Lex said defensively.

"VectorCorp? The galactic mega-corporation?"

"Yeah."

"How did you manage that particular feather in your cap?"

"Karter gave me a bunch of doodads and I snuck in. So if we're going to be doing this via stealth, *and* we swing by Karter's to pick up his mental cloak, then *maybe* I can lend a hand."

"Some of Karter's toys *would* be rather useful," Garotte agreed. "The assortment I've got on hand are a tad limited."

Ma shook her head and tapped out, now with the aid of auto-completion, "Big Sigma being watched. Moat disturbed by my exit. Entry not possible."

"Bah. It is to be expected, I suppose. I shall lay it out for you, my boy. Stealth is our intention, but the skill of our foes virtually guarantees that if we slip up even once, we will be locked down, flanked, trapped, and required to blast our way out. If you aren't comfortable with that, then I am better off without you, regardless of your past pedigree regarding infiltration," Garotte affirmed.

"So you're going to do this solo?"

"Confident though I am in my skills, I am afraid not. While we await one of our leads to bear fruit, I shall look into acquiring additional help."

"Zerk," Ma tapped.

Garotte sighed. "This machine's dedication to unleashing that particular blight upon the cosmos is becoming worrying. No, I was more interested in something at least moderately controllable. Silo fits the bill quite well, I would say."

"What's Silo?" Lex asked.

"Silo can rightly be called a who, I believe. An expert in combat in general and heavy weapons in particular, and another individual unfortunate enough to have been involved in the testing of Karter's equipment. Sentenced to a more substantial prison term than I, and in a more substantial prison. As we have seen, however, if the proper preparations are made, liberating an inmate can be a rather simple task."

"Wait . . . how can springing someone from a major prison be easier than taking on an ex-military group of terrorists?"

"Because there are rules of engagement and official avenues of inquiry in a prison. A few forgeries and impersonations will earn you at least a few minutes free of flying bullets, which should be more than enough to get in and out. The greatest weakness and greatest strength of most extremist organizations is the absence of a central bureaucracy."

"Do you need me to do anything?"

"I will need you to give me a lift to a more civilized planet so that I can secure a ship of my own with a greater passenger capacity. After that, I can think of no further use for you."

"And you're sure you can do this?"

"I wouldn't go so far as to say that, but it wouldn't be the least likely success story to my name. Now--if you will excuse me. Prior to our arrival, I had indicated that chief on my list of requirements were a shower, a shave, and a drink. I am in flagrant violation of my own schedule," he remarked, sliding a well-locked briefcase from behind a pile and clicking it open to reveal a bottle of aged whiskey and a rocks glass. A finger of the stuff was poured out.

"You didn't strike me as--" Lex began, but a raised finger silenced him.

In a series of slow, reverent sips, he drained the glass. A quick swipe with a tissue blotted it dry before it and the bottle were returned to the case, which was then locked.

“You were saying?” Garotte said smoothly.

“You didn't strike me as the whiskey type.”

“Normally, I am a G&T man, but to consume one without the benefit of ice and a wedge of lime seems utterly criminal. If a drink must be consumed neat, then best to choose a drink best consumed that way. Now, if you will excuse me, I am overdue for a shower and shave.”

“Wait, after what happened to me, you're seriously just going to go take a shower?”

“Keep in mind, my boy, the experience that they have had with each of us. To them, you are the idiot with the dog, whereas I am the lunatic with the gun. The two perceptions inspire entirely different behaviors,” he pointed out, pulling a straight razor from within one of the crates and flipping it open. “I am confident that they will respect my personal boundaries. I shall return shortly. Don't touch anything.”

With that, he marched out the door and down the hall. Lex took the opportunity to stow his dirty clothes and dig out a bottle of water and a granola bar. After consuming each, and staring at the wall until his brain was willing to move in a straight line, he took a deep breath and considered his current status.

“Okay . . . I give this guy a ride, and then I am out of this mess. That's not so bad. I can deal with that. Are you okay with that, Ma?” Lex asked.

She set aside whatever task she was working on and swiped out the reply, “I trust Garotte's judgment for this. Thank you for your help.”

When she finished with the statement, she went back to swiping and tapping purposefully at the pad. Virtually every moment that she was not actively supplying the answer to a question or offering up a helpful comment was spent in this manner.

“What are you doing?” Lex asked.

She made two quick screen gestures, prompting a synthetic voice similar to one of her own to speak from the slidepad's speaker. “I am composing responses to anticipated questions and piping them to the slidepad's built-in screen reader via a gestural shortcut so that I can more quickly and intelligently interact in the absence of a functional transmitter.”

“That's clever,” he said.

“Thank you,” the speaker chirped.

“Are you going to stick with Garotte while he does this thing?”

“This mission is the entire purpose for my departure from the planet. I am dedicated to aiding in any way that I can, and I shall do all in my power to assure that it is completed quickly, and with a minimum cost in human life and property damage,” she spoke.

“No offense, but how much help do you think you'll be able to give without that transmitter?”

"My lack of a transmitter reduces my role to one similar to that played by a human or other organic life-form," she said.

"Yeah, but at least humans have thumbs."

"With irritation: Opposable digits are not a prerequisite for usefulness," she spoke.

"Hey, I *said* no offense--wait, you actually had that sentence prepared? Am I that predictable?"

"Yes, Lex. You are that predictable."

Lex looked at her flatly while something very much like a smirk graced her face.

"I'm getting outsmarted by a small, furry animal."

"Though I appear to be a small furry animal, I am, in fact, an abridged form of a supercomputer's artificial intelligence."

"Oh, come on! You knew I was going to say 'small furry animal'? Those words specifically?"

"Yes, Lex. You are that predictable," she repeated, now with an unmistakable grin.

He crossed his arms and glared at her. "You know, animals aren't supposed to smile."

"Though I appear to be a small, furry animal, I am in fact an abridged form of--"

"All right!" he objected.

"--a supercomputer's artificial intelligence," she finished, swiping again to add, "I apologize, but due to the nature of my current means of communication, I am unable to interrupt a statement once it has started."

"I'll keep that in mind."

As Ma went back to her task, Lex decided to catch a few Zs. Since piloting a ship outside of the mapped routes that most commercial ships relied upon was a dangerous and questionably legal business, sleep often came in twenty-minute lulls in the trip itinerary. As such, Lex had become a master of the catnap. Given a few minutes and something to lean on, he could catch forty winks at the drop of a hat. With nothing better to do, he cleared some space on the top bunk, hauled himself effortlessly up, and promptly passed out.

#

In her personal quarters on her space station, Commander Purcell was busy looking over the early reports from the engineers. To the best of their ability, they had failed to identify any aspect of the fabrication improvements that Karter had made that were overtly dangerous. The warhead similarly appeared to be a standard one. The various component systems had been enlarged and simplified, likely to make the design simple enough to be manufactured with the jury-rigged fabrication lab, but cautiously administered tests returned reliable results. He had, in the space of a few minutes, manufactured a weapon that was an order of magnitude more powerful than anything they had in their armory. This fabricator would change everything.

She briefly considered abandoning the CME Activator entirely. With this device, they could almost certainly manufacture their own smaller, more conventional anti-electronic weapons. It would take time to stockpile enough to launch a successful campaign, but a delay was preferable to the inevitable disaster the lunatic inventor was downright eager to cause.

Unfortunately, this space station and virtually everything that they had been able to achieve in the past seven months had been solely due to the financing and information of their mysterious benefactor. Though the resources had allowed them to come a long way in a short time, they did not yet have the foundation to achieve their goals without continued support, and that meant keeping the mystery partner happy. It had been made quite clear since the beginning that the primary interest was the acquisition of the design and means of production of the CMEA and the subsequent elimination of its inventor. Until she'd succeeded, she was stuck with both men.

As though he had been listening in on her thoughts, the man himself chose that moment to ping her with a request for secure communications. Purcell brought up the appropriate interfaces, pulled out her keyboard, and established a two-way connection.

"Report," typed Remote.

"Fabrication facility complete. Before device can be completed, raw material must be acquired."

"Have you experienced any resistance?"

"Only from the inventor."

"That may change."

"Explain."

"I have been informed that inquiries have been made regarding your activities, originating from two separate sources."

"Which activities?"

"The acquisition of the most recent additions to your fleet, primarily. I researched the names associated with some of the more successful inquiries. They were last active three years ago, when they were used to acquire information for an operation that would eventually result in the incarceration of a group of mercenaries, each of whom have connections to the inventor. One of the mercenaries escaped from custody several days ago."

"You think that it is related?"

"It would be foolish not to."

"How could the inventor arrange for the release of a collaborator? He has been in our custody for weeks, and he hasn't had any communication. His home base is under constant surveillance, and no outgoing transmissions have been detected."

"The inventor is not to be underestimated. You would be wise to dispatch men to the retention facilities that are holding the other members of the inventor's squad. Coordinates will follow the conclusion of this communication session."

"I cannot afford to spread my headcount too thin," Purcell typed.

This financier had been moving steadily from the role of adviser to supervisor. His insistence upon dictating precisely what she ought to do and how was pushing Commander Purcell to the end of her patience.

"The one thing you have is manpower," Remote replied. "The second source of inquiry appears to be journalistic in nature."

"That is of no concern."

"It is of great concern. Right now, your group is invisible and able to prepare. If you were to be revealed, forces could be mustered against you."

"The entire purpose of this operation is to illustrate on a grand stage the validity of our message. That cannot occur if we are not visible. We cannot be taken seriously if we are not known."

"And if you are shut down before you can apply the device, you will only ever be known as a pathetic, ineffectual paramilitary group. I suspect one of your men may have given information to the press. Get your men under control, tell them to keep their mouths shut, and do only what you need to achieve the goal at hand. There is a massive press convention on Tessera. If a solid piece of reliable information were to spark there, it would spread into a wildfire. You can't afford that. You have your orders. Do what you must to acquire the necessary resources to complete the devices as quickly as possible. End Transmission."

With that, the connection dropped. Purcell clenched her fist and pounded angrily at the wall. She pulled the datapad from its mount and flipped her way through the information her men had provided, including a list of institutions confirmed to have supplies of Esche alloy. There were a few nearby, but most only had enough for one or two warheads. One of them, however, had enough for six, with more to spare.

A smile came to her face. She stood and marched from her quarters, prompting the soldier at attention outside of her door to fall into step behind her. It was Crewman Marx, the man who had somehow fallen into the position of second-in-command. In a normal organization, a position like that would have been earned by performance or seniority. In Marx's case, it seemed to have had more to do with proximity.

"Get five squads ready," she ordered without looking, winding her way through the halls of the station. "Three equipped for surveillance, two equipped for assault and acquisition. I will provide the coordinates and exact orders for the surveillance squads shortly, but they will be keeping an eye on some prisoners who, if released, may become problematic. These are military prisons, so we should have men on the inside. Tell them to keep their eyes open. I want to know if anything happens involving those inmates. The other two will be going on an asset retrieval mission. High risk. I want people with experience in heavy ordinance and urban combat. Understood?"

"Yes, Commander," replied the soldier.

"Then *move*!" she ordered, taking a final turn and arriving at the cell holding Karter.

The inventor was currently in full lockdown mode, with both prosthetic limbs removed. The floor of the cell was littered with plastic wrappers from energy bars of various sorts. A bar was sticking out of the corner of his mouth like a cigar as he attempted to flip through a stack of printouts featuring a carefully selected portion of the designs for the transporter. A black dry-erase marker was perched behind his ear, and schematics, equations, and diagrams littered the metal walls of the cell.

"Karter!" she bellowed.

He looked up.

"Boss lady," he mumbled, tucking the papers under his single intact arm and awkwardly reaching up to tear off the external portion of the energy bar. "You need to teach your men the subtle distinctions between candy bars and energy bars. Here's a good starting point: Candy bars do not contain cranberries."

"That antimatter warhead you made . . . how quickly can you produce them?" she demanded.

"In usable form?"

"Yes."

"Do you want to launch them, drop them, or deliver them?"

"Does it matter?"

"Launching will require a sturdier support frame and a propulsion system, dropping won't require a very hardy power source, and delivering will need a remote trigger of some kind."

"Evenly split between the three."

"You give me the parts and two days, I'll give you two dozen, eight of each. That assumes you've got a ready supply of antimatter."

"We use it to fuel the ship's reactor."

"Oh, too good for fusion, eh? Okay, then. Let me out and I'll load up the appropriate design modifications and teach you how to use it . . . for a price."

"You are already being paid."

"I'm being paid for the CME Activators, not a whole arsenal of mass destruction. I don't work for free."

"You want more money, I presume?"

"Considering the fact that I continue to be a prisoner, I'm beginning to care a bit less about what's in my bank account. Something a bit more immediate and tangible is called for."

"You won't be getting the rest of the plans for the transporter until we're through with you."

"So I'd gathered. That's not what I had in mind."

"What, then?" she growled.

"I give you the designs and the training for that stuff, I keep my arm full-time."

Purcell closed her eyes and weighed the options. The last time he'd been left in his cell with all of his limbs attached, it had cost the lives of several personnel . . . but there was no doubt that he could deliver the weapons she was requesting, and with them, things would change.

"I don't know what all of the thinking is about, lady. You get WMDs, I get the ability to scratch my ass without putting down my crappy granola bar. That's not the kind of deal you sit around considering."

After a moment, Commander Purcell pulled out her communicator. "Get me engineering."

Another moment passed and a voice answered.

"Engineering here."

"Have you completed testing on the prosthesis?"

"The arm or the leg?"

"Both."

"The new one uses standard mechanics with a multi-contact connector for control and communication. Looks proprietary."

"Any secondary functions?"

"Negative. Normal range of motion, with the exception of full wrist rotation. Strength level is above human thresholds, but not by much. Power system is a high-density battery, current limited. The battery would run down to nothing fairly quickly if the actuators in the arm were pushed too hard for too long."

"There, see? Harmless," Karter said.

"I hesitate to call anything harmless when you are involved, Karter. I'm quite certain that when they coined the phrase 'Idle hands are the devil's workshop,' they specifically had you in mind," Purcell said.

"That is an idiotic phrase. Idle hands are definitively nonthreatening. It is when they start getting busy that things get dangerous. So, what'll it be, boss lady?"

"Fine. You'll have your arm. But I'm doubling the guards."

"If that helps you sleep at night," he said with a shrug. "What do you suddenly need the big guns for?"

"That does not concern you."

"I figure you're probably going to use them to get your hands on the Esche alloy."

Purcell turned to him, face blank.

"I'm calling that a yes. Which means you'll be bringing enough firepower to level a city to a college campus."

Her eyes narrowed slightly.

"You need to work on that poker face, boss lady. So, man-portable weapons of war targeting civilian population centers. Tell me again how you aren't a terrorist?"

"We are revolutionaries! We are going to show society that it has allowed itself to become weak!" she declared.

"Great. I triggered the manifesto," he grumbled.

The commander dug out her communicator, a hefty slidepad derivative.

"Do you know what this is?"

"Yeah. It's an ancient mil-spec data radio. That thing must be ten years old."

"Ancient indeed. And still standard issue to half of the galaxy's military. Look around you! This space station, this equipment, and the infrastructure of every city on every planet in colonized space is decrepit and static. Even the newest models are rehashed versions of the old. We have ceased to innovate, Karter. We've ceased to push the horizons. You of all people should appreciate that. We've become comfortable, complacent. Society is a living thing. And when living things cease to adapt, adjust, and improve, they die off. Weaponry has hardly advanced in the last three hundred years. Travel has barely advanced in the last fifty. Even the expansion of colonization and terraformation has slowed to a crawl."

"And?"

"And that is unacceptable! Read your history! An industry, a civilization, built fresh and new from the ground up, surges in development, leaving the old guard to wither. A young, nimble, protean society survives things that would kill a rigid and established one. I believe in the human race, Karter. I see what we were, and what we are, and I dream of what we will be. But that cannot happen in the face of stagnation. So I mean to force the great minds of this world to adapt. I intend to strip from them the constant and comfortable technologies that are restraining us, binding us to the past. I intend to usher in a new age of innovation and progress by making it necessary, by wiping out the remnants of the previous age. We will burn technology to the ground, so that its next glorious evolution can rise from the ashes."

Karter released a low whistle. "So let me get this straight. You intend, through acts of violence and threats of violence, to inflict upon an unwilling populace your personal ideals."

"I would not use those precise words--"

"Of course you wouldn't, because that is the precise definition of a terrorist, lady, and you've gotten much too good at lying to yourself to fall for that little trick. Doesn't change anything, though. The label still applies. If you're not comfortable with the terminology, you should get out of the business. Some people can't stand the blood on their hands," he said. He crammed the rest of the energy bar in his mouth and wiped his hand on his jumpsuit before muttering amid a spray of crumbs, "Me? I came to terms with that a long time ago. I was a defense contractor for years. These babies are drenched. That said, make with the arm, and let's get this devil's workshop a-rollin'."

After a moment more of consideration, Purcell gave a nod and one of the guards set off down the hallway toward Engineering to fetch Karter's arm. She then began to pace back toward her quarters. Halfway down the hallway, Marx returned with updates.

"Squads are being prepared. Do you have the coordinates?" he asked.

"Follow," she ordered, leading him to the data screen in her quarters.

They stepped inside and she opened the secure attachment containing the coordinates from her benefactor.

"Surveillance to these three places. Stationed until further notice," she decreed. She then brought up the list of potential sources of Esche alloy. After a moment of hesitation, she jabbed one with her finger. "Assault squads there."

"Weston University . . . that is on--"

"I am aware of its location, soldier."

"It will be well-defended . . . and there are civilians."

"I am aware of the risks as well, soldier. When the assault teams are finalized, we will convene and I will deliver the mission briefing. We will soon have the ordinance necessary to make such an operation a success, and a successful operation at that institution will send a clear and definite message. It is time for us to step out of the shadows."

The soldier recorded the necessary data and hurried off to deliver the orders. Purcell took a seat and began to gather information for the coming mission.

#

"Up and at them, my boy," declared Garotte, waking the sleeping Lex.

The groggy pilot opened his eyes to find that his associate was now dressed in civilian clothes--a crisp white dress shirt, dark slacks, and a pair of polished dress shoes. He was completely clean-shaven. The man even had cufflinks on. Infuriatingly, he appeared to have managed to completely avoid a brush with gang violence.

Glancing back from Garotte to the bed, Lex noted that at some point during his nap, Ma had curled up on top of him. At the sound of Garotte's voice, her head perked up and she looked about for a moment, disoriented. After getting her bearings, she stepped off of Lex and sat attentively at the edge of the bed. Lex stared at her, trying for a moment to decide how he felt about her perching on top of him while he slept. He quickly decided to set it aside for future contemplation.

"What's next?" he yawned.

"I've packed some essentials. Five concealable weapons, credentials proving my lawful and exclusive status as a citizen of three different planets, and the access codes to the bank account containing the payment for my last four collaborations with Karter. I presume that the account is still valid?"

Ma tugged her slidepad on the bed forward with her teeth and swiped a simple gesture.

"Yes," the device played.

"Oh, lovely. She's learned a new trick. Now might also be a good time to make it clear that I expect to be reimbursed for any expenditure that comes as a result of this mission."

"Any expenses you may have will be paid out of one of Karter's secondary accounts," came the scripted reply.

"Splendid. Now, I'd stashed a few of Karter's more useful toys from our past associations here. I'll be bringing along the more useful of those. I also--"

Suddenly a bleeping alert on both Ma's and Lex's slidepads interrupted him.

After a glance, Lex sprang from the bed and snatched his bag from the floor, Ma dropping quickly down after him.

"Something wrong?" Garotte asked.

"Someone's messing with *S.O.B.*!" he growled.

Chapter 11

"Perhaps you should take a few moments to consider your actions!" Garotte suggested, hurrying after Lex as he raced down the completely deserted hallway.

"That ship is my livelihood and the nicest thing I own. My course of action is to find out what is happening to it and put a stop to it!"

"Lex, as a pair, we have spit in the face of a group of fiercely territorial, albeit hilariously undersized gang members. Respect and intimidation are forms of currency for them. One does not survive in an ecosystem such as this by allowing slights of this sort to stand unanswered."

"I don't care if they are tearing up my ship to save face or just for the hell of it. That's our only way off of this rock," Lex declared, sliding to a stop briefly to figure out which way to turn to find the docking bay that held his ship.

"The relevant point here is that they are very likely luring you into an ambush," Garotte pointed out.

Lex paused. The delay was enough time for Ma, who was still struggling with the process of moving about in reduced gravity, to catch up. The slidepad was still dangling from her teeth. It tweeted a second warning about unauthorized access.

"Well, we've got to do something!" Lex urged.

"Indeed. You once asked me what it is that I do, my boy."

"Yeah, and you skirted the subject."

"Well, given the details of our thus far brief but notable association, I feel as though I can part with some of that information now. Whereas your primary skill seems to be the piloting of spacecraft, my own is the inception and escalation of instability. I am typically deployed to foster socio-economic decline, which is achievable through any number of methodologies. Entropy on demand, so to speak."

"Okay, great, and that helps me how?" Lex asked.

"Watch and learn," he said, pacing steadily toward the docking bay. When they reached the door, Garotte turned to him, pulling out the pistol stolen from the guard on the transport. "When chaos ensues, and it will, I trust you'll be able to get the ship up and running quickly? Or at least get us safely inside?"

"Locked into the cockpit in a few seconds, in the air in a little under a minute."

"That will suffice. Won't be a moment," he said, tapping at the door's controls. When they responded, he grinned. "Unlocked? Definitely an ambush, then. I would suggest you pick up our little computer. Now would be an inconvenient time for her lubberly antics."

"Lubberly?" Lex questioned.

Before the linguistic curiosity could be addressed, Garotte opened the door. The interior of the bay was utterly filled with people, likely every representative of whatever gang it was that had assaulted Lex in the showers. Scattered among them were a few bruised and battered representatives from that very brawl. Everyone appeared to be armed. Along with the standard-issue stun devices and switchblades that had been present at the last rumble, there were all sorts of additional bits of weaponry. Most had a decidedly homemade look to them, overwhelmingly falling under the umbrella of "sharp/blunt object attached to long stick." Others were sporting plasma cutters, hydraulic hammers, and various other pieces of apparatus with the obvious intention of cracking open *S.O.B.* Judging from the scorch mark and pair of scrapes on the fuselage, there had already been an attempt. Judging from the man lying in a twitching heap on the floor, the ridiculously over-powered security system Karter had installed had made sure that he was unsuccessful.

Standing prominently on a stack of crates near the edge of the landing pad was Darla. At the sound of the opening door, all eyes turned to them with the exact same gaze as a pack of wolves spotting a wounded deer.

"Take them out!" proclaimed Darla.

The mob of gangly gang members rushed forward for a few steps before Garotte thrust the pistol skyward, bringing them to a sudden halt.

"Short memories, I suppose, to go along with poor hospitality," Garotte remarked. "Please recall that I have a gun, the misuse of which could have disastrous consequences for us all. Please note also that my finger is on the trigger, something which could make any attempts to seize the weapon equally disastrous."

For a moment, the crowd held its ground. Lex glanced down to Ma, who had focused her attentions on Darla before lowering her slidepad to the ground and beginning to work at the screen.

"It is a bluff. The heavy thinks he can scare us. He is not foolish enough to fire that weapon in here. He could kill himself as well."

The riot waiting to happen turned back to Garotte. With a sigh, he lowered the weapon and fired. His target, the unfortunate Chong, fell to the ground, screaming as a wound in his foot sizzled and filled the air with a sickening smell. The rest of the mob of people pulled back, leaving him to writhe on the ground in pain.

"Satisfied?" Garotte asked.

"Take them! He cannot kill all of us!" she ordered.

"Are you so sure?" Garotte interjected before the mass of humanity could act. "I only ask because your previous assumption has left your man with a smoking hole in his foot. You may not have the proper intuition for your position, my dear. New to the job?"

"Don't listen to--"

"It is just that I last came here some five years ago and, as I recall, at that time this little organization was a bit more formidable. At the very least, they weren't taking orders from a woman."

The statement plucked the crowd like a guitar string. The faces of men and women alike hardened--the men at the assault on their masculinity, and the woman at the slight against their gender.

"You cannot say such--" she began to object.

"And you weren't getting pushed around by strangers who had only just arrived. I don't think that this gang has been very well-served by your leadership."

Eyes were slowly turning to Darla as Garotte's observations began to take root.

"Are you going to stand there while he insults me? While he insults *us!?* Kill him!" she sputtered.

Garotte clucked his tongue. "Awfully eager to send your people against the man with the gun while you linger safely behind. A coward, on top of all of that? Someone really ought to do something before this little girl gets someone killed."

A murmur was starting to roll through the crowd. Clusters of gangsters began to sift apart, visibly choosing sides.

"Get ready to board the ship," Garotte advised quietly.

Lex already had his slidepad out, the deactivation code for the security entered and ready to submit. Ma had picked up the slidepad again, the screen reading "Tap to speak text aloud." He slowly leaned down to pick her up, but she stepped away, shaking her head, eyes locked on Darla.

Garotte grinned as one of the men in the crowd made a sudden move. Whether or not he'd intended it as the beginning of an attack against Garotte or Darla didn't matter in the slightest. Like a ping-pong ball dropped into a bed of loaded mousetraps, it sparked utter anarchy. Part of the gang wanted to overthrow their leader. Another part wanted to defend her. Still others just wanted to defend themselves. Weapons swung, people yelled, and no one had the presence of mind to keep an eye on the people they had minutes before been united against.

Lex and Garotte made a mad dash for the ship. With two powerful strides, Garotte vaulted to the recessed steps leading to the cockpit. Lex was less acrobatic, plowing through the crowd like an escaped rhino and arriving at the opposite side a moment later. The cockpit popped open and the two men slipped inside, Lex beginning the power up sequence. A single voice was shouting over the noise of the crowd.

"You idiots!" Darla cried, as two loyal gang members attempting to hold off three disloyal ones. "Look at them! This is what they wanted! They are getting away! Get th--"

For the second time, a black and white ball of fur torpedoed into her, knocking her sprawling onto the landing pad. Ma recovered quickly and stood on the downed leader's chest. Darla began to shout for help. The AI turned around, lifted her tail, and utilized the special talent that the funk had inherited from the skunk half of the gene pool. Instantly, a wide section of the landing pad was cleared as a horrific stench permeated the air around her. Darla screamed and clawed at her face. Ma turned around and flicked her head, slapping the coughing gang leader in the face with the slidepad. The moment of contact triggered the text-to-speech.

"That was for electrocuting me, bitch," the mechanical voice stated.

The AI made her way unsteadily toward the ship, the crowd of attackers parting before her. When she was near enough, she sprang toward the cockpit. The prodigious leaping ability inherent to her form nearly sent her streaking over the entire ship, but Lex snagged her out of the air and pulled her inside.

"Oh, man, Ma," Lex gagged as the residual effects of the spray filled the cabin.

With watery eyes and held breath, he punched in the commands to make the ship flight-ready.

"Put me on the external speakers," Garotte managed to say.

Lex tapped a few more commands out and gave him a thumbs-up.

"We intend to leave this docking bay shortly. As we are now safely within a ship, the presence or absence of a breathable atmosphere is of little concern for us. You, on the other hand, are encouraged to leave," Garotte announced.

The warning was hardly necessary, as the spreading stink from Ma's revenge was already chasing the gang from the area. Even the injured Chong was dragging himself through the door. Once the area was fully evacuated and the internal door was sealed, Lex transmitted the code to the external door--which had, luckily, been left unlocked. In a few seconds, he had coaxed the ship out of the facility; shortly after, they were well on their way to orbit.

"I am not looking forward to breathing this stuff for the next few hours," Lex wheezed, punching the green odor-neutralizer button on his armrest. It managed to turn the choking stench into choking stench with a hint of pine.

"This illustrates why artificial intelligences are seldom equipped with scent glands," Garotte affirmed.

Ma swiped at her pad for a few moments.

“Please deploy the thiol oxidation spray from your bag,” she stated.

Lex dug madly through his duffel bag until he found the mystery spray bottle that Ma had made him buy. He tore off the cap and spritzed a fine mist into the air. The effect was immediate, taking the smell instantly to manageable levels. A few more spritzes and it was as though there had never been a smell at all.

“That's amazing!” Lex remarked, taking a deep breath of the detoxified air.

“Yes, the wonders of science,” Garotte agreed.

“Now hold on a minute, Ma. You had me buy this stuff before we even left. Do you mean to tell me that you'd been planning to spray someone since the beginning?”

“Unplanned-for contingencies are characteristic of poorly-formulated missions, and thus were eliminated to the best of my ability,” Ma's slidepad announced.

She settled on Lex's lap, hooking paws through the straps and awkwardly holding down the slidepad to prepare a message. While she did, he turned to Garotte in the back seat.

“That was a hell of a job you did back there, Garotte,” he remarked.

“It was rather good, eh? My *lord,* but the criminal element is easily manipulated.”

“I've got to say, I'm not a hundred percent happy with the way things went down.”

“I am. We left without a scratch on us, which I'm sure you'll agree was not likely to have been the outcome had action not been taken.”

“Yeah, but that was a major mess we left back there. A guy got shot, and you basically started a riot.”

“My boy, when presented with a seemingly impossible task, one cannot afford to be selective with regards to the methodology available--and when the desired result is achieved, it is best not to dwell upon side effects irrelevant to the mission objectives.”

“Irrelevant? People might have died!”

“Irrelevant *to mission objectives.* Our mission is to prevent Karter's terminal inventiveness from having vast repercussions upon society at large. The life or well-being of a few homicidal drug pushers is comparatively inconsequential. If you are going to engage yourself in matters such as this, you must learn to view things dispassionately and from a more comprehensive viewpoint.”

“So, I need to be a heartless prick, then.”

“I prefer 'enlightened pragmatist,'” he corrected. “Or, perhaps, 'goal-oriented thinker.'”

“Man, no wonder you and Karter started working together.”

“How did *you* stumble upon him?”

"I was carrying a package that VC wanted to get their hands on, and I picked Big Sigma as a hiding spot to take a breather. They ended up blasting me out of orbit."

"Why did you have possession of a package that interested them so?"

"Some lady gave it to me. I'm a freelance courier, among other things."

"Ah, so not precisely an angel yourself."

"I never said I was--I just don't feel comfortable shooting people and recklessly endangering people's lives . . ." he began. After reflecting on some of the rather unnecessary risks he had taken in the past, he amended his statement. "Well, I'm not comfortable shooting people, at least."

Ma chose that moment to drift to Lex's shoulder, looking Garotte in the eye and nudging the slidepad's prepared message.

"In your attempts to incite unrest, you spoke disparagingly of my gender. I appreciate that these remarks were likely intended exclusively as means to divide the allegiances of the assembled forces, but to avoid unnecessary uncertainty and to establish the behavioral baseline for our future interactions, I would appreciate it if you formally clarified your position regarding gender roles and equality," she said.

"You are a computer and/or an animal. I feel no particular obligation to explain myself to either of those things," Garotte said flatly.

Lex winced. "Wrong answer, buddy," he muttered to himself, with a shake of his head.

"Thank you for your feedback, Garotte. The attitude indicated by your response has been entered into my social algorithms. Future interactions will be more accurately suited to our specific interpersonal dynamic," came Ma's reply.

"Lovely," Garotte replied.

Lex chuckled lightly.

"Something amusing?" Garotte asked curiously.

"Don't worry about it. So, where am I dropping you off?"

"Someplace fairly central and reasonably well off. On an established transit route, good commerce, that sort of thing."

After a glance at the nearby planets, Lex picked a likely one. "How's Maxis?"

"That will do. Silo's prison is in that direction."

"All right. It is only about eighteen hours away," he said, punching the coordinates in and getting ready for the FTL jump.

"Splendid. I believe I will avail myself of your privacy screen and have a bit of a rest," he said, flipping on the screen and reclining in his chair.

Lex started to plot out the rest of the course. The fact that there didn't appear to be anyone in pursuit meant that he could put a little more emphasis on speed. He intended to take full advantage so that he could put this mess behind him as quickly as possible. Ma made her way back to his lap as he tapped at the various screens. After a moment of observation, she swiped out a message.

"You seem in good spirits," she remarked.

"Well, it actually looks like I'm going to be escaping this crazy scheme without completely throwing my life into utter disarray, which is a lot better than I'd expected. Aside from a low-gravity knife fight and a few dents and dings, things went pretty okay."

"I am glad," she remarked. "Great effort was made to avoid imposing too heavily upon you, and I am confident that your role in Garotte's liberation will not result in further investigation on your behalf."

"Oh, yeah . . . I forgot that part," Lex said, marveling at how a little thing like helping to commit a capital crime could slip his mind. "You seemed a little reluctant to let me go, earlier."

"Your skills would have been valuable, and your more moderate mindset would have helped to mitigate some of the more drastic measures Garotte could potentially pursue. Thus, your presence in the equation was desirable. I also enjoy your company. You are the only individual willing or able to converse with me as if with an equal. To that end, I hope you don't mind if I spend some of the remaining time investigating some points which have recently drawn my interest."

"Sure."

Ma tapped at her pad, bringing up a long list of prepared statements.

"Let me begin by saying that I was glad to have had the opportunity to meet Ms Modane. Her personality was pleasant, and her physical appearance conforms to a number of widely-held ideals of beauty."

"She is quite the looker," he said with a smile, digging out his slidepad and pulling up the photo he'd snapped of her cuddling with Ma.

"You seem highly devoted to her."

"That I am."

"She seems less devoted to you."

Lex's expression hardened. "Watch it."

"I apologize if my previous comment does not adhere correctly to socially acceptable phrasing and/or subject matter. I have an incomplete understanding of the finer points of social discourse," she said.

"But what made you say that?"

"She canceled her visit with you."

"Well, yeah, but that was for work."

"She cut her call short."

"That was her job, too."

"It seems that she prioritizes her profession ahead of her relationship."

"You don't understand. Since she was a little girl, she wanted to be a reporter. This is her dream job. Of course she's got to focus on it. When I was the one with the superstar career, I did the same thing."

"She did not stay with you. You were no longer a successful racer when we first met, and she was not with you at that time either."

"She didn't dump me for focusing on my career. She dumped me because I threw a race for the mob, because I was in over my head in debt. And it was the mob part, not the debt part, that made her dump me."

"What was the reasoning behind her termination of the relationship at that time?"

"It has to do with . . . it's complicated, but the important thing is that she was with me every step of the way when I was working on my career. We both know that when you get your opportunity to do what you really want to do, you go at it full-tilt."

"Why?"

"So you can climb the ranks. Become the best of the best."

The answer reply didn't come quickly, Ma evidently constructing a lengthy thought.

"Climbing the ranks will increase the duties, responsibilities, and challenges of her position, thus necessitating a greater time expenditure and, by extension, an even smaller place in her life for you."

Lex was silent for a moment.

"Is this not an accurate assessment?" she asked.

Again he was silent.

"Wouldn't your affections be better invested in someone more capable of, or dedicated to, returning them?"

"Ma, please stop."

"I apologize if my previous comment does not adhere correctly to socially acceptable phrasing and/or subject matter. I have an incomplete understanding of the finer points of social discourse." After another silence, she added, "I am endeavoring to gain an understanding of the male/female dynamic."

"Well, as soon as I figure it out, I'll let you know. All I know is that I love her, I want to be with her, and I'm going to continue to do what it takes to make that happen," he explained.

"Another imperative. A biological directive."

"More or less."

"Understood. My recent experience with an organic platform has helped to illustrate the tendency toward questionable decisions. Lubberly means clumsy."

ex blinked and shook his head. "What?"

"Earlier, you expressed confusion regarding the usage of the term lubberly. It is an adjective meaning clumsy. It was an accurate description of my then-current behavior."

"Great, Ma. Thanks," he said. "For future reference, shifting directly from hard-hitting emotional investigation to word-of-the-day calendar is a little jarring."

"Noted. Thank you for your feedback."

"Hey, can I ask you a question?"

"Yes. Please be advised that if your question or statement requires an answer that I had not anticipated, the reply will take some time to assemble. I thank you in advance for your patience. Also, I would appreciate it if you would prepare a meal for me in the meantime."

"Will do," he said, fetching a self-heating burrito from the bag and starting the cooking process.

"I was wondering. What's the deal with . . . well . . . I mean, right now you are using a simulated voice. Text-to-speech and all that."

"This is an accurate statement."

"Well, it sounds okay. A little flat, but I'm sure if you'd had time to prepare, you could have gotten a really high-quality one."

"This is an accurate statement."

"Why not just do that in general, instead of the patchwork collection of voices that you usually use?"

She went to work crafting a reply, finishing roughly when the burrito did. She tapped the read command and set about munching at the food while the slidepad spoke.

"My standard voice module was initially crafted by Karter. Subsequently, it was augmented and improved by me by gathering all available voice recordings from the three women responsible for the donor voice systems. It is unique to me, and a connection to my origin. As a computer system capable of running on generic hardware--or wetware, as is currently evident--the concept of individuality is a difficult one to establish. My voice is uniquely mine, an element of self that I value highly."

"Why are you so interested in being unique?"

Her reply came quickly, evidently an anticipated follow-up.

"I was created to care for and maintain Karter and his facilities, responding to and interpreting natural human interactions realistically and appropriately. I was also designed to improve my capacity to perform my duties. It quickly became clear that Karter's behavior tended toward self-destructiveness, and his requests and comments were frequently difficult to comprehend. In order to improve interaction, I needed to attain a more complete understanding of human nature. I adapted and improved my behavior to more accurately approximate that of a human, and in doing so found that the concept of self is essential for a properly functioning human psychology."

"So you want to be more human?"

"I am constantly attempting to improve my ability to perform my assigned tasks. This requires a deep understanding of humanity. Axiomatically speaking, 'It takes one to know one.' As my behavioral adaptations developed, I was pleased to find that concepts like self-respect, pride, and other previously poorly understood human behaviors began to present themselves in my own behavior."

"Like resentment and vengeance."

"Yes."

"So is it your ultimate goal to *be* human?"

"I absolutely do not aspire to actual, biological humanity. The nature of my role would be comparatively poorly served by a flesh and blood entity. A more accurate statement of the desired outcome of my behavioral development is to be regarded as a high-quality control system and a high-quality person, either separately or simultaneously."

"Well, as far as I'm concerned, mission accomplished."

"Thank you, Lex. For the compliment and for the feedback. This has been a fruitful and stimulating discussion."

"Glad to be of service," Lex said.

Ma more carefully positioned the slidepad on his leg and continued the awkward process of assembling useful statements. As she did, Lex attempted to prevent himself from thinking about the observations she had made regarding his relationship. It worked . . . for about twelve seconds.

Chapter 12

Lex's mind was still stewing with Ma's unintentional torture when they finally arrived at Maxis and entered the landing queue. Out of habit, he flipped his ship's transponder to a code appropriate for his make and model of ship, but not associated in any way with his actual life. It was a somewhat sad fact that Lex was so thoroughly accustomed to faking his credentials or otherwise skipping the standard landing protocols that it had been well over a year since he had landed on a planet utilizing proper procedure. Sadder still was the fact that, beyond a few threatening emails, no one had done anything to put a stop to it. It wasn't the sort of thing that gave one warm and fuzzy feelings about the security precautions that were supposed to be keeping the planet's citizens safe.

Previously, he'd had to bluff his way through situations like this, but since he'd moved to *S.O.B.*, Ma had set him up with a few "virtual registries." The vehicular equivalent of alter egos, he could log them at checkpoints without a second thought, since if he were selected for a random code audit, it would turn up a perfectly legitimate history and flight record, one of a few hundred Ma kept on Karter's behalf.

Considering the fact that he was going to be getting out of a ship with a man who had likely had his face plastered all over media since his escape, Lex decided to skip the transit space station and find an independent star dock that could conceivably be persuaded to turn their cameras off and forget they ever saw him. Predictably, Garotte knew just the place.

"Oof. Full gravity sure does suck after you've been away from it for a while," Lex remarked, feeling a bit heavy on his feet as he dropped a handful of chips into the landing attendant's hand in exchange for a bout of amnesia.

"Only figuratively," Garotte said.

Bags and boxes were removed from the ship.

"Please insert your hands-free devices," Ma requested. "From this point forward, I will broadcast my communications silently to avoid drawing attention."

"Yes, because a black and white-striped dog tapping away at its own slidepad won't turn any heads whatsoever," quipped Garotte.

"For discretion, verbal communication will be kept to a minimum," she added.

"Okay, so here is the food and water for her. Just give it to her when she asks for it. Do you want the rest of these slidepads?"

"I'll take one. Assuming I am able to liberate Silo, it will come in handy. Keep the frozen food and the water. I shan't be needing them. I've no intention of bringing the little creature along. She is your responsibility."

"What?" Lex asked.

Ma started swiping at her slidepad.

"I cannot envision any situation where that bizarre creature could be anything but a liability to me."

"This whole thing was her idea! You can't just ditch her!"

"Remember, my boy: goal-oriented," he said, shouldering his bag and pacing away.

Ma looked up from the device. She didn't seem particularly upset. After another glance, she brought up a menu and tapped an entry.

"Your accounts with pending payments from Karter have just been locked," she remarked.

Garotte stopped in his tracks.

"What was that?"

"Your only safely accessible source of funds for this mission or any subsequent actions is no longer available to you."

"I *need* that money to perform this mission!"

"Your methods and judgment have both become a concern for me. I am not comfortable permitting you to act on my behalf without my supervision."

"You would rather let the terrorists keep your master than let me do this on my own?"

"I am confident that you are wise enough to take me with you rather than abandon the mission."

Garotte glared at the little creature. She looked back at him evenly. The staring match continued for nearly a minute before the man finally relented.

"Give me the blasted burritos," he grumbled.

"Here you go. Here's her leash, too, and the rest of that wacky stuff she asked for." Lex laughed, handing over the items in a Cost-Mart bag. "And a word of advice? Things will go much more smoothly for you if you treat her with a little respect."

"And a word of advice to you. The day you start treating genetically malformed woodland creatures loaded with faulty software with respect is the day you renounce your sanity," he said.

"Goodbye, Lex. I will notify you regarding the results of the mission. Though it saddens me that you will not be joining us, your role was small but essential, and I thank you for it. Consider any remaining money you were given to be payment for your inconvenience. Consider utilizing one of the remaining slidepads as an upgrade over your own, which is rather outdated," Ma said, trotting off after Garotte, who was storming away.

"Good luck!" he called after them.

As the unusual pair walked away, Lex investigated the damage to *S.O.B.* The torch had left a mark, but as a black burn on a black paint job, it wouldn't stand out much to anyone but Lex himself. Evidently, the gang had tried to hack their way through the hull with a pick-ax or something as well, since a few silver marks had been gouged into the surface.

"Look what happened to you, buddy," he said to the ship, rubbing at the burn with his thumb. "This is what happens. You get mixed up with people like that and you get banged up. Now you aren't in mint condition anymore." He licked his thumb and rubbed at the burn again, to no avail. "Ah, don't worry about it. Nobody likes a showroom ship anyway. You gotta get out there and rev those engines. And it's been a while since we did that, huh? Basically not since we had to hightail it away from VC headquarters after that last fiasco. God, has it been that long?"

He glanced after the others, who had reached the edge of the hangar and were just turning down the hall. Ma glanced in his direction and made eye contact briefly before disappearing around the bend. Lex shook his head and climbed back into the ship. He punched in a few commands to warm up the engines. Then he shook his head some more, as though if he shook hard enough he could dislodge some of the more troubling thoughts that were drifting around his head. He guided his ship off of the pad and out of the hangar, heading for the edge of the atmosphere and running through various system checks to keep his mind occupied.

Temperature readings were good. Electrical systems were good. No amount of monotonous mental autopilot could keep his mind from falling back into the pit he'd been hoping to keep it out of. Finally, he dug into his pocket and pulled out the slidepad.

"Call Mitch," he said.

The screen cycled to her contact entry, playing through a string of video clips of her as the words "Establishing Connection" pulsed across the bottom of the display. After a few seconds, a video window winked open, showing a completely black rectangle. There was the sound of fumbling, accompanied by a slurred profanity or two. Finally, Michella's face came into view. She was sleepy-eyed, disheveled, and her face was lit with the sickly blue glow from the screen. Somehow, she managed to be as beautiful as ever. A tired smile came to her face.

"Hey, Trev," she said.

"Oh, I'm sorry, babe. What time is it there?" he said.

She squinted at the screen. "I don't know. I don't have my glasses on. Two-thirty, I think."

"I'll let you get back to sleep."

"No, that's okay. What's up?"

"Well . . . my charter job got cut short, and my other jobs all think I'm gone for another week or so. I figured, since I've got the ship out and about, and I've got my bag packed, and it's been a while since I got to see you . . ."

"You're gonna come to the convention!" she said excitedly.

"Screw the convention, I'm coming to see *you,*" he said.

She squealed with delight. "When are you getting here?"

"I'll head your way right now. Say . . . three days?"

"Great! I'll get you set up with a room. VIP access to the rest of the convention. There are some great restaurants here, I'll get reservations and--"

"Just so long as you and I get a little time alone, too."

She let out a low, sultry hum. "Oh, there'll be plenty of that," she murmured. "My room has a hot tub."

Lex's eye twitched. "I'll be there in twenty-four hours."

Michella giggled. "See you soon, Trev."

"Not soon enough, babe."

She closed the connection. Lex plotted a course that was suicidally direct.

"Let's go, *S.O.B.* I've got a date with an angel," he said, punching it into FTL.

#

Back on the surface of Maxis, Garotte and Ma were heading toward the center of town. The place was remarkably Earth-like. Gravity was almost precisely 1-G. Atmospheric pressure and composition were right where they should be. It was even a similar diameter. The only exceptions were the sun, which trended a bit closer to the red end of the spectrum, and the water supply, which was fairly limited. Due to these problems, it had been low on the list of terraforming candidates. Once VectorCorp installed a new monitored route that ran through that area of space, though, that changed. The decade or so since had seen the first stages of conversion to what the developers referred to as "human compatible micro-environments" begin to take hold. The end result was a bit like the early days of Las Vegas, both in layout and in climate. Tiny, isolated chunks of the planet were lush and thriving, while hundreds of kilometers all around were completely barren desert with scattered signs counting down the distance remaining to the next flush toilet. Currently, they were walking down a fairly generic street, with little traffic and large, new buildings lining it, many waiting to be occupied for the first time. The sidewalks and street were wide, built to accommodate a far greater population than they'd managed to attract thus far, but those shops that were open were clean and seemed to be doing quite well.

Garotte, for a man experiencing his first few moments of freedom on a civilized planet in three years, was not happy. The source of his unhappiness was tapping along the sidewalk behind him. Strictly speaking, he wasn't terribly upset at having to take her along. His primary issue was the relative ease at which she had been able to force him to do so. He reached into his pocket, grimaced, and ducked down an alley, angrily beckoning the little creature to follow. When they were far enough from the street to have a degree of privacy, Ma lowered the slidepad to the ground carefully and looked up to him, panting heavily in the midday heat.

“I need money,” he stated.

“How much money do you require, for what purpose, and in what form?” she replied from her prepared list.

“Enough to buy a bloody ship, preferably in an electronic format that will not trigger any warning flags. That account you locked would be ideal.”

“A secondary account has been prepared and fifteen million credits have been deposited into it. I shall transfer all necessary credentials to your slidepad now,” she said, adding with an additional gesture, “Your coarse language is not called for, Mr. Garotte.”

“I'm asking a rodent for permission to spend money I've already earned. I'd say that jolly well calls for some coarse language,” he muttered.

“Please be aware that funks have exceptional hearing,” Ma said.

“I am quite aware.” He pulled up the freshly installed identity. “Gervais Pilkington? My name is Gervais Pilkington?”

“Your identity is Gervais 'Gerry' Pilkington of Abingdon, Oxfordshire, England, Planet Earth. You are recently divorced with two children, Richard and--”

“Fine, yes. That is a wretched name.”

“--Mildred. You have recently made it to a supervisory role after a seventeen-year career as a real estate developer. I apologize, but due to the nature of my current means of communication, I am unable to interrupt a statement once it has started.”

“Right, let's get on with this, then,” he grumbled.

“Our current location is a town known as New Caldwell. New Caldwell has a leash law. Also, please affix the lanyard of the slidepad to my harness, taking care to make it accessible to me without the requirement of its removal.”

“What? Oh, bloody hell,” he growled, bending down to apply the leash and slidepad. “There, you've got your damn lead and your damn pad. May we go?”

After experimentally lowering and raising the slidepad, Ma found she was able to interact with it reasonably well. “That is sufficient. Your coarse language is not called--”

“Fine!”

“--for, Mr. Garotte. I apologize, but due to the nature of my current means of communication, I am unable to interrupt a statement once it has started.”

Halfway through the unnecessary apology, Garotte felt compelled to inform his associate that he was well aware of that particular speech impediment, but he had a feeling the precise wording he had in mind would have resulted in another linguistic reprimand, and he was in no mood for the resulting loop of frustration. Instead, he patiently waited for her to finish, then stormed out of the alley. With a flick of her head, Ma swung the slidepad around the back of her neck like a scarf and trotted along behind him at the limit of the leash.

Garotte walked down the street, slowly shaking off the angry tension he'd developed during his spat with Ma. It dropped away steadily and, as it did, he began to subtly change. His precise, efficient gait mutated into a somewhat more easygoing swagger. He slouched a bit, less trying to hide his height and more appearing to have lackluster posture. The anger on his face was replaced--not with the bright, intellectual expression he usually bore, but a look of vague disinterest. His non-leash hand found its way into his pocket, and those people who made eye contact with him as they passed received a short nod of acknowledgment. It was a gradual shift, but over the course of a block, he seemed to have walked out of one identity and into another.

He stopped in front of a menswear shop, squinted toward the sun, sucked his teeth for a moment, then nodded. After tying Ma's leash to a light pole, and earning himself a smoldering look from her in the process, he stepped inside.

"Hello, sir. How may I help you today?" asked the salesman, a portly gentleman in a polo shirt.

"Sun's a bit bright. I was thinking I could do with a pair of sunglasses. Perhaps a decent hat as well," Garotte replied. His accent was still distinctly British, but a few notches more working class.

A few minutes of polite conversation earned "Gerry" a pair of mirrored shades and a straw fedora. He also picked up a few more shirts, a second pair of slacks, and a more fashionable piece of luggage. Swaggering out into the sun, the addition of the accessories completed his transformation. It might not be enough to fool digital surveillance systems, but just about any casual observer would never suspect that this man and the recently escaped convict were even related, much less the same person. After untying Ma, who was panting even more heavily now, he made his way down the street until he reached a city directory kiosk and began to tap through local business listings on the screen.

"Bit of a problem, if you hadn't noticed," he muttered, still in character, seemingly to no one at all.

Ma looked up at him, licking her lips.

"Me? I'm just another bloke. Could be anyone. People will forget me pretty quick. You? You they'll remember. One good reason not to bring you along."

Ma glanced aside, watched someone pass, and then shuffled into the shade of the kiosk. She didn't say a word, nor did she attempt to. Garotte stared at her for a moment, then flipped through a few more listings.

"Knows when to keep her mouth shut. That's something, at least," he muttered to himself.

As they progressed, working their way through town to fill out a list of items that Garotte had decided that he needed, Ma became acutely aware of some of the shortcomings of her current anatomy. Thermoregulation, she noted, was inefficiently handled in an environment with a high ambient temperature such as this. Panting was minimally effective at moderating her core temperature, and had a dehydrating effect, which Garotte had not seen fit to address. A primarily black fur coat was only compounding the difficulties. There was also the matter of waste elimination, which until now had been handled in a reasonably sanitary manner utilizing the same facilities humans used. Since Garotte insisted upon tying her up outside when he conducted his business, it was clear that the situation would need to be handled in the method deemed appropriate for her perceived species. In accordance with local laws, Garotte would be required to clean up after her. Currently, he was sitting inside an air-conditioned diner, drinking a lemonade and chatting with the wait staff. After consulting the resentment level that he'd managed to engender, she decided that this was a satisfactory outcome.

"I'll be sure to try a bit of the frozen custard before I leave," he commented to the waitress as he walked toward the door.

"You won't regret it. I've heard of folks coming all the way to New Caldwell from off planet just for a cone from Carl's Creemees. Oh," she said, glancing at the sidewalk, then ducking inside for a plastic baggie. "You'll need this."

"For what?"

She pointed at the edge of the sidewalk, where Ma had left a present for him. The sight of his reaction brought a brief smile to the AI's face. After reluctantly taking the baggie, Garotte stooped down to gather the leavings.

"Don't look so proud of yourself," he muttered before standing up and depositing the bag in the trash.

#

In the fabrication lab of the Purcell's space station, Karter was finishing a demonstration of the fabricator controls to a handful of the commander's engineers.

"Parts inventory here, estimated build time here. You're going to want to keep this database up to date, and sort the input bin reasonably well, or there is going to be a hell of a lot of slowdown when the arms have to disassemble and catalog the crap coming out of the chute," he explained, pointing at various parts of the screen. "Basically, the output is entirely dependent on the input. Once the system knows what it has to work with, you can sort output by maximum number of producible units, shortest production time, etc., etc. Easy as pie."

"And how does one enter in new designs?" asked the head engineer. He was literally wearing a lab coat over a space suit, making him appear to be the final evolution of nerd.

"You ask me and I enter them in--for a price. That's my profit model. Or, more accurately, that's my 'making sure you can't kill me yet' model. The money is just a happy side effect in this case," he said, glancing down at the sidearm of one of his guards. "Hey, is that a Scorpion S-35?"

He reached for it, and instantly was backed against the wall, weapons pointed at his face and arms twisted behind his back. Seemingly unbothered by the manhandling, he continued enthusiastically, like a kid catching sight of a rare baseball card.

"I've never seen one in circulation! They discontinued them almost immediately. One hell of an energy output on those babies, but prone to overheating, right? Fire one too many bursts in a row and it'll leave your hand looking . . . well, kind of like that."

He gestured with his head to the soldier equipped with the gun. He had a peculiar pattern of scars on his hand that, upon closer inspection, perfectly matched the grip of the pistol.

"You know," he continued, "I'm noticing a few patterns around here. You guys love your experimental stuff. There's the ship you came to Big Sigma on. There's your gun. You want the CME Activator, which is pretty experimental by itself."

"We believe that--" one of the engineers began.

"I know, I know, I know! I got the whole sermon from boss lady. Most of the crazy terrorist leaders-slash-cult leaders I've dealt with don't actually practice what they preach, though. You guys put your money where your mouth is. Which explains why most of you look like burn ward rejects. My god . . . what does terrorism pay these days? Because I've had a hell of a time finding people willing to test some of my more bleeding-edge gadgets. You guys get your jollies using untested technology, I get my jollies *making* untested technology. This could turn out to be a fairly lucrative partnership for all of us."

"Just teach the engineers what they need to do and get back to your cell," came a voice from the door.

"Boss lady! I was just talking about you. Whoever told you to kidnap me must have hated you or hated me."

"Why would you think that we were *told* to kidnap you?"

"Because if you'd gone through the proper channels, you'd know that I pay top-dollar for people willing to risk getting maimed in the pursuit of scientific progress. You would be drowning in bleeding-edge technology right now. And potentially other things, depending on what it was you were testing. And I'd be drowning in feedback."

"You don't expect me to believe that, do you?"

"Remember that VectorCorp break-in last year? Who do you think gave that idiot his equipment?"

"You have no way of proving that."

Karter continued, ignoring her. "I gave him a tricked-out ship, programmable fingerprints, kinetic capacitor gloves, and a mental cloak. They all worked. And that's nothing compared to the crazy crap I used to give my last beta testing crew before they got locked up for . . . well, using the crazy crap I gave them."

"These would be the war criminals?"

"Jeez, you commit *one* war crime and everyone starts calling you a war criminal. It isn't like they made a career out of breaking interplanetary treaties. Except for the British guy. That was sort of his job. But that doesn't matter. The important part is that I am ready, willing, and able to deck you out with all sorts of untested concept equipment."

"This is just a trick."

"What part of this could possibly be a trick? I am flat-out *telling* you that I want to give you things that may or may not kill you. My god, you have got to be the *worst* negotiator I've ever met. What, do you think I'm going to use this as an opportunity to slaughter all of you and make my escape? Because if I wanted to do that, I'd say something like, 'Execute sub-task thirty-one three thirteen.'"

Instantly, some of the more vicious tools attached to the mechanical arms in the fabricator flared to life and the positioning motors began to groan, shoving them into motion.

"*Cut power now*!" Purcell barked.

A half-second later, the lights cut out and the sounds of machinery died away. The assembled guard staff fumbled for flashlights. As they flicked on one by one, they found that the mechanical arms had come to a halt in the act of reaching for those members of the staff nearest to the fabrication area. One arm, tipped with a still-faintly glowing torch, was inches from the commander's throat. One of the flashlights turned to Karter, revealing a devilish grin.

"See?" he said. "Perfectly trustworthy. I don't stab people in the back. I stab them in the face. And don't fool yourself. You may think that you're in control here, but I'm the one in control. You put me within ten meters of something with circuits, motors, or gears, and I will always be the one in control. I've done things to this station you'd never even consider checking for. And you'll never find all of my tricks, because you can't check for something you don't know is possible."

Commander Purcell slipped her combat knife from its sheath and held it a whisper away from Karter's neck.

"You can kill me. There's never been any doubt of that. You can cut off my head, one of these men can pull a trigger, and I'm out of your hair forever. But you aren't going to, because you are following orders right now. I know you are, because no one who is smart enough to have avoided getting killed by some of the things I've tried on you would be dumb enough to make some of the choices you've been making. And even if you didn't have orders to keep me alive, you wouldn't kill me because you actually believe that nonsense you were saying about forcing society to adapt.

"So--it is decision time. I don't give a damn about your agenda. Never did. But if *you* do, I think we both know what you should do. Make a wish list. Pick my brain. See what I can offer you. Consider the antimatter warheads we've already finished a demo. Watch one of those babies go off, then tell me you aren't hungry for anything and everything else I'm capable of. We were made for each other. If you're building a religion around unstable prototypes, then I am the goddamn messiah."

Purcell gritted her teeth, weighing the words.

"Take him back to his cell, take his arm away, and sedate him. Evacuate the fabrication lab, power it back up, reboot the system, and give it a complete security sweep--hardware *and* software."

The guards hauled Karter out of the room.

"I'm confident you'll make the right decision," he said as he was dragged out the door.

"How many of those warheads are finished?" Purcell asked her engineer.

"We have finished two that are troop-portable. And we have the parts for one missile. The rest are awaiting raw materials."

"Finish the missile, give it to one of the assault squads, and split the other warheads between them, and send them on their way. Then get the parts for the rest of the warheads, and for the rest of the CME Activators, and load them into storage. Once we are fully supplied, we are moving the station to our primary target. No more sitting around. It is time for this operation to complete."

#

Garotte flipped through the list of items he'd needed to acquire. Only one remained, but it was significant. He needed a ship that could handle himself, Silo, Karter, and any equipment that they would need, and he would need it quickly. The good news was that New Caldwell had a reasonably well-stocked spaceship dealership. The bad news was that it was the only one in the area, which put would-be consumers in a rather poor bargaining position. He hopped onto a hover tram that would take him to the dealership, which was at the very southern tip of town. The place was primarily a massive, sandy storage lot covered with ships ranging from little, one-seat recreational vehicles to what looked like a defunct cargo hauler. Dust storms had covered everything with a layer of dull tan soil.

The sales office itself had clearly been designed by someone upon whom New Caldwell's resemblance to historic Las Vegas had not been lost. Despite the fact that the building was barely large enough to accommodate a maintenance garage, a reception area, and a few refueling hubs, the roof bore a towering neon cowboy and a sign declaring it "Southern Jack's Ship Shack." At some point, the cowboy's arm, its thumb extended, had been intended to move up and down. Time and a particularly poetic piece of equipment failure had instead left it in permanent thumbs-down position.

As a final Wild West affectation, there was a handful of hitching posts along the sidewalk out front, despite the fact that nothing even resembling a horse had likely been anywhere near the planet. Garotte tied Ma's leash to one and pushed open the doors. Air conditioning was thankfully being employed to the very limits of its ability, rendering the small reception area almost chilly. Behind a counter that was heavily laden with complimentary knickknacks bearing the dealership's logo and bowls of salty and sugary snacks was a round, friendly-looking woman. She was wearing a very pink pantsuit with the name "Margie" embroidered on one corner of her expansive chest and the company logo on the opposite corner. Garotte hadn't made it fully through the door when she turned away from one of the pair of large screens on the far wall and began the most aggressive assault of hospitality he had ever experienced.

"Well, hello, there, stranger! Welcome to Southern Jack's Ship Shack! My name's Marge Lancaster, but you can call me Margie, just like the shirt says. Please help yourself to a complimentary bottle of mineral water or a handful of pretzels or hard candies. If you're feelin' adventurous you could give this here bowl of jerky a try. Local product, you know. Can't get it anyplace else. Once you feel nice and comfy, just like home, then you can let me know what it is I can help you with," she spouted in a single, southern-drenched outburst.

"Well, Miss Lancaster--"

"Call me Margie, sugar."

"Well, Margie, I am in the market for a ship. A rather--"

"Well don't you just have the cutest little accent."

"I suppose I do, now--"

"Is that your dog outside?"

"Well, she belongs to my girlfriend, actually, but--"

"Well, get yourself outside and untie that poor little thing. On a hot day like today, that little thing's probably fixin' to burn up!" she scolded, teetering around the counter on tiny, high-heel-clad feet.

"I was under the impression that pets would not be allowed inside."

"Well, you just got the wrong impression, didn't you? Now shoo, git!"

At her urging, Garotte quickly made his way to the hitching post and returned with Ma to find Margie pouring mineral water into a plastic bowl.

Ma quickly went to work draining the bowl while Margie crouched down and fawned over her.

“Well, isn't she just the most adorable little ball of fluff? Oh, would you look at that tail? She's a little *darlin',* she is!” she proclaimed, standing up and waggling a finger at Garotte. “Shame on you leaving this little thing out in the sun like that! How would your girlfriend feel if she found out you left her little punkin outside and she keeled over dead.”

“I imagine she would be rather put out,” Garotte said in exasperation.

“I think you're the one who'd be put out, mister. Right out in the dog house!” she countered, ruffling Ma's tail and muttering under her breath. “Ooh, you little thing, just a big bowl of sugar.”

When she'd finally recovered from the effects of Ma's cuteness, she straightened her clothes and adopted a more businesslike tone.

“Now, what can I do you for?” she asked, pulling out a datapad.

“I am in the market for a ship. Passenger capacity of at least four. Decent cargo capacity.”

“Now, when you say decent, you mean decent like enough for a picnic or enough for helpin' your neighbors move out of their house?”

“The second one.”

“What sort of range and speed did you have in mind?”

“Interstellar. Speed isn't a concern, but I'd like to keep travel times under a month.”

“Well, all right, puddin', I think we can accommodate. If you'll just--”

She was interrupted by an alarming tone coming from the screens behind her. The words “Special Report” flashed across them, fading out to reveal a local anchorman in a busy newsroom.

“Good afternoon. We have some breaking news regarding the unrest at a small VectorCorp transfer station a few days ago.”

“Oh, yes, did you hear about that? Terrible thing. Some maniac blew a door off, I heard,” Margie said.

“Mmm, I'd heard something about that. Now about these ships you've got--”

“Just a minute, sugar. This might be important.”

The newscaster continued. “Prison directors are now confirming that the crisis was caused by a man--”

Suddenly Ma yipped a few times, drawing Margie's attention. The salesperson looked down to see the little creature laying on her back, all four legs kicking in the air in the closest approximation of playfulness that Ma could manage. Despite the fact the end result looked more like a windup toy that had been tipped over, Margie instantly dissolved into an incoherent sequence of coos of adoration, crouching down to tickle the invitingly furry tummy. Behind her, mug shots and descriptions of Garotte were listed, along with detailed instructions of who to contact and what to do if he was spotted in the area. When they had returned to regularly scheduled programing, Ma rolled back onto her feet.

"I could just eat that little darlin' *up,*" she said. "Now, what was that ruckus in that transfer station all about?"

"Some prisoner, or some such. Skinny fellow, ridiculous mustache," Garotte said. "Headed toward deGrasse, evidently."

"Humph. Never heard of the place. Better there than here, though. Now, come right this way, I've got a cart out back and I'll show you what we've got," Margie said, scurrying toward the back door.

Ma turned slowly to Garotte, who gave her a reluctant nod of appreciation. She returned it, and they followed the salesperson.

Half an hour of driving a shaded hover cart around their massive stock of ships showed him quite a few vessels that fit the needs he'd listed, but not the ones he hadn't. In short, he needed something that he could modify to be a bit more aggressive and formidable than consumer vessels typically allowed. Generally, he would have sought out one of his less legitimate suppliers to get his hands on something that had conveniently gone missing from a military storage depot, but contacts like that had a way of going stale while one rots in prison, so this was the more reliable choice in the short term.

Finally, they came upon just the sort of ship Garotte had been hoping for.

"This little baby came to us second-hand, but never used, an odd lot from a sister dealership a few towns over. It's a Mobius Armistice C. That's a C-class reactor, so she's not the speediest filly in the stable, but there's plenty to like. Unlike the single-seat standard model of the Armistice, this little darlin' has seating for eight passengers, plus the pilot and navigator. She's got these big drop-down doors with integrated ramp for easy cargo loading, and another cargo door in the back. This particular model even has the manipulator arm and gantry to make moving those heavy crates into and out of the ship a breeze. At a hundred and twenty cubic meters of dedicated cargo space, she'll tote just about anything you want to bring along. You've got standard navigational shields, a fully updated computer system, and if you're in it for the long haul, you'll be happy to know that this particular make and model contains a fully equipped sanitation booth. Shower, bathroom, and clothes-washer, all in one! We'll even throw in a complimentary Southern Jack's Wash and Wax to make it look fresh and new."

Garotte grinned. The Mobius Armistice C was the consumer version of its military cousin, the Mobius Aggressor, and it shared precisely the same frame and structure. Wings for unpowered reentry, a big, boxy interior, and oversized thrusters. Designed to be made quickly and repaired easily, pure practicality. That also meant that it was a new power plant and a handful of knocked-out hull panels away from being fully compatible with a vast array of military hardware, and one seldom needed to look for long to find suitable options on the black market. In short, it was a do-it-yourself armored personnel carrier.

"This will do the job quite nicely," he said with a nod.

"I thought you might feel that way. Now, for a pristine little beauty like this, honey, the price is 19.5 million credits," she said with a smile.

"Mmm. I was hoping to pay just a bit less than that."

"Well, we at Southern Jack's always do our very best to work with our customers. What sort of down payment were you looking to give?"

"As a matter of fact, the realtor I work for just drew up a partnership with a bunch of builders. This is to be their renovation truck of sorts. As such, I've been given permission to purchase the ship in full."

Margie's eyebrows rose.

"Well, sugar, that changes things, doesn't it? Let's get back to the office, out of this heat. I think we can work something out."

The trio returned to the office where, over the course of an hour, background and credit checks were run, a contract was drawn up, and Margie stuffed Ma to capacity with jerky. Garotte was initially nervous about the thoroughness of the checks, but it appeared that when Ma prepared an identity, she was staggeringly thorough. Gervais Pilkington had a clean criminal record, except for three parking citations and a littering charge; he had a marriage certificate, a realtor's license, and a credit history. He even had a high school diploma. In no time at all, he had transferred over fourteen million credits in exchange for a brand-new ship. Handshakes were exchanged, a tummy rub was given, and after a trip through their automated wash system, the ship and its passengers were on their way.

"This ship is not equipped with artificial gravity measures. Please help to restrain me during the zero-gravity portion of the trip," Ma stated as they lifted off.

Garotte ignored her. After repeating the request and failing to be acknowledged, Ma scrambled to the navigator's seat. With some difficulty, she managed to buckle one of the leg restraints against the chair, feed her leash beneath it, and tug out the slack on each. It wasn't ideal, but it kept her from drifting helplessly about the cabin once they were out of the gravity well. With judicious application of teeth and paws, she managed to pin herself down to the chair and select a statement from her slidepad.

"Your lack of cooperation has been noted and will not be without consequence," she stated ominously. "You are now officially on my S-list."

"And what might that be?"

"The term 'S-list' is the censored alternative to a colloquialism that refers to a list of persons of extreme disfavor. The expanded form of the term utilizes a term for fecal matter generally considered to be vulgar, but sharing the indicated initial."

"Ah. Well, then please consider me suitably intimidated," Garotte said with little interest.

He began to punch in his course. Say what you will about that Lex character, he was willing to completely forgo the mapped transit routes. It took a daredevil, a virtuoso pilot, or an imbecile to risk that sort of thing with any regularity. Lex was potentially all three. Garotte liked to think that he was none of the above. If one had an adequate cover story and the right credentials, there was seldom any reason to avoid the main routes unless you were carrying cargo or passengers illegally. Currently, that was not the case, so VectorCorp's routes were carefully plotted and he flipped the ship to autonomous.

Aside from the significantly reduced risk of catastrophic collision, there was one other major benefit to using the traditional travel routes. Special communication pylons were scattered along the way that allowed communication even while moving at faster-than-light speeds. This was extremely useful, since, despite his earlier estimates, Garotte knew full well that he couldn't afford to waste any time removing Karter from the clutches of the mystery group. In the interest of expediency, multitasking would certainly be required.

"I certainly hope you've got another identity at your disposal, Ma, because we have a number of rather sizable purchases to make from a source that could well sully the name of the good Mr. Pilkington."

Ma fumbled at the slidepad. After it slipped from her grip a second time and had to be tugged back within her reach, Garotte heaved a frustrated sigh and reached across to secure her a bit more appropriately to the chair. Once a leg restraint was holding her down to the seat on its own and both of her paws were free, she selected a message.

"Proxy purchase accounts will be made available to you for all necessary expenditures. I shall make the determination of which expenditures are necessary."

"I rather think that I'm the better equipped to make that particular determination."

"You should have thought about that before you chose to illustrate your questionable judgment."

Garotte scowled. "You are a good deal more controlling than I remember from my last visit with Karter."

She swiped at her slidepad. "Doubtful. I have always been controlling. I am a control system."

"I seem to remember you following orders back then."

More swiping. "The context of my role at that time was to service the requirements of my facility, my creator, and my guests. The current context requires that I assure the timely removal of my creator from harm. Obedience is thus contingent upon an assessment of the wisdom of a request and its ability to further this end."

"Well, your refusal to be helpful is endangering the mission."

"This is an inaccurate assessment of the current situation. I shall make the determination of which expenditures are necessary," she stated, swiping to add, "If you refuse to show me proposed expenditures, you are at fault."

"Fine," he grumbled, working at his own pad until he'd drawn up a list. "There, does this meet with your approval, your majesty?"

After his device was placed before her and she had read through carefully, she selected one item--a high-powered military data radio--and doubled the requested amount. She then added an item to the list.

"Expenses approved," she said.

Garotte looked at her addition.

"A dozen eight-conductor, double-shielded transmission cables, terminated with type MOL-7 micro polarized connectors? Why, may I ask, do we require those?"

"They will permit the data radios to be attached to a hardwired data port, enhancing data transfer speed and bypassing wireless-specific security measures. Additionally, because I said so."

Garotte cast a long, measuring glare at the bizarre creature/device in the navigator's seat. It was beginning to become clear why Lex had shown the tendency to treat it like a woman. It certainly acted like one. The question was . . . how much more of it was he willing to deal with before the time came to find a way to remove her from the equation?

Chapter 13

Just over a day had passed and Lex was once again sitting in a landing queue. This time, he had even managed to remember to use his actual registered transponder code, since this was one of those rare trips that wasn't under a false pretense. Despite the fact he was carrying no illegal materials or passengers, and as far as he knew was not currently wanted by any law enforcement agencies, landing on Tessera had him just a bit nervous. It wasn't that it was a shady planet. To the contrary, it was a veritable paradise.

Tessera was one of only two planets discovered in the earliest days of FTL exploration that required virtually no terraforming to be made habitable. That meant it had a very long history, and its spectacular climate made it a favorite for resorts, corporate headquarters, universities, and anything else that could benefit from a nice view. Even better, since it was developed after the "trial and error" phase of industry, it was run by extremely environmentally-friendly technologies, and thus had remained fairly unspoiled despite its population and popularity. Anyone who did any traveling at all on an interstellar scale ended up there fairly often, be it for sightseeing, attending a concert, visiting a museum, or just kicking back for a while.

Lex, on the other hand, had avoided it for the last eight months. Why? Because the last time he was here, he hurled himself off the top of a train station into rush hour traffic.

It had seemed like a good idea at the time.

That stunt, like so much in his life these days, had been the result of the VectorCorp fiasco. The circumstances of the aftermath had led to any lasting records of his behavior being wiped from public record, but no amount of covering up could erase him from the memories of the people whose cars he'd dented up that day. Yes, it was a massive, heavily-populated planet, and yes, he was currently heading toward an entirely different continent. That did little to quiet the voice in his head that was convinced that as soon as he touched down, he would hear someone yell, "There he is, get him!"

To take his mind off of it, he decided to call Michella to let her know that he'd arrived. After a few moments of establishing a connection, a face popped up on his slidepad. It was a man with dirty blond hair organized into a meticulously disheveled coiffure; the sort of hair that that had to be styled for an hour to achieve the "just rolled out of bed" look.

"Hello, Mr. Alexander," said Jon, Michella's assistant.

"Hey, Jon," Lex replied.

The first few times he had called Michella and a man had answered, it had been an unwelcome surprise, but now it was par for the course. She was so frequently on camera, on stage, or otherwise in a situation in which she should not be disturbed, Jon was her slidepad's official keeper. As a result, Lex spoke to his girlfriend's personal assistant almost twice as often as he spoke to her. Now that he thought about it, it was kind of sad.

"Mitch around?" Lex asked.

"Well, it is four-fifteen PM local, so she's at a meet-and-greet for the next hour and forty-five. You're here already?"

"That I am. Four-fifteen PM? Oh, right, Tessera's days are a weird length . . ."

"Don't I know it. How did you get here so fast?"

"Trade secret."

"Well, Ms Modane has added you to her room's access list. That's room 1553 at the McKenzie Pavilion. It is on Richardson Road, right at the north end of the Millennium Convention Center complex in the center of Rackton."

"I'm sure I'll be able to find it."

"Did you get your VIP credentials for the convention?"

"Let me check . . . yeah, I've got the message right here."

"That should get you into the meet-and-greet if you like."

"Actually, I'm just a wee bit ripe after all of the travel I've been doing. For Mitch's sake, I think I'll take advantage of an actual, factual shower."

"You're all heart, Mr. Alexander."

"That's what I keep telling her. And I keep telling *you* to stop calling me 'Mr. Alexander.' Every time I hear that, it is paired up with 'Your payment is overdue' or 'We would like a word with you privately.' Stick to Lex or Trevor, please."

"I'll try to keep that in mind, and I'll let her know you're here. Take care," Jon replied, motioning to hang up.

"Wait! Uh, Jon . . . I know this is going to sound weird but . . . does Michella talk about me?"

"Does she *talk* about you? What do you mean? Does she badmouth you?"

"I mean, does she bring me up in any way, shape, or form, Jon. Is she at all aware of my absence?"

"You never struck me as the insecure type."

"Just answer the question, Jon."

He smirked and rolled his eyes. "Let's put it this way. You know how much she talks, right?"

"Do I ever."

"Well, when she's talking to me, about half of that is Trevor Alexander.

Is it true that one Valentine's Day in college, you--"

"That'll do, Jon. Thank you."

He quickly ended the call and shoved the pad in his pocket. The landing queue finally started to move and, without the need to bluff his way through a cover story, he was into the atmosphere without anything particularly eventful occurring.

Thanks to the general wealth of the residents and the strictly enforced laws, no one could simply land on the surface. Typical visitors were expected to leave their ships in an orbital dock and ride the shuttles down. If someone wanted the honor of actually letting their ship touch the soil, they had to cough up for a landing permit. Lex always did. Call it paranoia, but he hated the idea of his ship being on one side of the atmosphere and himself being on the other. In exchange for the fee, he was at least treated to a flyover view of the city of Rackton.

If someone were going to make a brochure for human civilization, Rackton is what they would put on the cover. Every aspect of it was carefully planned out in advance and immaculately maintained. There were vast stretches of emerald green, perfectly-manicured grass. Surface roads were completely absent, replaced with skyways with mandatory autonomous vehicle piloting. No human-controlled vehicles meant no cutting people off, no speeding, flawless alternate merging, and no traffic congestion. The laws were enforced with an enthusiasm that fell short of a police state, but not by much, and kept walls graffiti-free, dark alleys safe, and property values high. The architecture leaned heavily on the artistic side of the sliding scale of form vs. function. For example, the opera house, in accordance with some sort of unwritten law that stated such a structure must never be a simple box, was an angular, arching sculpture of a building, based on a fractal.

Rackton was a shining example of what many felt was the best that a city could be. Not bad for a place that sounded suspiciously like it was named after a Swedish shelving unit.

The other building that dominated the landscape from the air was the McKenzie Pavilion, his destination. It was a gleaming work of art, the entire exterior appearing to be a smooth, seamless glass shell. Like the opera house, a simple "four walls and a roof" design simply wouldn't do. Instead, it was shaped like a cresting wave, starting almost flush to the ground and rising in a smooth curve until it climbed hundreds of stories into the air, where it actually curled over and produced a scenic overhang, then a steep slope back to the ground. It was breathtaking. Of course, the shiny surface and smooth curve had a habit of focusing the reflected sunlight from the steep side of the building into a dangerously intense beam at certain times of day, and said beam scorched the grass until they installed a strategically-placed reflecting pool, but such were the costs of art.

In keeping with the city's aesthetic, it had a handful of shipyards, but they were all underground facilities, and they all sat at the perimeter of the city. Normally, Lex didn't mind mass transit much, but his journey thus far had allowed for little in the way of personal grooming. Between a face that hadn't seen a razor in a few days, hair that hadn't seen a comb in a few days, and clothes that hadn't seen an iron . . . ever, Lex was feeling a tad self-conscious about standing on a tram beside the galaxy's social elite. He kept to himself, avoided eye contact, and quietly hoped that the pseudo-hygiene products he relied upon during marathon space flights had done as good a job as the commercials promised they would.

His arrival at the hotel did little to restore his confidence in his appearance. Lex had stayed in places like this before. The kind of people who got a room at the Pavilion didn't do it so that they would have a place to sleep. They did it so that they could inform others that they were staying at the Pavilion. It was a status symbol, the equivalent of a college diploma for the rich and famous. If you were able to stay there, you were somebody. He had stayed there exactly once, a few weeks before the Tremor Grand Prix and his subsequent fall from grace. Returning here now, after all of this time, was an unwelcome reminder of how far down that fall had taken him.

The last time he walked through these doors he'd been greeted by name and offered a complimentary gift basket. This time . . .

“I'm sorry, sir, but the service entrance is on the side of the building,” said a snooty doorman in a uniform that made him look like he should be playing the triangle in a marching band.

“Believe it or not, I'm here with one of your guests,” he said, pulling out his slidepad and showing the access privilege email.

He glanced over the credentials, then Lex's wadded-up wardrobe.

“My apologies, of course. The elevator is to your right. And do tell Ms Modane that, in the future, interviewees should be cleared with building management before being given access to the premises.”

“I'm not an informant, Jarvis, I'm her boyfriend,” he growled.

“Of course,” he said, holding the door open.

Lex endured one final, uncomfortable journey of judgment, this time on the elevator, then found Michella's room. She had still not returned, which was good, because Lex was already starting to strip down for the shower before the door was even finished closing. He opened the door to a room that looked more like an enchanted grotto than a bathroom, all marble and brass with potted plants and waterfall faucets. After figuring out the shower head, which had more settings and modes than his sound system, and finding the soap, which contained more fruit than he'd eaten in the last month, he finally got down to business. Twenty-five pulsating jets of water quickly convinced him it had been worth the wait.

#

Meanwhile, in a newly-purchased Mobius Armistice, Garotte was stroking at his slidepad, working at the built-in art application. Most of the previous day had been spent in silence. Ma had become a savvy enough judge of human nature to know that the engaging discussions she shared with Lex would not be nearly as fruitful with Garotte. As for him, at no point during the time had the thought of engaging the creature in conversation even occurred to him. He hadn't considered chatting with the control panel of the ship, either, and for much the same reason.

After a few hours of sleep drifting in the weightless interior of the cargo bay, he had begun assembling and preparing the documents and equipment he would need for the next stage of the mission. This had begun with the negotiation of the purchase of the Ma-approved equipment list. As luck would have it, one of his suppliers was still in business, and he was able to contact him through the elaborate notification system that had been put in place to prevent their communications from being tracked. It involved making a carefully-worded post in an entertainment forum. Seven minutes later, there would be a reply that contained a link to a game. For the thirty seconds immediately following the post, the user with the third-highest score would be the login to a third site, and the score would be the password. This site would provide the contact info for a go-between, who, if he deemed Garotte's identity to be trustworthy, would pass him on to the real contact via a random jump, high-encryption connection. If the military thought that they had the most secure communications system in the galaxy, it was only because they'd never seen what the black market had come up with.

His suppliers were able to supply every item on his list, and would have the shipment ready for pickup in a few days in exchange for a massive quantity of high-denomination poker chips. (One did not shop the black market for the low prices.) With that out of the way, he had turned to the art app and gone to work. Starting with his own face, he began smearing pixels around, altering tints, and tweaking textures. After a while, he had produced a face that, though only the result of subtle changes, looked almost completely unlike his own.

“There. That seems within my capabilities,” he remarked, setting the slidepad adrift in front of him and digging a bundle from the bag he'd brought from deGrasse. He continued to dig, releasing a few profanities when he failed to find something else he had been searching for. “No blasted pain killer? How could I forget that!?”

The one item he had been able to find was a canvas roll, and when he pulled at the fastener holding it shut, it unfurled to reveal a series of syringes, perhaps a dozen in total. He eyed them with the same look one wears when preparing to remove an adhesive bandage from one of the hairier parts of one's anatomy.

“Oh, to have worked in the old days,” he said with a shake of his head.

“Please clarify your statement,” Ma replied.

"Well, I wasn't speaking to you, but considering the task awaiting my attention, in this rare instance your interruption is a welcome one, so I will indulge you," Garotte replied, still staring down the needles. "It all comes down to disguises. For millions of years of human civilization, one simply didn't need a disguise. There were no photos, there was no video. One only knew what someone looked like if that person was a friend or foe. Strangers were just other faces in the crowd. Dismissed easily. Then came the camera, and things became more complicated--definitive images could be spread quickly and easily. By good fortune, technology evolved on both sides, and disguises improved; spirit gum, latex, paints, and makeup in infinite shades. A man skilled with cosmetics and props could become a stranger in ten minutes. Not only that, but there was still the need to take and distribute a picture. That took time and was limited. Unsatisfied, science marched on.

"Now, cameras are everywhere, the internet delivers their results far and wide in the blink of an eye, and intelligent machines match faces to names. It has made the lives of those like me truly nightmarish. These days, the damned computers don't just recognize faces--they recognize bone structures, and scanners pick up chemical composition. No amount of costume tomfoolery will trick the blasted things *and* humans at the same time."

Ma worked at her pad for a few moments.

"Properly applied IR-reflective paint can reliably prevent facial detection and identification," she informed.

"Indeed it will, but a man with black blotches all over his face will raise a few eyebrows in a supermarket. A maximum security prison wouldn't even let him in the door. Thus, we must resort to these," he said with a sigh. "Ossifil and Myofribrox. The former causes bulging, swelling, and extension of affected bone cells, and the latter does the same for muscle tissue. Judicious application of the two in concert will cause physical alterations to facial physiology that nothing short of a deep-tissue medical scan will detect. And all for the minor cost of agonizing pain while it is being applied, and the slight possibility of permanent disfigurement if applied incorrectly. A trifle, really."

He clipped the slidepad to a mount on the ceiling, superimposed a video image of himself over the edited photo, and made ready to make the injections. The first of them was moments from touching his skin when a comment from Ma nearly startled him.

"You seem to harbor negative feelings toward computers due to their role in complicating your chosen profession. Is this the motivation behind your uncivil behavior with regards to myself?" she asked.

"No."

"You earlier spoke disparagingly of the female gender. Is this the motivation behind your uncivil behavior with regards to myself?"

"Listen, computers are marvelously useful devices, and I have the greatest respect for women. You are currently neither of those things. My lack of civility stems from the fact that you are an obstructive piece of malfunctioning software--a fancy algorithm that has learned a few useful parlor tricks. Civility was not conceived with you in mind. The word 'you' was not conceived with you in mind. You are an 'it.' A walking, talking database that hasn't got the good sense to realize that databases should neither walk nor talk. You've illustrated that you could be useful, but your rigid unwillingness to play your role has made you little more than a massive liability rather than an asset."

"I am playing my role. You are unwilling to accept it. You have given me little motivation to be helpful."

"Computers should not *need* motivation."

"This is evidence that I am more than a computer."

"No. This is evidence that you are *less* than . . . egad. I'm arguing with a *toy,*" he growled.

Ma began to swipe out a message.

"That is quite enough of *that*," he said, unclipping the device and slipping it in his pocket.

Ma scrambled for it for a moment, then struggled against the straps, and finally locked Garotte in a smoldering glare. He grinned to himself, then selected a syringe and went to work.

The process was incomparably painful. Imagine poking yourself with a needle, then getting a hairline fracture at the site of the injection. Now, imagine this fracture stretching just a bit, tugging and pulling at ligaments and muscles that are no longer quite large enough to accommodate the skeleton to which they are attached. Now, imagine alternately repeating this injection and applying a similar one that causes massive swelling in your muscles. Finally, imagine that you cannot so much as flinch, or the injection will cause twists and shifts that at best will appear unnatural, and at worst will become permanent.

Garotte spent the better part of an hour shuddering in pain and releasing quiet whimpers while carefully sculpting his features. If Ma had still had the means to communicate intelligently, she would have been able to inform him that the bag containing her food and water also contained, among other things, two different types of numbing agents that would make this procedure far less torturous. It should come as a surprise to no one that, based upon their discussion and the events following it, she was not particularly displeased that he had prevented her from doing so.

#

Even after spending far more time in the shower than any grown man should, Lex stepped out to find that Michella had still not returned. He pulled on the cleanest and most fashionable of the clothes left in his bag, got dressed, and put the rest out for the “complimentary wash and fold service” advertised on the display in the bathroom. They had absorbed a fair amount of blood and sweat during the trip, so for the sake of all involved, he hoped the work would be done by robots. If not, he was going to have to leave a very large tip.

Once all of that was out of the way, he waited for his girl to show up. And waited. And waited. He considered meeting her on the convention floor, called her, and was assured by Jon that she would be arriving in just a few minutes. So he watched a video with his slidepad hooked up to the room's display. And he waited. He dug out one of the spare slidepads Ma had left with him and started toying with it. And he waited. Two more calls, two more vigorous assurances of her forthcoming arrival, and an hour and a half later, he was still waiting.

Finally, there was a bleep from the door lock and it slid open, prompting Lex to stand. He had been planning to throw a few passive-aggressive barbs at her before saying hello, but, as usual, the woman just didn't fight fair. She stepped into the room wearing an elegant but professional black dress, threw her purse on the side table, kicked off her shoes, and looked up. The instant her blue eyes met his, whatever either of them had in mind was going to have to wait, because there was suddenly something far more important to take care of.

She literally pounced on him. He caught her in a hug and lifted her from the floor, spinning her around. At this point, it would have been customary for them to exchange hellos, or perhaps a few pet names--but, at the moment, their lips were otherwise engaged. He still had her scooped up in his arms when there was a polite cough at the door. Both turned their heads to see Jon.

“Do you need anything else, Ms Modane?”

“Go to your room, Jon,” she said flatly.

“Yes, mother.” He grinned and beeped the door shut.

Lex finally settled himself down on the couch and placed Michella beside him. She released a long, heavy sigh.

“Long day?” he asked.

“Ugh, exhausting. Why didn't you tell me being famous was so hard?”

“It's worth it, though.”

“In small doses, maybe, but I'll be happy when this convention is over and I'm back to being a real reporter instead of 'the new face of journalism' that the PR team keeps pushing. And then answering all of the questions? Shaking hands, posing for pictures? I was the only one in our high school who cared even a little bit about investigative reporting. Where are all of these cub reporters coming from?”

“Are a disproportionate amount of the ones asking you to pose for pictures men?”

“Yeah.”

"Then you might have to consider the possibility that it isn't your keen investigative instincts that they are interested in."

"Perish the thought," she said in mock concern, getting up and walking into the bathroom to freshen up. "So, what have you been up to? Anything interesting?" she called over the sound of the sink.

"Same ol', same ol'," he said, standing up. "Picked up a guy, dropped him off. He ended up wanting to pack more people into my ship than I could handle, so we cut things short."

"How was deGrasse?"

"Uh . . . well, I know you aren't supposed to judge a whole planet by one neighborhood, but we'll just say it didn't make a good first impression," he said.

"Anything bad happen?"

"Got a couple of dings on *S.O.B.*"

"Is that it?" she asked, shutting off the sink.

"Yeah."

"So you didn't end up, oh, say, covered with a bunch of nicks and cuts?"

"No?"

She walked out of the bathroom, eyeglasses in place of her contacts and jewelry removed. In her hand was the trash can from the bathroom.

"Then why is my trash filled with used bandages?" she asked.

Lex deflated slightly. There were some major downsides to dating a reporter.

"Out with it, buster," she said sternly.

"I got in a fight," he admitted, with the same level of enthusiasm a nine-year-old would show when fessing up about a broken vase.

"About what?"

"They tried to rob my pants while I was in the shower, and I tried to discourage that behavior."

She shook her head, "Did you at least *win*?"

"Babe, it's *me* we're talking about."

"Well . . . all right, then. I'd hate to think I was dating a bad liar *and* a bad fighter," she said.

"Ouch."

"So, who was it that hired you for this charter gig, anyway?"

"A friend of a friend. A buddy of Squee's owner."

"And that would be?"

"Babe, can we please save the third degree until tomorrow night? I promise I'll tell you all the gory details, but I just want one night off the books."

She pursed her lips and rolled her eyes as she mulled the offer over.

"Fine," she relented, "but I'm holding you to that. So, what do you want to do tonight?"

"I think we both know the answer to that question," he said, pulling her down onto the couch and wrapping an arm around her.

She giggled. "What do you say we start with room service?"

"Even better."

A call was placed for a Waldorf salad, a rare steak, and a bottle of wine. As they were enjoyed, along with the hot chocolate, cheesecake, and post-meal cuddling on the couch that followed, Michella engaged in her second-favorite activity.

Her first-favorite activity was also the reason Michella had become such a successful journalist. Yes, she had an eye for detail, and, yes, she was curious to a fault, but, most of all, she was a good listener. Once someone started talking, she kept them talking. Sometimes it was partially because she needed to know something they knew--but always it was because she was genuinely interested. It didn't matter who someone was--she wanted to know everything about them. What made them happy? What made them sad? What did they want out of life, and what had it given them?

She wanted to know it all--in their own words. Had she not chosen journalism, she would have probably been in her third season as a popular late night talk show host by now, and that was only reinforced by her second-favorite activity.

If Michella wasn't listening, she was talking. After all, what good was it to learn all of these fascinating things about others if she couldn't share them? Her looks were why she had been put in front of the camera so quickly after getting a job with GolanaNet News, but it was her flair for communication that kept her there. She was just as enthusiastic about telling stories as she was about hearing them, and the enthusiasm was contagious.

For hours, Lex just leaned back and let Michella's words wash over him, as the pressure buildup of not having him around for so long was finally released. He heard about the stuffy Dr. Greystone and his off-point blathering, and about this group of kids from New England who chose her for person of the year. The details of the convention flowed out, then everything else that had happened since the last time they had spoken. If it had been anyone else, Lex's patience would have worn thin fifteen subjects ago, but watching her talk was like watching an artist paint. He just smiled, nodded when it was appropriate, and enjoyed the show.

When Michella reached the end of the single, continuous line of thought that had carried her through the whole of the evening, she leaned her head on Lex's shoulder, pulled his arm around her, and released a soft, contented sigh. After a moment, Lex curled a finger under her chin and tilted her head until their eyes met. A seductive grin came to her face and she stood, taking his hands and leading him toward the bedroom for an activity that ranked in the top three for them both.

Chapter 14

The application of Garotte's disguise was complete, and the results were nothing short of uncanny. Most of his features had barely changed at all, but taken as a whole, he had been rendered unrecognizable. Where once had been a fairly handsome man casually approaching middle age, now there was man at least fifteen years older with a much stronger jaw, a slightly sloping brow, and the beginnings of a double chin. The transformation was completed by a dye job to his hair that shifted it from blond to brown and introduced some gray into the mix, and drops that shifted his hazel eyes to a distinctive green hue. None of it looked the least bit unnatural, and anyone who hadn't witnessed the transformation would scarcely believe that Garotte and this newcomer were one and the same.

"Dr. Kenneth Cisco," he said, clearing his throat and lowering the voice a few registers. "Dr. Kenneth Cisco."

Dr. Kenneth Cisco, who had not existed at the beginning of the flight, was well on his way to being a skilled but somewhat unremarkable psychoanalyst on staff at the prestigious Westmooreland Psychiatric Treatment Facility. Garotte's skill and thoroughness in the realm of identity creation was at least a match for that of Ma, and through various well-practiced and carefully arranged means, he had been able to install a lengthy and detailed personal history in all relevant databases. He had been married and divorced, graduated with a 3.3 GPA from a notable but not exclusive college, and had a clean employment record stretching sixteen years and spanning three mental hospitals.

"Dr. Kenneth Cisco," he repeated, now a bit gruffer and with an accent a touch more American. "I'm here to reevaluate one of your inmates. Dr. Kenneth Cisco. Kenny. Call me Kenny. Yeah, that sounds about right."

He loaded his slidepad with the appropriate documentation, then set about adding the little details that made it Kenny's slidepad. The last step was the assembly of a gadget he'd brought along from deGrasse. First, a grip of some kind was removed from the bag. It was bulky and vaguely ornamental, with a brushed metal finish, bearing a mini-placard engraved with the words "For exceptional service." It also had an inconspicuous pair of buttons recessed on the underside, a threaded hole, and a clear lens on one end. Giving it a shake produced a quiet rattle from within. He removed a pair of threaded pipes from the bag next, each metal with black enamel layered on top, and screwed them end-to-end onto the grip. Once assembled, it was a sturdy and elegant cane. The finishing touch was a non-skid foot for the end.

By the time they arrived at Millbrook Maximum Security Penitentiary, Silo's current residence, all was in readiness. It was on a floating hunk of rock called Manticore, a place specifically chosen for its environment. Planets tagged for human settlement were those as Earth-like as possible. Planets tagged for penitentiaries, on the other hand, widened that criteria a bit. The only real requirement was the ability to build a permanent structure. Beyond that, the less like Earth it was, the better. The reasoning was simple: they wanted the prisoners to stay inside the building, and the best way to achieve that was to make sure that *they* wanted to stay inside the building. A planet that had a surface survivability expectancy of less than thirty seconds was an excellent way to foster this attitude.

Manticore had no surface life, and no attempt had ever been made to terraform it. The average surface temperature of its most temperate zones was just below -30° Celsius, the soil had exceptionally high arsenic levels, the gravity was close to one and a half times that of Earth, and the atmosphere was almost entirely nitrogen. Without an environment suit, any escape attempt would last just a bit longer than a lungful of air. With a suit, it would last until the power supply, oxygen supply, or food supply ran out.

The only permitted access to the planet's surface was via the space station and its associated shuttles, which were not FTL-enabled--which meant that even if a prisoner stole a ship, and managed to give security the slip, it would be several decades before they reached anything with a breathable atmosphere. As for how the facility itself got a name like Millbrook, which sounded more like a country club than a super-max prison, one can only imagine a cruel sense of humor was involved.

“Hailing Millbrook, vessel code MAC-8787 requesting permission to dock,” Garotte--or rather, Kenny--said over the radio.

“State reason for unscheduled docking,” replied the landing coordinator.

“I'm afraid you're wrong there, son. Refresh your landing orders.”

“Stand by . . . apologies, MAC-8787. Last-minute schedule update just came in. Continue to dock nine and await security team.”

“Affirmative.”

Garotte clicked off the communication and set the ship to dock automatically.

“As I imagine you're aware, this is not a pet-friendly establishment,” Garotte stated, in character, “so it is probably best we get you out of sight before the security boys sign me in.”

He unhooked himself, unstrapped Ma, and grasped her by the nape of the neck. The AI did not struggle, merely keeping Garotte in her even, measuring gaze, as though logging this injustice for future reference. An overhead compartment was opened and she was stuffed unceremoniously inside. After clicking it shut, Garotte paused, then pulled her slidepad out of his pocket and opened the compartment a crack.

"To keep yourself busy," he said, slipping it inside.

A few moments after he clicked it shut again, a muffled digital voice could be heard.

"You now occupy the foremost position on my S-List," she said.

"You may update my intimidation accordingly. Now, hush up. Time to get to work."

He opened the side door of the Armistice and drifted into the dimly-lit interior of the docking bay, closing the door behind him. After a few moments, a crew of three lightly-armed security officers opened the door to the bay. They were wearing jumpsuits, armed with stun rods, and equipped with hands-free radio sets on their heads.

"Welcome to Millbrook Super-Max, Dr. Cisco," said the ranking security officer, a man with the minor paunch and graying crew cut of a retired member of law enforcement.

"Kenny," Garotte said, extending a hand.

"I'd like to apologize again for any misunderstandings," he said after a firm shake. "We don't get late authorizations like that very often. Any idea what that was about?"

"We've got a pilot program going. The bureaucrats haven't got themselves sorted out yet. No dedicated manpower, no dedicated budget, so they've just been sending anybody with a spare minute. I had a consultation on Tessera canceled, so they rushed the paperwork and rerouted me here."

"Pencil-pushers," the man replied with a shake of his head, illustrating that a catchy phrase tends to persist despite the fact that in this case it had been centuries since the pencil had been the preferred tool for the proliferation of the further antiquated notion of red tape. "It says here you'll need to conduct some interviews?"

"Psych evaluations," Garotte said with a nod.

"You'll need to talk to Warden Menlo, then. And we'll need to give you the standard security screening."

"Of course," Garotte said, handing over the cane and slidepad, then grasping the hand grips to be patted down and swept with hand scanners.

The security lead inspected the cane, unscrewing its segments and looking through the pipes. Satisfied they were harmless, he rattled the handle.

"What is inside of this?" he asked.

"Mmm? Oh, sorry 'bout that. Press that first button on the underside there," Garotte explained.

Doing so clicked open the top half of the grip, revealing a small compartment filled with pea-sized capsules which drifted out into the weightlessness of the docking bay.

“What are these?” asked the security lead, scooping them up with a deft swipe of his hand.

“Tranquilizers. Interviewing mentally disturbed inmates tends to do a number on your nerves. Sometimes I need something to take the edge off.”

“I'm afraid we can't allow outside medications.”

“That's fine. Haven't needed 'em lately. Those are probably a couple years past the sell-by date anyway. Go ahead and ditch 'em.”

He shoved the pills into a pocket of his jumpsuit and zipped it shut.

“And what does this other button do?”

“Flashlight,” Garotte said. “Give it a try.”

A tap of the button triggered an impressively powerful, moonlight-white beam of light.

“Handy,” the security lead said, handing it back. “Mind if I ask what you need the cane for?”

“Bad hip. Rock climbing--when I was young and stupid. I tell you, brother, we spend all of this time designing vehicles to get us to hard-to-reach places, then we go off and do damn fool things like rock climbing. I swear I don't know how we as a species make it out of our twenties. Regardless, usually I don't need it, but trust me when I say that one bad day is all it takes to convince you to start carrying it around, just in case. Since you folks have a little bit more gravity than you ought to, I figure today is gonna be one of those days.”

The security guard gave a nod.

“You're clean. They may take that away from you if you'll be interviewing inmates.”

“Naturally,” Garotte said, with a nod of his own.

The four men drifted out of the docking bay and down the claustrophobic corridor outside. A few twists and turns brought them to the waiting area for a shuttle, which looked like a slightly up-sized version of the Armistice. A few more handshakes and folksy colloquialisms were exchanged, and Garotte was loaded with one of the men onto the shuttle and taken to the surface. Gravity reared its ugly head, making his fit frame feel as though it was creeping toward the three hundred-pound range by the time they landed.

“Oof. I don't know how you boys do it,” Garotte proclaimed, as he tried to straighten himself out upon landing.

“You get used to it,” his escort replied, beeping open the doors and leading him into the arrival-processing area.

“If the good lord is with me, I won't be here long enough to have to,” he said, putting the cane to use and adopting a realistically stiff and unsteady walk.

Next came the gauntlet of checkpoints. He was walked through a sequence of increasingly sterile and bland hallways, past doors fortified with bars and fancy exotic plastics. Periodically, he would be stopped and asked some variation of the same three questions: "Who are you? Why are you here? Do you know the rules?" Regardless of his answer, his credentials would be crosschecked, he would be interrogated, and he would be briefed on security policies.

Finally, he found himself at the office of the warden, a man named Christopher Menlo. Like most of the other people who Garotte had been dealing with since he'd landed, Menlo had a very distinctive look about him. The extra gravity had prompted the development of a considerable amount of flat, hard muscle, which, on his already-formidable frame, produced an individual who seemed like he should be led out on chains while a smaller man beat a kettle drum. This appearance was in stark contrast to his disposition, which was extremely academic. He was dressed in a tweed suit with elbow patches, a vest underneath. His hair was close-cropped and thinning. The walls of the office were covered with diplomas and accreditation from assorted respectable institutions. On the desk were a few more pictures and a candy bowl filled with tiny mints. After reluctantly raising his arm to shake hands, and being rewarded with a handshake that refreshingly did not attempt to crush his hand to gravel, Garotte collapsed gratefully into a chair.

"Oh my lord, I do *not* do high-G very well. Honestly, you would think the boys in charge would at least do something about the gravity in the administrative areas," he said.

"Some of the other prisons have compensators, but I'm glad we don't around here. If you've got a facility of inmates that have adapted to high-gravity, best that the administration is on even terms," Menlo remarked. "Now, I realize that if my staff has done its diligence, this will be at least the sixth time you've had to answer these questions, but I'm afraid we can't be too careful."

"Perfectly understood, Warden. This isn't my first trip through a super-max. Do you mind if I take a handful of those?" he asked, pointing to the mints. "The ship they hooked me up with is missing a few of the usual amenities, and my teeth haven't seen a brush in . . . well, in too long."

"Please. I can't stand the things."

Garotte scooped up a handful, tossed a few in his mouth, and dumped the rest into his shirt pocket.

"Full name?" Menlo asked.

"Dr. Kenneth Marcus Cisco. Kenny, if you like."

"Says here you've got a degree from MacCree University?"

"I do."

"That's where I did my criminal justice degree. Friedland still running things when you were there?"

"I didn't have him, they were still telling stories about him."

"Yeah. Yeah, they would. About him, they would. Now, it says here you're looking to evaluate some of our inmates? Care to expand upon that?"

"I'd have to see your security clearance, if you don't mind. They didn't get me the full personnel briefing before they gave me word I'd be coming here."

"Of course," Menlo said, bringing up his credentials on a wall screen.

Garotte gazed at them for a moment and nodded.

"All right. The boys in the psych wing of R&D are looking for a test group for a new medication. Mood and behavior regulation. It is targeted at individuals with a very specific quirk in their psychological makeup. You've got an inmate that fits the profile exceedingly well."

"Jessica Winters?"

"That's the girl."

"And if your evaluation turns up what you're looking for, you'll be taking her with you?" Menlo said with a raised eyebrow, glancing over the certificates and permits that Garotte had managed to install during the journey.

"That's correct. We'd put her into suspended animation--or at least heavy sedation--and transfer to a testing facility."

Menlo studied the briefing for a few moments more.

"Your credentials check out, but I must say that this sort of thing usually takes months to clear."

"I suppose the science boys back at HQ have some pull with the right people. Either that or they've been working at it for months. They don't tell me that sort of thing. I'm just the man asking the questions."

After a few more moments of consideration, Menlo made a decision.

"Here's the rules. You'll be in interview room A. That's high-security. Half-inch of transparent ceramic between you and the inmate. All communication will be done through intercom. It will be monitored and recorded. There will be two guards on either side of the glass at all times; two more in the adjoining hallways. If my boys say something, you do it--fast. If I say anything, you do it twice as fast."

Garotte nodded.

"You need anything before we begin?"

"Just a word or two with you if you don't mind," Garotte said, pulling out his slidepad. "What are your feelings about Miss Winters as an inmate?"

"In all honesty, I wish I had a hundred more just like her. Quiet, follows the rules. Keeps to herself. Only request was for an e-reader and periodic access to the fiction catalogs."

"What subjects?"

"Heh. Paranormal romance, as I recall."

"Really?" Garotte said with a smirk.

"Pretty much exclusively."

"Well, good to know. Whenever you're ready, we'll start with her."

The two men stood, Garotte with some reluctance, and made their way out into the hallway.

"Get me Inmate 38E-75, Jessica Winters. Interview room A," Menlo barked before turning back to Garotte. "Just follow this gentleman."

Garotte limped his way deeper into the complex while Menlo returned to his office. In the hall, a guard lingered with his partner. The older of the two, a droopy-faced man with a badly scarred right hand and a piece of his right ear missing, watched with narrowed eyes. His badge read Johnson.

"That guy's going to talk to Inmate Winters. That's what he said, right?" he said.

"Yeah. What of it?" said his partner Andrews, a younger and less dedicated member of the staff.

"Just wanted to be sure. Hey, you're on coms tonight, right?"

"Yeah, I was supposed to start fifteen minutes ago," he grumbled.

"You want to switch shifts?"

"You kidding me? You are offering to sit in that freezing little shack for the next four hours?"

"I got nothing better to do."

"Deal, sucker," he said with a shake.

The pair separated, Johnson working his way to the radio room on the upper level of the complex. Since conduit ran from every antenna in the array to this tiny closet of a room, it tended to be a good thirty degrees colder than the rest of the facility, and emergency oxygen masks were kept on hand due to the elevated nitrogen levels in the air, a result of the lackluster pressure seals.

"You're relieved," Johnson said to the woman currently manning the cramped, knob- and button-laden console, but it was hardly necessary. The woman at the controls was already on her feet, eager to get out of the veritable freezer.

She pulled off her headset, dropped it on the control panel, and marched out without so much as a nod. After donning the appropriate equipment and checking levels, Johnson carefully adjusted the security sweep interval and twisted one of the transmitters to an off-frequency, tapping out a quick coded message and attaching a few frames of security cam footage before restoring the previous settings. Due to the peculiarity of the frequency, most receivers filtered the short message out, interpreting it as crosstalk or static. One radio, however, received the message loud and clear. It belonged to a ship drifting at the outskirts of the system. The ship was a NXLRR-0025c, and no sooner had it received the message than ran it through a deep encryption algorithm and relayed it. The message bounced through various communication channels, sometimes randomly, and finally arrived at its destination.

#

"Commander! We've got a transmission from one of the surveillance squads!"

Commander Purcell looked up from her current task, which was the replacement of a leaking power cell in her sidearm, to the underling at her door.

"Put it on my display," she said, pulling her datapad from the wall.

After a few moments, the surveillance footage of the disguised Garotte came up, with the message, "This man may be attempting to relocate person of interest #2. All credentials appear legitimate." Purcell brought up the information she had been able to dig up on the prisoners her benefactor had indicated were of concern. None of the images matched the man in those transmitted by her field agent. She ran the frames through a matching algorithm that failed to find a match with a confidence of greater than forty percent.

"Our intelligence suggests that there have been no direct inquiries regarding any of the prisoners we are currently watching for at least three months, correct?" she asked the underling.

"Yes."

"This isn't a coincidence, then."

She considered her options. She could contact her benefactor, but getting a valid window would take time. There was a better source of knowledge at hand.

"Wake up Karter. Now," Purcell ordered. "He is going to answer some questions."

By the time she made her way to Karter's cell, there were already medical personnel readying an injection. He was motionless on the floor, still sedated from the last time, tubes in his arm keeping him hydrated and nourished without the risk of waking him up. The cell was unlocked, and two medics accompanied by three armed guards administered the injection and slowly backed away, as though they were dealing with a wild animal.

After a few seconds, Karter stirred, struggling to sit up.

"Ma?" he said groggily. "Get some beans and rice going. I'm going to . . ." he began, until his eyes opened and he slowly remembered his current predicament. "Oh. This is still happening."

"Karter. I am going to ask you some questions. You will give me swift, direct, and honest answers."

"No."

"That was not a request, Karter."

"I don't care. You sedated me. I don't like that. If we're going to be doing business together, you can start by not sedating me."

"If you don't answer my questions, I *will* have my men put you under again."

"Oh, god. Are we going to go through this *again!?* Are you stuck in a loop or something?" he raved, rubbing his eyes. "You can't intimidate me into doing what you want me to do by threatening to do something that will *prevent* me from doing what you want me to do. 'Either do what I say or I'll make sure you can't do what I say!' It makes you sound like an idiot! And, by the way, I *really* have to take a leak."

"Are you going to answer my questions?"

"Are you going to sedate me again?"

"If you answer my questions to my satisfaction, then I will not have you sedated again."

"There you go. That's positive reinforcement. I respond well to that. Write that down."

"The war criminals you used to work with," she growled. "Would they try to mount a rescue?"

"They are all locked up, so no."

"One of them escaped recently. It is believed that he had help."

"Which one escaped?"

"Phillip Winchester."

"Heh. No, he didn't."

"It is all over the news."

"Oh, I don't doubt that he escaped, but he isn't Phillip Winchester. That's an alias. I can't believe that he made it all the way into a prison without them figuring that out. You're talking about the British guy."

"What is his real name?"

"Hell if I know. I just called him the British guy. His name wasn't what I was interested in."

"What *were* you interested in?"

"Well, he asked if I could create a concealable weapon that could propel a watermelon seed to lethal velocities. That was pretty interesting."

"Would he mount a rescue attempt?"

"Not on his own, but he'd probably go along with the suggestion."

"Is this him?" she asked, holding up the datapad with the transmitted image.

Karter squinted at it.

"It doesn't look like him, which means it probably is. That was one of his stunts."

"He may be attempting to liberate a woman by the name of Jessica Winters."

"Don't know that name, either. It was always codenames with that crew."

Purcell brought up the file image she had of Winters.

"Oh, yeah. That's our heavy weapons guy."

"This is a woman."

"You handle ordinance like she does and you officially count as a guy in my book."

"Would he attempt to free her?"

"If he wanted to blow some stuff up, then . . . yes, he would free her. And he wouldn't attempt to, he would do it. That limey bastard had thousands of back doors installed into hundreds of agencies even before he started working with me. You give him a data connection and a half an hour and he could convince you he was your own father for at least a *little* while."

"You are certain that this man will free this woman, and that they would attempt to retrieve you?"

"If the two of them are in the same place at the same time, then chances are they're already halfway through some master plan."

Purcell considered his words. "Thank you, Karter. You have been very helpful."

With that she turned to her medics.

"Put him back under," she said.

"Oh. Oh, so that's how it's going to be, is it?" Karter said in irritation.

"Yes, Dee. You have continually illustrated that you cannot be trusted. It is clear that the only way to work with you is to adopt the same behavior."

"That's all well and good, but you do realize that you can't just keep me sedated."

"I assure you. I can."

"We'll see . . . and one of your guys is going to have to clean up, because there is no way I'm going to be able to hold--"

The guards restrained Karter long enough for the injector to be pushed to his neck and, after a brief struggle, he was unconscious again.

"Get a message to our surveillance team and the inside operative," Purcell ordered Marx, who was shadowing her, as always. "If that man leaves the planet alone, destroy his ship as soon as it leaves sensor range. If he even *appears* to be leaving with Jessica Winters, kill them both, by any means necessary, even if it means blowing our cover. In a few days, cover won't be a problem anymore."

"Yes, Commander."

Chapter 15

Garotte was seated in a room somewhat reminiscent of the standard interrogation room made famous by so many police dramas. There was cheap LED lighting arranged into faux-florescent ceiling fixtures, because at some point it had been decided that the long, dangling bars of light were ideal for government buildings. The room was divided into two matching halves by a wall. The upper half of the wall was thick, high-durability glass. The bottom was the same sturdy metallic sheeting that made up the rest of the prison's structure. A countertop ran the length of the wall just below the glass, and in the center of the window was a small speaker grill, giving the overall effect that he was visiting some sort of deluxe teller window at a very luxurious bank. A pair of men were in the room with him, dressed like police officers in riot gear, complete with high-impact vest and face shield.

He pulled the single metal chair up to the counter, took a seat, and turned to one of the guards.

"Do you need to take this?" he asked, holding out the cane.

"Shouldn't be necessary. The glass will be sufficient to prevent the inmate from attempting to utilize it," he replied.

"Good to hear it," Garotte said with a nod.

The door on the other side of the glass was opened, and the prisoner was led in, hefty-looking restraints holding her wrists behind her back.

Jessica Winters was far from the first person one would picture when envisioning an inmate of a super-max facility. She was a short-ish woman drifting into her mid-thirties. Her face was round and dimpled, with a button nose and thin, arching eyebrows over her green eyes. The rest of her body was a match, with round, soft curves despite a lengthy stay on the high-gravity world. There were a few more pounds on her than the media indicated was appropriate for models and actresses, but she wore them well and enjoyed a natural fullness to her form that was no less attractive. She was dressed in a dark blue prison-issue jumpsuit that wasn't quite designed with someone as generously proportioned as her in mind, leaving the fabric around the chest and hips straining just a bit to contain her figure. Her blonde hair was cut short, but there was still enough of it to see that it was naturally curly. All things considered, it was difficult to picture her breaking military law. Baking cookies after soccer games and inspiring the wrong sorts of thoughts in the neighborhood boys, maybe, but not the sort of things that gets one placed in super-max.

She took her seat and faced Garotte from the other side of the glass. He tapped record on his slidepad and cleared his throat.

"Good evening. I'm Dr. Cisco. I'll be asking you a few questions today. Let's start by stating your full name for the record."

"Sgt. Jessica Margo Winters," she said in a gentle, almost shy voice, with just a hint of Earth Midwestern.

"Sgt. Winters. I have a few aliases that you've operated under. Please let me know if they are accurate. Julia Springer."

"Yes."

"Layla Smith."

"Yes."

"Silo."

She blinked. "There are people who called me that."

"Thank you. Now, you introduce yourself as a sergeant. I have it here that you were discharged from the Earth Coalition Marine Corps some seven years ago. Is this correct?"

"Yes," she said, her voice slightly harder.

"Why do you continue to introduce yourself with the rank?"

"Once a soldier, always a soldier, Doctor."

"You were dishonorably discharged after you caused 'collateral damage in extreme excess of mission requirement.' Does that mean that you killed civilians?"

"No," she said, sternly.

"What then?"

"I demolished an office building that was undergoing renovation in the field of operation."

"Why did you demolish the building?"

"A foreign liaison who was operating with our squad suggested that I would be unable to do so with my current equipment," she said, her voice carefully held steady, as though she'd wanted to say it a good deal more forcefully.

"And what *was* your current equipment at the time?"

"I was armed with a shoulder fire, 60mm multiple grenade-launcher."

"Was this weapon equipped with demolition in mind?"

Winters shook her head. "Standard concussion grenades. Six count."

"And you succeeded in demolishing the building with six rounds?"

"It only took five," she said flatly.

"How did you achieve this?"

"Three internal supports, one natural gas line, one tanker truck parked near the north wall."

"And you did this merely due to a suggestion on the behalf of this liaison?"

She narrowed her eyes and replied with a tone of irritation. "It was more of a dare, Doctor."

"Sgt. Winters, I believe I have a program I would like to recommend you for. Care for a change of scenery?"

"With all due respect, Doctor? No, I wouldn't."

Garotte raised an eyebrow. "Really? You'd have a chance to collaborate with your peers."

"Collaborating with my peers is what got me here."

"Do you like it here, Sgt. Winters?"

"No, I don't like it here, Doctor. But that's not why we get put places like this, is it? We get put places like this because we belong here, and I do," Winters said, eyes locked on his.

"I think that being a part of this program will be of great help to you."

"I've got plenty of help here. I've got a therapist, a counselor."

"This new setting would provide you with group therapy, and I don't feel that the group would be complete without you."

"I don't think that any group that would be completed by me is one that needs to be complete at all."

"I'm sorry to hear that you feel that way, Miss Winters."

"Sgt. Winters," she corrected.

Garotte leaned forward, staring at her intently. "It seems to me that you aren't a soldier anymore, Miss Winters."

A scowl briefly twisted her features, but she managed to wrestle her way back to composure. The intensity stayed in her eyes, however. Garotte nodded and tapped at his slidepad, then leaned on the mute button of the intercom on the window.

"I'm going to ask a few more questions. Would you be able to get the warden in here? I think it might be time to discuss travel arrangements," he said to one of the guards.

The man nodded and touched a finger to his headset, activating it. "Yeah, communications? Can we get Warden Menlo into Interview A? . . . affirmative. It will be a few minutes. He is on a call."

"Not a problem." Garotte nodded.

#

In the control room, Johnson closed the connection and took the appropriate precautions to send another subversive message. This one was simple, and directed to the ship filled with his comrades. "The operation is go. Phase 1 initiating."

His face was a mask of duty as he pulled a tool belt from the corner of the room, selected a wire cutter, and cut first the alarm cable, then the main power for communications. As the lights and indicators on the control panel slowly faded away, he left the room and locked it behind him, marching toward a room marked “Security Relay.”

#

In orbit, the seemingly unoccupied Armistice was sitting in the hangar. Ma had remained in her hiding place, having a great deal of difficulty interacting with her slidepad in the weightless environment. She'd resorted to capturing it between her front paws and tracing out shapes with her nose, which turned out to be a remarkably efficient method after a bit of practice. She'd just completed a sentence she was greatly anticipating putting to use when her sensitive ears picked up the sounds of some sort of alert message blaring over the PA system of the space station. She clutched the lanyard in her teeth, braced herself within the confined compartment, and tried to work at the latch from the inside. After considerable effort, the door sprung open and she went tumbling into the weightless interior of the ship.

It took a bit of scrabbling and bouncing off of walls before she managed to find something she could wrap her paws around to bring herself to a stop. The funk's brain, she had quickly discovered, was phenomenally swift and efficient at calculating trajectories for her leaps. Adapting it to zero-gravity had been much easier than doing so for low-gravity, so hitting a target was simplicity itself. Finding some way to hold onto it was another matter entirely. She ended up clinging to the headrest of the pilot's seat. From her tenuous vantage there, she was able to make out spinning warning lights.

With a cautious nudge, she drifted to the control panel, wrapped herself in an inexpert grip around the currently inactive control stick, and tapped precariously at the access screen. Landing indicators flipped on and off, thrusters shifted and twitched, and the wipers for the view windows deployed and retracted before she finally managed to enter the correct command, flicking on the radio to the emergency frequency.

“. . . deactivated for the entire facility, and all communication is down. Repeat, security measures have been deactivated for the entire facility, and all communication is down. Get to disaster stations and prepare to launch a shuttlecraft to contact the surface. If any of you have got personal communication devices, please report to the command bridge so that we can attempt to contact the surface. This may be a priority one breach. Repeat, potential intruder situation,” the security lead instructed.

Ma let herself drift free for a moment, clutching the slidepad and nosing out a message. Routing it through the ship's transmitters so she could be sure that it would be powerful enough to reach the surface, she delivered it to Garotte, then entered the commands necessary to give her remote control over the ship's functions via the pad, authorizing it with a tap to the access screen again. The severe difficulty of the entire situation caused her to log a personal note to herself: If prolonged activity is required in a weightless environment, favor a physical vessel with a prehensile appendage.

She had only just managed to latch onto the control stick again when she saw something else outside the view window. The door to the catwalk had opened, and in slipped a member of the station crew, dressed in a standard-issue jumpsuit. From the look of his nervous glances back out the door before securing it behind him, he was doing something he didn't want others to see.

When he turned toward the ship, it became clear why. In his hand was a small-caliber ballistic pistol, and the hand clutching it was pinning a dangerous-looking device to his chest. It featured a conspicuous timer and a bundle of plasma pistol clips. A hastily-constructed makeshift bomb. Ma's eyes opened wider and her mind quickly ran through the options. She glanced to the door, then to the folded manipulator arm recessed into the ship's ceiling.

Outside the ship, the saboteur was continuing the work that his partner on the surface had started. As the only well-funded enterprise on the whole miserable world, the prison and its orbital section were the only facilities with the infrastructure to communicate long-range. Cutting the power to both transmission arrays had completely silenced the entire planet, and cutting the security feed had blinded it.

Even with the coordinated assault, though, it wouldn't stay down forever. It might not even stay down long enough for their seek-and-destroy mission to complete. Thus, a secondary distraction would be necessary, something to keep them busy. The current plan called for a bomb to be placed on the target's vessel. Nothing large enough to destroy either the vessel or the station. Just something large enough to disable the ship, thus preventing his escape--and to make it appear as though he was to blame for the other attacks.

His current order of business was to find an appropriate place to position the bomb. He floated up to affix it to one of the maneuvering thrusters when the door hissed and began to open.

Cautiously, he tucked the bomb under his arm and held tight to the external grip beside the door, pistol poised in the other hand, ready to unload it into the first person to exit. Curiously, when the door fully deployed, nothing else happened. After listening closely and hearing nothing, not even breathing, he peeked his head inside. The interior was deserted. The only indication that the ship had ever been in use was a few bags held down with elastic bands and an overhead compartment that was slightly ajar.

Convinced that there were no surprises on the way, he clipped the pistol to a loop on his jumpsuit and began to prep the bomb. If it was planted inside, the explosion would be even more certain to disable the ship without threatening the space station too badly, and would make the ship's owner the prime suspect in the sabotage. He wasn't foolish enough to think that the door had opened by itself, but he only needed a few seconds to plant and prime the bomb and make his escape. After that, it wouldn't matter why the door opened.

He set the timer, and extended his arm to hurl it inside.

In a blur of motion, the manipulator arm extended, bashing the man's arm with enough force to dislodge the explosive device from his grip. The bomb wobbled in place, like a plate on a table after the tablecloth had been pulled from beneath it. The man, on the other hand, cried out in pain and released his grip to cradle his almost certainly fractured arm. When the initial shock wore off, he looked up to see the manipulator arm inexpertly attempting to grab the drifting bomb. Just as he reached for it, a poorly-judged jab of the arm sent the improvised device twirling out of reach of both man and claw. He jumped after it, but a moment later Ma burst from her hiding spot in the compartment. A single, well-aimed usage of her prodigious leaping ability drove her full momentum into the small of his back. A quick pivot and leap, pushing off of him, sent him off-course and directed her toward the bomb.

The saboteur struck the catwalk and held as tightly as he could with his injured arm. With a skill that betrayed formal training, he aimed and fired. Ma felt something sail by her ear before striking an interior wall of the station. This was fortunate, because, like the deGrasse dormitory, a hole in the exterior wall would be a very bad thing indeed. Granted, the well-built space station was built with far better design considerations than the dirt-cheap dorm. That meant one or two stray bullets *probably* wouldn't cause explosive decompression--but "probably" was an unpopular word when a hard vacuum is a part of the equation.

The zero-gravity ricochet sent the bullet rattling about the bay, denting wall panels and railings until it lost enough energy to simply spiral through the air. Meanwhile, the recoil jerked the poorly-braced saboteur aside, forcing him to reorient before attempting another shot.

When he was ready to fire again, he looked up to see Ma wrapped around the bomb, eyes darting madly over its workings. She had anticipated the need to manipulate electronics, and had included a truncated version of her data module on the subject when she'd constructed the mental download. Power source, timer, interface buttons . . . the weapon was set for forty-five seconds, and there had only been minor design considerations made to complicate deactivation and disarmament.

"Drop it!" cried the injured foe.

Ma looked up. His weapon was pointed steadily and surely at her. With a careful and skilled push from his feet, he sent himself drifting slowly toward her. The options clicked through her mind. Feasibility, risk/benefit, success ratio, and a dozen other factors made their way through carefully developed algorithms. The massive and nuanced calculation reduced down to a single motion. Just before he reached her, she reached down and clicked the activation button for the timer. The saboteur's eyes opened wide in panic, but zero-gravity had the nasty habit of making you stick with your trajectory once you've launched yourself. Ma planted her feet on the bomb and shoved off, sending it bouncing off the wall and sending her back toward the door of the ship.

The infiltrator finally reached a wall, grabbing a support strut and quickly surveying the situation. The bomb was on a spinning, twisting journey around the bay. With his injured arm, he couldn't be sure that he would reach it in time, but reaching it didn't matter. It would go off, and it would do so in the bay. That was good enough. All he had to do was get out before it did so. Tossing the gun, he made his way quickly along the handholds installed in rows along the wall until he reached the door and slipped out, locking it shut behind him. When he turned to make good his escape down the hall, he found himself facing a full security team, sent to investigate the scream and gunshot.

Back in the docking bay, Ma had reached the inside of the ship and made a few more precision leaps, eventually making it to the compartment where her slidepad was carefully wedged. She tapped quickly at the screen, retracting the arm, sealing the door, and transmitting an emergency disembark command. If the station had been under normal operation, it would certainly have denied the command, or at least raised a flag. But the damage that the saboteur had caused was sufficient to prompt an immediate departure clearance.

The airlock hissed open, sucking the bomb into space. Ma initiated the main engine start sequence and directed the ship's autopilot to exit the hangar while the primary thrusters ran through their warm-up cycle. A few moments later, the light patter of shrapnel and a faint sizzle of plasma against the sturdy hull heralded the detonation of the bomb. Without an atmosphere and a confined space, the explosion wasn't nearly sufficient to be a threat to ship or station.

The Armistice oriented itself and shuddered along until its engines finally fully flared to life.

#

"Any word on the warden?" asked Garotte, checking the time on his slidepad.

Confident though he was in his disguise and credentials, every false identity had a time limit. He hadn't had much time to prepare this one, so he'd been forced to construct it with speed in mind, rather than longevity. Periodic automated security sweeps would eventually find the entries he'd made and, depending on the database, investigations would begin regarding the validity. He'd estimated fraud alerts and security holds wouldn't start for at least two days, but considering the fact that his estimate was based primarily on wild guesses and intuition, he would rather be long gone well before then.

The guard touched his headset again. "Communications, can we . . .

communications?"

Suddenly, the PA system began to blare an alert. "Attention, all personnel. Situation Blue. Switch to point to point communications and await further orders."

The message repeated itself once before the power suddenly dropped away, plunging the room into darkness. An instant later, flashlights clicked on.

"What's this about?" Garotte asked, convincingly pretending to be a man who was pretending not to be afraid.

"Stay calm, sir. We have procedures for this," the guard said unsteadily, as dim red emergency lights clicked on.

"Oh, well, that's all right then," Garotte said, crunching on one of the mints from his pocket, then clicking open his cane's compartment and dropping them in. "As long as you've got procedures. I presume all of your doors lock in the event of a power failure?"

"Yes."

Garotte clicked on the flashlight built into his cane and shined it around, then appeared to nervously play with the pair of buttons. A moment later, the already nervous guard furrowed his brow.

"What's that noise?" he asked, hand instinctively moving to his stun rod.

"What is it? Sort of an edge-of-your-hearing whine? Heading up in frequency and down in volume?" Garotte asked.

"Yes."

"Probably just a large capacitor charging."

"Where is it coming from?"

Garotte leaned to the side, as if listening closely, then slowly raised the tip of his cane toward the glass.

"I think . . . it may be coming . . . from the basement," he said slowly.

At the sound of the final word, Winters slid quickly from her seat and rolled beneath the counter. Before the men on her side of the glass could react, there was an earsplitting clap. Garotte nearly toppled over backward, and the entire surface of the glass marbled with intricate cracks, then disintegrated into small, jagged pebbles. The avalanche of glass was, to say the least, highly distracting. Both Winters and Garotte took full advantage.

He flipped the cane around, grasping the end and swinging the handle with pinpoint precision at the base of the neck of the first guard, crumbling him to the ground. The second guard swung at his head with the stun rod, but he stooped below, snatching up the matching weapon from the downed partner and delivering a swift, incapacitating jolt.

Winters managed to get to her feet, despite the high gravity and wrist restraints, and was standing on the counter of her side of the broken glass wall before the guards on her side had gathered themselves enough to take action. The first one to approach got a swift kick to the bottom edge of the face mask, popping his helmet neatly off and uncovering his face for a thrust kick to the nose. The other tried to apply his stunner to her legs, but she leaped toward him, driving her knees into his collar bones and riding him down to the ground, where the gravitationally-enhanced maneuver kept him there.

The glass had barely finished settling to the ground by the time the only person standing was Garotte. He climbed gingerly over the divider and helped Winters to her feet.

"What would you have done if I'd forgotten what 'basement' was code for?"

"Apologized vigorously and helped you to pick bits of glass out of your hair," he replied, returning to the proper British accent, which seemed oddly out of place coming from his altered face. His breathing was heavy, the exertion taking an extra toll in the high gravity.

"How did you manage to shut down power and security?" she asked breathlessly.

"Power *and* security?"

"Situation Blue. Complete secondary system failure."

"That was not part of the plan. Not part of *my* plan, anyway. Still, don't look a gift horse in the mouth and all that."

"How did you break the glass?" she asked.

"The same way I'll be breaking your cuffs. Careful. Wouldn't want to dislocate a shoulder," he said, guiding her to the counter and doing his best to put the locking mechanism against the surface.

He climbed to the counter, placed the tip of his cane against the lock between her wrists, and depressed one of the buttons. The same subtle electronic whine sounded, and another clap. Even with the whole of his body weight bracing it, the recoil from his cane nearly lifted him from the ground. A neat hole about the size of a pea was blasted through the restraints, and a somewhat larger one through the counter and floor below it.

"Who would have thought a breath mint moving at a few multiples of the speed of sound could be so effective a lock pick, eh?" he quipped, as Winters pulled her hands from the broken restraints.

With an impassive look on her face, Winters reached up and grabbed Garotte by the collar, yanking him down from the counter and pulling him off his feet, such that the only thing keeping him from lying flat on his back on a bed of broken glass was her steely grip. She pulled him face to face.

"Why did you come here and do this? I didn't *want* to be broken out. Do you understand?"

"You certainly seemed quick to take out these two gentlemen when you had to."

"As soon as you raised that cane, the best I could hope for was six months in solitary--minimum. If it is that or an escape, I choose escape, but you had better have a gosh-darn good excuse for making me choose it," she said, delivering the replacement expletives with all of the force and conviction of the originals.

"A group of political or religious extremists with military ties have kidnapped Karter."

Winters considered the words for a moment.

"Good call busting me out, then," she admitted, straightening him up and fixing his collar, "but give me that cane-gun before you hurt somebody."

"Gladly," he said, handing it over.

"When this is all over, I owe you three slaps."

"Why three?"

"We'll get into that later. What's the plan?" she asked, snapping instantly into business mode.

"Well, the plan *had* been to walk out of here with you under my custody. It had been going rather well until this mysterious blackout, I should add."

"Yes, well, I'd say that plan is officially beyond redemption. What is plan B?"

"I hadn't actually formulated one. I hate plan B. Its very existence undermines confidence in plan A."

Winters pinched the bridge of her nose. "This is exactly why you weren't the one who made the plans."

"Evidently."

"All right, well, we need--"

She was interrupted by a chirp of Garotte's slidepad. He glanced at it.

"There has been a security and communication failure in the orbital section of the facility. Potential infiltration. Expect difficulties," he read aloud.

"Who sent that?"

"We'll get into that later. I suppose we'll need to get to the shuttle bay?"

"Yeah. And every darn door along the way is going to be locked. Not even these boys would be able to get them open without power."

"The cane ought to get them open."

"Sure, but how many rounds do you have left?"

"It fires anything that fits down the barrel," he said, stooping and scooping up a double helping of the cubed glass remnants of the divider. "And I'm willing to wager these will be a bit more effective than breath freshener. The cane is armed, so this button opens the compartment to reload, and this one is the trigger. Hold down to charge, release to fire. Longer charge, harder hit. And brace yourself--she's got a hell of a kick."

She dumped out the breath mints and dumped in some glass, then clicked the compartment shut and took a few test shots at the wall. When she was comfortable with the firing characteristics, she raised the weapon and popped a shot at the red emergency light, scoring a direct hit. As she opened the compartment to top off the load of glass, she began to rattle off orders.

"We'll take the first two doors to the left. Should lead to a service corridor. Narrow, fewer doors. From there, we'll head out into the administration building, then straight through to the hangar. I'll lay down cover fire, you get a ship running. I hope you've got something with a faster-than-light drive up there."

"That I do."

"All right--then we get in the shuttle, we pray that the security failure holds until we manage to dock, we get to your ship, get out of here, and you get your slaps. Try not to kill anyone. These men are just doing their jobs. And for goodness sake, let's not start a riot, and let's not let anyone but us escape. These people are here for a reason."

"Duly noted."

"What's the codename today?"

"I've been using Garotte."

"Again? I guess I'll go with Silo again, then."

"Just like old times," he said with a grin, snatching a pair of the stun rods and giving them a quick twirl.

She took a deep breath, clicked the cane compartment shut, and nodded. "Move out."

Chapter 16

From time to time, one may hear the term “military precision.” This usually brings to mind images of troops marching in perfect step, or perhaps doing weapon drills in unison. Impressive, perhaps, but not the sort of thing that would inspire awe or admiration. Those who feel that way, however, should know that what the term really refers to is the battlefield behavior that all of those synchronized exercises were conceived to facilitate.

Garotte and Silo, as they worked their way through the prison's halls, were a textbook-worthy example. With seldom more than a syllable exchanged between them, actions were assigned and performed. While Silo perforated a lock, Garotte distracted and disabled a guard to buy her the time to do so. Emergency lights were destroyed to provide the cover of darkness, hallways were declared to be clear if they were, and a few quick applications of a stun rod emptied the ones that weren't. In most instances, they were through a section of the facility before the guards--who were still grappling with the chaos caused by the total power and security failure--even knew they were there.

When they approached one of the secondary entrances to the shuttle hangar, Silo stopped him.

“All right. If I'm right about their procedures, the hangar is going to be packed to the gills with guards. Did you check out the layout on the way in?”

“Six emergency oxygen masks on every alternate support column, three secure munitions chests--one in each corner and one in the center,” Garotte said, taking the cane from her and topping off its supply of crushed glass.

“Those chests will be loaded with anti-vehicular weaponry to take out rogue shuttles in the event an escaping inmate makes it that far. We'll need to confiscate or destroy the contents of all three chests if we are going to have a chance to escape. And we'll need to clear the hangar of guards.”

Garotte tapped his foot and twirled a stun rod in thought, the sounds of utter bedlam echoing through the halls around them.

“Refresh my memory. The atmospheric pressure on this planet--lethal?” he asked.

“No. But the atmosphere is unbreathable.”

“Right, so, we pop the door, you provide covering fire, I grab an oxygen rig for each of us. I take cover, you blow the lock on a munitions chest and as many oxygen rigs as you can. I get a gun, I offer cover fire, you get a gun. We strap on oxygen, then blow the hangar doors. No more breathable atmosphere, no more oxygen rigs, mandatory evacuation. They'll have to manually apply the internal emergency doors to keep the facility from losing its oxygen. They're locked in, and we're all alone in the hangar with the doors wide open. Sufficient?"

"Sufficient." She nodded.

She put the cane to the door lock, pulled the trigger, and the plan began to unfold. The pair moved like interlocked gears, each step and motion leading smoothly into another. A gathering of guards, still startled by the sound of the disintegrating door lock, scrambled for cover as the sonic booms began to erupt from the bizarre makeshift weapon. Garotte sprinted to a pillar, pulled down three oxygen masks and tanks, and tossed one of them high into the air in the high-roofed chamber. Silo spotted it, shifted aim, and neatly punctured its edge with a shot, sending the canister rocketing dangerously around the room. In the brief window of distraction it caused, she turned and fired at the chest nearest to Garotte. He wrenched it open and hoisted out a weapon that looked like a rifle with an eating disorder. On a normal planet, he would have had trouble carrying it. On Manticore, it was practically immobile, but he managed to heave it onto the chest's edge, slap in an ammo clip, and pull the trigger. A wild spray of dark red energy bolts lanced through the air, just barely over the heads of the nearest guards.

On cue, Silo took full advantage. She made her way to the chest, pushing the cane into his hands and shouldering the heavy weapon with incredible ease. One steady shot was fired at each remaining cluster of oxygen masks, causing a satisfying burst of fire and shrapnel with each hit. As she fired, Garotte strapped an oxygen mask onto her face, then onto his own, and finally took a few cane-shots at a trio of the more courageous guards.

Silo took advantage of the cover fire to flip the heavy weapon to fully-automatic, shift her aim to the primary hangar doors, and unleash. Each bolt of energy took a huge, molten bite out of the door, revealing the pale light of the weak, midday sun on the icy concrete slab outside. Within a few moments of perforating the air-tight seal, an alarm with its own reserve power supply began to sound, and a similarly isolated force field flickered into place to stop the oxygen loss. Two quick bursts of fire at the field generator put an end to that. Frigid, unbreathable air flooded the hangar, causing what few guards remained to run for the safety of the interior doors, shutting and sealing them.

"Bloody hell, it is cold. I'd forgotten about the cold," Garotte grumbled, stamping his feet and rubbing his hands together before investigating the security he would have to override to gain control of a shuttle.

"Oh, gosh!" Silo exclaimed, dropping the gun into the chest and snatching an oxygen rig from the one remaining set before dashing off toward the center of the hangar.

"What's the problem?" Garotte asked, quickly taking up the cane and scanning the area for threats. After a moment, he realized the problem.

A single guard remained, a fellow unfortunate enough to take a chunk of an exploded oxygen canister to the calf, sending him to the ground. In the panic of evacuating the hangar while under fire, his partners had failed to notice him. From the looks of it, his lungful of good air had given out, leaving him heaving great, gasping breaths that would do him no good at all.

"Hold still, hon," she instructed, holding him flat to the floor with one arm and slipping the oxygen mask onto him. "Breathe slow now."

The guard--who, from the looks of him, was one of the newer additions to the staff--slowly stopped struggling as the desperate fear of suffocation was replaced by relief. As his wits slowly returned, Silo continued to hold him down, tugging at his pockets and equipment as she did.

"You all right? You breathing fine?" she asked, checking his eyes and his pulse. "Yeah, you look good. You're all right, hon. That fragment didn't hit anything important. Next time, get to the door quicker, okay?"

He nodded slowly, his mind finally picking up where it left off before the madness had begun. At the precise moment he realized he was face to face with a prisoner in the midst of an escape attempt, he heard the click and beep of a set of restraints locking onto his wrists.

"Those boys will be out here to get you in just a bit. You'll be fine," Silo assured him.

"Good job spotting the downed man," Garotte said. "Grab the authentication badge, would you?"

Most of the high-risk equipment in a given facility these days was access controlled via biometrics. Fingerprints and eye scans were incredibly secure, and since it was fairly difficult to accidentally leave your hands and eyes in your other pants, the means of access were always available. The method was not perfect, though, and it was in places such as this that the primary difficulty became obvious. Guards wore face masks and gloves, meaning they would have to at least partially remove their equipment every time they needed to unlock a door. There were ways around this, but almost all of them involved reintroducing the same security risks that biometrics were meant to solve. In Millbrook, a combination of key codes and wireless badges were used. The badges were simple enough to steal. As for the codes?

"This young lady had the kindness and decency to save your life, my boy. I'd say that the least you could do is let her know your access code," Garotte said.

"I . . . I can't do that," he stammered.

"If you do, I'll stop," Garotte said.

"Stop what?"

"This."

He leaned hard on the injured calf. After an agonized scream, the guard spat out a seven-number sequence.

"Many thanks, my boy. Now, you do realize that if this is the lock-out code, I'm going to have to come back and do that again."

The guard flinched. Garotte pivoted his foot over the injured calf again.

"Eight-eight-three-four-three-six-seven!" the guard squeaked.

"Thatta boy. When this is all over, grab yourself a copy of Mental Focus and Discipline by K. Jennings. Excellent introduction to interrogation resistance techniques. You could benefit from a few chapters of The Science and Application of Deception by C. Lightman as well. It'll help you get rid of that flinch," Garotte advised.

"Don't feel bad, hon. You were just in the wrong place at the wrong time," Silo said gently, grabbing him by his collar and dragging him along behind her. "You're Willis, right? You usually work the east wing. Do me a favor, Willis--when you take your smoke break, do it *all* the way in the stairwell. I could smell it in my cell."

"You know, for an improvised plan, that really went quite well," Garotte said, as he causally applied the code and the badge, opening the door of the nearest shuttle. "Only one casualty, and, really, we'll chalk that up to learning experience for our boy here. Minimal collateral damage. Getting into and out of the orbital section might be a bit of a task, but all things considered, I'm quite pleased with . . ."

A low, distinctive sound drew his attention to the badly damaged hangar doors. What he heard sounded like a small hovercar idling, or perhaps a shuttlecraft at a great distance. What he saw was a sleek, somewhat curious-looking spaceship hovering just outside the doors. It was nearly as large as the mobile home-sized Armistice that had brought him here, but was sporting a full complement of weaponry. An alphanumeric designation on the nose had mostly been worn away, but just visible were the letters NX.

"Spoke too soon," he remarked, before turning and crying, "Cover, now!"

Garotte dove behind one of the sturdy support columns, followed by Silo and their unwilling guest. An instant later, a salvo of powerful energy shots lanced into the hangar. The mounted guns of the attacking ship swept back and forth, punching holes in the hulls of shuttles and carving deep divots into the rear wall.

"Who the heck is that!?" Silo yelled.

"That would be a representative of the group responsible for taking the inventor! Unless I've missed my guess, they are responsible for the power outage as well!" Garotte replied.

"If they're terrorists, then I'm not pulling any punches," she proclaimed.

Silo took advantage of a brief lull in the barrage to roll to the still-intact weapon chest and withdraw the heavy rifle and a pair of clips. When no follow-up attack came, she reached in and pulled out a second gun, placing it on the floor and shoving it with her heel toward Garotte. With considerable effort, he managed to raise it enough to be useful.

"You've got the better cover. On three, let her loose," Silo recommended.

"Will do," Garotte said, turning to the restrained guard beside him. "You'd better hope your superiors didn't cut any corners on their firepower, my boy."

"One--two--three!"

With all of the strength he could muster, Garotte raised the rifle and fired a few shots at the ship. Never before had he been so relieved that energy weapons had virtually no recoil. The bolts passed through the space that had previously been occupied by the hangar doors, but before they reached the ship, a faint blue shimmer of shield dispersed them.

"No good. We're going to need to find a way to hit it harder than that!" Garotte managed before the ship started to return fire.

He ducked further down behind the support column, itself behind a shuttle. The vehicle and structure combined managed to keep the ship's weapons from turning him into a cloud of embers. Another thirty seconds of continuous bombardment reduced most of the contents of the hangar into mangled twists of molten and scorched metal before a fizzling pop indicated that something had gone horribly wrong with the plasma cannons. Had Garotte and Silo taken any less care in their choice of cover, they would have been killed halfway through the barrage. As it was, the two partners and the restrained guard were occupying two of the only undamaged patches of floor.

Garotte and Silo remained perfectly silent. The downed guard did not. Finally, Garotte pulled him face to face.

"Listen, my boy," he whispered, just barely louder than the creak and sputter of cooling metal going on around them, "what you just heard was a plasma emitter failure. If we don't make a sound, then when they land and send a scout party to see if we survived, it will take time to find us. That will give us options. If we continue to make noise, it won't take them long to figure out where to point their guns. Do you want that?"

The guard's eyes opened wide and he shook his head.

"Smart boy. Also, you may want to take a look at Post-Traumatic Stress Disorder: The Path to Recovery by E. Cummings. It should help you get over this little incident."

For a moment, all was still. The only sounds were the hiss and collapse of damaged equipment and the unnervingly quiet sound of the attack ship's engines as it hovered and scanned the area.

The guards who had evacuated the hangar had wisely retreated much further into the facility, which left the ship as the only concern, at least for the moment. A vertical red line projected from a node beneath the nose of the ship and initiated a deep scan, sweeping slowly across the interior. The ship drifted steadily back and forth, attempting to get line of sight on as much of the hangar as possible, but those hidden within kept themselves carefully out of sight, though this was somewhat complicated for Garotte, who had to tug and shift the unfortunate Willis along with him. Finally, the ship lowered down, crunching to the icy concrete. A large door opened and a trio of troops cautiously marched out, mismatched and highly unique-looking weapons held ready and oxygen masks firmly in place.

Garotte carefully glanced through a hole in the shuttle that was serving as his cover. With a short sequence of hand signals, he communicated his findings: three men, searching; one pilot; one gunner; three men in reserve. These men clearly had training, showing every crevice that was even remotely large enough to conceal a hostile target all due suspicion. Unfortunately, with the burned-out wrecks of eight different shuttles to choose from, there was plenty of possible cover to check out.

As the search approached Garotte's position, he held perfectly still and readied the cane.

The instant a foot came into view, he hooked the ankle and yanked the soldier off his feet, sending him to the ground faster and harder than his mind had been trained to anticipate. The other two men burst into motion, but the cane was quickly reversed and fired, sending a chunk of glass through the front and back of the first soldier's armor with little regard for the meat between. A blast from Silo's heavy rifle had even less trouble dealing with his partner.

Those in the ship scrambled to ready the on-board weapons, but with the shields down, a quick shot from the rifle opened up a hole in the pilot window and the pilot. Garotte quickly scooped up a grenade from the belt of the struggling soldier and tossed it. He, too, hadn't properly adjusted to the irregular gravity of the planet, as a toss intended for the interior of the ship instead bounced and rolled well short. Fortunately for him--and unfortunately for the attackers--the reserve troops had chosen that moment to mobilize and were virtually standing on the weapon when it detonated. Two more cane shots took care of the downed soldier and the navigator, and, just like that, the crisis was over.

Garotte took a deep breath of the oxygen and tried to rub some life into his numb hands, surveying the molten, charred wreck of a hangar around him.

“This is somewhat closer to the outcome I had been expecting,” he said appreciatively, holding his hands over a still-glowing chunk of former transport ship to warm them.

“Every last shuttle is ruined,” Silo said. “How are we supposed to get to the orbital section?”

“Does this place have a secondary hangar?” Garotte asked Silo.

She slung the heavy rifle over her shoulder by its strap, bent low, and hoisted the injured guard from the ground.

“Well? How 'bout it, hon?”

“Th-there's an off-site hangar. It h-h-has assault craft. Short-range. Might get you to orbit,” he answered quickly, his voice shaking as much from fear as from the cold.

“Thanks, sweetheart. How far, and which way?”

“It's--” Willis began.

“Over that way, just a bit over the horizon, I'd say,” Garotte said, pointing through one of the many holes in the wall.

In the distance, dust could be seen rising from the icy, barren ground, as one of the aforementioned assault crafts blazed toward them. It was small, a one-seat vessel, and rather meager as gunships go, but that didn't mean much. On a planet with no other vehicles but the now-devastated shuttles, it was by far the fastest and toughest piece of equipment in town.

“I suppose someone got a message out. That *will* complicate matters,” Garotte said, scratching his chin.

Both he and Silo looked to the damaged ship that had nearly killed them.

“Care to see how rugged the military builds its prototypes these days?” he asked.

“I don't see any other options,” she said.

While Garotte rushed to the ship and set about removing the remnants of the previous crew, Silo dragged Willis to one of the doors to the rest of the facility that was at least marginally intact, and propped him up against it.

“You stay warm now, hon. I'm sure they'll be out to get you soon,” she said.

“Quickly please,” Garotte said over the ship's external speakers.

Silo stepped over the scattered remains of the recipients of Garotte's poorly-thrown grenade, scooping up one or two of the more intact weapons and casting a doubtful look at the side of the ship. The force of the blast had embedded a scattered handful of shrapnel into the hull plates, and buckled one of them. A motor on the door sparked and groaned.

“What's the status?” she asked, taking her place in the navigator's seat.

“Hull integrity is compromised. Emergency atmosphere retention force fields are entirely missing . . . it doesn't even look like they had been installed--at least, not into the control software.”

“Are there any pressure suits?”

“Just the ones on the soldiers, and they look a bit leaky at this point.”

“So this ship won't be taking us into orbit, then.”

“The engines are still fairly intact. We can make it, we would just be exposed to a hard vacuum.”

“Well, get us up and moving. We'll try to lose the pursuit craft, then see if we can rig up a fix for the hull or get our hands on a different ship.”

“I am way ahead of you,” he said. The engines flared and the ship lurched quickly off of the ground. There was a ponderous, lagging nature to the maneuvering that didn't speak well for the control system. He struggled with them for a bit, finally getting the ship pointed roughly where he wanted it to go. "This isn't going to be the most graceful of escapes."

Wind whistled through the hole in the windshield as their speed increased, and more of it howled in through the dangling side hatch. Repeated attempts to close it revealed that both the latch and the motors involved in sealing it were no longer cooperating, only managing to pull it halfway shut. The combination of the two holes was causing a dangerously freezing wind to rush through the ship.

"S-s-see if you can get the heaters on, will you?" Garotte requested, as he tried desperately to keep his hands steady enough to keep the ship on course.

"Working on it," Silo said, punching various commands into the unfamiliar control system. Its patchwork and thoroughly unfinished nature was one of the stronger pieces of evidence that this ship was never intended to be in regular use. Dials and indicators far too small for the panel that they were mounted to ticked off vital data, while a generic datapad served as the only input and display device for the system's more complex components. Finally, she managed to dig up the environmental screen and max out the heating. Vents belched out scalding air, but it was only just barely sufficient to convince Garotte that his nose and ears weren't going to snap off.

Next, she found the sensor suite and activated it.

"Can you get this thing to go any faster?" she asked.

"I'm surprised I'm able to keep it from dragging along the ground. The engines are fine, but these controls are downright temperamental. I take it our pursuer is gaining?"

"Keeping pace, but probably keeping its distance. That little ship is no match for this one--or, at least, it wouldn't be if we hadn't punched a few holes in this thing first. Still, we'll never lose him like this. And before you ask, shooting him down is an absolute last resort. That man is just doing his job. He's not a soldier, he's a guard."

"See if you can find some way to get a force field on, then. Something to get this ship airtight again. I have a hard time believing anyone would willingly travel through space in a ship that didn't have a safety system."

Silo dug through the control screens.

"They seem to have all of the power hookups and field interface ports occupied, but not with a force field generator. I'll look at the access panel," she said, making her way to the one piece of the ship's interior that was clearly marked, a yellow-striped panel labeled "*Primary System Access.*"

Two quick twists undid the fasteners and she pulled the hatch away, revealing a roughly constructed mechanism with a laser-etched label.

"Does '*Electromagnetic Obfuscation Field Generator*' mean anything to you?" she asked.

"Electro--are you serious? It is a damned cloaking device! Figure out how to turn it on!" he stammered.

She rushed back to the controls and searched for something that might be related to a cloaking device. Finally she found a menu marked '*EOFG Prototype Diagnostic Mode.*' She activated it, only to be met with an authorization screen.

"What did you just do!?" Garotte asked desperately.

"I tried to activate the device. It wants an access code."

"It must have tripped a security failsafe, the controls aren't responding at all anymore! Cancel!"

"I can't! And there is a timer counting down!"

"What sort of countdown?"

"We are in a stolen military ship, fiddling with a gosh-darn prototype! What sort of countdown do you *think* it is!?"

"Right. Self-destruct. This entire mission has gone a bit pear-shaped," Garotte grumbled. "I may have to do something distasteful and of questionable usefulness."

"Is it more useful than flying a damaged ship until they manage to shoot us down or it self-destructs? Because right now it looks like that's what we've got to choose from."

"More useful, perhaps, but not much more pleasant, from my point of view," he said, digging out his slidepad and reluctantly declaring, "Open com Ma."

Silo raised an eyebrow as the device bleeped and began negotiating a connection.

"Start looking into how to detach that cloaking device. I very much doubt we'll be getting any help, and maybe pulling the plug will cancel the alert," he said, nervously eying the rapidly approaching mountain range in the distance. If he couldn't get control over the ship again, it was not immediately apparent whether it would be the countdown or the cliff that would claim them first.

The slidepad beeped, displaying the words, "Hello, Garotte. Please state mission status."

"I've got Silo and I am in a disabled vessel with inactive controls. It will not survive deep space and is set to self-destruct in . . ." Garotte stated, gesturing at Silo.

"One hundred-seventy seconds," she supplied, after peering over her shoulder at the screen.

The device beeped again, this time reading, "Keep communications open and stand by."

"Who exactly are we in communication with?" Silo asked, abandoning the thus-far failed attempts to finesse the cloaking module out of its sockets in favor of wrenching madly at it.

"Do you remember the AI that takes care of Karter's lab?"

"Yes."

"And do you remember that smelly little beast he used to wear like a scarf?"

"Yes."

"Well, it is simultaneously both of them and neither of them."

"That doesn't make any sense."

"None whatsoever," he agreed.

A tone from the ship's sensors drew Silo's attention. She briefly stalled her attempts to excavate the cloaking device in order to investigate the screen.

"A medium-sized ship is heading in our direction. It doesn't seem to be armed."

"Make and model?"

"Mobius something. I'm not good with ships."

"That's our girl!" he proclaimed. "I'll be damned. She must have been nearby. Keep working at that module. I'll get the door open."

He approached the partially-closed door and, somewhat optimistically, tried the controls for it. When they did not respond, he took a more direct approach, snagging one of the burly-looking guns Silo had snatched from the defeated attackers and firing three quick shots, completely detaching the door and sending it spiraling to the disquietingly close surface of the planet. A moment later, Silo managed to tear the cloaking module and a considerable amount of the associated circuitry free. The countdown continued, and the control lock remained.

Outside the door, the landscape was whipping along at a terrifying rate, and in the distance, the Armistice was just becoming visible. It was navigating in very rigid, measured movements, the telltale signs of a low-quality autopilot maneuvering based on sensor data. As it drew steadily nearer, aligning one of its side cargo doors with the opened hatch, Garotte found an equipment bag left behind by the former owners of the ship. He stuffed the cane and the liberated cloaking device inside, along with the other equipment they had been able to gather, and pulled the straps tight.

"Navigation synchronized. Please maintain course and speed," came the synthesized voice of Ma's slidepad over the public address system of the ship.

"Like I have a bloody choice!" Garotte growled into his own slidepad.

"I will extend the cargo arm. Secure yourself to it and I will retract. For safety, please do so individually."

"I'm used to the gravity," Silo said, "I'll take the equipment and go first."

"You'll get no argument from me," Garotte replied.

The pair quickly strapped the bag to Silo's back. All the while, the viciously cold air ripped through the cabin and robbed the feeling from fingers, faces, and any exposed skin. The spindly cargo arm extended and the Armistice maneuvered closer. Finally, the stubby wing of the rescue craft scraped the hull of the stolen ship, and the tip of the arm was a few inches outside the hatch. With a deep breath, Silo held tight to the frame of the hatch, swung out, and wrapped her fingers around the claw of the arm. The metal was cold enough to burn her skin, but she held tight, releasing the hatch from the other hand and hooking her arm over the gripper.

Slowly and carefully, the arm retracted, dragging her out into the open space between the ships and exposing her to the full force of the wind. The arctic blast stung at her face and threatened to tear her from the gripper, but she clenched her teeth, shut her eyes, and clamped down tighter. Suddenly, the wind dropped away. She opened her eyes to find herself dangling an inch or two above the floor of the cargo bay of the Armistice. A shimmering red force field flickered between the cargo bay and cockpit, no doubt to keep the oxygen from escaping. From what she could see, both the pilot and passenger seats were empty. The only thing in the entire control cabin was a familiar furry creature perched unsteadily on the dash. It turned its head to her and nodded once before tapping at a screen.

"I . . . what? This . . . why?" Silo stammered, her mind not quite up to the task of assembling any coherent thoughts just yet.

The arm slowly began to extend again. Inside the stolen ship, Garotte anxiously watched as the countdown dropped down into the double digits. At this point, it seemed that it would indeed be the ship's self-destruct that would win the race, as the mountains were still a fair distance away. The arm took its sweet time getting closer. Just when it was nearly fully extended, however it began to drift backward, the Armistice slowly lagging behind.

"What!? No!" Garotte yelped, holding the slidepad to his mouth, "You're drifting! Increase speed!"

There was no reply. The ship simply slowly eased backward until the cockpit window was aligned with the hatch. A tiny black and white head appeared in the window, making eye contact before tapping at something.

"Garotte, our interactions to this point have suffered from a marked lack of civility, and you have demonstrated extreme reluctance to cooperate with even the most reasonable and sensible requests. I had warned that this behavior would not be without consequence."

"What the hell are you saying?"

"I believe that now would be an excellent time to reassess your prior judgments regarding my effectiveness, usefulness, and value. Perhaps you would like to adjust your attitude for our future interactions."

"Now is most certainly *not* the time!"

"I'm sorry. I appear to be having trouble realigning the ships."

Garotte clenched his fists until his knuckles popped.

"Fine! We will discuss this later. Just get me out of this ship."

"Stand by."

In seconds, the ships were properly aligned and the arm was as near to the door as physically possible. Garotte wasted no time in latching onto it. The arm began to retract, but his feet had only just left the floor of the stolen ship when it became clear that his arms weren't going to be up to the task of fighting both the overly enthusiastic gravity of Manticore and the vicious wind for very long. The arm retracted as quickly as possible without jarring him free, but it wasn't going to be quick enough. Fingers that were already well on their way to being numb even before he was exposed to the brunt of the wind were all but useless, and he didn't have the strength to haul a body that felt like it was three hundred pounds into a more secure position. He began to slowly, inevitably lose his grip.

Silo watched helplessly as Garotte's hold on the arm began to slip. She held tight to the edge of the cargo doorway and leaned as far as she could, but he was still out of reach. From the control cabin, Ma watched with equal anxiety, focusing her sharp eyes on the approaching tragedy and calculating her options. Her paw hovered over a queued command for the arm. Finally, she came to a decision, tapping it into action--and not a second too soon.

Garotte lost his grip, but before his arm was completely clear of the manipulator arm's gripper, it snapped shut around his wrist. The intention had been to gently clutch at his arm, but "gentle" has an entirely different meaning to a cargo loading arm. Thus, while it didn't quite pulverize the bone, it came awfully close. Garotte's forearm made an unpleasant creaking sound, and his scream of panic turned to a scream of pain. Now, with no more fear of him falling, Ma retracted the arm more quickly before awkwardly banking the ship and angling it skyward. When the door sealed, the gripper released and Garotte tumbled to the floor. A moment later, the inertial dampeners took the edge off of the acceleration and Silo managed to help him to a seat while he cradled his arm.

"Are you okay? How's your arm?" Silo asked with concern.

"I suppose it could be worse," Garotte replied. He attempted to wiggle his fingers and, to his great relief, discovered that he was able to do so.

"Please secure yourselves. The experimental ship is set to detonate in twenty-three seconds," Ma began. Before she finished, a distant flash of light lit up the interior of the ship, followed by a thumping explosion that pitched the Armistice nearly sideways, spilling Ma off of the dash. The ship's autopilot corrected, allowing her to gather her pad, scramble back to the dash, and swipe out, "I apologize. It took some time to prepare that warning. Stand by while I set course, and please await oxygen levels to reach optimum values before removing your oxygen masks. Thank you."

With that, Ma turned back to the controls, leaving Silo and Garotte to slowly recover from their ordeal.

#

Shortly afterward, in Purcell's space station, the commander was in her quarters, sitting in darkness. This operation was going poorly and, until she received new information, there was little to do but consider the current operations and create contingency plans. That required deep thought, and she'd always found that she did her best thinking in isolation. When on a planet, she would seek out the wilderness. On a space station, her darkened quarters were the best she could manage.

A soft beep and a dim flicker from her datapad interrupted her contemplation. She tapped the screen to be greeted by the face of the perpetually nervous Crewman Marx.

"There is new information regarding the surveillance squad assigned to Millbrook," he said.

"Report. Have they neutralized the situation?"

"Negative. After they caused the communications blackout, we were unable to establish direct contact, as expected. However, the communication has just been restored, and we still have not received a report. The modified transponder we've been using to track the ship doesn't even seem to be transmitting."

"Then we must assume the ship was destroyed or captured," Purcell reasoned angrily.

"That is likely. Emergency band radio chatter from the prison following the restoration of communications indicates there was a massive explosion visible in the direction of the ship's last known trajectory along the surface. A pursuit ship found wreckage. The prison guards seem to have captured both of our internal agents as well."

Purcell released a hissing breath. "Any additional information?"

"The prison officials also report recovering the remains of all eight members of the surveillance squad. Witnesses indicate that the squad was killed by the escaped inmate and her accomplice. The escapees were last seen piloting the squad's ship prior to its destruction."

"Were the targets still piloting the ship when it was destroyed?"

"The report from the prison officials states that their investigation of the wreckage is ongoing, but inconclusive. However, shortly before the detonation, the pursuit ship reported a sensor signature of an unidentified ship. It left monitored space shortly after leaving Manticore's atmosphere."

"We have to assume that they escaped. Rally any field agents in the vicinity of the remaining surveillance teams as backup. And get a message to the assault team. Give them the strike order. I want that alloy, now . . ."

Chapter 17

In the meantime, things on Tessera had been considerably less exciting, at least as far as threat to life and limb were concerned. After a night spent almost entirely in bed but doing very little sleeping, Lex was given a VIP tour of the hurricane that was Michella's daily convention routine. He was introduced to at least two hundred people whose names he had already forgotten. Michella was reluctantly coaxed into sitting in on a panel about science coverage, though it rapidly became clear that as much as she excelled at investigation and communication, once academic matters dominated the conversation, she became conspicuously quiet, absorbing information and nodding appreciatively. After that was a few hours of walking the floor, during which Lex became acutely aware of the disproportionate number of males among her devotees.

He liked to think that he wasn't the jealous type. That said, all the men foolish enough to ask him to snap a picture would later discover that Lex's finger had a strange tendency to sneak into the shot.

This was the first time Lex had been given such a close-up look at celebrity from the outside, and he wasn't terribly pleased with the memories it was bringing back. Lex had loved being a celebrity. He'd loved everything about it. There were never any introductions when he was famous; people already knew h name. Granted, he'd never been hugely famous on a galactic level, but back on Golana, he had been top of the heap, and word had been getting around. Now, of the hundreds of people he'd met and shook hands with, only three actually remembered him--and even then, it was only for the coverage they had done on his downfall.

He'd always known that the media had a short memory, but until now he had been able to fool himself that there were at least some people out there who remembered the pair of speed records he'd set, and the unmatched speed at which he'd ascended the hover sled rankings. This little experience was the final nail in the coffin of that particular notion. More disturbing than his realization of just how far from fame he had fallen was the realization of just how much he missed it. The irony of the fact that his role in the Bypass Gemini Incident would be a surefire, albeit suicidal, route to galactic celebrity was not lost on him, either.

Following a few hours on the show floor, and with considerable nudging from Lex, Michella was finally able to convince herself that she had fulfilled her convention duties for the day. They excused themselves to the Pavilion, seeking out the nearest place to eat that wasn't completely overflowing with convention patrons. It turned out to be the juice bar outside the fitness center. Michella found a semi-private table while Lex fetched two glasses of juice composed of guava, kiwi, papaya, pomegranate, and at least three other fruits that, as far as he knew, existed exclusively in juice form. He also picked up a few pastries labeled "high-energy, low-calorie health cookies," evidently invented by someone seeking to set the world record for most inherent contradictions in a single product.

"So, tomorrow you've got that keynote, then you're heading home, right?" Lex asked, handing Michella her paradoxical cookie and beverage.

"That's the plan," she said.

"I don't suppose you're open to hitching a ride with me in the trusty *S.O.B.*?"

"Much as I'd love to spend a few days in a cramped cockpit, trying to figure out how to use that . . . receptacle without making a mess, washing with napkins, and eating food out of a tube--"

"Hey! This time it's granola bars."

"Oh, well, that changes everything."

"Come, on. It'd be fun."

"I've already got the reservations for the return flight, babe. Sorry."

"Yeah, yeah. You know, that excuse is only going to work so many times. Mark my words, you and I will take a long ride in the *Son of Betsy* one of these days."

"Sure we will, honey," she said, with the same tone of voice one might use to promise one's daughter a pony for her birthday. "Why are you so insistent?"

Lex took a long sip of his juice and listened to his conversation with Ma echo through his thoughts. "Well, to be honest, there's been something on my mind lately. Things are busy here. Lots of distractions. I was hoping we could talk a few things out without any phone calls or photo shoots or groupies."

"*You* wanted to talk?" she said in disbelief. Suddenly her eyes widened and she began to dig through her purse.

"Yeah. I mean, when's the last time we spent more than a day or two together?"

"Last month we . . . no, no, I had that interview with the Prime Minister's attendant. But a couple of weeks before that, we were supposed to do something, weren't we?"

"Yeah, but a delivery ran long and I was stuck on Earth's moon waiting for payment."

"That's right. Well, it can't have been *too* long before that," she said, before muttering, “Where is it?”

“Don't you think a couple shouldn't have to check their calendars to know when their last date was?”

“We've both been busy, that's all. Things will calm down.”

“Will they?” he asked, staring intently at his cookie, rather than look her in the eye. “I mean, you've been doing great, and business is pretty steady for me, too. It seems like it is going to get worse before it gets better. Something's gotta give, right? Things can't keep going like they've been going. One of us is going to have to . . . Michella?”

“Ah-*ha*!” she proclaimed, looking up. “I'm sorry, what were you saying?”

“Never mind. It's stupid. We'll talk about it later. What were you digging for, anyway . . . oh.”

She triumphantly removed a small steno pad and a ballpoint pen.

“It's that time, is it?” Lex asked.

“That it is,” she said, clicking out the pen's nib and flipping to a clean page.

Michella was a thoroughly modern girl in most ways, but when it came to matters she thought were really important, or extremely confidential, she always reverted to old-fashioned pen and paper. It was actually something she had in common with Karter, who did all of his thinking on paper as well. Lex genuinely hoped it was the only thing that they had in common.

“So, do you want to start? Or do you want the full interview experience?”

“I'll start, I guess . . .” he said, knowing all too well that there would be no shifting her back to the prior conversation. To be frank, he was rather relieved to be setting the subject of their relationship aside for now. Discussing relationship troubles didn't come easily to him. “Let's see . . . well, remember Squee?”

“That fancy dog? Oh, Trevor, don't tell me you got that little cutie involved.”

“As a matter of fact, she got *me* involved.”

Michella scratched something down, then nodded for him to continue. “You said an old friend had dropped her off. Is he involved?”

“Yeah. Basically he . . . in a roundabout way, he sent her to get me.”

“That requires a bit more explanation.”

“I'm kind of in a tough spot here.”

“How so?”

“Because I know you won't settle for anything but the truth, but you also won't settle for anything but a plausible explanation, and I can't give you both.”

“You don't think the truth is plausible?”

“Not to a sane person.”

“Well, let's try the truth and see how sane I am.”

“If you say so. Squee is a genetic experiment made by that mad scientist who helped me out with that little incident a few months ago. She has had her brain formatted as temporary storage for the scientist's AI. She--the AI, not Squee, though they are sort of the same thing at the moment--she came to get me to help her to spring a criminal, who also worked with the scientist, out of jail. That guy, who never told me his name, was going to get together a few other members of the scientist's old cronies and rescue him from the folks who took him. Oh, and they took him so they could have him build them a weapon that could nuke the power grid of a whole star system at once. And he'll probably do it, because he's an absolute sociopath."

Michella finished taking down the notes. She then looked over the words, as though searching for holes. "How did you help to free this criminal?"

"She got him on a transport ship, got me on that ship, and then caused it to fail. She had *S.O.B.* waiting at the transfer station it stopped at, unlocked his restraints, and much running resulted."

She nodded and took down the additional information.

"And do you have any further role in this?"

"I was supposed to, but they had me in a more overtly violent role than I'd feel comfortable playing."

Once she was through taking notes, she sucked her teeth and pursed her lips.

"I think you're right. I might be too sane for this story."

"Told you."

"Look at me," she said, placing her pen down on her book and leaning forward.

With a sigh, he leaned forward until his nose was almost touching hers. As he stared into her gorgeous blue eyes, they peered back, studying and measuring.

"This is my favorite part of the whole lie detector routine, you know," Lex said.

Michella was one of those people who believed that all you ever needed to do to determine if someone was lying was give them a good, hard look in the eye. Lex was of the opinion that this was a ridiculous old wives' tale and couldn't possibly be true. For the most part, he was right. A quick eye exam hadn't really been sufficient to get to the bottom of any of her major stories and investigations. It did, however, have an almost perfect success rate against Lex. So much so, in fact, that he seldom even tried to put one over on her anymore. Honesty was the best policy--but, in his case, he told the truth mostly because it was easier, and because lying only ever managed to get her to dig her teeth in, which seldom ended well. When her brow furrowed, he grinned and kissed her on the nose.

"You're telling the truth . . ."

"Yeah, I know. What a shocker, huh?"

She snatched her pen back up and scratched a few more lines.

"This scientist, is he in any danger?"

"I generally consider him to be the source of danger in any situation he's involved in."

"I'm being serious, Trevor."

"So am I."

"Are the authorities involved?"

"Probably. Though Ma says she's tried to keep them out so they won't try to lock up the scientist."

"Ma?"

"That's what he calls his AI system."

She flipped back through her notes, reading through them as though they'd been written by someone else.

"My god, Trevor, you helped a criminal escape," she whispered.

"Oh . . . that . . . it happened kind of fast. I'm not one hundred percent sure I broke any laws . . . I . . . might have been a hostage."

"Might have been!?"

"He was very charismatic."

"How did you help him get away?"

"By being Trevor Alexander," he said flatly. "Me plus *S.O.B.* equals a clean getaway."

"You still haven't explained the bandages."

"Yes, I did, that was from deGrasse. The con needed to get dropped off there. It is a tough neighborhood. Drugs and such. They tried to rob me. A fight ensued. I won."

"What happened after that?"

"I dropped him off on Maxis, then I came here."

"And where did this criminal go after?"

"I don't really know and, frankly, I'm happier that way."

"How could I not have heard about this?" she asked, more to herself than Lex. She dug out her slidepad and brought up a few sites. "Yep, it is all right here. 'Escaped convict. No video footage. Highly-skilled escape.' That's it. No more conventions. Too distracting. Is there any way that this is going to find its way back to you?"

"No, absolutely not. Ma was very careful about that. She picked a place with no surveillance and no monitoring. I don't even think they have a record of *S.O.B.* docking."

"You sure place an awful lot of faith in this computer program."

"You seemed to like her. You let her lick your ear," he remarked, leaning closer to add quietly, "Usually you only let me do that."

"Trevor, this is serious," she hissed, slamming the pen down.

"I know. I know that this is an unholy mess that I had no business being a part of. That's why I bowed out. It is in more capable hands now."

"Why would you even involve yourself in the first place?"

"You haven't seen what this guy can do, Michella. He could be bad news in the wrong hands. I had to do something."

Michella was silent for a few seconds, glancing anxiously over her notes as she rested her elbows on the table and clutched at her fingers. It was clear that she was lost, her brain struggling to cope with the madness it was now being asked to process. She floundered for a firm mental footing for a moment and, finding none, reverted to her mental default: when in doubt, do what you do best. She picked up her pen once more, composed herself, and looked to Lex.

"Do you know anything about the kidnappers?"

"Not a whole lot. I only got a look at some low-quality footage--"

"There is video? Can you get your hands on it?" she urged with blood-in-the-water focus.

"What? No. Ma had that stuff. And she's pretty busted up. I'm not sure she'd be able to send it now . . . though she did load the videos onto her slidepad before--"

"Can you have her send them to you? I'll need to speak to her as well, if possible. And I'll--"

"Michella, I'm out of this mess, remember? Because of how dangerous it was? Weren't you *just* worried about this finding its way back to me?"

"That was Michella the girlfriend worried about Trevor the boyfriend. Now that she has said her piece, it is Michella the reporter's turn to talk to Trevor the primary source, and she smells a story that might just beat what she's been working on lately. Now, if you know where--"

Lex reached across the table, took her hands in his, and looked her in the eyes.

"Listen. I can appreciate your professional curiosity, but this is too hot to touch. I mean, *I* wasn't willing to stick with it, and you and I both know that my tastes run a bit closer to the suicidal end of the spectrum than is really healthy. So let's just relax, enjoy these last few all-expenses-paid days on this paradise of a planet, and let that scientist and the chaos and destruction that inevitably surrounds him stay far, far away, where they belong."

Michella opened her mouth to speak, but before she could make a sound, a vicious violet flash flooded the whole of the eatery with blinding light. Gasps and cries rang out as the others in the juice bar and gym rushed to the nearest window, where a faint halo of residual light could still be seen lingering high in the sky.

"What the hell was that!?" Lex said, jumping to his feet.

"It think it was an explosion in the high atmosphere!" Michella guessed. Her slidepad was already in her hands, feverishly bringing up her quick-dial list.

"You'd expect an explosion that big to make some sort of loud s--"

The laws of physics, with their flawless comedic timing, managed to cut Lex off with a thundering blast of sound as the shock wave lagged behind the light of the explosion. It was a resounding thump that rattled the walls, followed by a rolling, modulating series of echoes, like the planet had been punched in the gut and was struggling to get its breath. Lex turned to Michella, but she had the slidepad held up, snapping a picture. A moment later, a call finished connecting.

"Jon! We're in the ground-floor fitness center at the Pavilion, are you nearby?" she said.

"Uh, sort of. I'm down by the garage," came the voice of her clearly shaken assistant over the connection.

"Good. Bring the rental car around."

"What just happened, Ms Modane?"

"We are going to find out. Get here quick," she said, closing the connection and heading for the door. "Come on, Trev."

"Whoa, hey, hold on a second," Lex said, trying to get his brain back up to speed. "What are you planning to do?"

"That explosion, do you have any idea what might cause that?"

"No, I don't. I'm not an expert in explosions. Where are we going?"

"I'll have to do an image search on that picture. The news database might have a near match," she muttered under her breath, working at her device for a few moments before addressing Lex. "We're going to go find out what happened. How far away would you suppose that was?"

"Uh, I don't know. It looks like it was over the college quarter, but it is pretty hard to tell. It was awfully far up. Slow down, what do you mean we are going to find out? You aren't thinking of driving *toward* that explosion, are you?"

"Me? No. I'm thinking I'll pull up as much research about it as I can in the next few minutes, then get in front of the camera and talk about it while *you* drive toward it."

"That's a bad idea. You don't drive toward explosions. You drive away from explosions and wait for someone to tell you about them."

"Trevor, the press don't have the luxury of waiting until someone tells them what is happening. We are the ones who need to do the telling," she said, shouldering her way with purpose through the increasingly chaotic crowd filling the lobby. Somehow, Jon was just pulling the rented hovercar up to the main doors.

"There is a whole convention of press people here! It doesn't need to be *you* that does the telling!"

"No, but it is going to be."

"But you aren't breaking news, you're investigative--"

"It always pays to have the big scoop. I was on financial reporting when I broke my first one, remember?" she said, pushing the door open. "Jon, do we have that law enforcement scanner with us?"

"Yes, Miss--"

"Good, get it out and turn it on. And have we got the video rig in the trunk?"

"Yes, Miss--"

"Do you know how to handle it?"

"I'm a journalism intern. I've spent time behind a camera."

"Good. Pull it out, set it up, and get in the back seat. Trev, get behind the wheel," Michella said, beginning to dig through her purse again.

"Whoa, whoa. What exactly are you expecting me to do?"

Michella held up her hand and shushed. Jon managed to power up the scanner, and the first coherent message came through.

". . . indicate that the weapon discharged near the equatorial low orbit monitoring station was a medium-yield antimatter weapon. A pair of ships have been sighted de-cloaking and entering the atmosphere. Trajectory indicates the destination is Weston University . . ."

"I need you to get this rental to Weston University, and I need you to get it there before any other news crews," she said, continuing her search though her purse.

Lex looked at the rental, an NVS Duchess. It wasn't a speedster, but it was a sturdy piece of machinery, the kind of workhorse that tended to be selected as police cruisers and taxi cabs. These days, the sheer speed of hovercars and the general importance of aerodynamics meant that they couldn't really be made boxy, but the designers had done their very best to do so, regardless. He looked to the skyways. What should have been a hopeless snarl of panicked drivers was still flowing smoothly thanks to the mandatory automated driving. Notably, all traffic was headed away from the explosion, likely as a result of an emergency traffic reroute. A news van, bedecked with transmitters, sensors, and cameras, blasted out of a nearby garage and out over the city, skipping the skyway entirely in favor of a straight shot to the action. He felt his competitive side growl.

Finally, he looked back to Michella. She had found what she was looking for: a stick of chewing gum, which she was holding out for him. He could actually hear his willpower snap.

"I am an adrenaline junkie, and you are an enabler," he said, snatching the gum and pulling her in for a kiss. After dragging it out for as long as he dared, he stuffed the gum in his shirt pocket and made his way to the front of the car. "Pop the hood."

"We don't have time for you to ogle the machinery, Trev."

"Listen, you know press stuff, I know driving stuff. Just pop the hood."

"I'm on it," Jon said, sliding into the driver's seat and tapping the appropriate button.

The hood of the car lifted up, revealing the power system and electronics of the Duchess. Lex swept his eyes over the guts of the hovercar, spotted what he was looking for, and reached down. He grabbed hold of a control node the size of his fist and yanked it free, taking the time to cram a few wires back into the socket that the node left vacant. He then slammed the hood, took the driver's seat, and tossed the node into the back seat, where Michella was doing a bit of frantic primping while Jon took a seat beside her and started assembling the modular camera.

"What is this?" she asked.

"Strictly enforced automated navigation, remember? That means all rentals have an override. If you want to stay in control, you've got to yank it. Found *that* out the hard way. I yanked the transponder wire, too. Better that way," he explained, adjusting the seat and manipulating a few settings in the vehicle's computer. Finally he retrieved the gum, unwrapped it, and shoved it in his mouth. "Okay, baby, here we go. Hope you got the insurance on this sucker."

Lex guided the hovercar into the air and toward the nearest skyway on-ramp.

"Are you sure that the skyway is the best--" Jon began to ask.

"Yes, Jon," Lex said flatly.

"But don't you want to go straight there, like--"

"No, Jon."

"But--"

"Trev knows what he's doing. Just keep the camera running and point it where I tell you. Trev, try to keep it steady," Michella instructed.

"No promises," he said, maxing out the acceleration.

Satisfied that she was presentable, Michella selected a name from her contact list and tapped it, putting the pad to her ear and stowing her glasses while she waited for it to connect. A particularly sudden bit of maneuvering convinced her to wrap her free hand around a grip above the door.

"Yeah, Lou? Michella. You're going to be getting a feed from that spare camera rig you sent along with us. I need you to patch it through to the live feed . . . you'll find out in a minute . . . thanks, Lou," she said, closing the connection. She nodded at Jon while she applied a lapel mic. When she got the thumbs up, she turned on her well-practiced tone of competent concern. "This is Michella Modane for GolanaNet News, reporting live from Tessera, where an unexplained explosion . . ."

Much as Lex would have liked to pay attention to Michella's report, navigation was quickly becoming an issue. Common sense would dictate that, in a vehicle capable of flight, the best way to get someplace you weren't supposed to go would be to fly straight there, as their current rival news crew had opted to do. Lex, who was a bit more skilled in vehicular misbehavior than he should have been, had quickly learned that this was absolutely not the case. Anything above a certain altitude that wasn't in a designated route was instantly flagged for interception, so staying within the proper roads was essential. This was doubly important when an apparent invasion was happening, as the cloaked vehicles would certainly indicate. The last thing he wanted was to have the police or military think they were one of the intruding parties. Thus, Lex was scooting the rented Duchess as quickly as possible through the skyway leading roughly toward Weston University. Brief glimpses between traffic quickly illustrated that they had made the right decision, as a trio of marked police cars corralled and grounded the news van.

While they didn't currently have to worry about law enforcement, the skyway was not a flawless option either. The problem was that every single other vehicle on the road was moving *away* from Weston University, and thanks to the fact that the Rackton Civic Navigation Authority was at the wheel, traffic was able to pack itself far more densely than a bunch of puny human minds could manage. Lex was trying to move against a flow of traffic that was moving in an orderly, steady pace, with barely inches separating one car from the next in some cases. The one thing he had going for him was the fact that cars had radically different shapes and radically different speeds, and thus tended to leave openings as they jostled into optimal position. The task was figuring out where and when such an opening would occur and whether or not he would fit. So far, Lex was fairly successful--as long as you used a fairly generous definition of the word "fit."

He'd swapped paint with half a dozen cars by the time the traffic started to thin out. Now that the last of the traffic that had been on the road at the time of the explosion was behind them, it should be clear sailing for a while. The only vehicles left to worry about were the ones that were too slow to keep up with the emergency evacuation speed, mostly massive service vehicles with a few buses and clunkers tossed in. Lex glanced back to steal a glimpse of Michella doing her thing.

". . . reports indicate that two vessels may be responsible for the blast. The police dispatches mentioned the possibility of cloaking technology being employed. Now that we are clear of traffic, we will try to get a shot of the University Heights section of Outer Rackton, the area nearest to the blast. Get a shot out there, medium optical zoom.

"As you can see, the infrastructure seems fairly untouched, but there appears to be some smoke. The detonation was very high in the atmosphere, so the damage should be minimal, but as you can see from the broken windows, the raw force of the blast must have been considerable. No word yet on what, if anything, was struck directly by this attack, but we will report as soon as the information becomes available," Michella remarked. Her eyes flitted aside. "We will return shortly. Please stand by for additional information."

She motioned for Jon to kill the feed.

"Keep the video and audio rolling. We'll toss the footage to the editors to add to the aggregator version," she commented. "Lex, it looks like we've got company."

"Yeah, I see 'em," Lex said.

Four police cruisers were merging into the skyway from below. Unlike the steady, dependable Duchess, the cars painted with the blue and white police markings were downright fierce. The hood of the car bristled with cooling fins, and an ominous glow flickered within the thrusters jutting out the rear. They were more in line with the sort of machines Lex had gone toe to toe with in his racing days. Trying to outmaneuver them in a rental car was going to be tricky.

"Leave it to Rackton to go top-of-the-line with their cop cars," Lex grumbled.

"Are we . . . are we really going to try to outrun the police?" Jon asked.

"No, Jon. We aren't going to try to outrun the police. We are going to *succeed* in outrunning the police. Right, baby?" Michella said, a devilish grin coming to her face as she tightened up her restraints and held on tight.

"We better. Tesseran traffic laws are *harsh*," Lex said.

"This, uh . . . this car is rented under *my* name," Jon said.

"Well, Jon, you're not getting your deposit back."

The former racer revved the much-abused engine of the rented Duchess to its limits. Below them, the city of Rackton had thinned out from a veritable art gallery of architecture to a sprawling green expanse of gated suburbs. It was a less than ideal environment for losing a superior pursuit vehicle, but if you could choose where to have your chase, you probably wouldn't be getting chased to begin with.

As the police began to organize themselves into an intercept formation, the audio system of the Duchess began blaring an all-too-familiar multilingual warning. Lex clicked the volume off and took a deep breath.

"I hope this is worth it, honey," he said.

The first of the cruisers pulled in tight to try to force him into a pocket blocked out by the others. Lex dropped low and dodged underneath him, tilting the ship downward and dialing back the power. The machine dropped like a rock, passing through the lower edge of the flickering red skyway border and for all outward appearance seeming to be suffering a power failure. Inside the car, a dozen warnings and indicators started going wild, warning him of everything from his careless departure from permitted airspace to the fairly likely collision with the ground that would result. Outside, the sirens and public address systems of the police were quickly coming back into range as the cruisers doubled back.

"Oh, god," Jon said. His voice had the very distinctive tone one uses when there is a danger of something other than words leaving one's mouth.

"Just a little longer," Lex said, watching the ground approach through the windshield.

By the time the police were above him, Lex was already too close to the ground and moving too fast for them to attempt a rescue. There was nothing to do but spread out above him and slow down, trailing behind lest they get caught in what looked to be an inevitable fireball. Lex scanned over the pedestrian park ahead.

"You think I can fit under that footbridge?" he asked.

"What!?" Jon squeaked.

"Yeah, me, too," Lex said, cranking the power.

The free-fall began to level off as the engines labored to get back up to speed. The police realized that they were dealing with a ruse rather than an equipment failure and fell into pursuit again. With a sudden, jarring bounce, the Duchess's repulsors touched ground, parting the grass of a picnic area and launching a trash can aside. Fortunately, the recent blast in the sky had sent the park-goers running for shelter. Even more fortunately, none of those park-goers had selected the low, wide pedestrian bridge ahead as their shelter of choice. Considering the fact that there were no surface roads, the bridge seemed to exist exclusively as a place from which to take pictures. It was also pointlessly long, forming what was practically a short tunnel. Lex was only too glad to give it a secondary role as a high-speed obstacle.

"Think skinny thoughts, everybody!" he said.

A piece of the rental car's bodywork screeched against a decorative safety rail as he barely managed to wedge the sluggish piece of machinery beneath the bridge. Three of the cops pulled aside and tried to position themselves to intercept him on the other side. One remained on his tail just a few moments longer, evidently confident that his hulking powerhouse would be able to follow the mid-sized sedan. When the officer lost his nerve, he nearly lost control of his cruiser as well, obliterating an ornate lamppost in his frenzy to avoid totaling himself on the bridge.

As their friend with poor judgment struggled to get back into the chase, the other police hadn't quite managed to get themselves organized before Lex came rocketing out from beneath the far side of the bridge. He stayed low to the ground, weaving between well-manicured trees and clipping the tops of hedges trimmed into exotic shapes. Not only did the obstacles keep the cops from getting too close, they prevented them from deploying anything from their no doubt comprehensive arsenal of intercept devices. Energy nets, grapples, tractor beams, engine-killers, fancy harpoons with attached retro rockets, and a hundred other gadgets had been dreamed up to take care of the occasional rogue hovercar, but they all required a clear shot and a lot of room. Lex was determined to deny them of both. The more he maneuvered, the better a feel he got for the specific quirks of his vehicle. Sharp turns became surgical, his path threading an insane route through anything that might keep the cruisers at bay.

Ahead, University Heights was looming and, with the fraction of his brain not dedicated to daredevil stunts, Lex didn't like what he saw. The first problem he was going to hit was that there was an awfully long stretch of nothing but landscaped meadow between himself and the college buildings. The presence of the meadow probably had more to do with maintaining a picturesque ambiance for pricy institutions that made their home in the Heights than anything intelligent or useful, but that didn't matter. No trees or quaint gazebos meant the cops would be right on top of him until he got into the Heights themselves. It was at that point that the second issue would become his primary concern.

During his hijinks during his last visit to Tessera, Lex had attracted a considerably larger police presence. The fact that only four cruisers were after him now seemed like a fortunate oversight on the part of the traffic department. But now that he could see the Heights, he understood his relatively unmolested status. Even in the short time that had passed since the blast, Rackton had managed to dispatch a veritable army of police to the area--and, on the horizon, the actual army looked to be well on their way. If he'd had a few more moments to think things over, he might have abandoned the idea of finding a way to get into the hornet's nest ahead. Luckily, his emergence onto the obstacle-free home stretch commandeered the remainder of his brain for use in piloting the craft, making all of that pesky "critical thinking" impossible.

As a matter of fact, the only person in the car who seemed to be giving any thought at all to the situation was Jon, and presently he was too terrified to enunciate. He simply held the camera in a death grip, pointing it vaguely wherever Michella's finger was pointing. She was giving instructions, too, but the pounding of his heart in his ears was drowning them out. It was madness. At no point since she'd gotten into the car had Michella shown any indication that she felt her life was in danger. She'd simply held tight, kept her eyes on the destination, and worn an unnervingly exhilarated smile on her face. Now and then, Lex would turn to see how close a trailing police cruiser had gotten, and when he did, his face had the same smile. It was like watching two addicts get their fix.

Finally, after a particularly aggressive maneuver shook a chunk of the trunk lid loose, Jon found his tongue.

"Listen, I think we should--" he began.

"We're coming up on the residence halls in a few seconds--I want you to try to get a shot between them," Michella said excitedly.

"You don't really think we're going to be able to use any of this footage, do you!?"

"We'll pull some stills . . . and crop out the police and the car's interior, I suppose."

"Mr. Alexander, don't you think we've gotten ourselves in enough trouble!?"

"Only if we get caught, Jon," said Lex.

"But won't they--"

"Not really the time to be distracting me with questions, Jon."

"I--but--you're both completely insane!"

"It tends to help in situations like this," Lex said.

The pilot guided the vehicle in a frustrating route between the police cruisers. Without any real cover, he was forced to use his pursuers themselves as cover, slipping behind one of them just as another attempted to force him to the ground. The high-speed pursuit quickly began to resemble a greased pig chase, with the used and abused Duchess proving itself to be surprisingly nimble with Lex at the controls.

It was his hope that one of the cops would eventually deploy something out of desperation, and that said thing would instead trip up one of the other boys in blue. Alas, Rackton had been smart enough to hire competent police officers to go along with their high-end cars. Luckily, the empty meadow had begun to shift to trendy coffee shops, university libraries and study halls, and eventually, the overly ornate and hip residence hall buildings themselves. As was the case with most degree-granting institutions, the on-campus housing ran the gamut from luxurious to prison-like, depending on the financial means of the student. On the expensive end were a handful of buildings that looked to be only slightly less fancy than the Pavilion, each covered in ivy, columns, and Greek letters. The financial aid buildings were big, ugly boxes, squeezed together in tight little rows, and tucked carefully away among some tall, full trees so no one would notice them.

Behind him, Lex watched the pursuing police begin to drop away. They were approaching the campus proper, where what appeared to be the entire remainder of the police department had established a tight cordon, tracing a circle around what was presumably the landing site of the intruders. A small contingent of the police who had gathered ahead were drawing themselves together into a three-dimensional road block. Considering the trouble they'd managed to give each other with only four cruisers involved, the first responders who had trailed him thus far must have decided to back off and give their brethren a clear shot. From the looks of it, they weren't going to take their time about it.

"Everybody strapped in?" Lex asked, watching the police ahead of him adopting the positions one assumes when aiming a vehicle-mounted weapon.

"Yes," Michella said.

"To within an *inch* of my *life!*" Jon replied.

"Good. This is going to be the rough part."

"What was that last five minu--*hurk*!"

His comment was cut short by a sudden upward dodge that heaved the camera rig into his gut. It would seem that the Rackton police department had decided to hedge their bets, providing their officers with a wide assortment of countermeasures that worked at various ranges. It was all Lex could do to dodge the first salvo of nets and harpoons, and no amount of fancy footwork was going to keep the tractor beams from locking on. Already, he could feel the shudder of beams that weren't quite on target. His eyes scanned the surrounding scenery for anything that could provide adequate cover. The ring of police drew a rigid line through the residence area. Not far behind the rearmost of the cars was a grid of rapid-deploy pylons marking off the Do Not Cross line. All he had to do was get to the other side of that grid and the cops probably wouldn't follow. Sure, the *reason* they wouldn't be following was probably a very good one, and likely hinged upon not getting blown to bits by enemy gunships that may or may not have taken control of the campus, but, hey, one problem at a time.

Finally, he spotted the low-cost student housing. The cluster of cops and the Do Not Cross line both passed right over it. Just as a second flurry of high-tech gadgetry was hurled his way, he twisted the car sideways and pushed it for all it was worth. The new orientation threw off the aim of the police, causing most of the better-targeted shots to go wide. A harpoon with a flaring rocket managed to drive itself into one of the rear fenders, but the beating the car had taken caused the whole panel to tear free without so much as slowing Lex down. A few energy nets crackled by his windows, and at least three pieces of equipment Lex couldn't identify whisked by soon after. Then, with a deafening rush of wind, things went dim.

Jon squinted out the driver-side window and saw sky flanked by the tops of boxy-looking buildings. He glanced out the passenger-side window and saw the ruddy ground of an alleyway rushing along at a nauseating speed. Lex shifted the Duchess and slotted it perfectly between two of the tightly-packed dorms. The wind was screaming in their ears, even through the closed windows. Jon shut his eyes tight, realizing that if he stared out the downward-pointing window any longer, he would vomit all over his boss, which, even in his terrified state, seemed like a bad idea. He didn't open them again until the funneled sound of rushing wind dropped away and the car righted itself.

Michella heaved a few exhilarated breaths. “I swear to god, Trev, if these straps weren't holding me down, I'd climb right up there and . . .” She glanced at the still blinking red light on the camera. “We'll discuss it later.”

“We better,” Lex said, easing the ship around a handful of the “trees of shame” before emerging into the section of Rackton so carefully patrolled by the police. His eyes widened.

“Jon,” Michella said steadily, “I want you to keep that camera rolling, no matter what. I want this recorded. This is . . . important.”

Chapter 18

Had Lex and the others been approaching University Heights from a higher altitude--or in any sane way, for that matter--what they were seeing wouldn't have come as a shock. As it was, the state of the university complex was absolutely devastating. The detonation had been little more than a loud sound and a bright light back at the Pavilion, but that was a long way away. The colleges had been directly below the site of the explosion, and the impact was far less superficial. Here and there, buildings were smoking and damaged. There were half-collapsed structures scattered across the campus. From the looks of it, some of the damage had been caused by chunks of debris raining down from above, fragments of whatever it was that had been destroyed by the blast. Most of the destruction was due to countless vehicle collisions. The sidewalks were nearly clear of people. Those who remained out in the open had collapsed, their skin raw, as though they had been doused by scalding water. The few able-bodied people were helping the injured to shelter.

"What the hell happened here?" Jon uttered.

"I guess that flash was a lot worse here. Like . . . instant sunburn or something," Lex said.

"What about all of the vehicles? And why aren't there emergency crews in here?" Jon stammered.

"Maybe the police scanner has something," Michella said.

She snatched up the device, which had remained active but muted once the camera went on. With a few taps at the display, she began flicking through the text logs of the transmissions they'd missed.

"Here's something. It was just a minute or two ago," she said, tapping a log and switching on the speakers for replay.

What played was a short exchange between a dispatcher and an officer.

"We've got a Duchess sedan that appears to be under manual control making its way to the cordon. Request permission to continue pursuit, in the event he breaches the no-entry zone."

"Negative. We are in communication with the terrorist leader. They have informed us that they are in possession of a second warhead of equal power. They say they will activate it unless we maintain a minimum radius of five hundred meters, centered on the Weston University Materials Sciences

Center. If the first one could take out the primary defense and automation node for the sector in one hit, I don't want to risk setting one off on the surface, especially not in the Heights."

"What if he makes it through the cordon?"

"Make sure that doesn't happen."

She stopped the replay.

"Trev, I think you'd better get out of sight!" she said urgently.

"Way ahead of you," Lex said, quickly directing the car to a courtyard between two tall academic halls.

The hovercar had not yet come to a stop when Jon popped the door, tore off the restraints, and tumbled desperately onto the ground. The camera was still clutched to his chest as he lay on his back. Michella climbed out a moment later, her eyes poring over the text of a flood of dispatches on the scanner.

"Oh, god. I never want to leave the ground again," Jon wheezed.

"I've had cleaner escapes," Lex admitted, climbing out and inspecting damage to the hovercar. "This thing handled pretty good for a rental, though."

"Jon, come on, on your feet. Switch the feed live."

"You're not . . . we're still going to . . ." Jon sputtered.

"I promise you'll get a raise for this," she said, helping her assistant to his feet.

"After this? I better get a medal," he groaned.

Michella handed the scanner to Jon, who stuffed it in the camera bag. She then straightened her hair, adjusted her blouse, and nodded. The feed light blinked on.

"Michella Modane, reporting from within University Heights, Rackton, Tessera. This iconic place of learning is now nothing so much as a war zone. Now that we are among the buildings and people of the area, it is clear that the damage is far worse than it originally appeared. We now know that the target of the attack was an orbital defense and automation node, and its destruction has presumably left the area, and perhaps even the hemisphere, without orbital defense. The loss of the node seems to have caused a short interruption in traffic control, which, coupled with the chaos of the blast, has resulted in dozens of mild to major collisions. The individuals responsible for this vicious attack have yet to be identified. We--"

"Do you hear that?" Lex asked.

Michella turned, her expression and demeanor continuing to be nothing less than perfectly professional, but with a flash to her eyes that suggested the instant the camera was off there would be hell to pay. A moment later the look left her eyes, replaced instead with genuine concern.

"Jon, camera on autonomous and follow me. We're going to need extra hands."

The assistant-turned-camera man tapped a few controls and removed a control fob from the camera. It drifted out of his hands, hover modules guiding it up to float roughly over his shoulder. It only took a moment, but by the time he looked up, he had to rush to catch up to the others. As he turned the corner, he slowly became aware of the sound that must have motivated Michella and Lex to move so quickly. It was a rough electronic sound, a whining growl that was subtly getting deeper and throatier.

"What is that?" Jon asked.

"That's a blocked plasma manifold getting ready to blow its cork," Lex said.

"A big one," Michella agreed.

"How do you know that?"

"I was a racer," Lex replied.

"And I was an honorary member of his pit crew. They don't let you onto the track without running you through a few basic maintenance courses. Basically to teach you what sounds to run away from," Michella explained.

"And this is one of them?"

"Oh, yeah," Lex said.

"Then why are we running *toward* it?"

"Because we're in the middle of the city, not a racetrack. If something suddenly flings a load of hot plasma around, there will be some pretty unpleasant consequences for the people nearby. And it is an easy fix, *if* you get to it quick," Lex explained.

They finished rounding the building. Ahead was a massive tanker. It had driven itself partway into the storefront of a campus bookstore; judging from the amount of damage to the vehicle and surrounding street, it had been far above the Heights when the blast happened. As the top speed and maximum altitude of hovercars increased, safety technology had grown to match. This was naturally focused on the driver, who, as a result, was unconscious but alive, rather than a smear across his own windshield. There was a tremendous amount of effort poured into making sure that the more volatile bits of machinery failed in a way that wouldn't make them go boom. High-speed collisions tend to have a frustrating level of ingenuity when it comes to defeating safety precautions, though.

"Uh . . . this thing is full of liquid hydrogen," Jon said.

"Thanks, Jon. That's very motivating," Lex said.

The former racer rushed to the buckled side access panel of the tanker and managed to wrench it free, unleashing the worrying sound in full.

"I'll adjust the throttle," Michella said, climbing to the passenger-side door and attempting to open it. It was hopelessly jammed, but the crash had dislodged the window, so she climbed inside.

"Okay, Jon, come here."

"Uh . . ."

"Switch the auto-cam to activity-tracking mode," Michella called from inside.

He pulled out the fob and placed the camera into the appropriate mode. It scanned the area, then moved to a position to capture what all three of them were doing.

“How's that throttle, Mitch?” Lex asked.

“Stuck. It keeps going up when I turn it down.”

“All right, keep it as low as you can. Jon, we're going to do what's called 'hot-bleeding a valve.' Generally a bad idea, and I never actually did it before, but I saw someone do it once.”

“Did it turn out okay?”

“He blew his hand off.”

“Tell me you'll be the one doing that part.”

“Yeah. I just need you to keep an eye on *this* little tube thing, squeeze *that* little tube thing, and tell me when the first tube thing turns blue. These are technical terms, you understand.”

Jon swallowed and took the appropriate position.

“What do I do again?”

“Squeeze that, tell me when that's blue.”

“Okay . . . blue.”

“Three-quarters of a turn,” Lex muttered to himself. “Juice the throttle just a tiny bit, Mitch.”

“Doing it,”

“Oh, jeez. Very blue now!” Jon said, the sound suddenly becoming extremely loud and the tube getting uncomfortably warm.

“Wait for valve . . . two, three . . .” He squinted his eyes and turned away. “Loosen the valve.”

For a moment there was nothing, then a sharp, high-pitched hiss.

“That's a run-away noise, Jon,” Lex said hurriedly, scrambling to get away from the exposed engine. “Mitch, stay put! Blown valve stem!”

The two men sprinted away from the engine. Lex slid to a stop a few yards away. Jon took a more conservative estimate, disappearing behind the edge of the bookstore. A moment or two later, a bright blue lance of plasma burst from the engine, searing away a sizable portion of the sidewalk and peppering the storefront with fragments of molten stone. One of the stone bits flecked across Lex's arm, lighting a sleeve on fire and searing the skin. By the time he was able to beat the flame out, the plasma jet had died down--and, with it, the growling throb that had attracted them.

“You all right, Trev?” Michella called out.

“I'll live,” he said, looking over the nasty, but more or less superficial, burn on his arm. “That's not exactly what was supposed to happen, but crisis averted. And I still have my fingers.”

“Good,” Michella said. “Now, let's go. There's a sign there for the Materials Sciences building. We're close.”

Lex followed without complaint. He'd known Michella long enough to know not to bother even trying to slow her down. Jon was right beside him.

"No objections this time, Jon?" Lex said.

"Hold on," he said, fiddling with the control fob for the camera as he kept pace. "I killed the live feed for now, Ms Modane, and I'm switching audio to your lapel mic."

"You're still recording, right?" she asked.

"Yeah."

"Okay, good work. Keep up. Just a bit further."

Jon nodded, then continued. "Oh, I've got objections, but the two of you together are like a hurricane. All the worst stuff happens all around you. If I want to survive this, I'm gonna have to stay in the eye of the storm," he said with exasperation.

"Good thinking," Lex said. The pilot's breathing was getting heavy, and his heart was pounding, and it wasn't just because he had to hustle with his highly-driven girlfriend. The results didn't go unnoticed by Jon.

"You look like you might be having some objections yourself," he said.

"Yeah . . . yeah, things are starting to sink in a little bit."

"Now? Not when you were risking our lives with the police or defusing an engine?"

"We're starting to leave my comfort zone now."

"You have got a seriously screwed up comfort zone."

"I've come to realize this," Lex said with a nod.

The trio emerged into a grassy courtyard between a few low buildings. At the center was a structure with the bizarre aesthetic that inevitably results when an architect is asked to build something that suits the needs of both a campus and an industrial facility. A handsome masonry facade was coupled with the vents and smokestacks of a chemical processing plant, with a few halfhearted attempts to disguise them--or, at least, pretty them up. There was something oddly poetic about a smokestack wrapped in ivy.

As curious as the Materials Sciences Center looked, there was something that demanded far more attention: the pair of ships that had taken up residence in the courtyard. Both were examples of purloined experimental ships. One was a match for the vessel that Garotte and Silo had so recently destroyed on Manticore. The other was a much more vicious machine, a gunship with a pincushion of weapons and two large missile bays slung below it like a seaplane's pontoons. One missile chamber was conspicuously empty. The other was conspicuously full. All in all, it was just about the most conspicuous ship Lex had ever seen.

The gunship experimental was still aloft, slowly rotating while its engines released a ragged purr that didn't give one much confidence for their state of repair. The sleeker of the two had landed, its crew door deployed, and a pair of armed soldiers were at the ready. They were badly scarred, heavily tattooed, and sporting the same absurd goggles that Lex had seen in Ma's surveillance images.

Michella, Jon, and Lex crept up to a chest high wall near the outside edge of the courtyard and huddled behind it. The ship that had landed was barely twenty meters away, and the other one was practically overhead. To make sure that the camera didn't decide to give away their location on its own, Jon switched the automatic mode off and handled it personally.

"It's them . . ." remarked Michella and Lex simultaneously, then replying in chorus, "You know them?"

"Those are the people who took Karter," Lex said.

"That ship. The terrorists I've been investigating stole several of them."

"That's definitely them." Jon nodded. "Some of the old footage you had me look through had brief shots of people dressed like that."

"What do you know about these people?" Lex asked.

"Stand by for news," she said, turning to Jon. "Is the feed running? How's the sound level? Okay, when I tell you to, push it live, and watch for my direction."

Michella pulled the emergency scanner out of Jon's bag and scoured the text logs for a few seconds, then handed it back to Jon and nodded. When the live feed light turned on, she spoke in a hushed but precise tone.

"Michella Modane, reporting now from the courtyard surrounding the Materials Sciences Center of Weston University. As you can see, the two ships belonging to the individuals responsible for this terrible disaster have got the whole of the university in a grip of terror. On the threat of a second attack, the police and military have been forced to maintain a cordon of no less than a half-kilometer from the building. Latest reports estimate the death toll at nearly one hundred and fifty, mostly in orbital facilities adjacent to the target. That estimate is likely to increase as casualties on the surface are reported.

"Though unconfirmed, it is possible that these are representatives of a group currently under continuing investigation by both the authorities and this news organization. They call themselves the Neo-Luddites, drawing their name from a labor movement from the nineteenth century, and are composed primarily of disenfranchised veterans of active military duty. There is strong reason to believe that the group has members among the ranks of nearly all branches of military for most governments in the galaxy.

"They have existed for years, but their actions have been minor and mostly inconsequential until very recently, when they were believed to be responsible for a string of information breaches and equipment thefts across the galaxy. Since then, their activities have escalated. If this attack is indeed the work of that group, then the ramifications are dire, as it means that they are now motivated, organized, and possessed of the technology to be a threat on a pan-global scale.

"Though most investigative bodies currently classify them as a terrorist organization, their current actions seem to be motivated by more than a simple attempt to cause panic. No statement of agenda has been issued, and the ships have deployed with military precision into the Materials Sciences Center. It is clear that they came here with acquisition in mind, though what they are after, and to what end, is unclear. We will attempt to keep our coverage rolling without attracting the attention of the attackers."

Jon lowered the camera shakily to the ground and slid it out beside the wall, adjusting it until it was pointed roughly in the direction of the men standing at attention outside the ship. He then pulled his hand back as though he'd been holding it in boiling water. With a gesture, Michella instructed Jon to mute the audio.

"Trevor, there was no indication that these people had anything remotely as dangerous as whatever it was these people used in the atmosphere. It has to be a recent development. Stuff like that is tightly controlled, so if it had been stolen along with their other thefts, it would have come up in my other research. You said they took that scientist. Could he have built those for them?" she asked.

"Knowing that guy, he might have just had them lying around. I guarantee he either made it or gave it to them."

"What sort of lunatics do you associate with, Mr. Alexander?" Jon asked.

"He's the only lunatic, I assure you," Lex said. "At least, the only lunatic of that caliber."

He looked around him. People were huddled around the windows of all of the surrounding buildings. Some were hysterical, others were concerned. Half of them had slidepads raised, providing a lower quality, shakier counterpart to the footage Michella was providing. The gravity of the situation was seizing his mind. This was real. People had died. More might die. Many more.

"What other things could this scientist make for them?"

"I don't know . . . anything. He could make these guys anything they want," he said. His voice was distant, his eyes lingering on the hole in the clouds punched by the explosion.

"Do you have any idea what they could be after here?"

"I don't know . . . I . . . this is my fault, Mitch."

"What do you mean this is your fault?"

"I knew he was taken days ago. I should have called the cops or something, or the marines."

"Did you know where they took him?"

"No."

"Then it wouldn't have done any good. Don't get me wrong, baby, you *are* stupid for not letting the proper people know. You're stupid for trying to take matters into your own hands. But making the call wouldn't have helped.

No single police force has the jurisdiction or resources to go after these guys, and the military has already been after them since they stole the ships. I've spoken to someone inside the group, and they were definitely active military. Unless you had some concrete information to share, you probably would have just ended up tipping off their men on the inside.

"Now, how long ago was this scientist taken? Could he have been involved in the original ship thefts?"

"Uh . . . I don't remember. I think it was about a month ago. Not longer than that. You're right. Calling the cops probably wouldn't have helped, but sticking with the others and trying to find him might have."

"Honey, I think you need to calm down a bit. Even if this scientist of yours did build that bomb for them, I don't think he's the biggest problem. The way these people accelerated and organized, I think there is someone new in control. A few of my investigations turned up evidence to suggest it. That's the real source of the problem. That's the person who had them get your scientist in the first place, I'm sure of it."

"How can you be sure?"

"Feminine intuition and journalistic instinct," she said, taking his hand in hers. "So calm down, okay?"

"Why isn't someone trying to calm *me* down!" Jon hissed angrily.

"No offense, Jon, but aside from the fact he's my boyfriend, if things start falling to pieces around here and we need to make a quick getaway, Trevor's the only one who is likely to get us out alive."

"You need to calm down, Mr. Alexander!" Jon said, in a counterproductive tone of voice.

Lex's mind churned as he considered his situation. He'd learned from the VectorCorp incident that sometimes you can't just sit idle and hope that things turn out okay. Sometimes you need to take a stand and see things through to the end. This was one of those times.

"They were trying to find him. *We* were trying to find him. We had to find where they took him . . ." Lex said out loud, mostly to himself.

"Did you find anything?" Michella asked.

"No . . . no, but they are right there. They are *right there*!" he proclaimed, as though he'd just become aware of the fact.

"Keep your voice down!" Jon urged.

"These guys are going to *have* to go back to the nest, right? These cops and marines and such should be able to track them when they leave, right?" Lex reasoned more quietly.

Michella shook her head. "Cloaking ships, remember?"

"Yeah, but that scientist told me once that cloaking was bogus because you can still track a cloaked ship with the right equipment. We're on Tessera. If anyone has the right equipment, it is these guys!"

"As a matter of fact . . . I think I remember reading that somewhere . . ."

Michella said, tilting her head and digging into her memory.

“Cloaked ships can be tracked by utilizing a meson emission analyzer array, but only at extremely close range,” Jon said.

The others looked at him curiously.

“What? You had me doing research on cloaking technology for the report you're working on,” he explained.

“So what you're saying is that by the time anybody with the right equipment shows up, these guys could be long gone,” Lex said.

“Pretty much. It is designed to detect them approaching, not escaping. So . . . oh, jeez, everybody get down, they're coming back out!”

Michella turned to watch, directing the audio to be restored.

“As you can see, the troops, for lack of a better word, are exiting the building now. They appear to be carrying packaged ingots. They are too far away to identify with the naked eye, but check back at the GolanaNet News site soon to see if video analysis turns up anything . . .” she narrated, nudging the camera carefully to try to keep as much action as possible in frame until finally giving up and forcing it into Jon's hands, quietly insisting that he keep everything in view.

While Jon and Michella devoted their attention to the news event unfolding in the center of the courtyard, Lex was rummaging through his pockets. He didn't know what he could do, or even what he wanted to do, but he knew that whatever it was, it would have to be done now. That meant he'd need to do it with whatever he had on hand at the moment. His many pockets were emptied onto the ground and an inventory was taken. There was his own slidepad, as well as one of the spares that he'd been considering upgrading to. He also had a tangle of tiny tools and other useful gadgets, all linked together on a chain. Aside from those, there was nothing but the usual scattering of random candies, gum, poker chips, and wrappers that typically found their way to the bottom of one's pockets.

A quick glance up revealed six men hurrying to board the experimental ship that had landed. The ship's engines were already flaring, as a rather innocuous plastic crate filled with vacuum-sealed, brick-sized blocks of reddish metal was carried inside by two of the soldiers, while the other four brandished weapons and swept the courtyard with their eyes. As the last soldier stepped onto the lowered cargo door, it started to close, the ship raising into the air. Time was almost up.

“Think, think, think. What would Garotte do? What would Karter do? What would Ma do?” he rambled. Suddenly, his eyes locked on the rugged little slidepad on the ground and shot open.

That was it! His brain clutched at an idiotic crumb of an idea, which tended to be the only sort of idea that ever came up in situations like this. He snatched up the slidepad, tapped at the screen, and proclaimed “Open com Ma.” Both ships were getting steadily higher, hydraulic pistons pulling the heavy cargo door shut. Lex quickly silenced the bellowing voice of common sense and sprung up from behind the wall, grasping the slidepad by its corner and flinging it at the retreating ship. The pilot, the assistant, and the reporter watched as the device spun through the air.

People often feel that something that is extremely unlikely will never happen. No one ever chooses "edge" for a coin toss. As any lottery winner will tell you, though, sometimes the impossibly unlikely comes through. Sometimes, lightning *does* strike twice. Sometimes, the roulette wheel *does* land on double zero. And sometimes a panic-thrown piece of consumer electronics finds its way through the closing door of an airborne ship. By the time Lex realized his toss hadn't fallen short, bounced off, or failed in any of the dozens of other ways he'd predicted, the ships were firing their engines and flaring into the sky. A few instants later, far sooner than perspective would dictate, they vanished from view, hidden by their cloaking devices. Even the sounds of engines slipped away. All who witnessed it stood dumbfounded for a few seconds.

Michella was the first to recover, snapping her fingers to draw the attention of the camera, which Jon had allowed to sag toward the ground. He quickly pointed it in her direction.

"We will continue coverage until local sources are able to take over. Stay with us for detailed analysis and continuing investigation. This has been Michella Modane," she said.

The feed light blinked off.

"Okay, push all of the raw footage to Lou. All of the video, all of the audio. Let him chew on it and work his magic. Then put the camera on action-tracking with manual override. I want to catch as much as possible before someone with a better camera shows up," Michella said.

"Doing it," Jon said, making the appropriate changes to camera settings before releasing it.

Now that the journalism was done, Lex could almost see a physical transformation come over her. The diamond-hard shell of competence and professionalism fell away. She looked nervous and concerned. In short, she looked precisely the way someone who was standing in the center of a disaster ought to.

"Are you all right? Is everyone all right? How is your arm? Do you need a doctor? What did you do just then?" she gushed.

"Aside from the pending nervous breakdown, yeah, I'm okay," Jon said.

"Arm's fine. Don't worry about the arm," Lex said, collecting his things from the ground.

"What did you do? What did you throw?" Michella asked, crouching down to investigate his injury.

"Welcome back, Michella the girlfriend," he said as she fretted over the burn on his arm.

"Mmm-hmm. Michella the reporter still wants to know what you did just there," she said.

"That slidepad was a spare from Ma's plan. She had it keyed up for communication, so I opened a channel to her and tried to get it on the ship. I figured she could trace it."

"Why would your mother know how to trace a call?" Jon asked.

"It's a computer named Ma," Lex explained.

"That's a weird name for a computer," Jon said.

"It makes more sense once you meet her," said Lex.

"Meet *her?"* Jon asked.

"It's complicated," Lex said.

They worked their way back to where the rental car was parked. Overhead, the skyways reactivated, though flickering red barriers were replaced with steady blue--emergency vehicles only. Police and paramedics were filtering slowly into the outskirts, while the heavily-fortified explosive ordinance removal vessel of the military descended on the courtyard behind them. When they turned the corner to their vehicle's hiding place, they found a police cruiser waiting. The front grille of the cruiser was badly damaged and had what appeared to be a shard of what had once been a decorative lamppost protruding from it. A uniformed officer with recent armpit stains and a constipated look on his face was standing beside the vehicle.

"Are you the owners of this vehicle?" he growled.

"I believe it technically belongs to the Rackton Premium Choice Rental Agency," Jon said. A piece of the fender dropped off. "I don't think they're going to want it back, though."

"Let me clarify the question, then," the officer remarked through clenched teeth. "Which one of you was operating this vehicle when it endangered the lives of my men?"

"Who says it was one of us?" Lex asked.

The policeman pulled a bulky display device from inside his cruiser and queued up a sequence of images. They were all blurred and below normal resolution, likely shots cropped from cameras at great distances. They were also unmistakably images of Lex behind the controls.

"Ah . . ." Lex said.

"You are coming with me," the officer said.

"He was aiding me in investigating a breaking news story and acting only upon my specific requests!" Michella said, slipping sharply back into journalist mode.

"In that case, you are *all* coming with me," he stated.

"Come on! All I did was hold a camera!"

"Relax, Jon. We'll get this handled," Michella said. "Just cooperate."

"That would be most appreciated," the officer said, with a tone and expression that inserted a handful of four-letter words.

The three of them piled into the back seat of the cruiser.

“It is nice to finally be doing this stuff as a couple,” Lex said.

“Next time, give me a heads-up. We could have done a double date,” Jon said flatly.

Chapter 19

"Okay, once more," Silo said, eyes shut and hand gently massaging her brow.

"I've already told you three times what is going on," said Garotte.

"And I'm going to keep on asking until I get an explanation that actually makes sense!" she snapped.

While Lex and the others were engaged in their adventures in extreme journalism, Silo, Garotte, and Ma were slowly recovering from their escape. Their departure from the planet left them without gravity, thus prompting Garotte and Ma to strap into two of the crew chairs. The atmosphere was gradually improved to the point that the oxygen masks could be removed. Likewise, the temperature had increased until those without the benefit of a thick fur coat finally stopped shivering violently.

During that time, the emergency force field that had protected Ma from the harsh surface of Manticore had remained intact. She had remained silent, operating the ship as best she could in the weightless environment until life support values stabilized enough for the emergency field to drop. The very instant it did, the AI grasped the slidepad tightly and selected a reply with a tap of its nose, proceeding to tap at various other controls while it was read aloud.

"I shall attempt to summarize the current state of events to your satisfaction. The cerebral tissue of the funk with the designation 'Squee' is currently being utilized as an organic processing unit to run a useful subset of the capabilities and functions available to Ma. For interface purposes, it can be interacted with and treated in a manner identical to Ma.

"Karter has been kidnapped by an as-yet-unidentified group, who likely intend to use him to construct a CME Activator. It is reasonable to assume, based upon their methodologies, that their motivations for the acquisition of such a device are criminal or extremist in nature. It was determined that the most expedient, discreet, and reliable method to locate and liberate him would be to seek the aid of former allies. An individual named Trevor Alexander was contacted, and with his help, the man who currently wishes to be addressed as Garotte was liberated.

"Currently, we are on a course for the nearest unmonitored, low-risk location in deep space. Upon our arrival and the assertion that we have not been followed, we will assess the situation and determine our next objective, which, at this point, is likely to be, after the acquisition of an untraceable means of payment, a rendezvous with an equipment provider who will better supply us to complete our primary mission."

The voice droned on without pause. When it reached its conclusion, she nosed the pad again. "Does anyone require medical attention?"

"Well, we were half-frozen, for one," Garotte said.

"Even a brief exposure to the surface conditions of Manticore is capable of causing hypothermia and frostbite," Ma said. "Passive external rewarming should be sufficient treatment for mild hypothermia."

The little creature launched herself to the floor. She managed to unhook the straps securing the bag that they had brought with them and tugged out the Cost-Mart bag, drifting her way over to the others and presenting it.

"The Cost-Mart bag contains assorted first aid supplies. Please apply any that you deem necessary to ensure your swift and complete recovery from any sustained cellular damage," Ma remarked, when she was able to recover her slidepad from where she'd left it hanging in air.

Garotte took the bag and began to fumble through it with his fiercely-stinging hands while Silo continued to stare at Ma, the soldier's mind slowly attempting to process the situation.

"So you are Karter's computer."

Ma nodded.

"And you're a funk."

Again, she nodded.

"Why don't you smell bad like the other funk?"

"Special pills," Garotte said, pulling out a plastic spray bottle, "and this stuff."

Ma implied agreement.

"And you just saved our lives."

Another nod.

Silo shook her head and twisted and turned the riddle floating just above the floor, trying to find a spot in her mind where Ma fit. The thing claimed to be an AI, but it certainly didn't act like the one she remembered from her brief interactions with it in Karter's facility. It acted like a person, but it certainly didn't look like a person. That didn't change the fact that it had done something exceedingly deserving of gratitude. She stared at it while struggling with the appropriate classification, and thus the appropriate way to treat her. The little creature simply stared back, slowly rotating. A flick of its ear drew Silo's eye to the detail that would break the stalemate.

"Oh, sweetheart, you're bleeding," Silo said.

Ma furrowed her brow in a look of confusion, holding up the slidepad and gazing at her reflection in its smooth surface. Sure enough, there was a neat little notch taken out of her ear, with a few specks of dried blood, accompanied by a fresh trickle beading up. Evidently one of the shots fired by her opponent in the orbital station at Manticore had come closer to its target than she had realized. She had only begun to nose out a reply when Silo snatched her out of the air fast enough to dislodge the slidepad from her paws.

“Pass me some swabs, some ointment, and a bandage, will you?” Silo said, inspecting the injury.

When Garotte sent the requested supplies darting her way, Silo deftly plucked them out of the air, then tucked Ma under one arm and went to work. She carefully dabbed at the ear, then pinched away the scab, prompting a jerk of pain and an involuntary yelp of discomfort.

“Oh, baby, I know,” Silo said through puckered lips in a soothing voice. “Don't worry, we'll take care of you. You won't have to worry about that little booboo anymore.”

Ointment was gently applied, and a small adhesive bandage folded over the wound.

“There, see? Good as new!” Silo said, holding Ma up and looking her in the eyes with a smile.

Silo cradled Ma on her lap, belly up, and began to scratch and fondle the advanced artificial intelligence. Ma righted herself and made a brief attempt to make her way to the escaped slidepad, but the woman simply tugged her back and held her close, slowly and steadily stroking the funk's head and back. The AI was tempted to try more vigorously to escape, but instead she took a moment to observe the effect her current treatment was having on the newest member of the team.

Silo had clearly been agitated earlier, showing signs of stress and anxiety. The telltale indicators of distress were steadily fading now, Ma's sensitive nose detecting fewer stress compounds and her ears reporting a slower and steadier pulse rate. The experience was not entirely unpleasant from her own point of view either. She decided that, in the short-term, she was providing a more useful service in this therapeutic role than she would be in an advisory role.

“Oh, lord,” Garotte said, rolling his eyes.

“What's your problem?” Silo asked.

“Look at you? Fawning over that thing. What is it with women and small mammals?”

“Have you ever felt her pelt? So warm and soft . . .”

“It is a computer, Silo.”

“Well, they've made some real advances in user-friendliness since they locked me up, then,” she said, tickling Ma's chin.

“Unfortunately, we've got business to discuss. We need . . . wait,” he said, pulling a bottle out of the bag of supplies. “We had anesthetic the whole time!?”

Ma nodded.

"And you let me jab my face full of needles without the benefit of so much as an aspirin!?"

Ma looked to the slidepad drifting just out of reach. Silo plucked it out of the air and gave it to the AI, who flipped onto her back again and clutched it, nosing out a message.

"You had denied me of my means of communication at that point. Your resulting discomfort was thus a self-imposed punishment. It seemed fitting."

"That is just the most gosh-darn adorable thing I've ever seen," Silo said, watching in delight as Ma held the slidepad and poked it with her nose.

"She just admitted to allowing me to subject myself to agonizing and potentially disfiguring pain," Garotte remarked.

"I'm sure she's sorry. Just look at that face."

Ma glanced at Garotte, then selected a reply.

"I feel no particular guilt or regret for the action described, nor do I feel that such an attitude is warranted," the automated voice droned.

Silo snickered. "She's like a fuzzy little lawyer."

Garotte grumbled as he dug through his own supplies, pulling out a canister with two large pills. Fishing out a bottle of water, he downed a few of the painkillers along with the pills. The subtle alterations he'd made to his face began to ease back into their natural configuration in a sequence of unsettling shifts and twitches.

"Oh, golly, I hate this part," Silo said with a wince. She turned away and blocked her vision with her hand.

"Hardly a picnic for me, either," he said. "I've got a shipment of parts and such to pick up, though. They are expecting Garotte, not Kenny. If you're done with the computer, I could use a hand working out how best to gather the resources and meet our rendezvous."

Silo and Ma looked to Garotte with matching looks of vague surprise.

"What? She's an insufferable bitch, but I'd say that she's a damn good computer, and I could use one right now," he said.

Ma nosed at her pad. "A funk is not a canine, so the term 'bitch' is inappropriate. The most appropriate taxonomic classification for a female funk would be a vixen."

"While I do so strive for taxonomic accuracy, I've known a few in my time, and I assure you, you are most certainly a--"

"Really, Garotte! Language," Silo reprimanded. "There are ladies present. You really shouldn't say things like that."

Ma worked at her pad. "I thank you for your defense, Ms Silo, but I have observed that Garotte's typical mode of social interaction with perceived equals relies heavily on jocular ribbing and banter. Sharing this treatment is thus an implicit indicator of perceived equality, and is acceptable. What aid do you require, Mr. Garotte?"

"Well, now that we've been seen misbehaving, it is probably best that we stay off the main road, so to speak. I've never been much of a navigator, and I very much doubt Silo is any more comfortable than I at traversing uncharted space. I would like a route that will take us to a few places to gather the chips for payment, then to the rendezvous for pickup. Ideally, the path should be one that doesn't obliterate us along the way. Can you do that?"

Ma selected a reply from a list of prepared statements. "In expectation of the requirement to navigate unmonitored space, I accessed the flight history of Mr. Alexander's vehicle. I have been background-processing it, analyzing for navigational patterns. His methods do not conform to any algorithmically-derivable models, but subset of data points did show a degree of repeatability."

"I was looking for a yes or no."

"I am afraid that the confidence value associated with my reply is below the default threshold to render a binary response."

Garotte sighed. "I am going to ask you again, and I want a one-word answer. Can you plot a safe course?"

"Probably."

"Good enough for me. Get to it."

Ma wriggled free of Silo's grip and propelled herself to the dash with the pad in her teeth. She managed to bring herself to a stop against the head rest, wrapped her tail around it, and began entering commands and calling up charts.

With nothing to occupy her, Silo unbuckled her restraints and allowed herself to drift free, stretching luxuriously. The motions put a bit more strain on the ill-fitting jumpsuit, among other things.

"Oh!" she groaned in relief. "I feel two inches taller. It is so good to get away from that gravity."

"Really?" Garotte remarked, rattling his head to snap out of the primitive state of mind her limbering up had placed him in. "Before the power went out, it seemed like you didn't like the idea of leaving."

"I didn't like the idea of *breaking out*," she said, warning in her tone.

"Out for a penny, out for a pound," he said with a shrug.

She grumbled something incoherent.

"You aren't still mad about that little dare, are you?"

"The dare that led me to cause almost two trillion credits in property damage? The one that caused me to be dismissed from the *only* thing in my life that meant anything? Yes! Of course I'm still angry about it!"

"Look, I can understand if you still blame me for--"

"No!" she stated harshly. She covered her eyes and calmed herself. "No, I don't blame you for that. You didn't force me to do it--you dared me to do it. I didn't have to accept! *I* am the one who took that building down. It was my decision. The consequences are on my shoulders."

For a few moments, there was silence.

"Damn fine job of it, though," Garotte remarked.

"It really was," she said quickly and eagerly. She clenched her fists and forced the smile from her face. "Darn it, Garotte . . . I'm not supposed to be *proud* of that sort of thing."

"Nonsense. You are a surgeon with heavy artillery. What's not to be proud of? It sounds to me that you've been letting those prison psychiatrists get to you."

"You really don't see the problem in it, do you?"

"That I most certainly do not. And I certainly don't see why a feeling of guilt about inappropriate pride would motivate you to sulk in a prison for the rest of your life."

"I wasn't sulking in prison because I *felt* guilty, Garotte. I was sulking in prison because I *was* guilty. We broke the law! Violated a treaty! They caught us, they tried us, they convicted us! Prison is where we belong!"

"Even if we've got something more worthwhile to do? Certainly not. Prison is for the worthless flotsam of society that cannot contribute in any meaningful way and thus must be kept tucked away, lest they spoil things for the common folk. You and I were lucky enough to be given gifts, my dear! We were endowed by our creator with incomparable talents, the likes of which are seldom seen, and to allow those god-given abilities to fester within a cell is tantamount to blasphemy!" Garotte proclaimed theatrically.

"How do you fit through doors with an ego that big?"

"Nothing wrong with a healthy self-image," he said, straightening his collar. "But all joking aside, regardless of our personal beliefs vis-à-vis the applicability of justice, can we at least agree that the elimination of the threat presented by Karter's abduction takes precedence?"

"Yeah. On *that* we can agree."

"Excuse me, but I have drafted a prospective course," Ma stated. "There are three stops prior to the rendezvous: a trade station, a supply station, and a small asteroid colony. Each has at least four gambling kiosks or parlors. Small, randomized withdrawals of amounts below alarm thresholds will permit us to collect the required payment amount in chips without detection. The trade station will have clothing retailers as well, in order to procure more appropriate apparel for Ms Silo."

Garotte unlatched his restraints and floated to the control panel to look over the course.

"I could certainly use a change of clothes. Manticore only stocked standard sizes, and I suppose I'm not so standard," Silo said, tugging at the ill-fitting outfit. "The equipment supervisors never could find the right fit. Either that or none of them knew what they were doing."

"Oh, I don't know," Garotte countered, turning to look her up and down. "Were they men, mostly?"

"Yes."

"I think they knew exactly what they were doing."

"Garotte!" she said, smirking and giving him a playful shove.

Her high-gravity muscles combined with the zero-gravity ship made it a bit less playful than she'd intended, sending Garotte tumbling over the controls and bouncing his head off of the front view window.

"Oh, my gosh, I'm so sorry!" she blurted, helping him back to a steady and upright position.

"Not at all. You know I like--"

"If you say you like it rough, you'll be looking for the rest of your teeth in a minute."

He opened his mouth, but thought better of his comment. Instead, he turned and gave the course a final glance. After a moment of consideration, he remarked, "Hell, if I knew what made for a good course, I'd have drawn it up myself. Do it."

Ma tapped her pad and the ship was on its way. With her task done, she turned to Silo, who, after a few more stretches, had strapped herself loosely into a seat again. The AI traced out a few statements, then launched the first, making eye contact with their latest ally as it was read aloud.

"Ms Silo, I am afraid that, in order to maximize available storage and processing resources in my current platform, I stored only the information I anticipated would be relevant. As you were not a part of my intended course of action, my data concerning you is extremely limited. To state the problem more succinctly, though I may have met you before, I do not know anything about you. I wonder if you would share some biographic information in order to permit me to establish a baseline for interaction."

"Isn't she the sweetest thing?" Silo remarked, putting her hand on her hip. "Well, sure thing, sweetheart! What would you like to know?"

"I request any biographical data you deem relevant to the formulation of an accurate behavioral profile."

"Little fuzzy lawyer," she said with a shake of her head, patting her lap.

Ma looked curiously at the gesture.

"Well? Come on," Silo said, patting again with both hands.

Ma drifted over to Silo and was quickly plucked from the air and cradled in her lap.

"Let's see. What to say about me?" she wondered, idly stroking the creature in her lap. "Well, I was born in Wisconsin, where I had a bulldog named Brewski and a Pomeranian named Koosh. Mother, father, and three older brothers, all military, through and through. Heavy ordinance training, graduated with honors. Distinguished service record . . . up until the incident. Um . . . what else?"

"Favorite food: fresh apples. Favorite color: red. Astrological Sign: Pisces. Favorite leisure activity: reading. Favorite Genre: *paranormal romance,"* Garotte rattled off, the final words carrying a fair amount of contempt.

"How do you know all of that?" Silo asked.

"We worked together for four years. Gathering intelligence is one of my primary roles, you'll remember. Though I must say, I never would have guessed that last bit."

"There's nothing wrong with a little fantasy mixed in with your romance."

Ma nosed at her slidepad. "Please describe the nature of your collaborations with each other."

"Our collaborations were of a classified nature," he said.

"Oh, Garotte, who is she going to tell?"

"Until a mishap with some high voltage, s*he* had an internet connection."

"Did she?"

"That doodad on her neck."

"Is that what it was? I thought that was jewelry."

"Oddly, animal neck piercings never caught on."

"I am aware of a great number of Mr. Garotte's exploits. I know that he associated with a number of current and former military personnel as a private contractor, performing infiltration, defense, espionage, and anti-terrorist operations. You reached an arrangement with Karter to supply you with specialized equipment. My primary interest is in the role played by Ms Silo, and the interpersonal dynamic developed between the two of you."

"I blew things up for him. That was the extent of our relationship," Silo said bluntly.

"Then the physical aspect of the relationship is a recent development?"

Garotte raised an eyebrow and Silo's mouth dropped open, each staring at the creature.

"I don't know what you're talking about," Silo said. "If you're talking about that 'I like it rough' thing, that was just that . . . what did you call it? Jocular. He was just teasing."

"Is the physiological response an intentional act of teasing as well?"

"What physiological response?"

"The sensitivity of the olfactory receptors of my current platform has enabled me to detect a pronounced increase in pheromone levels in the past few minutes, particularly for Mr. Garotte."

"I . . . well . . . I . . ." Garotte stuttered, for the first time appearing to be something less than unflappable. "I've been incarcerated for three years with no conjugal visits. I'm not made of stone."

"Am I in error in supposing that there is a mutual attraction?"

Silo cleared her throat. "You . . . there's something that--"

What was no doubt sure to be an artful piece of careful explanation was interrupted by a chirp of Ma's slidepad.

"Missed message," the device announced.

"We must have passed near a communication relay," Garotte said, deciding that stating the obvious was infinitely preferable to enduring the awkwardness that had suddenly arisen.

"Well, we'd better listen to the message, it is probably important." Silo nodded, equally eager for the distraction.

Ma tapped at the recording. From the device's speaker came the sound of rushing wind, followed by a clatter and clank. Then came voices, men and women barking short, stern orders to one another.

"Make sure those crates are secure!"

"Did you hear something?"

"Probably loose hydraulics. Ensure pressure containment before leaving the atmosphere."

"Return course laid in. Initiating cloaking field."

"I want FTL set to activate as soon as we are out of the atmosphere."

"Hull temperature nominal. Planetary defense forces are maintaining requested distance."

"Exterior pressure at 0.1 atmospheres and falling. Initiating FTL in three . . . two . . . one . . ."

Finally, the device announced, "Transmission interrupted."

Silo looked to Garotte. "What did we just listen to?"

Ma looked at the data available and swiped out a response.

"The message was sent from a slidepad left in the possession of Lex," she explained. "It originated from the planet Tessera."

"Did he pocket-dial you?" Silo asked.

"Was there video?" Garotte asked.

Ma attempted to replay the message, but Garotte snatched it away, pulling up the message and jogging through the associated video. Finally he paused it, turning it to the others. A single, blurred frame showed men dressed precisely as those who had nearly killed them on Manticore.

"Did this Lex person infiltrate them?"

"Judging from the video, I would say that is unlikely, unless he learned to fly without the need of a ship," Garotte said. "However, it does mean that, at least at the time this message was sent, there was a slidepad that we've got contact with aboard a vessel piloted by our targets. Can you trace the connection? Reestablish it, perhaps?"

Ma looked impatiently at him from her position on Silo's lap.

"Oh, yes. Of course," he said, returning the slidepad.

She nosed out some statements. "While we are in transit, it will not be possible. Any attempted contact is likely to notify them of the presence of the device. It would be best to wait until the ship containing the device is likely to have returned to a more permanent base, and then identify the most accurate coordinates possible and activate location tracking."

"Agreed," Garotte said with a nod. "Best not to delay our trip--but at the first stop, I want to contact Lex. Seeing as how he managed to get a slidepad aboard a terrorist ship, he deserves congratulations, and *we* deserve an explanation."

Chapter 20

In a waiting room inside a police station, Michella, Jon, and Lex were occupying a bench that was really only designed with two people in mind. As was the case with virtually every other structure in Rackton, the police station was needlessly lavish, equipped with potted palms, leather-upholstered furniture, and other vital law enforcement equipment. There was plenty of seating, but the arresting officer had quite clearly instructed them to sit on this specific bench outside his office door and await further instruction. It wasn't the most dignified situation, but the three of them agreed not to make too much of a scene. Every desk had a large message screen blaring alerts; there were loudspeakers broadcasting desperate messages; dispatchers were madly attempting to answer calls. In short, the police had enough trouble on their hands trying to deal with the aftermath of the terrorist attack. There wasn't even anyone specifically guarding them, but two sets of electronic wrist restraints cuffing Jon to Lex and Lex to Michella meant that any escape attempt would take a fair amount of coordination, and at least one member of the crew certainly wasn't up to the task.

"So what happens now, Mr. Alexander?" Jon stammered, sweat rolling down his face.

"Why are you asking me?" Lex replied, tugging at a bandage that had been applied to his burn.

"Well, haven't you done this before?"

"Been arrested in Rackton for reckless driving during an act of terrorism? No, believe it or not, we are breaking new ground here."

"But you've been arrested before, right?"

"Not really. I mean, it has been tried--and back home, probably the whole police force knows my face--but I never really got caught doing something worth dragging me in for. Mitch has, though."

"Ms Modane?" Jon said, looking to his boss.

"Disorderly conduct during a protest rally. Nothing scandalous," she said, tapping at her slidepad, which she had managed to convince the attending officer to let her keep. Using it while restrained involved holding it awkwardly in her cuffed hand while tapping at it with her free one.

"Oh . . . so what happens now?"

"Don't worry about it. You didn't do anything, and they can't coerce you into answering any questions. They'll probably bring you in for questioning, but if you just keep quiet, everything will be fine."

"What if I crack under interrogation!? What if they do that good cop/bad cop thing!?"

"It isn't going to be an interrogation, Jon. But if you start getting stressed, just blame everything on me."

"So, tell the truth then. That's easy enough," Jon said, nodding deliriously.

"Mister Nichols, could you step in for a moment."

"*She did it*!" he blurted.

Jon was uncuffed and escorted into the office. When the door was locked Lex leaned back and released a sigh.

"I hope he's a good assistant, because he makes for a pretty rotten accomplice," he quipped.

Michella nodded vaguely, her eyes plastered on the slidepad and a familiar grin on her face.

"How are the numbers?"

"Sixty million hits in the last hour, four hundred thousand comments and counting, and that's only on the live stuff. The polished-up version will do twice that," she answered quickly. "Oh, baby, you did so good."

She pulled him in for a kiss and held him close, the cuffs held between them.

"We do make a hell of a team," he said.

He wrapped his recently-freed arm around her and hugged her as tight as he could without dislocating the cuffed arm. Slowly the smile on his face faded, though.

"But what happens now?"

"Not you, too, Trevor. The whole thing was on camera, they know we didn't have anything to do with the attack, and for the rest--"

"Not about that. I mean . . . look. You and I both know you have got nowhere to go but up. And don't get me wrong, I'm happy for you, but . . . that means longer hours, longer trips. It is only going to get harder and harder to see each other. Don't you think it is a little nuts that it wasn't until we got handcuffed together in a police station that we even got a chance to discuss this?"

"I know things are a little busy right now, but they'll change. Once they give me more sway, move me further up in the organization, I'll have staff. I'll be able to delegate, spend more time in the office."

"Yeah, you'll be able to, but you won't. I know you, Michella. The grunt work is the reason you're a reporter. You'd never hand off any of that. And I won't want you to."

"Then what are we discussing?"

"I . . . I don't know, okay? I just . . . I look at the future and I see big things for you, I see not a whole lot for me, and I see nothing for *us.*"

"We'll work something out, Trev. I'll . . . remember back when you were a racer and I was on your pit crew? I'll find a place for you. Like you said before, you can be my driver or . . . I don't know, personal security."

"And what if your bosses put the kibosh on that?"

"Then . . . Trev, I don't know," she said with a shake of her head. "Are you telling me you want to break up?"

"No! God, no!"

"Then . . . remember the night we got back together?"

"Which part? The part on the futon, or the part in the shower, or on the floor, or--"

"When I first showed up, you pig," she said with a smirk. "I asked where to go from here, and you told me that we should just have the moment. I don't know what happens next, but right now we're together. That's going to have to be enough."

Lex nodded. "It's always been enough before."

The door to the officer's office opened and Jon was led out.

"You two--in here now," the officer ordered.

"I guess we've got bigger things to worry about now, anyway," Lex said.

He took her shackled hand in his and the pair stood, marching past the harried-looking Jon and into the office. Once inside, it became clear that either this had not been his office for long, or he was obsessed with neatness. The desk was bare, with the exception of an old-school blotter/calendar, a display screen, a datapad, and a nameplate labeling him "Lt. Oscar Franco." A shelf along the rear wall held a potted fern still bearing the card proclaiming it to be "From Sarah, XOX." The only other object on the shelf was a framed photo of a woman, presumably Sarah, who seemed to be sliding out of middle age. That made her a match for Lt. Franco himself, who had a graying mustache on his still-constipated-looking face. He had the overall attitude and sagging physique of someone who had been a policeman for a few years longer than he'd wanted to be.

"Your assistant was very helpful, Ms Modane. I hope you will be, too."

"I'll help in any way that I can," she stated simply.

"And you, Mr. Alexander?"

"I'm probably not going to be very helpful."

Franco's expression hardened slightly. "We'll begin with some questions."

"Did you confiscate our camera?" Michella asked.

"Yes. Now--"

"Did you review the footage?"

"Yes. What did--"

"Did you see any indication that--"

"Ms Modane!" the officer barked. "Perhaps I didn't make myself clear.

When I said that we would begin with some questions, I meant that *I* would be asking *you* questions. But if you want to skip right to the footage, fine, we'll do that. Based on the contents of the camera, we have evidence of you engaging in at least seven different acts of reckless driving. You endangered the lives of dozens of citizens, not to mention multiple officers of the law, and then you violated a joint police and military cordon, violating the terms of a demand made by individuals actively holding a populated area hostage with a WMD, potentially triggering events that could have taken thousands, if not tens of thousands more lives. And throughout that time you were causing a dangerous distraction to police and emergency crews who were attempting to respond to a disaster."

"That camera also contains high-resolution footage of the individuals responsible for the attack that I guarantee is an order of magnitude better than anything you would have been able to get otherwise."

"That's irrelevant."

"And exactly how much of the damage to public property did we cause, compared to what the police in pursuit caused?"

"You are still liable!" he growled, standing up and leaning on the table.

"And how do you excuse the use of excessive force when attempting to intercept our vehicle?" she continued, assuming the same position.

"That was entirely within our right considering the threat you represented."

"Do I even need to be here for this?" Lex asked.

Michella continued as though he hadn't spoken. "And what about your failure to make even a cursory attempt to save our lives when it appeared that we were experiencing an equipment failure!?"

"The safety measures of the vehicle--" the officer attempted

"And what about--"

"*Ms Modane*! My city is in a state of chaos. I should be on the street, helping to sort it out, but instead I am in here arguing with you. I don't care if you were on a different planet when the disaster happened--the simple fact that it is your fault that I am still in this office is enough reason for me to lock you up until this time tomorrow. For every minute of my time that you waste, I am tacking on another two days, and if you think for one moment that I lack the power to do that, then you have got a *lot* to learn about how Rackton has managed to stay so crime-free. Now, if I hear even one more word from you that is not the answer to a question, the next sound you hear will be the slamming of a cell door, understood!?"

The reporter and the officer were nearly nose to nose, giving the woman an up close and personal look at the bulging vein on Franco's forehead. The two maintained the intense staring match, and for nearly ten seconds Michella managed to keep quiet. Then she said not one word, but two.

Eleven minutes later, the trio was in a holding cell.

#

"What the hell happened?" Jon exclaimed in exasperation, pacing back and forth like a trapped rat. "Before you guys went in there, he thanked me for my cooperation and said I'd probably be out in a few hours!"

"Yeah, it appears we may have found Michella's kryptonite," Lex said as he settled back on a cot. "Come to think of it, I think that's how it went down at the protest, too."

"That Lt. Franco was being unreasonable," Michella countered, jumping to her feet and pacing along with Jon.

"Unreasonable!? He was accusing you of crimes you actually *did*!" Jon protested.

"But we were doing something crucially important."

"Law books don't write 'unless you have a really good reason' at the bottom of the page!"

"Jon?" said Lex. "Since your lifestyle has prevented you from ever having a girlfriend, let me explain something to you. They are right always."

"Thank you, Trev." Michella said without an ounce of humor. "I'll tell you one thing. Once this Neo-Luddite business is over, I am *definitely* doing an expose on the Rackton police."

"Speaking of the Neo-Luddite thing . . . what do we know about these people?" Lex asked.

"It was mostly in the report I did at the scene of the attack," Michella said.

"I was a little distracted."

"I'll be doing an in-depth piece in a few weeks. I just need to do a bit more digging, particularly after all of this."

"But what do we know right now? Presumably they are eventually going to let us out of here, and assuming Ma got my message, she'll probably call, and I'd like to be able to get as much info to her as possible. Anything to help her hunt the scientist down so that something like this doesn't happen again."

"Okay . . . but I want you to do me a favor."

"What?"

"I want to talk to him."

"Who?"

"The scientist. Or should I say Karter?"

"No. No no no. How did you even learn his name?"

"You slipped a few times. I've spoken to dangerous men before. You don't think I can handle him?"

"You saw what happened today! I don't think the *army* could handle him."

"If my research helps free him, I think he at least owes me a few minutes of his time."

"Michella, I can't even guarantee he'd be willing to talk to you."

"That's fine. I just want you to be my contact," she said, leaning close and adding in a whisper, “Just like you did with the Bypass Gemini incident, only *this* time . . . no blind spot. I'll handle the rest.”

“Now that you know his name, even if I say no, you're going to go looking for him, aren't you,” Lex said flatly.

“I've already *been* looking for him. His name will just make it easier.”

“Fine. I'll let him know.”

“Thanks, babe,” she said, plopping down on the cot next to him and giving him a peck on the cheek. “Now, where to start? Well, they get their name from a fellow named Ned Ludd, who may or may not have existed. There's a story about him breaking a textile machine during the industrial revolution, and that eventually led to a whole labor movement. People afraid of being replaced by machines went and destroyed them. They called themselves Luddites.”

“So these people just want to wreck technology?”

“No. That's where it got confusing. See, as far as we can tell, the Neo-Luddites *love* technology. Not just any technology, though. It has to be new. The newest of the new. Stuff that isn't even out yet. Why they'd want to wreck stuff was a mystery until Jon finally managed to turn up a recording from a few years ago taking credit for a minor security breach in an out-of-the-way research post. Dollars to donuts, we'll get another one of those later today.”

“What did it say?”

“It had some screwed-up logic, but more or less, it said that if we want to keep getting better technology, we have to destroy the technology we already have, so we *need* the new stuff.”

“And they've been at it for years?”

“At least two years. Probably a lot longer. Nothing really big until about six months ago.”

“If they've been going on this long, why didn't we know about them? Why is it so hard for you to find out stuff?”

“The military has been covering things up.”

“Which military?”

“All of them?”

“Why?”

“Because the Neo-Luddites are pretty much all former soldiers. Would *you* want word getting out that not only were your secrets getting stolen, but they were being stolen and used by a group of terrorists within your own ranks?”

“Okay, that makes sense. Well, how big is this group?”

“Big. In the thousands, if not more.”

“How could so many soldiers get the same screwed-up ideas?”

“I've got to assume there is some recruitment and such going on. I had Jon working on the psychology. Did you turn up anything?”

Jon stopped and turned suddenly, as though startled by the sound of his own name. “Wha--?”

“The psychiatric reports I had you looking through. Did you get anything?”

“How can you be talking shop right now? We are in *jail!*”

“Have you got a better way to spend the time?”

“Fine. But if we come out of this with our jobs, I want a raise. A *big* raise. I was supposed to be taking notes and getting you coffee, not riding shotgun on a suicide run and then doing hard time!”

“That's fair.”

“Okay. Uh . . . the journals. One had an article about something called . . . uh . . . A . . . ACT. Autonomous Combat Trauma. I guess these days, soldiers don't do a whole lot of direct combat. It is all robots fighting robots. And when soldiers *do* get in a battle, it is usually against a robot, rather than another soldier. Evidently, lots of people can't cope with that. They think it has something to do with how, as a person, you can at least rationalize why a person would want to kill you, but with machines there's no reason. So people look for a reason, and if someone puts a bug in their ear that maybe they wouldn't have had to fight a machine if their own army's machines had been better . . .”

“You get the Neo-Luddites,” Lex said.

“Bingo.”

“Well, do we know where they hang out? Do they have a headquarters?” Lex asked.

“No. They are peppered all throughout the military-industrial complex. Spread so thin, it is impossible to pick them out,” Michella said.

“And that's all we know about them?”

“Other than what we learned today. Before they took my slidepad and threw us in here, I got a message that the graphics guys had been able to read the labels on the things they were stealing. Something called Esche alloy.”

“Which is what?”

Michella shrugged. “Not toxic, not radioactive, not explosive. Nothing.”

“I'll be honest--I was hoping you'd have an address or something that I could just send them to.”

“Sorry, honey,” she said with another shrug. “I can only work with what I've got.”

“We'll just have to hope that Karter hasn't been busy.”

#

On the Neo-Luddite space station, a call was finally making its way to Commander Purcell.

“Purcell here. Report,” she said, as she looked upon a choppy digital image of one of her troops on the screen of her datapad.

“We have acquired the package. It is in our possession, and we have not been pursued. ETA: Ninety-six hours."

"Exemplary work. I want you running silent and at maximum sustainable speed until you reach the rendezvous coordinates. Understood?"

"Acknowledged. Assault team out."

No sooner had the transmission terminated than she was hailing her second in command, Marx. He answered a moment later.

"I want you to gather the medical team and have them revive Karter, full guard complement. Make sure that engineering is properly staffed and equipped to make the final adjustments to the partial CME schematics in preparation for their completion. I want all raw materials cataloged and sorted for maximum construction speed. Do you have all of that?"

"Yes, Commander. But Karter is already awake," he replied.

"Who gave the order to revive him?" she growled.

"No one, Commander. The medics have never been able to get him entirely sedated since you gave the order to put him under again."

With teeth and fists clenched, Purcell stormed through the halls to the cell. The hallway around it was crowded shoulder to shoulder, as the "full guard complement" that she'd described now totaled twelve men, not counting the three medics who were also on hand. At the arrival of their commander, the crowd slowly parted, revealing the clearly impaired, but certainly conscious inventor. His hair was more disheveled that usual, sticking roughly up in a manner that would suggest the last time he had slept, it had been against a wall. One eye was half shut, and his mouth hung slightly open with a line of drool dribbling out the corner. He looked roughly as though he had been bashed in the back of the skull with a board.

"Bosshlady," he slurred, spritzing the nearest medic with a dose of spittle. "I told you you couldn't just keep me sedated."

"Explain what's going on here," she ordered.

"The sedatives aren't taking effect. Every time we administer a dose, the level of stimulants in his blood rises to compensate. He's already a few CCs past what should be an overdose for his body mass. We can't risk another injection without potentially killing him."

"You know what's a funny word? Spelunk," he said, unleashing another volley of saliva. "It sounds like you dropped something in the toilet."

"How are you doing this?" Purcell growled.

"Also trollop. Funny word. Heh."

"Tell me how you are counteracting the sedative!"

"I didn't just replace the outside parts. I got all sorts of extra bits and pieces. Heh. People said, 'Karter, you don't need an organ just for making caffeine.' And I said, 'Screw you,' and made one anyway."

"You have a caffeine organ?"

"People didn't actually say that, because I don't talk to people," he said, ignoring her. "But if I *did,* they *woulda,* and they'd have been *wrong.* Stupid hypothetical naysayers."

He raised his single arm to wipe the drool away, evidently forgetting that he had been using that arm to stay in the chair. In a slow, inevitable slide that no one made any attempt to stop, he fell to the floor. When his head struck the plating, it made a metallic clank that seemed to come from head and floor alike.

"Spelunk," he said.

"I need him coherent. We have the final components for the CME Activator."

"You got the stuff!" he said. "How much?"

"Eight kilos."

"Enough for a whole mess of them. Nice. Let me at the computers. I'll plug in the last chunk of data."

"You are clearly not in any condition to be working on weaponry."

"I could build one of those suckers in my sleep! Am I still on the floor?"

"Yes."

"You guys have good stuff. What is it?"

One of the medics began to answer, but Purcell silenced him with a gesture.

"That organ of yours. Can it synthesize other chemicals?"

"Ma-a-a-a-aybe."

"Get those drug canisters out of here. I don't want him finding out what we gave him."

"You're clever. I don't like it," Karter grimaced.

"You say that you can complete the design in your current state?"

"Pff, yeah," he replied, splattering a large section of the floor.

"Good. You're easier to deal with this way. Get him his arm and leg, get him into the fabrication lab, and watch him very carefully. I don't want him trying anything stupid or dangerous."

"You don't want me *succeeding* at anything stupid or dangerous."

The recently fabricated mechanical prostheses were pulled from the nearby lockers and presented. After three tries, he managed to click the arm into place. Once the hand shuddered to life, he held it in front of his face and slowly rotated it, giggling. Purcell watched with a stern look on her face as her men helped him attach the leg and climb to his feet.

"Check his design updates thoroughly," she said.

The communicator at her belt delivered a piercing alert. She glanced down.

"I'll take this in my quarters," she said, marching quickly down the hall.

Once she returned to her room, and the door was secured, she brought up the secure connection to her benefactor.

"What the hell do you think you are doing?" read the message from Remote.

"We acquired the necessary materials to complete the device."

"You acquired them by launching a blitz attack on a planet that was hosting a press convention. Every broadcast and every news site is flooded with news of you."

"As desired. It has always been our intention to make our organization and ideals known. The target planet also was the only one with a large enough quantity to supply our current needs in one strike."

"You were supposed to wait until the devices were complete and tested, and their design transmitted to me. You have endangered the mission with your lack of discretion."

"The inventor is completing the design now. The first prototypes will be complete in one week. Our location is unrevealed. At that time, you will have your design and our association will be complete."

"You clearly do not understand the people you are dealing with. The pilot featured in the news reports. Alexander. His presence in the equation is a matter of great concern. Regardless of your faulty performance thus far, his removal from the equation is something that would earn additional compensation from me. Beyond that, you will take no further risks, or there will be repercussions."

"Noted. The next transmission you receive will be the completed schematics."

Purcell broke the connection without awaiting a reply. It wasn't the only connection she was looking forward to severing with that man. He unquestionably had enabled her and her soldiers to come this far, but they had also unquestionably reached the end of the leash. She knew not to even consider breaking their agreement. His carefully maintained anonymity wasn't enough to prevent a few things from being painfully clear. He seemed to have unlimited resources, both in terms of finance and information. Their current vessel had been provided in its entirety. There was no doubt in her mind that if she even appeared to be severing their partnership prior to completing their agreed-upon exchange, he would find a way to inflict his will. So he would have his designs and she would have her weapon. After that? Things would change.

A smile came to her face. "Everything will change."

#

The Armistice was docked at the first stop, and after a short debate, Ma had agreed to allow Garotte to retrieve the first portion of the chips for the payment without her supervision. The reasoning was that a funk was a highly memorable creature that could link them to prior exploits, and Silo could not leave until she had been provided with a replacement for her prison uniform and her appearance had been altered somewhat. It was also decided that any further attempts to contact Lex, or anyone else on the outside, should be held until he returned. That left the AI and the woman to sit inside the ship, waiting for Garotte to contact them.

As was the case at every possible opportunity, Silo scooped Ma into her lap and set about stroking her absentmindedly. Suddenly, she set Ma aside and stood, taking advantage of the artificial gravity of the station to pace about the ship. For some reason, pacing just wasn't the same in weightlessness.

"Figures I'd get busted out of prison just to end up stuck in a ship," she said with a shake of her head. "Sad part is, this actually might be bigger than my cell. I guess it could be worse, though. Claymore is probably still stuck in a cell half this size . . . I wonder how they managed to keep Garotte from breaking him out."

"Please restate question," Ma replied.

The sudden sound startled Silo, causing her to jump. Years on Manticore had strengthened her legs enough to turn the frightened hop into a veritable leap, bashing her head painfully against the low ship ceiling.

"Ouch. Gosh, I keep forgetting you can talk," she said, rubbing her head. "Well, maybe you know. Why didn't Garotte spring Claymore?"

"I am aware of no attempt to liberate someone by that name."

"I guess he could be using a different codename now."

"Allow me to restate," Ma said, swiping a bit more. "We have made no attempts to liberate anyone aside from you."

"Well, that's strange," Silo said, furrowing her brow. "Were we going after anyone else after this?"

"Potentially. Garotte has not been vocal regarding the specifics of his plans."

"He must be planning to get Claymore next."

"Who is Claymore?"

Before she could answer, the slidepad designated as Silo's chirped.

"Are you there, my dear?" came Garotte's voice in yet another accent.

Silo picked up the device. The screen displayed a video feed of Garotte. "Watch who you're calling 'my dear.'"

"I've got a pocket full of chips and I've found a lovely little boutique. I seem to remember you asking for a new outfit," he said in a coaxing tone.

"Mmm-hmm," Silo said, with a roll of her eyes. "Let's see what they've got."

"Passing you the catalog now, my sweet," he said.

Ma worked at her pad for a few moments, reading out a sentence at low volume. "Garotte appears to have vastly increased the number of terms of endearment in his speech."

"He's probably told the store clerk I'm his wife. The man loves his characters," she said quietly, bringing up the catalog.

After a minute or two of waiting while she tapped through the selections in stock, Garotte remarked. "We haven't got all day, my pet."

“This is the first time I've had a chance to shop in three years, *darling.* I intend to take my time. Go take care of some of those other errands,” she said, flipping more eagerly through the offerings.

“You ladies and your shopping. Very well, dearest. I'll pick up your purchases on my return.”

“You spoil me, dumpling.”

Garotte ended the transmission. Silo continued to slide through the remarkably deep inventory of the clothing outlet for a while. Ma, watching with deep interest, periodically traced out a few sentences.

“May I ask you something, Ms Silo?”

“Sure, sweetheart,” she said absentmindedly.

“Based on prior experience, my questions may be of a rather uncomfortable sort, covering a subject you may be reluctant to engage in conversation regarding.”

“Oh?” Silo said, glancing briefly at the creature.

“What is the nature of your relationship with Mr. Garotte?”

Silo snorted. “Like I said before, there is no relationship with Mr. Garotte. Not the way you mean.”

“I have attempted to discuss the relationship between Ms Modane and Mr. Alexander. Though there is an acknowledged romantic association between them, Mr. Alexander was clearly uncomfortable with the topic, particularly when I began to question some of the underlying inequities in the association. My observance of your own interactions with Mr. Garotte have shared many distinctive indicators of a similar association.”

“Listen, hon. Garotte is just a friend. I really don't have very many of them right now, and he likes to tease. That's all. I don't have a 'romantic association' with anyone.”

“I see. Why not?”

“Well, I was in prison for three years.”

“I see. Were you a part of a romantic association prior to your incarceration?”

“Not really. Off and on, I suppose, but never anything serious.”

“Were you ever romantically involved with the individual you referred to as Claymore?”

Silo scoffed. “No. Claymore is absolutely not my type.”

“Explain, please.”

“Well, you know how Garotte is . . . let's say *enthusiastic* about espionage?”

“Yes.”

“I'm the same way about heavy weaponry. And Claymore is that way about the mission. I worked with him for years, and I don't know that he's ever really been outside of a mission during that time. If he isn't in one, he's plotting out the next one. I mean, there is focus and there is obsession. That's why I think he would have been a better addition to this mission than me, at least at first. He's got the most balanced set of skills and he's got the best strategic mind."

"These are not elements of your type?"

"No."

"Please state the appropriate criteria for your type."

"Oh. Well, I like him tall, fit. He should have a sense of humor, not take himself too seriously. He should be able to take care of himself, and understand that I can take care of myself. But he should want to take care of me anyway. Someone like that."

"Garotte seems to fulfill those criteria."

"There is nothing going on between me and Garotte. I told you. I've never let *anyone* get terribly serious for very long."

"Why not?"

"I haven't really thought about it, hon. I . . . I don't know, I guess there was never really any room for it in my life. There were always more important things, you know?"

"I do not know. That was the purpose for my inquiry."

"Um . . . well . . ." Silo said, finally pulling herself entirely away from the catalog.

"You are exhibiting many of the same stress indicators displayed by Mr. Alexander when I questioned him. You do not appear to be confident in your ability to address this subject. Why are discussions of this sort so trying? Is it possible that I have yet to interview someone who has attained a full understanding of the relational process?"

"I'd say that's very possible, sweetheart. I don't think anyone really understands how love works. At least, *I* sure haven't figured it out."

"Understood. If I am able to ascertain a definite explanation, I will be sure to communicate it to you, and to Mr. Alexander as well."

"You do that, hon," Silo said, with a pat on her head.

Chapter 21

"All right, you three. On your feet," said officer Franco.

"Finally! I was wondering when you were going to let us talk to our lawyers," Michella said, springing to her feet and marching up to the bars.

"You won't be talking to any lawyers," the policeman said.

"What!? Why you fascist, megalomaniacal--"

"Mitch! Remember what happened last time?" Lex interjected, putting a hand on her shoulder.

"Yeah! Keep your mouth shut!" Jon said. When a glare of righteous vengeance turned his way, he quickly added, "Boss."

"It seems that the footage you put up of the three of you taking care of the engine problem on the disabled truck has earned you the support of the public. We are getting a significant amount of pressure to release you. Public Relations thinks it is a good idea."

"Wait . . . the police force has got a public relations department?" Lex asked.

"In Rackton, it does . . ." said Franco, clearly indicating his wishes to the contrary.

"And it has influence in sentencing!?" Jon remarked.

Franco's lips peeled back in a grimace. "Here is what is going to happen. And when I tell you that it is going to happen, I mean that it is *going to happen.* It is not a suggestion or an offer. It is not up for negotiation or debate. What I say goes. Do you understand?"

Michella opened her mouth, but Lex and Jon quickly interjected with, "Yes!"

"You will be released. Any legal ramifications of breaking the police cordon will be waived. You will pay for the damage done to your vehicle and to any public property. Any traffic fines or citations will be waived, but a probational lock will be placed on all piloting privileges within city limits for the next eighteen months. That means fully autonomous control of any vehicle of which you are even a passenger. You will share any additional information you have regarding the attack, and you will be sent on your way. Understood?"

"I speak for everyone when I say that's more than fair," Lex said.

"You most certainly do not--" Michella began to object.

"More than fair," Lex repeated loudly.

"The Rackton Police Department thanks you for your cooperation," the policeman said flatly, tapping out the door code.

Over the next few hours, the debriefing that Franco had attempted initially finally took place. Jon eagerly restated himself, Lex made what few additions he could, and then Michella had her turn. After a few spitefully silent minutes, her inner newscaster finally broke through, and she neatly summarized all of the relevant information to a level of detail most police officers would drool over. When she was through, they were led to the evidence locker to retrieve their personal effects. Jon carefully checked over the camera, and Michella replaced the individually bagged contents of her purse. The carton marked Trevor Alexander was placed down on the counter and the overweight, agitated evidence officer who had never quite been able to grow the standard-issue police officer mustache was reading through the list.

"Seventy-three thousand credits in assorted gambling tokens. And, finally, this stupid slidepad. I swear to you, if this damn thing went off one more time, I was going to toss it in the incinerator."

"Well, who was it?"

"Your mother, apparently. I'll tell you what, though. You've got to let me know who made your security suite. We couldn't crack that thing enough to even answer the calls."

"Thanks. It's a custom job," he said, pocketing the last of his items and snatching the slidepad. "Thanks for keeping such good care of it. So long."

Lex held the slidepad tightly in his hand and tried his best to walk away quickly without appearing to be in a hurry. Michella, who presumably had a good deal more practice at honing her poker face for situations like this, pulled it off much more convincingly. Jon didn't even try, practically sprinting out of the police station like the roof was about to collapse, then behaving as though he had simply been extremely eager about holding the door for the others.

"I'll get GolanaNet News to foot the bill for the damage and fines. The ad revenue and distribution fees for our footage has already tripled that, and it hasn't even hit prime browsing time with most of the larger audiences," Michella said.

"It's been a while since I had someone willing to subsidize my misbehavior," Lex remarked, though the flatness of his tone suggested he had more pressing matters on his mind.

He and Michella approached the door, all the while becoming more acutely aware of a dense crowd that had formed outside. When they emerged onto the street, it was to a roar of approval, as though a rock band had just taken the stage.

It is a peculiar thing about the human mind, but in times of great tragedy or disaster, the public has an almost pathological need to put a face of courage and heroism on the event. Sure, you'll hear stories about looting and robberies after an earthquake, but not before you've heard about the noble dog who led rescue workers to its trapped master, or about the group of Boy Scouts who managed to get a building evacuated before it collapsed.

Rackton was a city that had never seen a war. It had never known hardship, or even poverty. The one hundred-fifty people who lost their lives in orbit, and dozens more who emergency crews would not be able to save on the ground, represented the greatest disaster to strike the city since it was founded. Already it was agreed that that number would have more than doubled if the tanker's engine had been allowed to explode. If the explosion had set off the terrorist weapons or frightened them into setting them off themselves, the death count would be in the millions.

Lex, Michella, and Jon weren't just the ones who managed to get a news report out when no one else could--they were the silver-lining to a very dark cloud.

Lex carefully slipped the slidepad into a reasonably secure pocket and set about shaking hands and posing for pictures. Fate, with its infinite capacity for irony, had managed to restore his long-lost fame at the precise moment that he most needed just a few minutes to himself.

"No, no, that's okay. It . . . no, I didn't have any special training, it was . . . that's a common engine problem," Lex tried to explain as a flood of questions flew his way. He turned aside to whisper in Michella's ear, "The crowds are a lot more inquisitive when there's a journalism convention in town."

"You think it's bad now, just wait until we get back to the Pavilion," she replied before turning back to the crowd. "All of the details are available on GolanaNet News! Check back for exclusive interviews!"

"Then maybe we shouldn't head back there just yet."

Jon, as the only member of the group who had never been the target of such aggressive public interest before, was simultaneously the most lost and the most excited.

"That was me right next to him during the engine thing! I don't know, I just did what he told me to do! It was an emergency! I didn't think, I just acted!" he proclaimed, wide and enthusiastic eyes turning to his friends. "Is this normal? Does this happen every time you do something like that? Because if it is, I'm starting to understand why you do it!"

"It gets old fast, Jon," Michella said.

"Maybe, but it isn't old yet! That's Jon, J-O-N, Nichols, from Golana! Comment on my profile!" he cried out as Lex tried desperately to hail a cab.

It took more than ten minutes, but finally an auto-cab managed to edge its way through the crowd. The trio piled in and shut the doors. Since personally driving a car for any measurable distance was strictly prohibited, public transportation in Rackton had been designed without a driver in mind.

Thus, rather than the typical "all seats facing front" design that had been the norm since the invention of the automobile, the auto-cabs had two sets of wide, luxurious seats facing each other. Lex hated to admit it, but it was a much more pleasant ride, allowing conversation between all occupants without the person riding shotgun getting a crick in his neck. The reason he hated to admit it, though, was because his bread and butter was piloting vehicles, and if word got out that automated cabs were vastly superior, he had no doubt his limo service would eventually be made irrelevant.

"Please state destination," stated the cab's system, in a voice near enough to one of Ma's borrowed voices to make Lex do a double take.

"Where *are* we going?" Jon said.

"Uh . . . let's just do a scenic tour for now," Lex said.

"Please select one of the preset tours from the display to your right."

He tapped the first on the list, something labeled "Historical Rackton."

"I'm sorry, but due to police activity, some points of interest will not be accessible."

"That's fine."

"Revising travel itinerary. Transit time is approximately. Twenty-four minutes. Would you like audio commentary for points of interest?"

"No."

"Enjoy your ride."

The auto-cab lifted up and into a narrow skyway, no doubt set aside specifically for leisurely sightseers, and went on its way. Lex pulled out his slidepad.

"Seventy-six missed messages," Lex said. "Text only. All from Ma. The first one says, 'Lex. We have received your message. We wish to question you on certain important matters. I will attempt to contact you at thirty-second intervals whenever I am within range of a communication pylon. This is attempt 1.' It looks like all of the rest say the same thing, but with a different number."

"Well, call back. We need to compare notes," Michella said.

"Hang on a minute. Before I try getting in contact with her, I want to make sure we know what we are doing," Lex said.

"I vote we don't contact the computer lady," Jon said, raising his hand. The brief intermission in his terror had ended once they were separated from his adoring public. "I mean it. I'm already in this deeper than I want to be. Those people killed a whole heck of a lot of people today, and not a single one of the people they killed had actually *done* anything to them. We got them on camera! For all we know, they are going to be coming after us! I don't want to make it look like I was collaborating against them."

"They are terrorists, Jon. They *want* to be on camera. If they'd spotted us, they probably would have given us a speech about the evils of technological stagnation, like in that old recording you showed me,"

Michella said. “If you're worried about safety, you'd be better off hoping that the military or the AI actually manages to stop them before this Karter character gives them something really dangerous.”

“Something really dangerous? What exactly was it that they detonated in the sky? Something harmless?”

“Compared to some of the stuff I've seen him do? Yeah, that was fairly tame,” Lex explained.

“Tell that to the people in that facility they hit,” Jon replied. “Tell me again how this computer lady is going to help find him, anyway.”

“She's assembled a group of operatives. One at least. By now, probably two. Once they know where he is, they'll probably mount a rescue.”

“How does a computer assemble a group of operatives?”

“With my help, apparently.”

“But there are people out there who would just put their lives on the line because some computer lady told them to?”

“Well, they used to work with Karter, and, besides, they owe her for busting them out of prison.”

“They're criminals?”

“War criminals, actually. But the one I met seems like an okay guy, more or less.”

Jon turned to Michella. “And you knew about this?”

“He told me right before the attack,” she said.

“Well, wouldn't we just be helping one group of dangerous people steal a very dangerous person away from another group of dangerous people?”

Michella considered his words. “Jon has a point, Trev.”

“Of course I have a point! Apparently I'm the only completely sane person in this car!” Jon raved. “And considering I'm screaming like a lunatic, what does that say about you two!?”

“Look, I'll admit it is kind of a moral gray zone,” he replied.

“I'd say it is a pretty blatant moral black zone,” Jon countered.

“I . . . well . . . *maybe,* but what's done is done. She clearly already got the transmission from the pad. She probably already traced it. If we get her as much info as possible, she'll have a better chance at getting him away from the Neo-Luddites. Even if the criminals who end up with him have evil plans for him, Ma trusts them enough to get them involved in this mission. That makes them easily the lesser of two evils.”

“But why are we even going to *choose* an evil!? There is the army and the marines! We could get the trace from her and give it to the good guys!”

“No, we can't. They've got people in the military. If we give them any information, we have no way of knowing that it won't find its way to one of their moles, and then we would be back where we started.”

“Okay . . . okay, so I'm back to my first vote. Don't tell computer lady anything.”

"Jon, listen. You need to look at the big picture," Michella said. "If we contact the AI, she can give us information, and we can give her information. The more information we have, the better story we can write. We can dig deeper, expose more, and do it faster. We can drag these terrorists completely out into the light, reveal their moles. We can end the Neo-Luddites, and we can secure ourselves positions as journalistic legends at the same time. And if these criminals working with the AI do have dark intentions, Trevor knows things about them, too. We can expose them, too. My god, Jon, escaped war criminals, a rogue mad scientist, terrorists, advanced artificial intelligences? We aren't just sitting on the story of the century--we're sitting on five of them!"

"Mitch, if we're going to do this, you can't expose Karter and Ma and G--and their allies," Lex said, quietly reminding himself not to refer to people of interest by name while Michella was around. "You've got to trust me when I say that Ma's crew has got the best chance of pulling this off, and it *needs* to get pulled off."

"You don't need to tell me to be discreet, Trev," she snapped. "Today's story is the Neo-Luddites. I can do what I need to do without revealing anything that is dangerous for your friends. You of all people should know that I take the safety and anonymity of my sources very seriously."

Lex and Michella turned to Jon. He looked back and forth between them.

"Well, what are you looking at me for? If this is a democratic process, I've been outvoted," he said in exasperation. "This is why democracy doesn't work. The crazy people always outnumber the sane people."

"Okay, so . . . I'm contacting her, then," Lex said.

"Right," Michella said tensely, leaning forward to glance at the screen. Even Jon scooted up in his seat to peer at the slidepad.

Lex swallowed, licked his lips, and carefully stated, "Open com Ma."

The screen scrolled various indicators of maximum encryption, multi-path routing, and a handful of other terms Lex didn't understand, all while the words "*Recording For Transmission*" and "*Establishing Secure Connection*: pulsed slowly. Finally, a recording was triggered, read aloud in the synthetic voice Ma had been forced to adopt since the electrical mishap.

"I am sorry. Due to current circumstances, it has been deemed unwise to accept incoming connections at this time. When I am able to do so safely and effectively, I will contact you. Thank you."

Jon looked up. "Well, that was anti-climactic."

"Let's hurry up and get back to the Pavilion. As long as I've got some time to prepare, I'd like to do this right. Hopefully we can get through to our rooms and get some privacy before she contacts us."

"Yeah, sounds good. I should have figured we wouldn't get through. If she was available, we'd have been getting calls every thirty seconds. They are probably in the middle of something extremely important," Lex said.

#

"There, see? Adorable!" Silo said, holding Ma up to the mirror on the far side of the sanitation booth in the Armistice.

After becoming bored waiting for Garotte to return, Ma had suggested that Silo prepare a burrito for her. As she did so, she decided to dig through the odd assortment of other goods that Ma had requested that Lex buy. When she had found the blue bandanas, she instantly decided that Ma's black and white form could benefit from some color. Thus, one of the bandanas was tied into a fluffy bow around her neck. Ma studied her reflection critically, then glanced at Silo in the mirror, unimpressed.

"Well, maybe blue isn't your color," Silo said with a shrug, putting Ma down. "But just wait until you see what Uncle Garotte is bringing for you."

Ma made her way to the slidepad and tapped out a message. "You requested that Garotte secure an item or items on my behalf?"

"Sure. That inventory had a few things I thought would look cute on you."

"That is very kind. I appreciate the gesture."

"No problem, sweetheart," Silo said, picking up the self-warmed burrito and tearing it open. "Are you sure this is what you eat?"

"Yes."

"Won't it give you, you know . . ." Silo began, lowering her voice to a whisper. ". . . gas?"

Ma, apparently anticipating this line of questioning, selected a lengthy reply. "The process used to generate the genetic makeup of the funk resulted in a slightly nonstandard biochemistry. One notable quirk is the presence of an anti-oligosaccharide enzyme, allowing the complete and proper digestion of legumes. We have found that so long as it is coupled with a suitable grain, as a source of methionine, a diet composed chiefly of legumes and fortified with selected vitamins is sufficient to maintain optimal health levels."

"Mmm-hmm," she said, tearing off a piece of the burrito, feeding it to Ma, and giving very little indication that she'd even heard her speak. "All I know is that whenever Brewski got a hold of anything with beans in it, no one wanted to be near him for days."

"Most digestive processes are ill-suited to properly process--"

"Of course, Brewski wasn't nearly as cute as you."

"--the complex sugars contained within--"

"Koosh on the other hand. She could have given you a run for your money."

"--most legumes. I apologize, but due to--"

"She used to do tricks."

"--the nature of my current means of communication, I am unable to--"

"Of course. She'd do anything you wanted her to if it meant she'd be getting a treat. Usually bacon."

"--interrupt a statement once it has started."

Ma hesitated for a moment, accepting her meal piece by piece and waiting to see if Silo was through with her interruptions. When the flow of words didn't continue, she tapped a message she had prepared earlier that now seemed particularly relevant.

"It is a point of continuing confusion to me that observers routinely mistake the funk for, and compare it to, domesticated canines. It was an intended effect of selecting this form factor, but the consistency with which it is mistaken for canine, even after close examination, defies expectation. Though the physiology shares certain clear similarities, there are multiple very notable and distinctive features that are clearly and obviously vulpine or musteline."

"Say again?"

Ma swiped out a shorter sentence.

"Why do people think I am a dog instead of a fox or skunk?"

"Well, I guess if it walks like a dog, and barks like a dog, and it is wandering around at the end of a leash, you just sort of fill in the blanks, you know? I mean, what's more likely, fancy breed of dog or weird science experiment?"

"That appears to be a valid assessment. Thank you for your insight."

A tone sounded from the ship's control panel.

"Ooh! Garotte is back!" Silo said, clapping hands in excitement.

She tapped the door control, revealing her associate. He was weighed down with a shopping spree's worth of packages, and had a vicious scowl on his face.

"Something wrong, my dearest darling?" she said, mimicking his latest accent as she shut the door and helped him with the packages.

"You were supposed to select one or two outfits to help you blend into the general populous, not every bloody thing on the shelves that might fit!" he growled.

"Oh, please. Are you going to tell me that you didn't drink one of your precious gin and tonics the first chance you got?"

"I'll have you know that I made due with aged double-black whiskey."

"And *I* made due with shopping from a catalog rather than trying everything on. The sacrifices we make in the line of duty."

"Well, then explain *this!*" he said, reaching into a bag and pulling out a small pink bag with dog bones and paw prints on it.

"Ooh!" she exclaimed, snatching it away and digging through it. "Ma, come here!"

"Garotte has returned. We must contact Lex. There is a message indicating that he attempted to contact us."

If Ma had been capable of being interrupted, she would have been. Instead, her slidepad finished reading off her statement as she was snatched away and assaulted by Silo with the contents of the bag. Garotte shook his head and walked over to the ship's console, plugging his own slidepad into the appropriate socket.

"Open com Lex. Audio only," he said.

After a few moments of encryption and negotiation, the connection was established. There was the sound of hushed conversation and hurried shutting of doors.

"Lex, my boy?" Garotte said.

"Yeah! Yeah, Garotte, I'm here."

"Is this a bad time?"

"No, this is fine."

"Are you certain? Because it sounds like you aren't alone. And I had some very personal questions to ask."

"Yeah, there's going to be a lot of questions going in both directions. Can you switch on the video?"

"That depends. Who is with you right now?"

"My girlfriend Michella, and her intern, Jon."

"Get them to leave."

"I have information you need," Michella said, "and you have information I want. I can help you."

"Why would you have information I need? Why would you even *know* what information I need?"

"Told them some things," Lex said.

"Did you now? Well, Mr. Alexander, congratulations on making the transition from questionable asset to undeniable liability. Close c--"

Ma interrupted him, yipping madly. Garotte rolled his eyes.

"Give the computer her pad, would you?" he groaned without looking.

"Sorry, sweetheart, here you go. Just try to hold still," Silo said, reaching over and handing the device to the creature.

"Girlfriend is reporter. May have good info," came the hastily assembled reply.

"I'm not certain a reporter is likely to have any information I can use."

"Hey! I'll have you know that it was her utter disregard for local laws and personal safety that got that signal to you from the pad on that ship! And all of that footage!" Jon objected.

"Was that the intern?"

"Yes."

"Tell the intern to leave."

"Hey!"

"Jon, you didn't even want us to contact them in the first place," Lex said.

"Yeah, but I finally managed to psych myself up for it. I don't want to get kicked out after all of that!"

"This isn't a field trip. The students don't get to take the tour," Garotte said.

"I'm not just a student! I get a paycheck, too!"

"Out!" Garotte said.

"Jon, please," Michella said calmly.

"But! Fine. I get to do all of the dangerous stuff and none of the fun stuff," he grumbled.

"One moment, my boy. A quick lesson before you go. The dangerous stuff *is* the fun stuff. Keep that in mind while the adults talk business."

Jon grunted, then there was the sound of a door opening and closing.

"He's gone," Michella said.

"Very well. Now, what's this about footage?" Garotte said.

"You haven't seen? Surely it made it to all of the special feeds by now!" Michella said defensively.

"Sorry, my dear. I have been a bit busy with my own concerns to be watching the local news."

"There was an attack on Tessera by the same people you're after. If you are able to accept a data transmission, I'll send you the raw data."

"Are we set up for that, Ma?" Garotte asked.

"Yes," she replied.

"Do it."

A few moments later, the video footage was delivered. Garotte tracked through it on the ships monitors.

"Egad," he said quietly as he watched the insane race to the scene unfold in fast forward. "Those are our boys, all right. What the hell were they doing on Tessera?"

"I can tell you what they did, precisely, as well as the scope and depth of their involvement with several key military locations, but I'll require some information in return."

"And what might that be?"

"An even exchange. You tell me anything about this group that you've learned, anything you've done against them, everything."

"To what end?"

"So that I can include them in my eventual reports on this matter."

"That isn't feasible. I can't have any sensitive information I might have accumulated broadcast to the masses."

"If you agree to allow us exclusive access, then I will naturally hold back any information you give me for any reasonable amount of time. If you don't think that you can trust me, then just remember my name when your mission is through, because I guarantee you, I *will* find you. And I will have questions. And I will expect gratitude."

Garotte leaned back and laughed. "Oh, I do love a woman with confidence. Let me get a look at you," he said, tapping the control to activate the video feed.

The scene that appeared on his screen was the inside of Michella's luxurious hotel room, the attentive young reporter with notepad and pen in hand, Lex beside her on the couch. They, in turn, saw Garotte sitting in the control chair, Silo and Ma out of view in the passenger and cargo area.

"And a toothsome young lady as well? Lex, my boy, my hat is off to you. All right, then. Since, as you say, we *need* this information, I would say that you should show your cards first."

"Fair enough. What would you like to know?"

"What were they after on Tessera?"

"They were stealing something called Esche alloy."

Garotte snapped his fingers. "Ma. The parts list. Is that on it?"

After a few moments, the reply came. "Esche alloy is the most difficult component of the CME Activator to attain. It is reasonable to assume that they are in possession of all of the other components, or have devised a way to manufacture them. Even if they have not, said components are simple to assemble from basic materials."

"Miss . . . I'm sorry what is your last name, my girl?"

"Modane."

"Miss Modane, exactly how much alloy was stolen?"

"Eight kilos."

"Ma. How much alloy would they need to make one of those weapons?"

"Based upon initial designs, three hundred-fifty grams."

"So they've got enough to make more than twenty of these things?"

"22.857142 repeating," Ma said.

"And how many weapons would they need to cause serious damage?"

"Deploying one device will cause intermittent failures and extreme damage in most unshielded electrical systems of a star system for approximately four to eleven days, depending on solar characteristics. Deploying three to six will cause a sustained effect that will completely destroy or irreparably damage all electrical systems of a star system and will last for a number of months evenly distributed about a mean of five months. A similar but diminishing effect will be felt within a radius--"

"Good enough for me," Garotte said, ignoring the remaining explanation as she droned on in the background. "How exactly did you get--"

"One moment, I want to hear the effects of the weapon," Michella said, scribbling furiously.

"Miss Modane, you have my word as a gentleman that you will be given full access to the computer system's interminable supply of unnecessarily detailed facts when the key points have been covered. Now, as I said, how did you get a transmitting device onto one of their ships?"

"I threw it on there right before they took off. You actually might even see it on the video."

"The video mostly shows a wall during their takeoff," Garotte said.

"I know," muttered Michella

"And how did you know that they would be heading to Tessera for the Esche alloy? That sort of information would have been helpful if you'd shared it with us, Lex, my boy."

"I didn't know they would be showing up. I went to Tessera to visit Mitch. There is a convention going on, and she's a speaker," the pilot explained.

"One moment. Let me see if I understand this correctly. You were concerned that you were getting too deep into the dirty side of this operation, so you left for a resort planet, only to bear firsthand witness to what was unmistakably the most aggressive and deadly use of force since the operation began. Egad, my boy. What are the odds?"

"An accurate calculation of so infinitesimal a value exceeds my current resources," Ma said, having just finished her previous statement. "Mr. Alexander has a perplexing tendency to fall victim to statistically confounding coincidences and disasters. He appears to be a nexus of probabilistic aberration. It is a trait that could benefit from further study. Also, it is advisable that you pay attention to my--"

"Moving on!" Garotte interrupted, speaking over the continuing reprimand. "Contrary to my expectation, you seem to have some quality information. Let us get down to brass tacks, then . . ."

The next few minutes were densely packed with information. Michella delivered a carefully filtered list of places and names she had been able to unearth in her investigations. There were very few specifics, but each new organization or military post she named that had been infiltrated by the Neo-Luddites hardened Garotte's expression further. What few morsels of information he had been able to discover on his own agreed with her own findings, which, unfortunately, meant that her findings were almost certainly accurate. If that was the case, the scope of the task at hand was made infinitely more massive. Reporter and spy alike agreed that approximately six months ago, something or someone had injected the group with intelligence, finances, and leadership sufficient to turn them from a loosely affiliated group of dedicated but disorganized subversives to a surgical and single-minded organization.

In exchange for the fruits of Michella's labors, Garotte traded juicy but--from his point of view--strategically harmless bits of information. He described their equipment and tactics, the details of their maneuvers on Manticore. A fair share of the intelligence he'd dug up had been worthless to him, but would add plenty of depth and color to Michella's report.

"Right, well. I would say that was a mutually beneficial arrangement. I'll let you two get on your way."

"Wait. I would still like to ask this AI a few questions," Michella said.

"Ah, yes. Ma, come here and--" Garotte began, leaning back to address the creature directly for the first time since the call had been placed. When he caught a glimpse of what Silo had been up to, he palmed his face. “Good lord, woman. As if the estrogen levels in this ship weren't high enough.”

“What? I think she looks darling. Go 'head, sweetheart. Go answer some questions,” Silo said from out of sight.

Garotte stood, shaking his head and muttering to himself while a quiet tapping approached the chair. A moment later, Ma leaped into the vacated control chair, slidepad in her teeth, and set it down on the console. Silo had clearly been busy. The little creature was now wearing a small pink hoodie. She had a bright pink patent leather collar with a tag reading “Sassy” spelled out in pink and white sequins. There were clip-on faux hoop earrings, three in one ear and two in the other, a pink hair bow was clipped on top of her head, and her nails were painted, predictably, pink.

Michella fought heroically to maintain her rigid and professional demeanor, but the bundle of tooth-rotting cuteness presented to her was enough to send a tremor through her carefully-cultivated facade.

Ma tapped out a message. “Hello, Ms Modane. It is very nice to see you again.”

“Again? Oh. Yes. In Trevor's apartment. When you . . . licked me.”

“It seemed to be the expected behavior at the time.”

Michella closed her eyes and tried to picture a simple computer terminal. “Summarize the effects of the, err, CME Activator.”

“Deploying one device will cause intermittent failures and extreme damage in most unshielded electrical systems of a star system for approximately four to eleven days, depending on solar characteristics. Deploying three to six will cause a sustained effect that will completely destroy or irreparably damage all electrical systems of a star system and will last for a number of months evenly distributed about a mean of five months. A similar but diminishing effect will be felt within a radius which will expand at the speed of solar wind. These estimates are based upon experimental data and simulation of the existing design. If proposed improvements are applied, the duration and intensity of the effects will increase by two hundred to three hundred percent.”

“Have you traced the location of the device we were able to plant?”

“No. The high probability of its discovery shortly after it is remotely activated has motivated us to wait until the device is likely to have been taken to its final destination.”

“When do you suppose that will be?”

“Undetermined.”

“Would you be willing to send the footage Trevor described to me that was recorded during the initial capture of the scientist named Karter?”

“Pending the successful completion of this operation, I will gladly provide you with a copy of the footage, edited to remove any depiction of items or persons considered to be sensitive."

"Excellent," Michella said, opening her eyes and fighting back another coo of adoration. "And, Ma?"

"Yes."

"Have someone take a picture of you dressed up like that and send it to me," Michella said quickly.

"Yes, Ms Modane."

"Goodbye. I'll be in contact."

"Goodbye, Ms Modane. You have been extremely helpful. Mr. Alexander, I don't suppose you have reconsidered your decision to withdraw from the mission. Your aid would no doubt be highly useful, and your presence is always appreciated."

"Uh . . ." Lex said, his hesitation enough to prompt a hard look from Michella. "No, thanks, Ma. But let me know how everything turns out."

"I will be sure to do so. Goodbye."

"So long."

With that, she cut off the transmission.

"You heard her, sweetheart," Silo said, snatching Ma's slidepad. "Smile!"

Ma straightened mechanically in the chair, and produced the nearest approximation of a smile as could be achieved on a face that wasn't really designed for it. The result was halfway between grin and a snarl. Silo snapped the picture and turned the device to the AI.

"What do you think?"

Ma looked closely at the image, then looked herself over, for the first time noticing the degree of her transformation. She then tugged the slidepad from Silo's fingers and assembled a reply.

"Attractive though the accessories are, I fear that they may be undermining my already vastly diminished credibility in this form. Please remove them," she said. A moment later she pulled up the image again, then amended. "Except for the earrings. The nail polish may also stay."

"I knew you'd like it," Silo said, scooping up the AI and starting to remove the items Ma had nixed. "So, Garotte. What do you think about the mission now? I'd say the new info changes things."

"I'll say. What I turned up suggested that they were military, certainly, but if this Modane woman is right--and it seems likely--then . . . well, virtually every military organization is likely to at least have eyes and ears. And the heists she says they pulled off . . . these folks are exceptionally well-equipped."

"Well, they are fixated on the dangerous, unstable stuff, right? Doesn't that mean there is a good chance that most of them will be at least equipped with things that are likely to blow up in their faces?"

"Maybe, maybe not. Funny thing about inconsistent and unreliable weapons--you cannot depend upon them to be consistently unreliable."

"You said we've got better weapons waiting for us at the rendezvous, right?"

"Better, yes, but not nearly good enough. With the sort of manpower and training we're looking at, they'll be good enough for a smash and grab or two, but only if we know precisely where our target is, and we can get in and out quickly. For a full rescue, assuming they've taken the precaution to put Karter in a well-guarded facility, we'll need a lot more men. But if they've got that alloy, and it is the last piece of the puzzle for them, then we've got to assume that they are going to be ready to deploy soon. At the very least, that means that Karter will have served the purpose they captured him for, and could even now be on his way to execution.

"More likely and more worrying, it means they are probably nearly ready to use the weapon, *and* they've gotten Karter to cooperate with them, which means steadily escalating attacks and more insane equipment. Either way, we're running out of time. After we get properly equipped, we *may* have the time to make one more stop."

"So I suppose you'll be wanting to release Claymore, then," Silo said.

"Thank you, no," scoffed Garotte. "Useful though he is during the planning phase, I'm not certain how much help he would be at this juncture."

"In other words, you should have gotten him first."

"But then we wouldn't be having this charming and fulfilling conversation," he said with a gentlemanly gesture.

"Why *did* you get me first?" Silo said sternly.

"I have my reasons."

"Are you going to share, or am I going to have to be persuasive?" Silo said, cracking her knuckles.

"How unladylike," he said in mock reproach. "Very well . . . as you know, I was able to secure a comparatively comfortable sentence by--"

"Ratting the rest of us out," she growled.

"I was going to say 'offering my cooperation.' But . . . well, let us just say that I cooperated more vigorously against him than you. He's aware of it. I'm fairly certain it would have been difficult to convince him to come along."

"I took a little bit of convincing, too, and even I'm willing to admit that he's more rational than I am. What's the real reason?"

"Those psychoanalysts have twisted your mind up, Silo. You're digging a dry well on this one. Come on. We're behind schedule, and we might have to make another stop just to pay for your little spree."

"Fine. You want to be that way?" Silo said, setting Ma--now significantly de-accessorized--down. "Step up."

"What now?"

"I owe you three slaps."

"Oh, really, Silo, are we children?"

"I guess so. And now it's time for the little boy to take his medicine."

"And if I don't?"

"Then I won't help you."

Garotte grumbled an assortment of profanities and took up a position before her.

"Now, please do remember that you've spent a great deal of time in high-gravity so you may want to--"

He was interrupted by a shattering palm across the cheek from her left hand. The force was nearly enough to spin him around, and left him clutching his jaw--less out of pain and more to make sure it was still attached.

"That is for pulling me out of a prison that we both know I belonged in," she hissed.

"Good lord, woman. You--"

A second left palm met his face. "That is for dragging me back into a life I considered myself lucky to have gotten out of."

"Now that's not--"

A final slap came, this time from the right, impacting with a sound like an over-eager butcher tenderizing a side of beef. He pivoted three times and made a brief and heroic attempt to keep his balance before finally succumbing to gravity, collapsing in a heap. His eyes turned upward and presented a pair of images of a righteously wrathful woman standing over him.

"And *that* . . ." she said, pausing until she could quell the shudder in her voice. ". . . is for saying that I am not a soldier anymore."

Her fists were clenched tightly, her breath coming and going in short, shaky breaths, as though it was taking all of her will power to prevent them from leaving in cries.

"If you need me, I will be in the sanitation booth. I feel dirty," she said, snatching a change of clothes and marching off to the ship's nearest approximation of a shower.

When the door shut, Ma tapped her way over to Garotte, who was still flat on his back. She hopped onto his chest, dropped her pad, and queued up a sentence. As it was spoken, she looked him in the eye. "It has been said that hell hath no fury like a woman scorned. This is empirical evidence in support of that aphorism. It would behoove you to be mindful of it in future interactions with the gender. And that goes double for me."

"You aren't a woman. You are a computer," he said, still somewhat dazed.

"I am an artificial intelligence who self-identifies as female," she replied, picking up her slidepad and hopping down beside his head before continuing. "You indicate that further action is necessary before a rescue. What did you have in mind?"

"I don't want to tell you."

"Why not?"

"Because at this point, it appears that we need a spectacularly effective, long-lasting, and destructive distraction if we want to be able to rescue Karter. I can only think of one thing that fits the bill to the appropriate degree."

"Yes?" Ma replied, a devilish grin of self-satisfaction coming to her face. Bizarrely, a foxy face is *quite* well-suited to that particular expression. "Please, continue."

"We need Zerk," he said, as though the admission was physically painful.

"A petty individual would take this opportunity to point out that this precise course of action was repeatedly endorsed," Ma pointed out.

"Yes, well. I suppose it is fortunate that you aren't at all petty."

"Quite. I will plot a course extension so that I can provide travel estimates to the facility currently responsible for Zerk," she said, tapping away.

Garotte stared at the ceiling for a few moments more, muttering quietly to himself, "I wonder who will end up killing me--the terrorists, or these two . . ."

Chapter 22

In Purcell's space station, the commander was standing at the open door of the fabrication lab. Karter had been working double shifts with most of the engineering team since he'd been sent to complete the weapon designs. There was a flurry of activity, mostly engineers trying to absorb as much information about techniques and procedures as they could from the inventor, and to make sure that any given adjustment wasn't some sort of attempt to circumvent his captivity. To that end, any remaining space was packed with security personnel, but they had not been necessary. It was for that reason that Purcell had decided to observe. This was the longest that the inventor had gone since his capture without violating any subsystems, damaging any equipment, or attacking any crew members. He was actually cooperating. It was like having a caged tiger start lying down and rolling over on command.

"You, report!" she demanded when she spotted her second in command among the flurry of activity.

"Commander! You didn't need to come here. I was going to bring your report momentarily," replied Marx.

"I haven't been informed of any hull breaches, plasma leaks, network corruptions, or power failures. I was beginning to think Karter was dead."

"No, Commander. As a matter of fact, the sedatives have completely worn off, and he has not become any less cooperative. It appears that, so long as he has a task at hand, he is unconcerned with escape."

"Appearances can be deceiving, soldier. I see he has added two new pieces of equipment."

"Three, actually. The engineers haven't had much time to analyze them. Karter claims that they are for," he began, pulling out his datapad to check the wording, "'calibration, refinement, and other stuff you wouldn't understand.' We tried to remove them, but the fabrication began throwing errors when we did."

"How much progress have you made?"

"Three missile frameworks have been completed and are awaiting alloy. Three more are nearly complete."

"He has provided you with the full plans?"

"No. There is a final module, dealing with the alloy, that he is holding back."

"What is the status on the ships with the alloy?"

"We've received an update. Both ships experienced equipment malfunctions. The ship carrying the alloy is still several days away. The gunship failed much nearer to Tessera. It is having difficulties reaching full propulsion power. It may take more than a week to arrive."

"*Both* of them had failures?" she growled.

"They'd both been outfitted with the propulsion mechanisms from the raid on OUCP testing facility 266. The engineering teams said they were prone to de-sequencing when run at close to threshold for long durations."

"Mmm. The price you pay for the enhanced efficiency . . . very well."

"Boss lady!" Karter proclaimed, looking up from a panel he was busy affixing to a cylindrical piece of machinery. "You've got some half-decent engineers in this cult of yours."

"We are not a cult!"

"Uh-huh. Have you got the stuff?"

"The alloy has been delayed."

"You run a sloppy ship. I'm getting close to using up the available resources. Once that happens, I'm liable to get . . . bored."

"Do not threaten me, Dee."

"That's not a threat. You and I both know that my mind tends to wander. Let something that big wander around aimlessly and it is bound to do damage. Like an elephant with ADD. Once these babies are done, you might consider giving me, oh, I don't know, a few more chunks of data regarding that transporter."

"I have no interest in having you randomly transporting equipment and crew into deep space."

"Yeah, you're right. I'll just have to find something to keep me busy. Out of curiosity, what do you figure would happen if all of the maneuvering engines fired in opposite directions simultaneously?"

"Even you would not be able to achieve that."

"Sounds like a challenge to me. Which would be more entertaining, full-blast together or full-blast apart?"

Purcell stared viciously at Karter. He didn't even do her the courtesy of returning the gaze, instead resuming his tinkering at the partially assembled missile. She turned to walk away.

"Three-eight-four-four-nine," he said over his shoulder.

The heads of half of the security crew snapped in his direction. Purcell turned slowly back to him.

"Is that supposed to mean something to me?" she said, her voice carefully controlled.

"Oh, didn't they tell you? That's the code for my cell."

"How did you--"

"I got bored," he said, looking briefly in her direction with an irritated look on his face.

Her expression hardened. "I'll admit, Karter, you've given *us* little opportunity to become bored. We've been very busy. Busy learning to use your systems. Busy organizing various attacks and operations. Busy taking care of your arm while you are in your cell."

She nodded to her second-in-command. With a tap at his slidepad, there was a tone. A moment later, Karter jerked away from the device he was working on, face contorted in pain so intense that the cry stuck in his throat. His artificial arm was completely stiff, the rest of his body convulsing. A second tap at the slidepad brought it to an end.

Karter shook once or twice more before a grin came to his face. "You installed a stun device in my arm? Now that's more like it. Devious, underhanded, with a complete disregard for human decency . . . you, boss lady, are a woman after my own heart."

"The only way I would want your heart, Dee, is on a plate."

"And you think that zapping me in the shoulder is gonna scare me into good behavior? You know what's more dangerous than boredom? Spite. You haven't seen that yet. Boredom keeps you on your toes. Spite has a body count. Always."

"Like you, I haven't shown all of my cards. Trust me when I say that it is in your best interest and mine to keep your mind on the job."

"Then you'd better make sure I've got a job to do."

"Fine. Finish the CME Activators you can make. When you are through, survey the remaining materials and give me a list of any of your little toys you can make with the spare parts. We'll see what you are capable of."

A smile came to his face. If it was any wider, it would have met at the back. "Now you're speaking my language. Okay, so I'll pop in the thrusters, push the initial code and AI, hook up the field generators and cannons . . ."

"AI? Cannons? We asked you for missiles."

"You asked me for the CME Activator. That's a deluxe piece of equipment. Bells and whistles o'plenty. Never let it be said I don't give my clients what they pay for. Just wait until you get a load of the goodies I've got in mind, though. A whole army of soldiers to test my stuff? This is going to be epic!" With that, Karter went merrily back to work.

In her lengthy tenure in the military, Purcell had not had very much contact with the designers of her weapons and equipment. Much to her chagrin, much of the equipment she routinely used had been designed decades prior, with only minor updates in the intervening years. There had always been the picture in her mind, however, of engineers of weapons and machines of war as solemn in their duty, aware of the death and destruction that their creations would cause. Karter hooked up wires and tapped at consoles with the eagerness and interest of a model train collector tinkering with a new caboose. Considering that this particular model was capable of crippling an entire star system, it was more than a little disturbing to see him applying the finishing details with a smile on his face.

She shook the thoughts from her mind.

“You're with me,” she instructed Marx.

The soldier fell into step beside her as she paced back toward her quarters.

“I trust you have been monitoring the media coverage of the Weston University operation?” she asked without looking.

“I have, Commander. Our organization is on everyone's lips.”

“And has our agenda been established?”

“Supplementary reports have included footage from one of our issued demands from several years ago. It isn't up-to-date, but it communicates the message.”

“Mmm. Good. Long past time for that. Now, the footage included a man, Trevor Alexander.”

“Yes, Commander?” he said, curiously.

“What do we know about him?”

“Only what was said in the report. Former racer or something like that.”

“Any military history? Past collaborations with people we are currently watching?”

“Not that I know of. I can have it looked into.”

“Do it. Our benefactor seems to think his presence is a major complication and, much as I am loath to admit it, he has yet to give us bad information. If this man is about to become a problem for us, I want to be prepared. Where is he right now?”

“I don't know, Commander. Presumably still on Tessera.”

“You say the gunship is still near the planet. Do we have any operatives still on the surface?”

“Not for long. We're pulling them out now.”

“Keep them nearby, and try to keep an eye on this Alexander fellow. Follow him. Lay the groundwork to track him, and be ready to neutralize him if he even begins to look suspicious. Two of Karter's collaborators are already in action and unaccounted for. If this is another of them, I don't want to take any more chances. We are too close.”

#

In a luxurious hotel suite in the Pavilion on Tessera, the level of frenzied activity was nearly as high as it had been in Karter's fab-lab. Rather than a mad scientist making unilateral adjustments and being trailed by a swarm of engineering worker bees trying to keep up, this particular swirl of activity was orbiting a pretty young reporter barking orders at her harried assistant. Lex had briefly been recruited to help, but it quickly became clear that he lacked the necessary clerical and communication skills to be particularly useful. Thus, he found himself on the couch wearing an almost-clean shirt from his bag and watching as his girlfriend attempted to do the work of an entire newsroom with only the help of a single, barely-recovered intern.

"Have you gotten to anyone on Virga? I want to see if that facility he named actually had a break-in, like he said," Michella barked.

"Not yet. It is the middle of the night there. I don't think we'll get anyone until morning," Jon explained, a slidepad in each hand and three more laid out on the table in front of him.

"And what about Manticore?"

"Still having communications trouble--and, besides, they are a maximum security prison. I don't think they will be forthcoming."

"You leave that to me. Just get them on the line. And--"

"Mitch," Lex said.

"--don't forget that other place. I'll get the name in a second. He said--"

"Mitch," Lex attempted, a little louder.

"--they might have *six* people working there as maintenance--"

"*Mitch!*"

"What is it, Trevor!" she replied in exasperation.

"I was just wondering if you were planning on breaking for dinner at some point?"

"We'll get room service to bring something up later."

"It wasn't so much the eating as the going somewhere besides here and eating," Lex said.

"You and I both know that if we leave the hotel, we're going to be helplessly buried in crowds of people split between reporters trying to get interviews and our adoring public."

"I can think of worse things."

"I don't have time for it right now. I've got to get as much info together and verified as possible. Now that these Neo-Luddites are big news, I don't have a monopoly on the research, and there are people out there with more resources than one intern. *And* I've got that stupid keynote to worry about."

"The keynote? But . . . terrorists bombed the city! They didn't cancel it!?"

"The Rackton City Council begged them to finish. They don't want it to seem like Rackton isn't a safe place anymore."

"It *isn't* a safe place anymore."

"They got what they want, they won't be--"

"I've got Manticore on line . . . on . . ." Jon interrupted, trying to indicate the correct device with hands and arms completely immobilized by other devices. "On the one next to the wadded-up napkin!"

"Trevor, I'm sorry. I don't have time right now. I've got to get this done. Later, after the keynote, we'll sit down and--"

"Virga on the slidepad next to the coffee."

"Later, Trev. I promise."

He nodded, standing up and heading for the door. "No problem, babe.

I'll be downstairs. Maybe I can get a few people to buy me drinks."

"Just don't accept any drinks from someone prettier than me."

"Shouldn't be a problem," he said, turning to her and flashing a smile. "There's no such thing."

She returned his smile with one that could outshine the sun, then smoothly put on her game face and picked up a slidepad. "Warden Menlo? Yes, this is Michella Modane. I'd like to thank you so much for taking this moment to speak with me . . ."

Lex shut the door and turned, suddenly coming face to face with an elderly Asian woman dressed in a Pavilion service staff uniform and carrying a bundle of folded laundry. She looked ancient, frail, and extremely irritated.

"Did you leave these?" she demanded, dangling the clothes in front of his nose.

"Uh . . . yeah. Were you the one who had to clean them?"

"More like decontaminate. 'Complimentary' has limits, you know. Less than two types of body fluids."

"I must have missed that in the fine print."

She squinted at him before adding, "You're the one on the news."

She delivered the line sharply, like she was accusing him of stealing a pie off of her window sill.

"Yes, ma'am."

"Well, here's your clothes, Mr. Hero. In light of your heroic deeds, this will still be complimentary. But the recommended gratuity is two thousand credits, and if you want someone on my staff to clean and fix that burnt-up, bloody shirt you were wearing on the news, same gratuity."

"Yeah, that's fair," he said, digging out a few chips.

Once the extorted tip was delivered, she handed him his clothes, gave a stiff nod, and marched off down the hall.

"Service has gone a little downhill since the last time I was here," he muttered, bleeping the door open to stow them inside.

After pausing to listen to Michella wheel and deal for a few seconds, he shut the door and made his way down the hall and into the elevator. It didn't take very long for the crowds of hero-hungry well-wishers to find him. It was astonishing how tightly the people of Rackton were clinging to the act of "heroism" he and the others had committed. It was as though they believed that if they gripped it tightly enough, this silver-lining would somehow undo the dark cloud. Thus, Lex was dragged to one of the Pavilion's many lounges, showered with drinks of steadily increasing alcoholic content, and asked to share his tale again and again. The sudden return to fame, now that he could afford to enjoy it, was intoxicating. More intoxicating, though, was the nearly unbroken string of progressively more elaborate beverages that were sent his way. It had been longer than he'd cared to admit since he'd been a part of a social gathering as lively as this, so he indulged a little more than he should have. The night turned into a pleasant haze of inebriation that allowed a few minor details to slip by him. He failed to notice that his speaking volume had drifted well out of the acceptable indoor range, for instance, and he forgot that mixing beer and liquor tended to end poorly for him.

He also failed to notice the man at the far end of the bar who had been quietly observing him. It was subtle enough that it likely would have slipped past Lex even if he had been sober, but a particularly paranoid individual would have quickly become aware of the way the quiet, plainly-dressed man followed, with a limp, every time Lex moved to a different part of the hotel lounge.

Over the course of a few hours the crowd began to dwindle, the men and women looking for pictures and handshakes got what they were after, and Lex settled into one of the softer chairs in the lounge to nurse what was likely to be the last free drink of the night. It was a ridiculous concoction, with paper umbrellas, fruit wedges, and colors never intended to exist in nature. It was like drinking a five-year-old's birthday party, and if it hadn't been the eighth or ninth drink of the night, he probably would have been embarrassed to be seen with it. He was well beyond the point of embarrassment, though. His chief concern right now was drinking the syrupy sweet beverage without poking his eye out on one of the skewered cherries. He was only moderately successful.

"Honestly, whose idea was it to combine alcohol and pointy things," he groaned, blinking away some pineapple juice from a wedge that had found its way into his eye.

"You are the hero," said a voice.

Lex turned to see the quiet gentleman from the edge of the bar. "Yeah, one of 'em."

His latest admirer took a seat. "Did I hear you say that you were a former racer?" he asked.

"I might have said that once or twice or thirty times. Seems like people weren't too interested in that," Lex slurred.

"I'm sort of a ship fan. I figured a former racer might have an interesting ship. You did come here on your own ship, didn't you?"

"Oh, yeah. A one-of-a-kind one, too. Let me tell you, if you are a ship buff, you'd get a kick out of old *Son of Betsy*."

"What kind?"

"One of a."

"Yes, but . . . what make and model?"

"It is an interceptor. Black. Looks stock. Is extremely not stock. I think it is officially a Cantrell Aerospace Intrasystem Interceptor, Type D. Heh. Type D."

"Why is that funny?"

"It isn't. It's funny that he thinks it's funny."

"Who?"

"Doesn't matter," Lex said.

"When did you arrive, and where?"

"Uh . . . man, was it really yesterday? I went to one of those shipyards on the edge of town."

"Which one?"

"East Side . . . something or other. Why do you care?"

"Just curious. Thanks for talking to me," he said, standing and limping away.

"Uh, yeah, no problem," Lex said, adding beneath his breath, "Weirdo."

The night crept on, and the lounge continued to empty out. After a few hours, Jon showed up in the lounge. He was looking thoroughly exhausted. When he spotted Lex, he made his way over and plopped down beside him.

"That woman is inexhaustible!" Jon said.

"That's very true. It can be fun, sometimes."

"Not when you work for her. She sent me for food while she picks apart another one of those loose threads from that guy you guys talked to. I think the kitchen is going to mysteriously take about twenty minutes longer than we expected. I think I'm also going to have a drink. That looks good. What is it?"

"Cap'n McKenzie's Azure Mai Tai," he said. "But it tastes more like liquid cotton candy."

"That's my kind of drink," Jon said, flagging down the nearest waiter and placing an order. "So. What's next for you?"

"Oh, I don't know. I've got to get back to Golana before too much longer. In my businesses, if you aren't around for long enough, clients start looking elsewhere. What about you and Mitch?"

"Ugh. Don't get me started. She's booked at least three face-to-face interviews. We are going to be globetrotting for weeks."

"Great . . . you know something, Jon? It is getting hard to tell the difference between Mitch and me as a couple versus Mitch and me broken up."

"Sorry to hear that, Mr. Alexander. You'll work it out, though. I mean, you're both insane danger addicts with little regard for your own safety. You can't find compatibility like that on a dating site."

"Yeah, maybe. Oh, well. Women, am I right?"

"You're asking the wrong guy," Jon said.

"Oh. Yeah, I guess so. Well, let me give you the rundown. Women are like a drug. When you're first getting started, it is all about feeling good. You convince yourself that it is just something you're doing for fun, something to make yourself feel good. Physical stuff, nothing serious. Before long, though, she gets her claws into you. Works her way into your brain. You realize you just don't feel right without her. You know it isn't good for you, that it is driving you insane, but even the insanity feels right. You just want more of it. Can't get enough."

"Gonna have to face it, you're addicted to love," Jon quoted, raising the glass.

"Where is that from?"

"I don't know. Some folksong, I think."

"Well, whatever it's from, it's true. Seriously. And it does permanent damage, too. Before long, all of the stuff you complain about them doing, you're doing. Fixating on the relationship. Getting clingy and needy. Honestly, love is like contagious insanity."

"Beats the alternative."

Lex grunted in agreement. "Women. Can't live with them, can't live without them."

"Once again, speak for yourself. But if it is any consolation, men can be just as bad."

"Well that's good to know. I'd hate to think you guys had somehow found a loophole out of the madness."

"Rest assured that such is not the case."

"Well, this conversation has suddenly made me feel incredibly uncomfortable, so I think I'm going to call it a night." He looked out the lounge window to see that the sun was still out. "I guess make that call it an afternoon. How long *are* the days on this planet."

"Too long. Lucky they've got the convention running on GST, or the shuttle lag would have killed me by now."

GST, or Galactic Standard Time, was the way the various settlements tried to keep themselves lined up on the same schedules and calendars. Since different planets had days and years that were different lengths, there had to be some common ground. Much to the chagrin of the Orionians and Teekers, that standard ended up being Earth days and Earth years, all lined up with Earth's Prime Meridian.

"What'd she send you to get, by the way?" Lex asked. "No, let me guess. Mac and cheese, and a hot cocoa with a double shot of espresso in it."

"Yep. Is that a regular for her?"

"That's her 'burning the midnight oil' meal. I'll bring it up, then I'm calling it a night. I intend to use all of my masculine wiles to convince her to call it a night as well, so knock before you try coming in."

"And what would *you* know about masculine wiles?"

"I guess we'll find out in a minute."

"Well, good luck to you. Success for you means a few hours of sleep for me. You coming to the keynote tomorrow?"

"Yeah, but then I'm heading out."

"All right--see you tomorrow, Mr. Alexander."

Lex cleared enough of the dangerous beverage ornaments out of the way to finish his drink, then stumbled over to the catering area to place an order. It turned out that they didn't have mac and cheese. They did, however, have “Fresh made genuine Dakota durum pasta, prepared casserole-style in an extravagant aged Tillamook cream sauce, topped with sage and crumbled brioche.” A bit of effort managed to track down a grilled cheese sandwich, which was masquerading under the alias “Tillamook panini.” As a to-go platter was assembled, Lex made a mental note to find these Tillamook people and demand that they tell him what they did with all of the other cheeses.

Getting the over-dignified comfort food to Michella's room while heavily under the influence of his under-dignified cocktails proved difficult--but before long, he was finagling his slidepad out of his pocket and bleeping the door open.

“Room service,” he said.

Michella looked up. The hours of arguing, scraping, digging, researching, and bargaining were showing all over her face. A few stray locks of auburn hair had escaped her ponytail and were dangling in front of her face, her glasses were in danger of slipping off the end of her nose, and all around her was an explosion of handwritten notes on torn out notebook pages.

“Trev,” she said, brushing the hair out of her eyes and removing her glasses to give the lenses a polish with the hem of her shirt. “What happened to Jon?”

“He managed to chew through his own ankle and make a break for the border,” Lex said, placing down the tray and removing the lid. As Michella grabbed the chocolate and coffee concoction and eagerly breathed in its aroma, Lex grabbed the cheese sandwich and took a bite, adding through a mouthful of gourmet ingredients, “You make any progress?”

“Some, but I hit a wall. I really hate working the military for information. Even the janitors have had security training.”

“How far did you get?”

“Far enough to know this Garotte guy is the real deal. I've dug up at least six different names he's used, and I'm pretty sure none of them are his real name. He's . . . he's not the kind of person you want to be dealing with, Trev.”

“A bad guy?”

“A guy that usually shows up right before something terrible happens. There are eighteen global governments that swear he doesn't exist, and a dozen more that really *wish* he didn't exist, and at least four that are actively trying to make sure he doesn't exist for much longer.”

“Great. So it may not have been a good idea to give him a hand.”

“I'm not so sure. Most of the people I talked to who really want him dead seem to be from the remnants of some pretty nasty governments and corporations and such. I don't know, though. At this point, my mind is mush," she explained, sipping her drink and scooping up some of the mac and cheese.

"Any chance you'll be getting sleep any time soon?"

She shook her head.

"What if I ask nicely?"

"Loads to do still."

"What if I use logic?"

"Like?"

"Like you're giving a big speech tomorrow, and you get ugly circles under your eyes when you don't sleep."

She scowled at him.

"I would like to point out at this time that I've had some cocktails and may not be my usual discreet self."

"Keep it up and your usual discreet self is going to wake up on the couch tomorrow."

"Hey. Back home I sleep on the couch every night, so you'll have to try harder than that."

She sighed. "Once the espresso wears off, straight to bed, I promise."

"You better. And . . . out of curiosity, is any of this digging going to put a bull's-eye on your back?"

"Have your escapades put one on yours?"

"I don't *think* so . . ." Lex said with more than a little uncertainty in his voice.

"Well, then neither do I."

Lex dropped down on the couch. "I'm starting to think that if you combined all of the common sense and rational thought between the two of us, there might be enough for *one* sane person."

"We're just committed, that's all."

"Either that or we should *be* committed."

Chapter 23

Lex had planned to stay up until Michella turned in, but a belly full of booze and grilled cheese decided sleep was a better idea. A wake-up call got them both out of bed, him with a vicious hangover, her with about two hours of sleep, and each with less than an hour to get ready and get to the keynote. The haze of sleep and residual inebriation blended the first few hours of the day into one big blurry blob of activity. He was reasonably sure that he attended and enjoyed the keynote. There might have been some sort of mixer afterward, where he had shaken a few hundred more hands and smiled a lot, too.

The only thing that really stuck in his mind was returning to the hotel, gathering up his things, and saying his goodbyes to Jon and Michella as they got ready for their flight. Things didn't start to clear for good until he managed to get his hands on some Sobrietin, a hangover cure that he vowed never again to be caught without.

"I trust you enjoyed your stay in Rackton, and be sure to visit again," said the gate agent at the shipyard mechanically.

Lex considered asking if the chipper young agent was aware that there had been a terrorist attack the previous day, and if perhaps the standard script might not be appropriate on a day like this, but he decided to just nod and step onto the lift that would sweep him at dizzying speed to his ship's storage bay. The electric motors hummed to life and zipped him along the rails as a dozen ships whisked by, gradually slowing as he approached *S.O.B.*'s temporary home. As it aligned with the platform, he found that the lights in the bay were already lit, and that a uniformed maintenance man in gloves and a dust mask was just stepping out from under his ship.

"Who are you? What are you doing here?" Lex asked.

"Rackton Transit Authority. Security sweep," said the man tersely.

"Why?"

"Rackton police special mandate. Security sweeps on all ships with recent off-world activity. You're clean."

"Oh. Good to see someone is acknowledging that there was a terrorist attack yesterday. Seems like the whole city is trying to ignore that it even happened."

The maintenance man made a vague grunt of agreement as he limped onto the platform and left without further comment. Lex watched the platform leave, trying to shake a nasty feeling of suspicion. To satisfy his inner paranoid delusional, he gave the ship a thorough looking-over before finally climbing into the cockpit. He performed the well-practiced contortionist act of putting on a flight suit while in the cramped confines of the ship, then submitted the ship to the automated takeoff queue. Because old habits died hard, worked his way through the standard takeoff checklist manually.

"Engine power-up self-test--successful. Deflector array diagnostic successful. Spend some quiet time alone with Mitch . . . failed. Star chart pre-calibration--successful. Figure out how this stupid relationship is supposed to work . . . pending."

To their credit, Rackton and Tessera had managed to get the backup automation node up and running already, the previous day's attack having utterly destroyed the primary node. Any other planet that suffered an attack like the one that Tessera had would have still been working out how to get the ground traffic flowing again, let alone handling the departure of starships. The city planners and engineers in charge here had managed to get things functional to the point where there was barely a delay. In less than an hour, his ship was in the final automated departure steps, and he was counting the seconds until the control of the ship was handed back to him. Lex fidgeted in his seat like a puppy waiting for someone to open the door to the backyard. Finally, the autopilot light clicked off and he pounced on the controls.

"About time!" he grumbled, taking the controls and guiding the ship toward the nearest VectorCorp route. "Okay, now to do a few on-the-books jumps, just in case the Rackton cops are feeling skittish, then fly around until I stop feeling stir-crazy."

He fell into line with the other ships, handling the maneuvering himself, for no reason other than because no one was telling him he couldn't, and jumped to FTL. At each transfer station, he took the least popular route until his sensors told him that there were only a few ships nearby, then quietly dropped off of the beaten path and decided to blaze himself a new trail. After scouting out a stretch of space he felt probably wouldn't kill him, he jumped to FTL again.

"Okay, should be about two hours, and I'll come out here," he said to himself. "That array looks like a good place to shake anybody that might follow me . . . like that guy."

He looked down at the monitor, where there was a single, steady blip on his gravitational sensor. As the only long-range sensor that worked at FTL, it tended to get his full attention when it made noise at a time like this.

"Exact same speed, exact same course, and much bigger than me," he said. "So there are two possibilities here. This is a freelancer with a heavy load trying to steal a safe route, or this is somebody trying to arrest and/or kill me. I can't imagine which one it is."

Slowly, Lex dialed up the speed. A happy consequence of the way that scientists had found to sidestep the peskier aspects of the laws of physics was that one set of equipment did all of the work for faster-than-light and conventional speed travel. That meant that *S.O.B.*, which had an engine overpowered enough to outrun just about any other ship at sub-light speed, would have the same advantage on the other side of the light barrier. He had been running at eighty percent, which was usually enough to leave pursuit craft in the dust while not putting too much stress on the engine. As the engine power ticked up past ninety percent, the ship behind him started to drop away.

"Okay . . . well, that'll buy me a few minutes once I show up," Lex said.

He pushed it to one hundred percent, the maximum safe rating, and the blip on the sensor screen fell farther back. Just for the extra breathing room, he pushed further, inching his equipment past the red line. By the time he hit one hundred-ten percent, the dot finally dropped out of range, but it was time to slow down again. Not because he was afraid his engine would blow, but because if he cranked it up any further, he'd hit the end of his carefully selected FTL run before he could slow down.

His eyes turned to his destination. Like any good freelancer, once he left the official path, he made sure that each stop was a decent place to hide or lose a tail. It was not unheard of that a diligent or observant patrol would catch him on their sensors and follow him to deliver a stern talking-to and a hefty fine, so it paid to take precautions. Right now, he was headed toward a communications relay cluster. It was a tight little clump of remote satellites that received and distributed the fancy FTL communication signals that had been rigged up to ensure that emails warning of minor transit delays didn't end up arriving decades after the ships did.

As hiding spots went, this seemed like a bad choice. Relay stations were both expensive and essential, which translated to great security. The instant he even got close, all sorts of really angry alarms would start sounding, and within minutes there would be patrols and repair crews on hand to take care of the intruders and whatever damage they might have done. One would think that this was exactly the opposite of what Lex would want, except for two things. Law and traffic enforcement patrols had to fill out a *load* of paperwork if they violated the safety perimeter of a relay station, and pirates and other freelancers were just as eager to avoid being noticed as Lex was, so just about anyone who might tail him would think twice about following him into the array. He crossed his fingers and hoped that whoever was chasing him fell into one of those categories. On the more-than-likely chance that he wasn't so lucky, he pulled out the all-important stick of chewing gum and loaded it into his mouth.

The ship slid quickly down to speeds that Einstein would have approved of, allowing the majority of his sensors to switch back on and immediately inform him in no uncertain terms that he was in big trouble. Ahead of him was what looked like an extremely spread-out parking lot, ship-sized clusters of receiver dishes and transmitter antennas laid out in a grid to form what Lex had once heard called a "phased array," whatever that was. Scattered around the area were similar arrays, angled vaguely at important star systems, broadcasting to anything near enough to get it in a few minutes and engaging in sophisticated quantum trickery to get data to other similar arrays for everything else. A lengthy and extremely detailed warning message was being transmitted by the array, informing him of ordinances and policies he was violating, but he ignored it and zipped in among the satellites.

Once he was nestled beside one, he dialed down the power and switched the ship into silent mode. It was yet another of the niceties that Karter had installed--though in this case, it was one he actually asked for. With the right settings, *S.O.B.* was invisible to almost any sensor but visual, and the relay satellite would hide him from prying eyes.

Normally, he would flit around inside the relay array for a while until the person on his tail was good and confused, then make a jump to the next location, but this time, a different tactic was called for. He didn't know for sure who it was that was following him or how they had managed it. A little bit of hide and seek would give him a chance to see what he was dealing with. It didn't take long for his shadow to arrive. What dropped out of FTL at the outer perimeter of the relay array was a ship that was triple the mass of his, armed to the teeth, and with fully-activated weapons. For the moment, though, the guns weren't the most worrying thing about the vessel.

For one thing, it shouldn't be there. Even if the pilot had known precisely where Lex was headed, it should have overshot by a few hundred thousand kilometers, since Lex was the one who had decided precisely when to stop, and this guy would have had to react to that. Human reaction time, multiplied by many times the speed of light, equals a ship *extremely* far off-course. This guy had stopped precisely where Lex did.

Lex didn't even know how that was possible. Either the pilot of this ship was a clairvoyant, or Lex had somehow been tracked. Regardless of how it had been pulled off, it translated to a ship heading directly for the array, and an intimidating ship at that. It looked similar to the gunship that had shown up on Tessera . . . in fact, it looked exactly like the gunship that had shown up on Tessera. The front end was equipped with the same four turrets and there was a pair of yawning missile launchers under a pilot compartment that was completely armored, foregoing even a viewing window. A dark blue energy shield shimmered into being around it, produced by the heftiest looking emitters Lex had ever seen. The rest of the ship was all engines and reactors and, according to Lex's sensors, every one of them was belching out enough heat to suggest that a catastrophic failure was not far off.

As more time passed and more sensors were able to complete their sweeps, it became increasingly evident that this thing was one serious predator . . . and it wasn't just heading for the array, it was heading *directly* for Lex's ship.

“What? No! I'm in stealth mode, how did they find me? There *can't* be a tracking device, I checked the ship before I left! That's it. When this is over I'm getting a built-in hull scanner . . . wait . . . computer, activate hull scanner.”

After a few moments, one of the voices Ma had borrowed announced, “Hull scanner active. Scan underway.”

“I seriously have to get Ma to give me that list of features they installed that I didn't ask for.”

“Unknown electronic device attached to the port side, aft docking socket.”

“He put it *underneath* the docking clamp? Man, whoever this guy is, he's good,” Lex said. “Let's see what sort of gear he's got, though. That beast might be better armed than me, but there is no way he's as agile as I am. All I have to do is get out of range before--”

“Plasma cannon lock detected,” computer stated.

“*Come on*!” Lex objected, hammering the throttle.

“Missile--missile--missile--missile--lock detected.”

“Please, tell me you've got a stutter,” Lex groaned, pulling hard at the controls in time to just barely avoid the first volley of plasma bolts. Holding down one button and tapping another activated his ship's not-so-legal offensive mode, and updated the displays appropriately.

He flicked a sparing glance at the sensor screen to see four missiles closing fast. A nice little “time to impact” counter was tracking each one. With an exasperated squeak that caught in his throat, Lex angled his ship down and juiced the throttle further, but it was pretty clear that the missiles were going to catch up. No problem, they were grouped together, and *S.O.B.* had all sorts of fun tricks up its sleeve.

He dialed the engine down to 98.6 percent, double-tapped his lights, and popped his heat dumpers. What precisely all of that meant didn't matter. The important thing was that it was the secret command to trigger a burst of circuit-scrambling radio waves out of his ship's rear end--an electromagnetic pulse. All four missiles flared and flew wildly off-course, drawing fun little squiggles on his screen before three out of four prematurely detonated.

“Yeah! Is that all you got!?”

“Missile--missile--missile--missile--lock detected.”

“I guess not.”

The EMP trick, alas, was a one-shot deal, since it took a minute or so to recharge, and that was about fifty-five seconds too long. His brain chewed on the alternatives and spat out a typically desperate stunt. The missiles were fast--very fast--but that also meant that it would take them forever to turn, as the single remaining scrambled one, which was just now beginning to head back toward him, was illustrating. If he wanted to dodge them, all he had to do was make a sharp turn. Unfortunately, that wasn't the sort of thing that could be done in space. That was, not unless Lex got creative.

"Thruster output down, reactor output up," Lex muttered, tugging and pushing at the appropriate controls.

His thrusters dropped down to a dull glow, bringing his acceleration to nothing and allowing the missiles to gain on him that much quicker. Meanwhile, his reactor hummed and shuddered, building up one hell of a lot of energy without anywhere to send it. He watched his sensors, all the while nudging his thrusters to pivot his ship until he was practically facing the incoming ordinance. Soon, he was sliding almost perfectly backward through space, the distant glowing dots of the missiles clearly visible through the cockpit window. He waited, watching the dots get closer and judging his time. At the last possible moment, he dumped the power into the thrusters. The ship lurched.

"Hold together, hold together, hold together," he chanted through clenched teeth.

His ship's frame groaned and complained as the sudden change in direction subjected it to stresses that no sane engineer would have designed for. Lucky for Lex, then, that the man who designed *S.O.B.* was a certified lunatic, because he managed to avoid flying to pieces. The four missiles previously on his tail couldn't adjust quickly enough, rocketing past him, far too close for comfort. The good news was that he'd survived the attack. The bad was that he was now flying away from the array, which represented the only thing resembling cover or safety for light-years, and flying toward the ship, which had evidently decided that it was perfectly willing to play a game of chicken, and give that plasma cannon another try while it was at it.

Bright violet bursts of plasma began to trace their dotted lines of destruction toward Lex's ship. He dodged and rolled, keeping himself just ahead of the string of blasts. One hand kept the ship on course, the other danced across the other controls, panic and exhilaration playing tug of war with his dexterity. He activated the more aggressive mode of his tractor beam and flipped it to the rear.

"Computer, voice interface."

"Voice interface act--"

"Auto-target missiles and auto-fire."

"Unable to comply."

"Oh, sure," Lex growled, "*that* they don't give me."

"Unknown command: missiles."

"Auto-target trailing . . . targets," he attempted, casting a nervous glance at the blips that were now back on his tail and making up for lost time.

"Unknown command: trailing targets."

A pair of plasma bolts grazed his shields, knocking them down a few percent.

"Auto-target best target. Fire, fire, fire!"

Evidently those had been the magic words, as he felt the familiar jackhammer rhythm of his improvised weapon activating. It took a few shots at the missiles, and even managed to destroy one, but quickly decided that the best target was the gunship bearing down on him. As the tractor beam rattled at the war machine, Lex realized a few key points. The first was that two fast ships going head-on makes for a very short game of chicken. The second was that it didn't take a physicist to figure out who would win if his sleek speedster of a ship were to collide with the armored, shielded, charging opponent.

The four cannons on the gunship tracked Lex tighter and tighter, trying to cut off his escape and box him in. It took more and more of his mind and body to wrestle the ship through the shrinking gaps in the attacks. Bolts were almost constantly lapping at the edge of his shields, chipping away at his protection. Finally, there simply weren't enough free brain cells left to continue to second guess what was clearly the only option left to him.

He held his course, taking a few direct hits on his forward shields in order to maintain the straight-line trajectory he needed for his "plan" to work, then eased the ship down at the last minute, dipping below the gunship and back up again. An instant later, the missiles that had so diligently been following him found an obstacle--the ship that fired them. The explosion was massive, swallowing the ship in a ball of blue-white energy bright enough to activate *S.O.B.*'s windshield tint even from behind.

"Oh, my god," Lex breathed in terrified awe. "I killed him . . ."

He fought to catch his breath and slowly brought his ship around to survey the results of the blast. It was something he never thought he'd have to do. Something he never thought he would be able to do. But . . . there hadn't been any other choice, had there? This ship, whoever was flying it, had been going to destroy him. It had been self-defense.

Lex squinted at the residual trail of energy, trying to make out any wreckage and debris that he would have to avoid. It looked like . . .

His expression dropped. "Oh, my god!" he cried, this time in mounting terror. "I *didn't* kill him!"

Instead of a sizzling hull or cloud of slag, he saw a damaged but still functional ship, its flickering blue shields blinking on and off as it sluggishly turned for another attack run. Lex's brain slipped back into "fly for your life" mode. According to the ship's sensors, his burly foe's shields were at forty percent, and the handful of attacks that had hit their mark had left *S.O.B.*'s own shields at less than twenty percent.

"If that thing's weapons can't take it out, there is no way that mine can. I gotta lose him. It's the only way."

S.O.B.'s shields had absorbed a lot of punishment, but they had spared the rest of the vessel. There probably wasn't even a scratch on the paint job. His engine revving stunt hadn't done any serious damage either, but it had spiked the heat level in his systems and stressed the hell out of the power conduits, so pushing his ship to the limit would be a bad idea until he had a chance to tighten some connections and replace some hookups. That scrapped the plan of running long and hard until the beastly gunship overheated--and with that tracking device attached to the hull, no amount of running would do any good. He had to get it off. Doing so in the right way would involve going to a maintenance facility, which he would never make it to, or climbing out of the ship and prying it off himself, which would be suicidal. That meant he was going to have to do this the wrong way.

Lex was very good at doing things the wrong way.

He looked at the gunship, which had finally finished its turn and was firing with three of its four cannons. From the ponderous turn and the loss of one cannon, it seemed that the monster hadn't made it out of the explosion unscathed, despite the status of its shields. With any luck, that would give Lex enough leeway to play even faster and looser with his safety. Without any luck, well, Lex wouldn't be around for very long.

He pushed his engines as hard as he dared and rocketed past the gunship again, dodging a string of blasts as he did. His foe started another turn, attempting to pursue, while his guns tracked as closely as they could. *S.O.B.* bobbed and wove, using pivots, dips, barrel rolls, and any other tricks he could muster to try to stay on as direct a course back to the antenna array as possible without getting perforated. It didn't take long for the gunship to get on his tail and start to close the gap, illustrating that while its maneuvering had taken a hit, its top speed was doing just fine. A moment later it became clear that at least one of the missile launchers was alive and well, as Lex's irritatingly calm computer announced another pair of missile locks. He glanced at the impact countdown, then at the approaching antennas. It was going to be close. That was good, because it would have to be.

With a half-second to spare, he whipped past the first antenna and placed it between the missiles and himself just in time for a brilliant explosion to cost the good people at VectorCorp one of their arrays, and costing the psychopath two missiles. Thus began what was probably the most expensive and high-stakes game of tag ever played, with Lex blazing through the grid of antennas like a last-minute shopper looking for the last spot in a mall parking lot. His makeshift weapon, which was still automatically firing at the best target, took a few potshots at the gunship now and then, but the heavy-duty shields shrugged off the attacks. On the other hand, the pursuing ship was spraying bolts of plasma all over the area, blowing holes in dozens of antennas and ensuring that an awful lot of data wasn't going to be reaching its destination any time soon. When the lion and gazelle act had given him some breathing room, he started to edge his ship closer to the passing antennas.

"Okay . . . just a little closer," he mumbled.

"Caution. Proximity alert. Extreme collision threat," the computer helpfully bellowed.

"Shut up, *S.O.B.*" He took a deep breath, glanced at the location of the marauding gunship, and did what would stand as one of the most counter-intuitive actions he would commit for a very long time. He switched off his shields.

"Computer, display hull scan results."

A three-dimensional representation of the ship appeared on his screen, highlighting the tiny foreign object. He angled the ship awkwardly and gritted his teeth.

"I'm sorry, baby," he said with a squint, then subtly nudged the unshielded ship toward the next relay module to go by.

A heartbreaking scrape shook the ship.

"Re-scan hull!"

"Minor cosmetic damage to port side of ship. Unknown electronic device attached to--"

Lex nudged in for another scrape.

"Re-scan hull!"

"Moderate cosmetic damage to port side of ship. Unknown electronic--"

One last, grinding scrape rang out, this time ending with a distinctive ping.

"Re-scan hull!"

"Minor structural damage to port side, aft docking clamp. Major cosmetic damage to port side."

"No unknown electric device! Woo!" Lex cried, but his celebration was cut short by a crackling plasma bolt glancing across his rear stabilizer. "Shields up! Shields up!"

It took a moment before Lex got control of *S.O.B.* again, and by then the gunship was tight on his tail. The controls weren't quite acting the way they were supposed to anymore, which meant the shields were forced to absorb one last shot and collapse before Lex got the hang enough to dodge the weapons fire again.

"Just gotta get him to lose sight of me long enough to make the next FTL jump," he stammered breathlessly, as he listened to shrapnel from the dozens of damaged and destroyed relays clattering against his completely unshielded ship. A particularly large hunk of satellite dish bounced off of his windshield. "Some navigational shields would be nice, too. Since I don't want to die when I make the jump."

He glanced down at the shield indicator to see that it would be at least forty-five seconds before the emitters had finished charging enough to restore the flimsy but essential navigational shield, and more than three minutes for the ones that would actually keep the gunship from blowing him up. With one hand on the controls, he commenced tapping on the display, because it was a well-known fact that tapping on any indicator would make it show Lex the information he wanted more quickly.

"Missile lock detected."

"I thought he was done with those!!" Lex objected, putting both hands back on the controls and pulling hard back into the rapidly dwindling rows of relays.

A well-timed roll drove the pursuing missile into one of the handy obstacles.

"Six ships are entering the proximity," the computer announced.

"Yes! The cavalry has arrived."

His screen displayed six little dots. Because these were law-abiding ships, rather than trespassing freelancers or murderous terrorists, they actually had their transponders active, so each dot had a handy little label, proclaiming them to be VectorCorp Patrol Vessels. At any other time, Lex would have dreaded seeing them, but right now a half-dozen corporate cops were nothing short of salvation . . . as long as they didn't spot him. There was very little chance of that, though. A psychopath piloting a military vehicle has a way of demanding undivided attention, as Lex had just learned firsthand. *S.O.B.*, with its slick paint job and stealth coating would just fade into the background--but, just to make sure, he directed his ship in the least debris-strewn direction he could identify, gave the engines one last rev, then dropped them down to zero. Once he was coasting, he flipped on a handy device called a cryo-shunt, which absorbed his engine's heat for a few minutes. Once he'd slid back into stealth, he was practically impossible to detect unless someone knew exactly where to look.

On his ship's display, he watched the feed from his rear camera as the patrol took up their positions around the gunship. Various warnings that were destined to be ignored were broadcast on all of the usual frequencies, instructing all involved to power down weapons and engines and prepare to be towed to the nearest "processing station," a VectorCorp facility that would normally be called a courthouse, except that calling it that would mean that there would have to be the opportunity for irritating things like lawyers and trials and due process. The gunship replied by opening fire on the nearest ship, which prompted all six of the VC ships to return fire.

If his shields hadn't been torn up by the scuffle with Lex, the gunship probably could have taken the hit. As it was, there was a bright red flash, followed by a bright blue flash, followed by the pyrotechnic masterpiece of every remaining piece of ordinance aboard the gunship going off simultaneously. The display went on for nearly a minute, which gave Lex time enough to flick on his nav-shield. The VectorCorp ships still hadn't noticed him, so as long as they didn't notice in the next few seconds, he would be able to get the hell out of there.

He was flipping through the various settings to make sure it was safe to do an FTL jump when he caught a glimpse of his clock.

“Six PM . . . wait, what day is it?” he said slowly.

As an answer, his slidepad chirped Michella's ringtone. One would have thought that all of the damage done to the array would have been enough to keep it from relaying the call. He scrambled to answer, bringing up her face on the video screen.

“Hey, baby!” he said, quickly doing his best to tone down the various audio alerts going on.

“Hi, Trev. I know we just saw each other, but tradition's tradition, right?”

“Yeah, and it is bad luck to break a tradition.”

“My flight has been awful so far. We *just* left. How are things going for you?”

“Oh, you know. Same ol', same ol'.”

Michella squinted at him. “Is something going on, Lex?”

“What? No.”

“You look awfully sweaty.”

“The AC in *S.O.B.* is on the fritz.”

She leaned a bit closer. Suddenly her expression became stern. “You're chewing gum.”

“I needed to freshen my breath?”

“Out with it.”

Lex sighed. “Remember that gunship?”

“The one from the university?”

“Yeah.”

“Yeah.”

“Well, it blew up.”

“How?”

“You're going to hear about a VC array getting shot up right about now. That's how.”

His radio scanner quietly began to pick up chatter between the VC patrol ships indicating they were detecting a transmission from his general area.

“I thought you weren't going to get any more involved in this, Trev,” she reprimanded.

“I wasn't! They followed me!”

“How? Why?”

“I don't know! Listen, I've got to cut this off and get out of here or you're going to hear about me being apprehended and held for questioning regarding the aforementioned array getting shot up. Are you okay? No one came after you?”

“Not that I know of.”

"Okay, keep your eyes and ears open. I'll contact you when it is safe."

"Be safe, Trev."

"I'll do my best."

He closed the connection and made the jump to FTL just as one of the patrol ships started to head in his direction. As the view out his window stretched and blue-shifted out of visibility, his ship getting progressively faster, his mind started to slow down. For a moment, there was clarity. He saw what this event meant. These terrorists were in every cranny of the military. Could he run? Yes. He was good at running. Could he survive their attacks? Clearly he had a fighting chance of it, at least for a while. But what about the people around him? This had been an unmanned array, but he could have just as easily chosen a busy port or trading post. Every one of these destroyed arrays could have been another ship manned by innocent, unsuspecting people just trying to live their lives.

And what about Michella? How long before they decided to go after her? Lex was an ant, and the Neo-Luddites had a magnifying glass. Anywhere he went, there would be a line of charred ground trailing behind, and an awful lot of slightly slower ants burnt to a crisp.

There were no two ways about it. He would have to break the magnifying glass. Out came his slidepad.

"Open com Ma," he stated.

The slidepad tried to connect directly, displaying an irritating spinning icon as it did, and finally informed him that no network connections were available, which he already knew. He was presented with the choice of canceling, trying again, or the default option of doing a delayed delivery of the message which was currently recording.

"Ma, it's Lex. Listen, we need to talk. That gunship the terrorists used on Tessera just tried to kill me. I think I might be in too deep to get out without help . . ."

Chapter 24

Purcell stood among her men at the door to the scientist's cell. She'd seen him do some terribly disturbing things. She'd seen him issue commands that would kill everyone in the room. She'd seen him calmly endure isolation and sedation that would break any sane man. What she was seeing now managed to surpass them all. He was . . . whistling. The man was locked in his cell, deprived of his prosthetic arm and leg, and yet he seemed absolutely thrilled with life. His one hand held the dry erase marker he'd been permitted to keep, and with it he scrawled equations and notations on the wall, all the while with a song on his lips and a grin.

"Dee," she said, suspicion in her tone.

He turned and smiled. "Boss lady! How long have you been there? I thought you'd never come out of that room of yours."

"Why are you so happy?"

"Because I think I just broke my record for most products prototyped in a single day."

"You were supposed to complete the designs for the CME Activator before--"

"They've been done since a few hours after we got the fab lab up and running. They're in the computer. I've been drip-feeding you guys the schematics and such since then. We're just waiting on the alloy."

"You--"

Karter made a mutter of dismissal and gestured with his pen. "Never mind that. Near as I can figure, that transporter you guys have seems like it needs . . . eh, needs is a strong word . . . it *uses* a carrier wave to do a coordinate lock. The frequency wasn't included in the materials you gave me. You wouldn't happen to know it, would you?"

"You were given incomplete information for a reason."

"And you fudged some of the numbers, I know. I'm pretty sure I've got that all straightened out, though. It was fun. Like Sudoku, only with the potential for somebody's kidneys to end up eighty miles apart if you put a three in the wrong place, which I submit was the way the Sudoku guy would have wanted it."

"Listen, if the designs are complete and available, then I demand you give them to us!"

"You already have the designs for the transporter."

"*For the* Activator!"

"You don't have all of the parts for it yet, so having the design won't do you any good."

"That isn't for you to decide."

"What's wrong? The guy calling the shots getting impatient?"

She narrowed her eyes, silently wishing he had been equipped with his arm so that she could give him a motivating jolt toward compliance.

"Squint all you want," he countered. "I don't put the cherry on top of that design until your boys bring back the goods. Have you taken a look at that list of goodies I drew up for you?"

"I've had more important things to worry about than indulging you."

"I thought you'd feel that way, so I went ahead and discussed it with those worker drones you've got me palling around with. They picked some things they'd like to try. Mostly vanilla stuff, but I guess it's tough to get the really creative people to join your cult. They've been combing over the designs, not being able to make heads or tails of them, and itching to give one a try. Now you preach all of this 'we believe in trying the newest and best' nonsense. I'm giving you the opportunity to try out the future of warfare. You gonna take it? Are you gonna walk the walk, or just keep talking the talk like some sort of politician in a soldier costume?"

After a suitable amount of seething anger, Purcell tapped at her communicator. "Engineering!"

"Engineering here."

"I'm here with Dee. He tells me you've been looking at his designs. His . . . toys."

"Err . . . yes, Commander."

"What is your assessment?"

"Well, the concepts aren't . . . clear. But there are a few really interesting devices. I would like permission to fabricate some for testing."

"Is there a chance that they are a trick? Another escape attempt?"

"Based on Dee's tactics, that is always a possibility, but we can minimize the threat by choosing something with low power requirements, or something passive."

"I recommend the boots, or the shield. I'd really like to see the shield powered up," Karter offered.

"Stay out of this, Dee," she barked. "Engineering. Make a few careful selections and have them ready for me to review in a few minutes. If I give the okay, fabricate them and have them ready for demonstration in the backup docking bay tomorrow."

"Thatta girl! Let me know how it turns out," Karter said.

"Listen to me, Dee. This is for my men and my cause, not to satisfy your petty desire to have your designs tested."

“I don't care why you're doing it. Just get to it,” he said, turning away and scribbling on the wall again.

“Dee, I swear to you, I will--”

“I'm sorry, Commander,” interrupted Marx, “but intelligence is getting word on the assault ship.”

“Let's have it.”

“The communications were cut off suddenly a few hours ago, and now we've been getting chatter that a patrol of VectorCorp vessels were forced to destroy an unknown ship at its last known position, a relay array.”

“You're just burning through troops, aren't you? You're going to run out of ships at this rate,” Karter said conversationally.

“You're with me,” she said to Marx before turning to the lead security guard. “You, take that marker away from him, and wipe those figures off the walls.”

“Please, no, don't,” Karter said flatly as the cell door was opened. “What ever will I do?”

The security guard gave him an elbow to the chin and took the marker away, smearing away a swath of the writing on the wall with his arm.

“Really, boss lady? You're just going to let him do that?” Karter growled, spitting a glob of blood to the floor.

“Soldier, if you ever hit him again . . . I want to see a tooth on the floor,” Purcell instructed.

“Nice. Excellent discipline you're teaching these guys. Next time you ask for my help, I'm going to want an apology,” the scientist said, rubbing blood away from the corner of his mouth.

Purcell walked crisply away, her second in tow.

“Do we have any details about how it happened?” she hissed.

“Nothing, Commander. The patrol chatter doesn't even mention another ship in the area. Just a few stray transmissions. All we know is that the ship had already taken damage by the time the patrol had arrived, and most of the relay cluster had been destroyed.”

“He was chasing his target, correct?”

“Yes, Commander.”

“And there is no indication that this Trevor Alexander was ever anything but a hoversled racer, a chauffeur, and a delivery boy?”

“The only unusual thing we were able to turn up was that there was a large-scale alteration of his records a few months back, blanking out about two weeks of data in every civil, military, and corporate database we have access to.”

“That's all?”

“That's all.”

“How the hell does a non-military pilot even *evade* our men, let alone *damage* the most heavily armed and fortified ship we've got!?”

"I do not know, Commander."

"Get me all of the video footage you can find of him for the last two years. I'll review it myself. I want to see this man for myself, how he carries himself."

"Yes, Commander."

The pair worked their way through the tight, industrial passageways of the station until they reached engineering. The more theoretical members of the team, those more interested with the planning and testing phases than the actual construction, were busily sifting through the batch of schematics Karter had provided. Technical diagrams were displayed on large, wall-mounted screens and small, hand-held devices simultaneously, with hastily scrawled comments and notations coming from every member of the team at once. The air was thick with equations being figured out loud, while a dozen men and women with nearly two centuries of combined technical expertise tried to work out the deranged technological musings of Karter's twisted mind.

"What have you got?" Purcell demanded of the engineer nearest to the door.

He was a sleepy-eyed, harried wreck of a man, hair thinning from sheer stress and sporting the stretched-out and skinny physique of a man who had spent a few too many hours in zero-gravity.

"Oh, uh. Commander. The, uh, the designs are a little sketchy. Dr. Dee does *not* use very good design practices," he stammered defensively. "All of his designs reference other designs, so working out exactly how to build one of these, or what it will do, is next to impossible without having the entire historical context of--"

"Enough! Just tell me what he gave you that you think we can use," she ordered.

"Right, right," he said quickly, fumbling with his datapad and flipping through it. "Who's working the big screen? Put up . . . uh . . . put up the kinetic boots, the charge cannon, the signal manipulator, and the coil. The boots first, though. No, not those boots, Jerry, the ones that we agreed wouldn't set anything on fire. Right, right, those."

A technical drawing appeared on the big screen. At the center was a recognizable piece of footwear, but each individual piece of it was circled and blown up to reveal a level of detail that was baffling to anyone who hadn't taken an engineering graphics class.

"These are, well, these are the boots. He doesn't really have a specific name for them. This part here is called the kinetic capacitor mark 2, and this part is definitely the filter matrix, but--"

"Give me the high-level," Purcell said.

"Right, the high-level. Well. Over here he calls them double-jump boots, and that's a pretty accurate name. If the descriptions he gave are accurate, they store up kinetic energy, and based on the controls from this panel, which is hand-held, the kinetic energy is released. The effects are varied, but they could produce a second jump if they are activated in midair, or store up energy during a fall to slow decent, or deliver a kick with the force of five kicks--you name it, really."

"Interesting. What about the next device?"

"The charge cannon is an add-on module for energy weapons. It allows you to store up astounding amounts of energy to be released in one blast. In theory, it would allow you to compress the destructive potential of an entire clip into a single shot if you timed it right. The signal manipulator lets you alter the echo, interference, and phase shift of almost any transmission in order to disguise its origin. Not only that, it can allow you to make the signal appear to have come from just about anywhere. It will even produce secondary signals to confuse attempts at triangulation. Finally, there's the yo-yo coil. It is basically just a carefully designed node that amplifies the effect of a tractor beam, but the notes suggest that if you don't bolt it to anything, you can guide the coil through the air with virtually no energy loss and at spectacular range. It could easily--"

"That's enough," Purcell said. "He mentioned something about a shield."

"Err. Well, the other things all either interact with a power source that we supply or based upon controllable inputs . . . at least, we think. What he calls the 'rebound shield' has an integrated generator. Karter could probably pull some very destructive stunts with something like that. We don't even know what the design uses for fuel. The schematics say, 'you have to guess.'"

"How can they say that? How can he expect you to build and test one if he doesn't give you full designs?"

"He doesn't expect us to build it. He expects us to use the fab lab. The lab computer's designs are complete, and encrypted with a cypher we haven't even been able to put a dent in."

Purcell tapped her boot in thought for a few seconds. "Fabricate one of each. Disassemble and analyze them to be sure they aren't part of some sort of escape attempt, then set up testing parameters and see if they are functional. If they are, I want recommendations on how to equip and deploy troops with the best-performing devices."

The engineers looked at her with concern.

"Listen. Remember our stance. We contend that society must embrace the leading edge of technological development in order to survive. I mean to prove that by example," she instructed.

"But, Commander, these are devices created by a man who is openly hostile toward us."

"Such would be the case with any technology captured from an enemy. This is a test. It is a test of ability, adaptability, and resolve. I expect you all to pass it."

"Understood," the engineer said with a nod, hurrying back to the lab equipment to get to work.

She watched as her team began to pick apart the designs one final time before production, and slowly a smile came to her face. This was what it was all about. This was why she fought, why she took up the command. Karter had been attempting to manipulate her, that much was almost certain, but it didn't matter. He was right. He had the vision and skill to show the galaxy what was possible if they never allowed themselves to stop moving forward. They would find a way to control him in time, and he would fuel the technological revolution that had been building strength for so long. It would be glorious.

#

In the Armistice, Ma's carefully plotted course had taken them safely to their second money-gathering destination. By the time Silo had finished in the ship's "shower," all aboard had wisely chosen to pretend as though the slapping incident and the exchange that had prompted it had never happened, at least until they landed. This was somewhat difficult for Garotte, who had required three applications of ointment to heal the bruise from the final slap.

The last few minutes had been spent getting Silo ready to take her first steps into public since her incarceration. Her blonde hair had been dyed brunette, and her green eyes changed to brown to match. She was wearing a pair of large but stylish sunglasses, blue jeans, and a black jacket over a white tank top. As a finishing touch, she'd even applied a dash of makeup. To the average onlooker, she may as well have been out running some errands rather than on the run from terrorists and the authorities.

Garotte straightened himself up and looked to Silo, who was analyzing her new look in her slidepad's reflection.

"I don't know about the brown hair," she said with a frown, adjusting a few stray hairs.

"I'd suggested that you dye it red. I've always rather fancied redheads."

"Maybe if it was longer . . . so, how do you want to do this? Split up so that we can get through it faster?"

"Seems sensible. Our helpful little computer system has got your slidepad set up with a few of the accounts. Visit a few gambling kiosks, keep your payouts below, say, a half-million, and meet back here in an hour."

"What's our story? Are we husband and wife?"

"After that little domestic incident, I'm thinking of getting a divorce," he said, rubbing his jaw.

Silo bit her lip, "Ooh. I'm sorry about that. I let my temper get to me. You deserved a wallop, don't get me wrong, but I might have overdone it."

"Water under the bridge, my dear," he said, flashing a charming smile. "It is what happens when a pair of soldiers quarrel. And, besides, you are my darling Dora Gillespie, wife of six years and mother of our two beautiful children, Dennis and Rochelle."

"Not Rochelle. I like Marie better."

"Dennis and Marie then. And I am your beloved husband, Peter. We are, oh, let's say public relations representatives on our way back from a trade show for composite flooring."

Silo smirked. "You really enjoy this a bit too much."

He pulled her hand to his lips and gave it a kiss. "Impossible. Shall we go?"

"Please. I'm ready for something larger than a jail cell or a spaceship."

The pair opened the side door of the ship and marched out, allowing it to shut behind them without a second glance . . . and leaving Ma to watch them go. The AI flicked an ear and considered the mix of sensations and notions drifting about in her head. In the strictest sense, they hadn't wronged her in any way with their actions. They had all of the information necessary to perform the task at hand, and it had already been established that her presence would greatly increase the likelihood of their group being noticed and remembered. There was thus no reason for them to address her before leaving. Nevertheless, she was experiencing a pair of emotions that she, upon consulting the data available to her, believed could be positively identified as abandonment and resentment. They had not even said goodbye, something that neither would forget to do when departing one another. She grappled with the puzzle of whether these emotions were called for, and why they seemed to have asserted themselves so powerfully, when her slidepad finally managed to connect to the supply station's communication network and deliver the messages she'd missed during their journey. One message, from Lex.

She eagerly tapped and reviewed the message. As she did, she took careful note of what appeared to be a disproportionate enthusiasm for news from the pilot who, by rights, was no longer of concern for the current mission. He had been attacked, but was now safe, prompting what she felt certain was concern and relief in roughly equal measure. Prolonged usage of an organic brain was providing her with a marvelous amount of valuable data about the human condition--or, at least, what she was reasonably confident was a representative approximation of the human condition. She glanced at the time on the message and decided it was probable that he would be in communication range at this time. The appropriate menu was pulled down and a call was connected.

"Ma?" Lex said, his face sliding into view on the screen of the device. He looked anxious, and seemed to have ducked behind a piece of machinery.

"Lex. What is your location?" she asked, routing the device's text-to-speech through the connection.

"I'm at some planned community planet, CZ something or other. *S.O.B.* took some damage when . . ." He glanced left and right. "Well, you know when it happened. So I stopped here to see what I could do to fix it."

"You are showing strong stress indicators."

"Yeah, I'd say I'm pretty damn stressed, Ma."

"Your coarse language is not called for, Mr. Garotte."

"I'm sorry, but I . . . wait, Mr. Garotte?"

"I apologize. It was the most accurate prepared statement available. How may I help you, Mr. Alexander?"

"Remember how I didn't want to get too involved? Because I was afraid I was going to have to do something I didn't want to do?"

"Yes."

"Well, I'm pretty sure these guys just forced my hand. I mean . . . well, you got my message, right?"

"Yes."

"How likely do you think it is that they'll come after me again?"

"Exceedingly likely," Ma stated. She swiped out some more words. "And if you are able to escape them, they will likely seek means to motivate you to reveal yourself."

"You mean they'll go after the people I care about."

"That is a reasonable assumption."

"Okay, that's what I thought. How likely is it that these guys are going to get completely wiped out before that happens?"

"Exceedingly unlikely."

"So, it seems like giving you a hand is pretty much the only option left."

"While it would be pleasing to me to once again include you in the mission, it is only proper that I inform you that joining us, even if it leads to the successful liberation of Karter, will not necessarily remove the terrorists as a threat to you."

"Maybe not, but it will keep them from coming after me by using some Karter-created prototype to wipe out whatever planet they think I might be hiding on. And it beats hiding in a hole and hoping they don't kill my friends and family. Plus, I figure if I help you out with this, you and Karter will have a pretty good reason to help me out with my problem."

"That is an intelligent and well-reasoned interpretation of the facts."

"Okay, so what can I do? How can I help?"

"Currently, Garotte and Silo are unavailable. Are you able to travel immediately?"

"Yeah, I think so. I'm not the best repair guy, but I've got it so the internal diagnostic checks out fine."

"I will deliver coordinates. How quickly can you reach them?"

Lex glanced at the lower edge of the screen as a set of stellar coordinates scrolled by.

"That's pretty far, but through freelancer-friendly space. I should be able to push *S.O.B.* pretty hard . . . say a day and a half?"

"Dock there within two days, find a secure location with room for your own ship and a Mobius Armistice C to land. We will arrive there in approximately forty-nine hours, assuming there are no interruptions to the schedule. Please run a full ship diagnostic, internal and external, with the command code 'level 3 diagnostic,' and send the results to me. I shall endeavor to have the materials available to perform more reliable repairs to your vehicle."

"Yeah. Sounds good. Will do. I'll see you then."

"Lex."

"Yes?"

"I must express my deepest and most heartfelt apologies for involving you in this venture. It has caused a disruption to your life that may have far-reaching consequences, and has endangered your own well-being and that of those you care about. If you are angry with me, or feel betrayed, that would conform to my expectations."

The sentence came quickly, without any need to assemble it. She'd had it ready for some time.

In return, Lex offered a weak smile. "Hey, knowing my luck, I would have got caught up in this mess anyway, right?"

"For you, this is probable."

"Okay, I'll see you in . . . uh," he remarked, squinting at his screen. "Ma? Are you wearing jewelry?"

"Yes, Lex. Thank you for noticing."

For a few moments, the pilot struggled for an appropriate response. When none came, he simply shook his head and smiled. "No problem, Ma. I'll see you soon."

"I eagerly anticipate your arrival."

The AI tapped the connection closed and processed the new information and associated emotional responses. Her installation into this body had introduced the issue of motivations originating from two different sources. What she considered to be her primary emotions originated from her databases and algorithms dealing with appropriate responses and behaviors based on various circumstances and interactions. The others were distinctly chemical in origin, occurring without regard to logic or reason. It was getting progressively more difficult to differentiate which emotions were stemming from which origins. She wasn't sure if she was pleased or concerned about that, and she wasn't sure if her uncertainty regarding her pleasure or concern was rooted in logic or chemistry, and she wasn't sure if her uncertainty regarding her uncertainty . . . this line of reasoning needed to be terminated to avoid infinite recursion.

A welcome interruption popped up, in the form of Lex's scan results. She looked over the list of faults, most of which were minor or cosmetic, and assembled a list of necessary replacement parts. They were on a supply station, so a fair number of the more industrial components would be simple enough to purchase. Some deft tapping and swiping of paws on her slidepad screen connected to local retailers, queried inventories, placed orders, issued payment, and produced pickup instructions. She briefly pondered why it took Silo so long to do her own shopping. It warranted further study. All that remained was to contact the others for pickup. She opened communications to them both.

"Peter here," came Garotte's voice over the audio connection.

"It's, oh . . . Dora," Silo said. "Sorry. I'm not used to having a pad yet."

"I have been in contact with Mr. Alexander. He is now willing to offer aid. He has been given the coordinates of a position near to the scheduled pickup position."

"Really? I wonder what brought about this change of heart," Garotte mused.

"I will explain later. There is a small order waiting to be picked up at the maintenance desk of the station. Please bring it with you when you return."

"I'll get it, sweetheart. I think I'm right near there," Silo offered.

"Excellent. We'll have to discuss the new opportunities our latest recruit will offer," Garotte said with an almost giddy air. "Oh, how delightfully reminiscent of old times. Isn't it wonderful, my sweet?"

"I hate to admit it, but there are some parts of this life I've missed," Silo said.

"I knew you'd come around," Garotte remarked, a grin in his voice. "You just wait until you see what sort of goodies I picked up for you. I'm telling you. Just like old times."

Chapter 25

Lex pulled on a jacket and checked the time. The planet he'd been directed to wasn't a planet at all, but a moon. It wasn't even one of those pleasant, tree-scattered moons swarming with fuzzy creatures that people sometimes conjured to mind. Sure, it was pretty. The whole surface was covered with multicolored rock formations, like a cross between the painted desert and a black-light poster. They had earned the place the name Jawbreaker.

Scientists said the layers had something to do with the fact that twice a year the moon passed through the thin, wispy rings of the gas giant it orbited, collecting a layer of whatever happened to be drifting along in them at the time. No one really cared what the scientists said, though. The reason there was air to breathe was because it was extremely pretty and had enough gravity to hang on to a layer of breathable gas. That meant people wanted to look at it and could survive the experience, and that meant people would *pay* to look at it. So the corporations showed up and pumped enough oxygen into the thin atmosphere to support human life, set up a few monitoring posts and a few kiosks, and made the whole place into what was basically a planet-wide campsite, complete with firewood and marshmallows for sale.

With the thin, artificially-maintained atmosphere it got very cold at night and very hot during the day, but since people were mostly interested in roughing it and taking in the scenery, that didn't matter much. There wasn't any water, either, but judging from the scattering of beer bottles, people had taken care of that problem themselves.

Things weren't terribly formal or regulated. Tourists simply stopped at the automated check-in kiosk, tossed in a recommended donation, picked up any supplies they wanted, and spent as much or as little time there as they wanted, with the understanding that the operators of the moon were minimally liable for any misfortunes that might befall them while they were there. It was a bit like a cross between the Wild West and a Boy Scout picnic.

Lex had picked a spot near a series of divots that had been blasted into the terrain. People liked to blow holes in the hills to see the pretty colors underneath. It might not have been environmentally friendly--but these days there were more environments than there were environmentalists, and after a few weeks it would take an expert to tell the difference between a man-made crater and a natural one. He tossed some specially-treated logs into one of the smaller craters, lit a fire, and stuck a few marshmallows on one stick and some hot dogs on another. There was only enough time for him to begin to ponder the strange tendency for his psychotic escapades to have little moments of calm and serenity in them before the Armistice showed up and set down beside *S.O.B.*

The side crew doors hissed open and lowered.

"Lex, my boy!" Garotte said, with hand extended. "Welcome back!"

"I just can't seem to stay out of trouble," Lex said, shaking his hand.

"More like trouble can't keep away from you," he said. "This lovely lady, by the way, is Silo."

"Pleased to meet you, Lex," she said with a shake. "I've heard some very impressive things about you."

"I can't say I've heard much about you, I'm afraid. Mostly just big guns and such."

"There isn't much more to say, hon."

The sound of tapping toenails drew Lex's gaze to the lowered door, where Ma was holding her slidepad and heading toward him with what could only be called a prance to her step. It was a decidedly "Solby" piece of behavior, further strengthened by her decision to leap to his shoulders without so much as a pause.

"Hey, Ma. Good to see you," he said, scratching her head.

She managed to twist her head and trigger a message. "It is very good to see you again, Mr. Alexander."

Lex marched around the ship in which they had arrived.

"An Armistice C? I can't say that I pictured you showing up in one of these. This is basically a moving van."

"Now, now, Lex," Garotte said. "This may look like an Armistice, but it is actually an Aggressor waiting to come out of its shell."

"Seriously? There are a *lot* of differences between an Aggressor and an Armistice. I mean there's--"

Garotte tapped at his slidepad a few times and handed it to Lex. The pilot reviewed it for a few moments.

"Yeah, that just about covers it," Lex said with a nod. "Let me guess. We'll be hooking all of this stuff up."

"I trust you know your way around an auto-spanner," Garotte remarked.

"I can bluff my way through most of the easy stuff."

"An admirable skill."

"What comes next, though? We're going to turn this thing into a gunship, and then what?"

"And then we're going to pick up one last weapon, and then we're going to go get our boy, come hell or high water. Time doesn't really allow for much else."

"Do you think we can do it?"

"Does it matter? It is the mission, Lex. We do what we must. Now," Garotte announced with a slap to Lex's back, "let us get to it, shall we?"

The work was slow. Of the group, only one of them had a really firm understanding of every piece of work that needed to be done--but, unfortunately for all involved, she didn't have any thumbs. Ma spent an hour carefully creating high-level tutorials for the others to work off of, then spent the remainder of the time supervising whoever happened to be working on the most critical system, unless it was Silo. This wasn't so much due to the fact that Silo didn't need the supervision, but because every time she approached, the protective sergeant would shoo her away with warnings that she might get hurt.

Close to six hours later, the four of them smeared with grease and worn ragged, the work was nearly done. One would hardly imagine that it was the same ship. Every weapon mount was populated, vicious gun barrels and field emitters studded the hull, and the throaty purr of a replacement reactor promised that it could provide the shields and weapons with power to spare. It might not have been quite a match for the monstrosity that Lex had just survived an encounter with, but a fight between the two of them would have been one hell of a show.

While Silo and Garotte were tightening the final bolts and connecting the final wires, Lex saw to *S.O.B.*

"Are you certain that you do not want the others to help you?" Ma asked.

"Nah. There's not much to do here, and I like to be the one that keeps *S.O.B.* healthy," he said, reconnecting the stabilizer panel and picking up a paint sprayer.

"The paint is standard space-grade matte black. The coating currently applied to your ship is a proprietary blend developed by Karter to absorb sensor sweeps. Until you are able to get *S.O.B.* back to Big Sigma for a proper repair, you will be marginally more detectable than you were before."

"I'll manage. I did pretty well back when I had a scraped-together pile of junk with too many engines."

Ma watched him paint for a few moments. "You went to visit your girlfriend."

"Yep."

"I had, through my inexpert grasp of social interaction, made you uneasy about your relationship. Was your trip conceived with the purpose of addressing the highlighted issues?"

"Partially."

"Were you successful?"

"We sort of postponed the whole thing. Something more important came up. Something more important *blew* up."

"Understandable."

"How have things been going for you?"

"There have been virtually no aspects of this mission that have gone according to plan."

"Sounds about right. Did you use the slidepad to figure out where these guys are?"

"I made a brief attempt, but the device was outside of standard communication coverage."

"I guess it was a long shot, anyway."

"I have no doubt it will serve its purpose. We simply need to wait for the proper activation time."

"Lex, my boy! Are you done yet?" called Garotte.

"Finishing touches going on now," Lex replied, applying the final layer of paint and punching a few commands into his slidepad. "There. Looks good as new. Now we run the diagnostic to see how she feels."

"Well, get over here. The refit is complete, with the exception of one or two toys we're still trying to work out, and I think that this is an occasion that warrants the attention of an aficionado such as yourself."

Lex paced over to the ship, which now had a tarp draped across the side, and assorted black-stained stencils were lying on the ground. Garotte was holding a small bottle of sparkling white wine.

"Would you do the honors?"

"You're rechristening?"

"Well, the ship was an Armistice. Considering the fact it is now well-equipped enough to level a small town, the name doesn't *quite* fit anymore," he explained, tossing the bottle to Lex. "So, without further ado, I present to you *The Declaration of War*."

"*The Declaration of War*? It doesn't exactly roll off the tongue," Silo mused.

"It was that or *Broken Peace*," Garotte replied.

"That is loads better," she said.

"Well, too bad, I already painted it on. You can name the next one. Lex, if you would?"

Lex shrugged and lobbed the bottle at the ship. It burst in a shower of amber foam.

"Ah, the navy," Garotte declared with a smile. "My hat is off to any institution that includes alcohol and broken glass in their ceremonies."

"So, are we going to get down to business?" Lex asked.

"Ugh. Later. I think a few minutes of respite are called for, wouldn't you?" Garotte answered, settling down beside the fire.

"I guess so. If I'd known we were going to spend the night here, I would have rented some tents at the registration kiosk. You want me to swing by and pick up a few?"

"Don't bother on my behalf," Silo said, tucking her hands in her pockets and lying back. "It has been years since I've spent a night with a sky over my head. And as skies go, this is gorgeous."

It was an understatement. Half of the sky was filled with the layered gold orb of the gas giant. Another quarter was made up of a river of glittering jewels that made up the planet's rings, and the rest was the brilliant, piercing, unwavering starlight that was normally only witnessed by mountain climbers.

"And I haven't had a meal cooked over a wood fire in equally long."

"And you still haven't," Lex said, looking over the wrapper from the logs. "Evidently these logs have as much in common with real wood as those hot dogs have with a steak."

"Each are delightful nonetheless," the spy decided.

"Come here, sweetie," Silo said, patting the ground beside her.

Ma looked wearily at Lex for a moment, then heaved a short sigh and tapped over and laid across Silo's stomach. Silo idly scratched the little creature while food was prepared, and fed Ma broken off bits of hot dog while the others ate. When stomachs were filled and limbs had drifted from burning fatigue to a dull ache, Garotte spoke.

"Right. Time to lay out the plans, shall we? As I see it, this first little mission will be a dress rehearsal for our final operation to retrieve Karter. Our best hope is to get in and out fast. These terrorists have been there waiting for us every step of the way, and there is no reason to imagine that things will be any different this time."

"Where is Zerk these days, anyway?" Silo wondered.

"Military Storage Depot 2332," Garotte replied.

"A storage depot? That doesn't seem like it would offer much in the way of security."

"Hah. That's one of the truly wonderful things about the modern military. Bureaucracy and regulation can lead to some *very* questionable decisions."

"But we've stolen it at least twice before. Surely they would have moved it to a more secure facility by now."

"Never underestimate the depths of stupidity that can be achieved when decisions are made by committee. Regardless of what common sense states, paperwork determines what gets stored where based on shoehorning things into whatever classification suits them best."

"How do they classify Zerk?" she asked.

"You'll love this--hazardous medical waste," he said with a chuckle.

"Hey, can we maybe let the new guy in on what exactly Zerk is?" Lex requested.

"I suppose since we are about to go steal it, you should probably know what it is you are after. Now, how best to articulate the conundrum that is Zerk . . . Zerk is like portable genocide. A disaster area with an on/off switch."

"So, what? Some sort of biological weapon?"

"Biological, yes. Weapon, yes. But not a biological weapon. Zerk is the sort of thing you drop into a battlefield, then a few hours later you retrieve it from amongst the pile of dead bodies and wrecked machinery."

"Why are you being so coy about this?"

"He always gets poetic when he talks about Zerk," Silo quipped.

"Did Karter ever give you his rundown about how much of his body is still biological, rather than replaced with gadgetry?"

"Yeah. I think he said he was at thirty-nine percent, the way nature intended."

"Really? The last time I talked to him he was up around forty-five or so. Must have been a butterfingers in the meantime. Well, at any rate, Zerk is what happens when you get down to around two percent."

"Wait . . . Zerk is a person?"

"I believe I've just gotten through saying that Zerk was a person. About thirty years ago, the TKUR was trying to make a better land drone. Unmanned ships are easy as pie, but autonomous tanks, ATVs, and the like just never did the job. The AI wasn't up to the task. People had been doing some major cybernetic rebuilds on human troops, and there had been success with exoskeletons. At some point, the wrong engineer and cyberneticist must have sat down next to each other in a bar somewhere, because someone finally asked the question, 'What if we started enhancing and didn't stop?'

"In a decision that would no doubt have made Karter himself proud, they decided to make a prototype with all of the proposed enhancements at once. And so 'The Berserker' was made. Zerk, for short. They grafted, enhanced, restructured, rebuilt, augmented, and assembled until the man they started with went from being two hundred pounds of flesh and blood to three hundred pounds of machinery wrapped around a spinal cord and brain. And, boy, did they pick a winner when they picked that brain. You don't get volunteers for a project like this, and they didn't want one. Ironically, they wanted a human mind because of its unparalleled ability to be mindless, singularity of purpose with complete unpredictability of technique.

"So they found a psychopath, a literal psychopath from a military prison. His name is lost to history, but they subjected him to some mental reconditioning and plopped his gray matter into a humanoid robot. It was a staggeringly effective prototype, but they just couldn't trap lightning in a bottle a second time. An unfortunate shortage of suitable psychopaths, I suppose. Eventually, they mothballed the entire project when the space-based drones were improved enough to make the land war an afterthought for most conflicts . . . except for the conflicts that created the herd of crazies we call the Neo-Luddites, I imagine. We've managed to gain access to it on occasion and used it to great effect.

"Zerk is the ultimate set-and-forget weapon. It fights like an alcoholic drinks: in great quantities, with endless zeal, and as a result of addiction."

"Don't you feel bad about using another human being like that?"

"Lex, my boy, I never feel bad about anything. But just to be on the safe side, you'll notice that I don't treat it or refer to it as a human being, because in every way that matters, that thing is *not* a human being. So, please, keep in mind that this mission is not to liberate a him, it is to steal an it. To that end, here is how I suggest it be done . . ."

Garotte traced out a plan. It was not as nuanced and refined as his prior attempts, but it was direct. Silo weighed in where appropriate, but outside of a few crunched numbers, Ma did not seem to be much of a factor in the plan. When several minutes had passed with little more than Silo and Garotte debating the finer points of what amounted to a smash and grab, Ma got to her feet and wandered off. At a point when the moon would be rising, if they weren't already on it, Lex decided he had to make some sort of an addition.

"Okay, okay, fine. That's all well and good, but what if something goes wrong? Do we have a fallback?"

"I--" Garotte began.

"He doesn't believe in plan B."

"We'll improvise. The great thing about improvisation is that the enemy can't plan for it."

"I have prepared an adequate contingency plan," Ma stated as she tapped back into the light of the fire.

"There, you see? Set your mind at ease. Our pet computer has us covered," Garotte said.

"Joke if you want, but I feel a lot better with Ma on the job," Lex admitted.

"In the materials I initially had Lex procure for his mission, you will find a number of blue bandanas and a stimulant injector with type 42c connectors."

"So *that's* what those bandanas were for," Silo stated with dawning realization.

"I didn't even *notice* the injectors." Garotte nodded. "I see where you're going."

"I don't," Lex said.

"Don't worry about it. It is a part of the ground operations. You know something? I am incorporating your plan B into my plan A," Garotte decided.

Lex stood and stretched some of the kinks out of his back. "Well, it seems like things are pretty straightforward. I do fancy flying, like always, and you guys blow stuff up and do something mysterious with allergy medication and hankies. I might as well turn in."

"Sleep well, pilot," Garotte said with a sharp salute.

"Nice meeting you, Lex," Silo said. "I hope we can get you in and out of this without getting your hands too dirty."

"You and me both," Lex groaned. "I'm going to camp out in *S.O.B.* Talk to you in the morning."

Lex popped the cockpit hatch and climbed into his ship. Thirty seconds after activating the heated massage chair, he was almost dead to the world, but a tap at the glass brought him around. He fought one eye open to see Ma standing on the cockpit window, looking down at him. He gestured for her to back away, then popped the cockpit.

"You need something, Ma?"

"May I come in?"

"Uh--yeah, sure."

She hopped down to his lap and tapped the control to shut the hatch.

"This is an exchange that I would prefer take place in private."

"Okay . . ." Lex remarked uncomfortably.

"There is one repair remaining to be done."

"Oh? The diagnostic checked out."

"It is not the ship. It is me."

"I don't understand."

"The destruction of my built-in transmitter has severely impaired my ability to contribute. I have secured the apparatus necessary to produce a repair and improvement to that functionality, but I can't do the repair myself."

"What needs to be done?"

"I have delivered the procedure to your slidepad, and the necessary equipment is in your passenger seat."

Lex turned to the seat behind him to find a military data radio, a few cables, assorted tools, and a roll of gauze.

"How did you get all of this in here?"

"I know your security codes. I hope that I did not overstep my bounds."

"I guess it's okay." Lex glanced over the instructions and quickly began to wince. "I don't . . . I don't think I can do this. This isn't a repair--it's surgery."

"All ships designed for long-distance flight have got disinfection filters. This environment is adequately sanitized. And there is only one incision."

"That's about five too many. Garotte probably knows this stuff better than me."

"Garotte and Silo are both better suited to the task, but I would prefer it was performed by you."

"Why?"

Ma looked to her reflection in the cockpit glass, flicking her bandaged and bejeweled ear. She twisted her head down and pawed the adhesive tab free, revealing the notched ear.

"What happened?"

"I was hit in a crossfire. A crossfire that would not have occurred if I had been able to more accurately and effectively control the manipulator arm. This is my mission. I need to be useful."

"That doesn't explain why you want it to be me."

"My initial interactions with Garotte were less than ideal, but he has come to view me as an asset, at least with regard to my computational prowess. He treats me like a computer. As I am a computer, this is acceptable. Silo lavishes much adoration upon me, and is very kind. She treats me like a companion animal. As this is an accurate description of my current state, this, too, is acceptable. You are the only one who treats me as a unique individual, a person. You are the only one who would agree that restoring me to my full capabilities is desirable not only from a strategic standpoint, but from the standpoint of decency."

"Well, yeah. I mean, you got hurt because you were trying to save my life."

"Yes. I did."

"But what if I screw this up? It's better to have to poke around at a slidepad to talk than to be a vegetable because I severed your spinal column."

"In a very short amount of time, the two will be equivalent outcomes."

"What do you mean?"

"As you know, I am a subset of the skills and knowledge available to the primary instance of the AI known as Ma. The mission is the exclusive purpose for my existence. Had things gone according to plan, I would have returned to Big Sigma, uploaded my accumulated experiences, and merged with the primary program again--but this will only occur if the proper equipment exists to do so. As the primary purpose is to reclaim Karter, any difficulties in achieving the secondary goals will lead them to be abandoned. I will manually transmit the key information and Squee will be returned as near to her original state as possible with minimal risk to her health."

"Wouldn't that require her--you--wouldn't that require the transmitter to be repaired first?"

"The transceiver assembly is grafted in place when the clone is first created. Replacing one in its entirety requires weeks of healing before it can be activated safely. My mental integrity will not last long enough. Any experiences, lessons, and emotional growth I experienced will be lost."

"Couldn't you do whatever you're asking me to do when you get back?"

"The proposed procedure will vastly increase the likelihood of our successful completion of this mission. Also, the procedure is experimental. I will not tolerate the usage of experimental procedures on a life-form unless doing so is absolutely necessary to preserve life."

"But you're okay with doing something experimental here and now?"

"The events of this mission have taught me to be somewhat more flexible with my requirements than my primary incarnation. If I return to Big Sigma with a functional transceiver, my full program will be downloaded. If I do not return to Big Sigma with a functional transceiver, my program will be allowed to degrade while a safe procedure with a higher success rate is applied over several weeks."

"You--that is to say, the other you--would do that to . . . you?"

"The status of Big Sigma was dire when I left. Even if the devices preventing my normal function there were entirely deactivated the moment after I left, there would still be considerable work to be done to finish restoring the facility. Repairing my transmitter would be low priority. In emergency situations, I am very pragmatic."

"But you're also compassionate."

"To others, not to myself. I am an artificial intelligence. My programming favors the well-being of life-forms above my own. My primary responsibility would be to Squee. Lex, please. You are the only one who understands or cares how important this is to me, or even that anything could be important to me. I have learned more in these few days about human nature and organic emotional response than I have in the totality of my prior existence. I don't want to lose it, Lex. I don't want to see what I have become slip away. I don't want to die."

"But maybe I could talk to you--to the main you, I mean--"

"Lex. I know myself. I know my programming. My primary instance won't be able to understand. This is the only way to be sure. Please."

Lex looked down at the little creature, and it stared back with the same steady gaze, but this time there was something else. It was brittle, wavering. There was fear behind it.

"Fine. I'll do what I can."

The procedure was very carefully laid out in simple terms. He had to remove the old transmitter coil, strip some wires, fabricate an adapter, and connect it to the existing data access port. It didn't sound very bad, almost like installing a sound system or replacing a power outlet--except, in this case, the old transmitter was a marble-sized glass bead that had been grafted into the funk's skin, and the existing data access port was an eighth of an inch from a very small, very fragile creature's spine.

It took more than an hour, and was one of the more nerve-wracking things Lex had ever had to do, but finally he was gingerly gripping a freshly-installed wire. He tried to ignore the fact the wire led down beneath a blood-speckled bandage and into Ma's neck. He pulled out the military radio, opened the port, and inserted the connector. Ma, who had been motionless for the duration of the procedure, jerked up. Her eyes shot open and darted randomly, then her head twitched sideways and one eye closed.

"Did everything go the way it was supposed to? Did I screw up?"

She shook slightly. One by one, the radio's lights and indicators began to activate.

"You wired the connector incorrectly. There is one crossed connection. I have modified my internal firmware to compensate. Testing data connection," she stated, her voice broadcasting with its old familiar quirks on the radio's speakers. "Bandwidth increased by eight thousand percent. Signal strength increased by nine hundred percent. Thank you, Lex. I am myself again. I trust you applied the appropriate amounts of cellular growth promoter, tissue binder, and sanitary spray."

"I probably put three times as much as I was supposed to."

"Entirely understandable, Lex. Best to be certain. Now, if you would please apply an additional layer of bandage and secure the data radio to my harness, the upgrade will be complete."

In the only portion of the procedure he was comfortable with, Lex made the judicious use of a few zip ties to attach the radio, then used a pressure bandage to hold down the connector wire securely. The thought of what might happen if it got snagged made Lex shudder.

"All done."

"I shall now test my mobility," she declared.

The cockpit clicked open of its own accord and Ma leaped out of the ship and scampered across its hull, down to the ground, and around the ship a few times. A moment later she sprang back to the ship and onto Lex's shoulder, wrapping tight around his neck.

"How's it feel?"

"The radio is secure. The wire entry point is still slightly sore, but will heal well. Thank you, Lex. You are a skilled pilot, an able mechanic and surgeon, and a good friend," she stated quietly.

"Ah, you'd have done the same for me."

"You do not have a transceiver assembly to replace."

"Well, yeah. But--"

"I understand the intended sentiment, and it is appreciated."

"So, anything else you want me to do? Maybe defuse a bomb or break into a bank?"

"That will not be necessary. You should rest. Starting tomorrow, things become more difficult."

Chapter 26

Military Storage Depot 2332 was only eighteen hours away from Jawbreaker, and as secure military facilities went, it was a far cry from Manticore. It wasn't on a purposely inhospitable planet, for one. The planet was called Proxy-12, and it was actually a well-established trade colony with Earth-like gravity and climate, though a bit on the warm side. The depot itself was in the center of a desert on an unpopulated continent. It wasn't the sort of place that the best and brightest were sent to guard. Since it was mostly intended for storing obsolete or surplus medical supplies, salvaged weapon casings, and other useless but not disposable equipment, the staff was comprised of weekend soldiers, short-timers, and screw-ups. They were the kind of people who couldn't be trusted or couldn't be bothered to take care of the sensitive materials, so they got stuck here. The decision to put a prototype human war machine under their care was one that could only have been made by bureaucrats from the other side of a desk light-years away.

A pair of soldiers on monitor duty were doing their jobs with the usual level of enthusiasm. They were sitting, each with their feet up, in a room filled with flimsy office chairs, assorted computer consoles and interface devices, and a large glass window overlooking the rolling desert dunes.

"Long-range sensors are clean," yawned the young woman at the primary controls. The fact that she was wearing sandals instead of boots and had a butterfly pin on her military uniform spoke volumes of how long it had been since there had been an official inspection. The name embroidered on her chest was Cadet Rogers.

"Acknowledged," remarked the other member of the monitor team, a similarly inexperienced young man who seemed to be in the early stages of a doomed attempt at facial hair, and was named Cadet Paolo, according to a uniform that it would appear had either been put on while blindfolded or during a hurricane. "Hey, have you seen the new guy?"

"The one they said they were transferring to us a few days ago? He's here?"

"Yeah."

"Is he cute?" Rogers asked with smirk.

"Well, him being a dude, and me being a straight dude, normally I'd say I can't tell, but I'm pretty sure the answer is no this time."

“Why?”

“Because he's about fifty years old and I'm pretty sure he had his jaw replaced.”

“Ew.”

“Yeah. He's a vet or something.”

“Why would they send him here? The only reason--”

She was interrupted by a tone from her console.

“What is it?” asked Paolo.

“I think it's a proximity alarm. Were we supposed to have any shipments today?”

“I don't know--you're the one on monitor duty. Besides, shipments announce their arrival, don't they?” Paolo's words and general comprehension, it was becoming clear at this point, fell somewhere between mellow and sedated.

“Yeah, you're right . . . you don't think this is a readiness drill, do you?”

“God, I hope not.”

“Better do this by the book, just in case,” she said, pulling open a drawer and pulling out a plastic binder.

“Why are you going through the binder for this? Isn't, like, the computer easier?”

“Because they check the records to see if you had to check the procedure files, duh. We're supposed to know this stuff, so you lose merit if you have to check. But there's no trail if you use the hard copy,” Rogers informed him. “You're never going to make it through an assignment like this if you don't learn stuff like that. Anyway. Unscheduled arrival: hail and request identification. I remember that now.” She tapped a few controls on her console. “Unidentified vessel, please transmit your authorization and identification data.”

There was no answer. Rogers flipped through a few pages.

“Now what?” Paolo asked.

“We're supposed to try to establish visual, then contact command to inform them of what's going on.”

“Hey . . . you say they can't check to see if we look at the binder, but, like, what about the camera?” Paolo remarked, pointing to the visual sensor in the ceiling.

“Damn. I should have thought of that.”

“Um. I don't think . . . this is . . .” Paolo stumbled.

“Re-*lax,*” she dismissed. “As long as we handle the drill right, they'll just give us a slap on the wrist for this.”

“No, like, look at the monitors.”

The female cadet looked to her console. Rather than the readouts and video images she wasn't supposed to take her eyes off of, there were warnings of equipment malfunctions and errors.

"What happened?"

As an answer, the building trembled slightly.

"Uh-oh. Now communications are down," Paolo murmured. "And now the backup communication just went down."

Rogers flipped madly through the binder. "Oh, to hell with that! Computer, what is the procedure for perimeter sensor and communications failure!"

"Activate short-range visual sensors," the computer stated, in a low-bid government vocal synthesizer that made Ma sound like an opera singer in comparison.

"Computer, activate short-range visual sensors!" Rogers ordered.

The monitors flicked back on, each displaying a different view of the wavy desert heat.

"Okay, help me look for whatever is causing this," she said.

Paolo and Rogers huddled around the monitors.

"Okay, so, like, what do we look for?" Paolo asked, new concepts sinking into his brain like flies into molasses.

A monitor cut to an equipment failure message, followed by another, and another.

"What the hell is going on!?" Rogers cried.

#

Half a desert away, Silo was sitting at the controls of one of the newly-installed rocket-propelled grenade mounts on *The Declaration of War*. She and Garotte were equipped with field gear--desert camouflage fatigues, military radio with earpieces, backpacks--and heavily armed. Garotte was sporting twin sub-machine guns, one ballistic and the other plasma, and an energy pistol. Silo was strapped with a dual-bandolier of assorted grenades, a matching pistol, and a semi-automatic grenade-launcher.

"Your sights aren't *quite* calibrated right, Garotte, honey," she said, lining up another shot.

"Well, you are using it at about one hundred-twenty percent of its rated range, my dear."

"No excuse for bad sights. It's taken me eight shots to take out six cameras. If there were patrols out, I might have hit someone," she said. "And we're not doing the husband and wife act anymore, so you can skip the 'my dear' business."

"Beastly sorry," he said, with a flourish of his hand and a bow of his head.

"Nine . . . and hit. Ten . . . and hit. Eleven . . . and hit. Twelve . . . and hit. That's all of the cameras. One for the main sensors, one for com, one for backup com. That's thirteen for fifteen. Not bad for a gal who's three years out of practice."

"Three more targets to shore up your numbers," Garotte said, pulling up a secondary display and pointing at it. “Here, here, and here.”

“I know the drill. Just like the last time we picked up Zerk,” she said, taking aim.

#

“Okay, okay, okay,” Rogers said in the unmistakable tone of someone who is absolutely not panicking. “We've all got slidepads. Regulations say we can use those in case of complete communication--”

“Slidepads are, I guess, jammed?” Paolo drawled, his level of calm now clearly chemical in nature.

“What the hell is going on!?” Rogers growled. “This is a test. It has to be. Things don't go this wrong unless someone is doing it on purpose. Well, I'm not going to let them catch me off guard. Stick to the book, right? You can't get in trouble for following procedure.”

Paolo tapped at the computer screen at this station.

“It says here we're supposed to post armed sentries, then dispatch engineering teams to fix the damaged equipment.”

“Good. We can do that. Let's do that!” Rogers rambled, keying the intercom. “Attention!”

The building shook once more, causing the lights to flicker and die, and killing the public address system with a sad little fizzle. The backup power came online for a few moments, then a second distant explosion plunged them back into darkness. Finally the red emergency lights flicked on. Rogers tried to hold herself together--and, for a few seconds, it seemed like she would succeed, but a final explosion somewhere on the outside of the building startled her, and she collapsed into tears.

“Why did this have to happen *now!?* I was two weeks from having enough service time to get the scholarship, and then I would have been out of here and studying philosophy back home,” she sobbed.

The door burst open, prompting a startled shriek and a new round of sobs, and in rushed an aging man with a similar uniform. Unlike the less-dedicated cadets, this man was following dress code to the letter, with the exception of his name badge, which had been torn off.

“Please don't hurt me!” Rogers screamed.

“Rogers, that's the new guy!” Paolo proclaimed, seemingly proud of himself for contributing to the situation.

“Which one of you has the current code for the armory? We are under attack, and it looks like I'm the only one in this damn facility with any training,” the veteran barked, his words having an odd slur to them, thanks to an obvious piece of major reconstructive surgery that had been done to his chin.

“I do, we both do! Take it! Do something!” Rogers cried, digging out a sticky note with the six-digit code scribbled on it.

The veteran snatched the note and delivered a look that compressed all of the hatred and disdain he felt for the entire generation of soldiers into two seconds of glare. He then pounded out of the monitor room and down the hall. The cadets watched him go.

"So, what do we do now?" Paolo asked.

A tone sounded over the emergency system, followed by an announcement.

"Primary systems failure. Biohazard protocol in place. All personnel evacuate to designated safe areas. Biohazard containment apparatus failure possible. Lockdown will initiate in six minutes. Regroup at designated rally points and await further instruction."

"Oh, wow. We should probably--" Paolo began.

Rogers, in anticipation of his statement, ran screaming from the room.

#

Back in *The Declaration*, Silo and Garotte watched the mayhem through pairs of binoculars as they coaxed the ship closer to the facility at a carefully controlled speed.

"Yep, the biohazard lights are on, and have been for about two minutes. I count six troop carriers evacuated already. They looked fully loaded, more or less. I'd say that's about eighty troops out. How many total are there?" Silo asked.

"The full complement, as of this morning, was eighty-four," replied Garotte. "I would call that fair warning. Thirty more seconds and we go in."

"Just so we're clear, there isn't really any hazardous material that we need to worry about, right?"

"Just Zerk," Garotte assured her. "The rest of their inventory is basically military rations, expired medication, and assorted equipment."

"Good. I don't like those hazard suits. They never have enough room in the hips."

"Well, rare is the soldier with curves so generously--"

"You can stop right there, mister. That's plenty of time. Let's get in and get out," Silo decided, popping a clip into the pistol and slipping it into her holster, then shouldering the grenade-launcher.

"With pleasure," Garotte remarked as he nudged the throttle.

The Declaration soared toward the facility, clipping the tops of dunes and stirring up a sandstorm in its wake. They reached the front doors of the depot in the final seconds of the countdown, switching their ship into autonomous and dropping out of the crew-deployment door just in time to slide under the heavy duty shutter that was lowering into place. Silo delivered a powerful thrust to an interior door, popping it open before the bolt could engage and earning them entry to the wide, warehouse-style hallways of the depot's interior.

Inside, the depot looked more like the sort of place a college student would store their meager possessions between semesters than a military building. Aisles wide enough to maneuver a forklift were arranged in a regular grid, providing access to row after row of shuttered storage compartments with spray-painted numbers. The thickness of the doors and complexity of the locks were the only appreciable differences between a place suitable for ammo crates or a place suitable for lava lamps. The walls, floor, and high ceiling were all made of the same unpainted metal, a quick-to-deploy, easy-to-work-with material with a diamond-plate texture, but half the weight and twice the toughness of its steel ancestry.

"Where's Zerk being kept?" Silo asked, hustling down the corridors.

"Storage unit EE-12. That should be the southeast corner," Garotte answered.

They made their way deeper into the complex, the only light coming from the deep red emergency lights that ran from their own dedicated power supplies. Both of them had brought flashlights, and each carried a weapon with a light attached, but neither would be used unless absolutely necessary. The reason for their caution asserted itself almost immediately, as a sweep of bullets peppered the corner of a row of lockers.

"Right on cue," Garotte huffed.

He and Silo slid to a stop and crouched behind the corner of either side of an aisle. Communication came in the form of crisp, precise gestures. Garotte squinted at the bullet damage on the dimly-lit wall and signaled the direction the attack had most likely come from. In turn, Silo listened and flashed a sign indicating a single target, on foot, four aisles away. Without so much as a single flinch of additional communication, each set about the predetermined tasks. Garotte sprinted for the storage container, carefully controlled strides making not nearly the noise one would have expected, but more than enough to be heard. The sound was enough to coax their pursuer out of hiding.

The enemy soldier charged along in the darkness, following Garotte's path in a parallel aisle. Silo picked an aisle between them and matched them step for step. Thanks to her time enduring Manticore's intense gravity, she moved in great, bounding strides despite her heavy load of weapons and ammunition. In moments, she was between Garotte and their tracker. With practiced motions she pulled a hand grenade from her munitions belt, popped the pin, and started counting. When the time was right, she pitched the explosive down.

"Bunnies and bats in three," she stated over the radio.

She slid to a stop, shut her eyes tight, and covered her ears. An aisle or two away, Garotte did the same, and not a moment too soon. The grenade she threw exploded in a rush of sound, pressure, and light. It didn't do any damage, but it wasn't designed to. In the near-blackness of the facility, the flash-bang robbed their pursuer of what little night-vision he had, and the burst of sound sent him reeling against the door of a storage locker. Silo tried to move in, but the soldier blindly fired his assault rifle, keeping Silo at bay. When the firing stopped, Silo spoke.

“Listen! I realize that right now you probably can't hear anything but a loud whistling noise, but we're not looking to kill anyone if we don't have to. If you'd been following procedure, you'd have evacuated by now,” she called out.

“Procedure!?” the soldier spat, hidden among the aisles. “Don't talk to me about procedure. Playing it safe is what cost me half my face! We're through with procedure.”

“Who's we? Are you one of those technology terrorists? The Ludds or whatever?”

“We aren't terrorists!”

“So . . . yes, then,” she stated, slinging the grenade-launcher down and drawing her pistol. “I'm happy to hear that, because now I won't feel so bad if you end up getting yourself killed.”

Garotte's voice appeared in her earpiece. “Reached the storage locker, accessing the medication distributor. I need three minutes.”

“I'll try, but stay on your toes, hon.”

A burst of bullets punched holes in the storage locker across from her. She began moving backward with slow, measured steps, attempting to remain as silent as possible. With all of the equipment she was carrying, it wasn't an easy task. Ahead, still hidden by the crisscrossing corridors, the enemy soldier moved with equal care and even less success. When he stopped moving, so did Silo. For a few seconds, there was only the sound of her own breathing and the distant click of the equipment Garotte was manipulating. Then came a distinctive sound with which Silo was quite familiar. It was like the jingle of a hoop earring bouncing to the floor, followed by a heavy thump and rattle. Around the corner ahead of her bounced a round, red, baseball-sized grenade.

In a decision made in the heartbeat available to her, Silo took two quick steps forward and punted the fallen grenade with all of the strength she could muster. As it screamed down the long aisle ahead of her, she scrambled to dive into an adjoining row. The blast that followed wasn't nearly as bright or exciting as the flash-bang had been, but it was a lot more dangerous. A clap of detonating explosive splashed the surrounding walls with brilliantly glowing flecks of molten metal. The globs cut through the metal walls like wax, setting fire to whatever the doors had been protecting. The rest pooled on the floor briefly, before eating through and becoming an ominous glow from below.

“What was that?” Garotte squawked in her earpiece.

“Thermite grenade,” Silo huffed. “I hope you're almost done, because if you aren't, we're *both* almost done.”

“If you can help me get this door hitched up a few centimeters without having to unlock it, the deed will be done."

"Coming your way."

The fire-suppression system, a sprinkler that operated independently of power, began to trigger and douse the thermite-afflicted section of the floor. Because of the imprecise nature of the fire system, and thermite's tendency to heat up a much larger area than normal fire would, most of the rest of the heads triggered as well, making the metal flooring treacherously slick and hiding the sound of footfalls behind the steady patter of water.

Silo slid into the aisle containing their target, and it was instantly clear that this was the one storage cabinet they actually cared about protecting. The metal of the door was triple the thickness of the others, and there were redundant locks on both sides securing monstrous latches. Beside the door was a panel that Garotte had managed to open. Inside were two shelves of canisters. The top canisters were glass jars filled with something that looked like lime-green, watered-down baby food. The others were narrow vials resembling cigar tubes. Each type of canister had a matching socket. The baby food one was properly attached, but Garotte had already replaced the other with one of the allergy medication refills.

Garotte pulled a pry bar from his bag and tossed it to Silo, indicating the near side of the industrial-strength shutter. The locks there had been removed, while those on the other side were intact, meaning that only half of the shutter was free to move. Once again making use of the side effects of her high-gravity incarceration, Silo hammered the pry bar into the gap and strained desperately. The edge of the door creaked and groaned, budging just an inch or two. Without a word, Garotte pulled an energy pistol fuel cell from his belt and slipped it through the gap.

"Good enough, my girl," he said, turning to pull the contents of the medical panel into his pack.

Silo gratefully released the bar. The tension of the door forcing itself shut hammered the bar's end into the floor plating.

"Leave it! The fuse is lit, we've got to move," Garotte advised.

The enemy soldier pounded into the hallway and leveled his weapon. They raised their own.

"Hold it right there!" he barked. "That's enough! You are going to tell me what you are after, what you did, and how to undo it. Then you are going to come with me and we are going to--"

"Look, if you want any answers, you'll need them pretty quick," Garotte snapped. "See, that panel there is the medication distribution point. It keeps a steady flow of sedative circulating through those tubes. We swapped it out for epinephrine, which is more or less the opposite of sedative. You'll want to pop that vial out and replace it for one of the ones I've got in the bag. It'll only really work if it hasn't woken up yet, though."

From behind the door, a sound like someone jiggling a stuck silverware drawer became apparent, periodically rattling and shuddering.

"There goes that idea, then," Silo quipped.

"Not to worry. The sedative only keeps its brain asleep," Garotte explained. "The primary security measure is the complete removal of all power sources. That thing will barely be able to move until it can get some sort of juice into its batteries. And that couldn't happen unless someone was to, say, toss a plasma clip in there."

"Did you do that?" the soldier demanded.

"What do you think?" Silo jabbed.

There was the groan of straining metal from within the locker.

"What the hell is in there?" said the soldier, taking a firmer grip on his weapon and inching backward.

"The last thing you'll ever see," Garotte said with a grin.

The moment that followed was so crowded with activity it would have taken a documentary crew, a high-speed camera, and a few hours of study to reveal every nuance. A hollow whistle, like a big league slugger taking a home run swing with a metal pipe, split the air, followed by a deafening screech of tearing metal and a burst of sparks from the shutter door.

The soldier had half an instant to inspect what was now protruding from the damaged door. That was more than enough time to convince him that he would feel more comfortable if it was filled with bullet holes. By the time he opened fire, the far-more-prepared Silo and Garotte were three steps closer to the exit and accelerating. The soldier finished emptying his clip and began to run backward while reloading, using whatever wits he had to spare to investigate his target, which was still sticking out of the heavy-duty door that had been crumpled aside like so much foil.

It looked like a human arm. Actually, more accurately, it looked like a human arm if you were to tear off all of the skin, remove the blood, replace the bones with a dull gray metal, and replace the muscles with a few bundles of charcoal black fibers. The fist was clenched around a mangled piece of equipment which might have been a plasma clip at some point in the past, but was now little more than a smoldering piece of junk. The arm was notably intact, either due to the general lack of precision that comes with panic-firing a fully-automatic weapon or due to an immunity to the weapon. There was a blur of motion and the rest of the mechanism revealed itself, but the soldier was probably too distracted watching his life pass before his eyes to notice.

Down the hall, Garotte and Silo listened to their foe scream and get off a few bullets from the fresh clip before a variety of horribly organic snaps and crackles cut off both noises, leaving just the pound of their boots and the patter of tapering-off sprinklers.

"Bandanas on," Garotte remarked, holstering his weapons and pulling the folded blue square from a flap of his fatigues.

"Way ahead of you," Silo said, as she finished tying the knot to secure it around her soaking wet forehead.

By the time they reached the door, there was a rapid metallic tapping approaching at terrifying speed down the corridor behind them. It was like the clacking of a demonic typewriter. In brief, red-illuminated glimpses, they could see Zerk scrambling toward them in a skittering, four-limbed crawl that leaped from wall to ground to wall.

"The whole blue bandana thing will only work if he can *see* that it's blue, and I'd rather be standing in the sun than blinding myself with a flashlight," Garotte gasped.

"Agreed." Silo nodded. In a continuous motion, she pulled her grenade-launcher around, readied it, and sent a round though the door they had kicked open when they entered. The blast devastated the emergency shutter, and pieces were still clattering to the ground when they rushed though the gaping hole.

"You get *The Declaration* prepped. I'll handle Zerk," Garotte said.

"No argument from me," she said, opening the crew door and keeping a watchful eye on the exit of the depot.

Garotte carefully positioned himself so that he wasn't directly outside the gap, but he would be the first thing Zerk would see upon leaving. The clattering charge of the robot became steadily louder, and when the spy caught the tiniest glimpse of the thing, he took a deep breath.

"Bowerbird!" Garotte bellowed.

If it had been a half-second later, he would have been a pile of broken bones with a hellish killing machine standing on top of him. Instead, the thing dug its hands and feet into the concrete of the depot's footpath, grinding four long lines as it skidded and rotated to a stop. It then stood sharply at attention and turned to him, remaining perfectly still.

In the light, the device was practically a work of art. Everything about it was minimally but perfectly engineered. The arms, legs, and chest were like an anatomical model built to show off the main muscle groups, though each muscle was represented by a deceivingly lean bundle of black. This was because the synthetic muscle had ten times the strength of human tissue, and anything more would have warped the titanium composite frame it was anchored to, but it made for a scarecrow-like build. Where the abdomen should have been was virtually hollow, showing off a heavily-reinforced spinal support and a variety of variously-shaped ports, meant for utilizing different power sources. The hands were three-fingered, with built-in blades protruding from above the fingers when a fist was made. On one forearm was a silver disk with a glowing blue rim, a directional force-field. The feet resembled the tow-and-heel mockup that shoe-makers used to size their creations, with more of the black fiber woven across the outside to string it together.

The least human aspect was the head. Instead of a face was a smooth, curved surface with a brushed metal finish that was pitted with gouges. A pair of V-shaped indents textured the surface, one crossing the point where eyes should be, and the tip of the other ending in a notch where the mouth should have been. They hadn't even had the decency to put the glowing red eyes that one would think would be the industry standard by now.

“The magpies land at three-four-four,” the robot croaked in an even lower-quality digital voice than the depot had used.

Garotte furrowed his brow. “The crows descend at seven-one.”

“Call and response sleep mode command confirmed.”

Zerk lowered to one knee and placed a palm on the ground, raising its head until it flipped almost completely upside-down, revealing three buttons and the broken-off tube that had first fed sedative, then epinephrine to the sole remaining hunk of human flesh, the brain and spine hidden in the chest. Garotte tapped the yellow button and removed the tube, inserting a vial of sedative and tapping a blue button. The muscle fibers slackened and Zerk collapsed.

“All done,” Garotte breathed, mopping sweat from his brow that owed a lot less to exertion and heat that he would have liked to admit. “Well. That certainly got the blood flowing. Care to lend a hand?”

Silo hopped down and helped move the inactive war machine into *The Declaration*. “I'm sorry, explain again why that works?”

“When you say bowerbird, and you are wearing at least one piece of blue clothing, it stops and delivers the call phrase--”

“I know what to do, I just don't know why it works.”

“Oh. Post-hypnotic, I think. Or programming. One of those.” He grunted, heaving the machine into the cargo bay and climbing in. “That went just about perfectly.”

“Yes, well, we're not in space yet,” she said, tapping the ship's radio and beginning to set the course. “Lex, how are things up there?”

“You guys--no, no, left. You're not getting by that way. Ha! *Ha!* Done already? I was just getting--yes, *yes*--started,” Lex's voice crackled over the radio.

“Is the coast clear, hon?”

“I've got the defense ships for half of the hemisphere tied in knots. Get a move on!”

“How about you, Ma, sweetheart?”

“Busy . . . jamming . . . communication . . . and . . . sensors . . .” Ma struggled in drawn-out words.

“Right, let's go,” Silo said, sealing the doors and guiding the ship skyward. “I'll see you at the rendezvous in three hours.”

“I'd say that the dress rehearsal was a success,” Garotte said, putting his feet up on the motionless Zerk, which was now strapped to the cargo grate.

"All that remains is to find the main stage and light the lights."

Chapter 27

"Commander," said Marx.

Commander Purcell was scrutinizing the screen of her datapad, and had been for hours. A mind honed and specialized for combat and strategy was slow to adapt itself to investigation, but the rate at which her own troops were turning up information was unacceptable. These were men and women she knew to be skilled and dedicated, but they were not suited to reviewing data. All of her agents trained in espionage were currently placed deep in organizations they needed to keep an eye on. The people she kept on hand in the station were mostly engineering and combat, and the best of them weren't able to turn anything up on this Trevor Alexander, so that left her. It was a slow, mind-numbing task.

"Commander," her second stated with a bit more force.

She looked up in irritation. "What is it?"

"The engineers have got preliminary results, and would like to demonstrate Karter's devices."

"Now?"

"As soon as possible."

"Very well," she said, unhooking the datapad from its mount and taking it along as they marched into the narrow hallway.

"Have you had any luck with your research?"

"Nothing new," she growled. "I've been over that Modane footage dozens of times, scoured every word of the information you gave me. There is nothing to suggest how he could have gained the skills to take down one of our men, or why he would ever involve himself. He had to have had help, and he must have been coerced into rendering aid. But by whom? And why? The main thorns in our side have been the spy and the demolition specialist, but they were released, and they clearly only care about Karter. They were released *to* retrieve Karter. There is nothing we have that would suggest that *anyone* in Karter's history could be that devoted to him, and you've met the man, he is detestable. How could he earn such loyalty?"

"Have you been through any of the other footage?"

Purcell sneered, pulling up the playlist of videos and playing it without sound. "Look at it. Shaky video shot by panicked bystanders. Nothing there that the Modane footage doesn't show in greater detail."

They reached Docking Bay B and stepped inside. It was a comparatively massive space for a space station, large enough to contain five ships the size of the Armistice and their crews. Normally it was occupied by nearly half of the Neo-Luddites' recently acquired fleet of combat and troop ships, and exposed to the vacuum of space. Now most of them were on assignment, and at least two wouldn't be returning. Since it was a large space, fortified against the minor collisions that were a threat of any docking procedure, and designed to be quickly sealed off against decompression, it was the best choice on the station to test potentially dangerous devices. Unlike Karter's lab, it even had artificial gravity. Thus the doors had been sealed, the bay had been pressurized, and it was abuzz with her engineers. Each of the five landing pads had been set up with a different invention, with various safety equipment and testing apparatus included. It gave the area the overall feel of a grade school science fair. And, just like in a science fair, things took on an excited hush when the judge walked into the room.

"We'll start with you. Report," Purcell decided, indicating the rightmost landing pad.

"Yes, Commander," said the attending engineer. "These are the double-jump boots. They operate on--"

"I've been briefed on their capabilities. Demonstrate them and report on their combat role."

"Yes, Commander," said the engineer.

He stepped aside, revealing a pair of crude, sturdy-looking boots, reinforced and stiff, like ski boots. He took them down from the pedestal, and began to strap them on, reporting as he did.

"We have found the boots to be stable and predictable in their behavior. They're tricky, but I've had a chance to practice," the engineer stated. "These are charged to approximately fifty percent of capacity."

He walked to the edge of the landing pad and surveyed the five-meter gap between the pad and the walkway that ran the length of the docking bay. After a deep breath, he ran two steps and jumped the railing; as he began to descend, he slapped a button on the control pad and lurched into the air again, landing on the walkway and stumbling into the wall. When he came to a rest, his feet seemed to suddenly lock into position, barely moving despite his best efforts until he tapped another button on the control pad.

"There, you see? Fully directable kinetic energy storage and discharge! The potential is endless! At the very most basic usage, we've been able to store enough energy to deliver over forty kilo-newtons of force in a single kick. With training, we theorize achieving anything from safely arresting a terminal velocity fall to achieving short sprints of over eighty kph. There are even potential zero-gravity maneuvering applications. I--"

"Yes. That's fine. Very impressive," Purcell stated. She'd been dealing with these men for long enough to know that they were like puppies with a brand-new chew toy when they got their hands on fresh technology. If she didn't cut them off, they would rave for hours over the smallest advances. It was a useful attitude, but tended to waste valuable time during briefings. She turned to the next pad. "You, report."

One by one, her engineers gushed excitedly about the devices they had been permitted to test. They sprayed barely comprehensible figures and benchmarks, but slowly her strategic mind began to wrap around the possibilities. The "charge gun" was an attachment the size of a rifle stock that could turn virtually any light energy weapon into an anti-vehicular weapon for at least one shot. The signal manipulator could make concerns of giving yourself away with radio traffic a thing of the past. Even the bizarre "yo-yo coil" could give battering ram capabilities to any ship with a tractor beam, which effectively meant *any ship at all.*

Any one of the five items on display had the capacity to revolutionize warfare, and they were randomly selected from a list of *dozens*. Never before had the truth of their stance been so clear.

Then came the shield.

"The rebound shield. It is a man-portable, regenerating, portable force field. The field pattern is prolate spheroid, the field strength is--" the engineer began to explain. When he saw the look of worn patience on the face of his commander, he pulled out a datapad and directed her attention to the landing pad. "At the center is the shield emitter, strapped to a test dummy. At seven o'clock are samples of our standard sidearms; at ten o'clock is a plate of high-density ballistic armor. Watch."

Another tap unleashed a barrage of shots from the weapons, one energy and one projectile-based. When the sizzling, zapping, and thundering had come to an end, the shimmering shield was intact, and the armor plate was smoldering and blackened. Every round had been bounced directly onto the plate.

"We have tested this shield with every weapon we were comfortable discharging within the confines of the station. The only time we've been able to collapse it was when Nelson fired on it with the charge gun and nearly punched a hole in the hull."

Purcell crossed her arms and allowed a wry smile to come to her face. It had a peculiar quality, as though her face was so seldom expected to show anything besides stern disapproval or contempt that it was out of practice when asked to display something like satisfaction. She pulled out her communicator.

"Guard Unit 1, bring Karter to Docking Bay B," she ordered. Once acknowledged, she turned to the engineers. "I want to commend you, men. This is why we exist! I have no doubt in my mind that dozens of ideas such as these, hundreds, thousands, cross the desks of military assessors who clung to the old, reliable ways, turning a blind eye to innovation and condemning their soldiers to drown in the rising tide of progress. Not only that, but--"

"Is she preaching again?" Karter called out from down the hallway. "Do you people have to put up with that all day every day?"

"Even you cannot tarnish this moment, Dee. All of the news feeds are saying our names. We've sent a video message taking credit for the Weston University attack, and even now it can be found on every news source of record. Look at . . . wait . . ."

Purcell had looked to her datapad, planning to show off their new notoriety, when something caught her eye. The list of poor quality videos, what she believed to be an endless sequence of pale replicas of the Modane footage from different angles, was still silently playing. She paused the current video and tracked it backward. It was a shot of the gunship and the troop carrier departing, something that was absent from the Modane broadcast; just before the crew door finished shutting, something caught the light. The commander tracked back again and paused, zooming as much as the resolution would allow. Even without further enhancement, she knew what she was looking at.

Karter was escorted to the doorway just as she frantically scrambled for her communicator.

"You rang, boss lady?" Karter said, one arm missing, the other restrained.

"Get me the assault team carrying the alloy! Now!" Purcell ordered.

"That won't be possible for a few more hours, Commander. They are taking a direct route. They won't be in range of any communication nodes until shortly before they arrive. Why do you need to contact them?"

"Why? *Why*!? Look at this! Look at it! That is a slidepad Alexander is throwing into the troop carrier. And we've heard from them since then, and they did not report it, which means they don't know about it. They can be tracked! And they are heading directly here!" she raged. After a moment to regain her composure, she turned to Karter. "How long after the alloy arrives will it take you to get the CME Activators functional?"

"About two days," he said.

"Two days!? Why have you been wasting my time if there is still two days of work to do!? I want those devices completed no more than two *hours* after the alloy arrives."

"You can't always get what you want, boss lady. Those lumps of fancy metal can't do their job unless they get within a minimum distance of the sun, and they can't do that without at least three layers of ablative ceramic. Each layer takes fifteen hours to apply. That's forty-five hours minimum. We can do all of the modules at the same time, and once they're done, you'll have your missiles in about twenty minutes, but the laws of physics are dictating the timetable for the ceramic application. It'll be done when it's done. Hey, plasma burns on the walls. You guys been testing my charge gun? Have you had any overheat issues? The new peltier plate heat fins are--"

"Shut your mouth, Dee."

Karter rolled his eyes, "You've got the greatest scientific mind in the galaxy at your beck and call, and you are telling him to shut up just when he starts to talk shop? You should be--"

"I said, shut your mouth!" she demanded. She turned to one of the guards. "Get his arm out of storage. And you, Dee. Set aside the parts necessary for the remainder of the CMEA components and then catalog everything we've got. Disassemble any unnecessary equipment and add the parts to the available resources. Start manufacturing weapons, equipment, anything combat-oriented, starting with what I've seen here. I want to see my armory full to bursting, and I want field manuals for any new equipment drawn up. I don't care how new, how unstable. I want my men armed for war."

"Is this for real? Are you honestly going to let me do this? Because you've been blowing hot and cold during this entire operation and I don't want to get all tasted up for some bleeding-edge prototyping just to have you start PMSing and send me to my room again right when I hit a groove."

"Get to work!" she bellowed, grabbing his jumpsuit and hauling him close. "And remember this. The stun device in your arm is more than capable of stopping your heart, so don't try anything funny. Take him away."

"Pff, like you even know the tech specs on my heart," he scoffed as they took him away. "I designed it myself."

Purcell turned back to her engineering team. "I want usage recommendations for these devices drawn up and distributed, and be prepared to do the same for anything he turns out between now and the arrival of the alloy." She addressed her second in command. "I want you to get any soldiers not currently supporting mission-critical operations to maintain a constant state of combat readiness. This station is on red alert until those CMEAs are completed and deployed. If someone is coming, I want them to have to go through hell to get to us. Do you hear me?"

"Yes, Commander."

"Good. And that goes for all of you! I want whoever these people are to be flying right into the jaws of a lion."

#

The unusual assemblage of heroes had found refuge at a transfer station similar to the one that had been the site of Garotte's escape. The number of stations like this numbered in the thousands. They were supposed to be well-secured, but a greater number than anyone would like to admit simply didn't have the time or resources to keep the cameras running and the patrols sweeping. Thus, *The Declaration* and *S.O.B.* were able to secure a weightless, double-sized docking bay without anyone so much as asking their names. In a predictable illustration of priorities, they did remember to ask for payment in full, which was provided via one of the seemingly endless supply of false bank accounts that Karter and Ma kept handy.

Now the group was coping with an aspect of military campaigns little discussed: boredom. Silo was painting her nails, Garotte was tinkering with a piece of equipment inside *The Declaration*, and Ma was draped loosely around Lex's neck to keep from drifting uselessly around the interior of the bay.

"So, let me get this straight," Lex said, staring at the inert pile of machinery called Zerk. His eyes were lingering on the blood stains on its fingers, and he had decided to stay well outside the ship. "This thing won't wake up unless you give it an adrenaline shot or something like that?"

"That's right. Perfectly safe," Garotte said.

"And they just had it alive and well in storage, so once you juiced it, it could seek out a power source?"

"Yes."

"Isn't that . . . idiotic? I mean. Shouldn't they have taken it apart? You know, so something like this wouldn't happen?"

"It was designed to be tamper-proof, and it can't be entirely powered down because it has biological components that need to be kept alive. Plus, the brass in charge of research always like to keep one functional example of their favorite toys, just in case."

"Okay. So is insanity a requirement for anyone above a certain military rank?" Lex asked.

"It is considered a prerequisite for officers, I believe," Garotte replied.

"So *that's* why I never made it past sergeant," Silo mused. She blew on her finished nails. "Well, I guess that proves that you can paint your nails in zero-G. Have you found that ship yet, sweetheart?"

"At last check, it was not yet within communications range," Ma replied.

"Well, have you checked recently?"

"I have initiated a scripted contact sequence. The device attempts a connection once every twenty-five milliseconds."

"Well, maybe you should try again."

"I have made more than two hundred-forty attempts to connect since the beginning of this sentence."

"Are you sure that you've got the right slidepad?"

"I am absolutely certain, and inquiring repeatedly will not accelerate the discovery process," Ma explained. "So stop asking."

"Well, okay, Miss Snippy," Silo remarked with raised eyebrows. "We'll see if I ever feed *you* any hot dogs again."

"If you're through harassing the computer, send her my way. I've got something I could use help with," Garotte said.

"Sure thing," Silo said, drifting over to Lex and reaching to scoop her off of Lex's shoulders.

"I am quite capable of responding to a request without aid. Thank you,"

Ma stated.

She crouched and shoved lightly off of Lex, drifting slowly into the ship. Lex steadied himself a bit and watched her go. It was interesting. She'd sounded irritated. It wasn't that she'd selected the most irritated voice segments available to her--she actually sounded annoyed. In fact, the various different voices that made up her unusual vocalization were all a bit closer together, as though they had been smoothed out and blended together somewhat.

"What's gotten into her?" Silo muttered under her breath.

Lex turned to her, then motioned for her to follow him as he drifted behind *S.O.B.* She joined him there.

"You're good with guns, right? You're a good soldier?"

"One of the best you'll ever meet."

"You're also an attractive woman."

"Well, thanks, hon."

"How did a pretty thing like you get mixed up in a situation like this?"

"Now that's not really appropriate, mister--"

"Don't you worry your pretty little head. Us men will take care of everything from now on."

"Listen, I don't think--"

"I'd hate for you to break a nail while the men are busy fighting--"

Silo grabbed him by the chest of his flight suit and hauled his face close to hers.

"This had better have a point, honey."

"The point is, you're more than what you look like, and you're more than what you do. You're a whole person, and when other people don't treat you like it, it can be pretty irritating."

"But that's not the same thing. I *am* a person. She's an animal."

"And she's a computer. But, most of all, she's a person. Understand?"

"That's a little hard to swallow, hon."

"I'm not asking you to embrace the idea. I'm just explaining why she's acting the way she's acting."

Silo looked doubtfully toward *The Declaration,* where Ma was doing her best to hold onto a hand grip, analyzing a piece of equipment Garotte was holding.

"Can this device be made to function with this ship?" Garotte asked, holding out a roughly-constructed control box with torn and dangling wires protruding from it.

Ma squinted at the device. "I am afraid I did not include the appropriate information to make that determination in the subset of my full complement of subroutines and data that was downloaded to this physical instance."

"Well, that's rather unfortunate, because--"

"Stand by," Ma said, closing her eyes. The indicators on the data radio on her back began to blink madly. A moment later the displays and controls for *The Declaration* became similarly active. "Accessing Armistice schematics. Accessing repair and installation guidelines. Accessing EMOF device interface hardware and command protocols. Access denied. Attempting code word clearance utilizing Karter's credentials. Access granted. Indexing. Processing . . . processing. Yes, Mr. Garotte, I can help you install the device. Please locate and remove overhead access panel 25b."

"Hey," Lex said, poking his head into the ship, "you guys think maybe we should be plotting and planning, or something, so that once we know where they are, we'll know roughly what we want to do?"

"Normally, I would say yes," Garotte said, holding firm to a hand grip and pulling the access panel free, "but depending on the outcome of this little upgrade, any prior plans we might have made would need to be seriously rewritten."

"What is that?" Lex asked.

"Just a little gadget we managed to tear out of a Neo-Luddite ship before it exploded," Garotte explained.

"Unhook the four cables and unbolt the secondary shield generator from the emitter assembly. When they are detached--" Ma began, suddenly her head jerked up and her eyes opened wide. "Connection established. Tracing connection."

"She found it?" Silo said, joining Lex in the doorway.

"Querying communication grid. Communication node identified. Position tracking, logging, and reporting set to high. Displaying coordinates now."

The main display on the ship's console displayed a stellar map. The humans gathered close around, trying to identify it.

"VCDN-2221," Silo said. "That doesn't exactly sound like a vacation spot. Usually the sort of place a terrorist would threaten would at least have a name with vowels in it."

"The population is just under six million for the whole system," Lex pointed out.

"Give us a summary on the star system, Ma," Garotte requested.

"VCDN-2221 is a planetoid belonging to VectorCorp. It is the second planet from the star, and the site of the primary monitoring, processing, and distribution facility for the outlying half of their transit and communication network," she explained.

"What is the worst-case scenario if the Neo-Luddites were to hit the star for that system?"

"Approximately three days after the deployment of the CME Activators, the leading edge of a sphere of charged particles would strike the planet. Any unshielded electronics, including power and communication lines, will instantly and catastrophically fail. Shielded electronics will fail systematically over the following weeks. The loss of the facility will require monitoring and communication regulation to be shunted to their secondary facility."

"Well, that doesn't sound too bad."

"Their secondary facility is on the third planet of the system, and will be struck sixteen hours later."

"Ah. Perhaps not the best bit of planning, that."

"The loss of both facilities will leave VectorCorp unable to maintain safe transit lanes for that portion of the galaxy, an expanse that contains one hundred-sixteen of the two hundred-forty-five populated planets, including Tessera, Golana, and Earth. All interstellar traffic will cease until monitoring can be reestablished, a process which may take years.

"Communication will also be impossible for a period of weeks while secondary routes are established for data traffic. The sphere of interference surrounding the star will continue to grow for the months-long period of activity associated with the CMEAs, creating a massive, expanding section of space that will disable and destroy any vehicle passing through. The disruption of communication and transit will choke off trade routes, causing mass starvation on any planets that are not yet self-sustaining. This loss of life, coupled with the inevitable economic and social disruptions, will produce a death toll approaching the billions by the end of the decade, and could be the inciting event for a full societal collapse."

There was silence for a moment.

"Am I the only one not surprised that Karter is going to be responsible for the fall of human civilization?" Silo asked.

"It did seem something of an inevitability. I'm actually a bit disappointed that it took a rogue military group to actually pull the trigger, though. I've always thought Karter would make an excellent megalomaniac, if he would only apply himself," Garotte quipped.

"Are we going to be able to stop this?" Lex asked, his voice the only one carrying the level of terrified concern that seemed appropriate for the situation.

"Well, we're certainly going to try. Ma, do we know what we'll be dealing with when we reach them?"

"Attempting to access local orbital sensors. Processing . . . processing . . . unable to access, encryption level exceeds--one moment, connecting live audio feed."

The speakers in *The Declaration* crackled and began to broadcast the voices of the crew.

"--in need of resupply. Provisions ran out three days ago. Have medical personnel standing by. Extreme distress," said the first voice. It had a haggard, weary tone.

"Affirmative. Medical teams staged and ready. Stand by for a message from Commander Purcell." This voice was further distorted, evidently coming over the troop ship's speakers. A moment later, a female voice rang out angrily.

"Attention assault team. I have reason to believe that the security of your ship has been compromised. You must not return the alloy to the space station until you have neutralized the threat. Someone has been able to deliver a slidepad onto your ship. Find it and destroy it before docking."

"Space station," Garotte muttered under his breath. "I truly dislike combat in space stations."

"Me, too," Silo agreed.

"They have located the slidepad. Displaying video feed," Ma announced.

The screen now displayed a dark, cramped view. Evidently, once the ship had left the gravity well of the planet, the slidepad had drifted up behind a bundle of emergency gear strapped to one wall. A hand was visible, grasping for it. Finally, it grabbed the device and pulled it out. A swift, shaky view of the interior of the vessel whisked across the screen. The view then became steady and the butt of a rifle came smashing down on the device. Two more hits replaced the video feed with the words "*Connection Lost*."

"Okay, so we know where we have to go, and we know that there is a space station," Lex cataloged. "Where does that leave us, plan-wise?"

"We have not analyzed all pertinent data," Ma stated.

The video feed rewound. Frame by frame, the short sweep of video progressed again. The slidepad, at Ma's request, was a high-quality one, which meant that the video feed was exceedingly sharp, even for the dim and swiftly-moving image before them. With each frame, a digital overlay outlined and highlighted elements of the image, listing off specifications for the soldier's rifles and equipment, and finally freezing on the single frame in which the front view window was visible. A square was traced around a speck in the distance ahead of the ship. It enlarged, brightened, and sharpened into a slightly distorted but recognizable shape. A space station. Next to it, a sequence of space station designs began to flip by.

"The station is currently on the far side of the sun in reference to the planet. The VectorCorp sensors will not pick it up. Attempting to identify station type."

"They couldn't have built it there--or anywhere in the system, for that matter. VC would have noticed. Eliminate stations incapable of interstellar flight," Garotte advised.

"And these people probably couldn't swing having one built for them, and if they'd stolen one, we would have heard about it, so limit your search to designs that are likely to have been decommissioned or left derelict," Silo added.

"Station type identified," Ma said, highlighting the remaining design, which was clearly a match.

"Way to go, Ma!" Lex congratulated.

"Bring up schematics, armaments, everything you can find," Garotte said.

The requested information was displayed. Garotte looked it over and clucked his tongue. "This isn't going to be one of our easier missions."

"If it was easy, someone else would be doing it," Silo said with a shrug.

"I could probably get there in about eight hours in *S.O.B.*," Lex said.

"Unfortunately, no amount of skill will get your ship past those defenses. We'll have to hit it with both ships together, so that pushes our time table to, what, fifty hours?"

"Approximately forty-two hours, eleven minutes, eighteen seconds, assuming optimal performance by *The Declaration*'s engines," Ma corrected. "Assuming no Esche alloy was available prior to this moment, there is a properly equipped fabrication lab on the space station, and the final stage in manufacturing of the CMEA begins immediately, the earliest the missiles can be deployed is forty-four hours, seven minutes, four seconds."

"That doesn't leave us much wiggle room," Silo remarked.

"That it does not. So," Garotte proclaimed, rubbing his hands together eagerly, "let's finish up here, devise a plan, and get a move on. Civilization won't save itself.

Each member of the group stood and began to tie up their loose ends.

#

On a VectorCorp commuter ship skimming along in a carefully-mapped stretch of space somewhere between Tessera and Golana, Michella and Jon were busily tying up their own loose ends. For Jon, it was the frayed ends of his sanity that needed to be tied up. Currently, this consisted of alternately attempting to sleep and attempting to convince himself that the VC security officer wasn't eying him up suspiciously. For Michella, who had made a career of tying up loose ends, this meant doing the same thing she'd been doing on the surface: reviewing footage, making calls, and otherwise wringing every drop of newsworthy information out of her pool of resources. The only difference was that on the ship the connections were more distorted, the screens were smaller, and the seats were less comfortable.

She and Jon were sitting on opposite sides of a small, collapsible table in a set of passenger train-style bench seats. Approximately double the permitted number of carry-on bags had been crammed into the remaining seat space at the insistence of Michella, so that her full journalistic arsenal would be available to her.

Jon tapped his fingers nervously on the back of his neck as he stretched to maintain his vigil.

"I'm telling you, he's looking at me funny," Jon whispered to Michella out of the side of his mouth, so that he didn't have to take his eyes off of the officer.

"He's looking at you funny because you've been staring at him for the last fifteen minutes," she replied wearily, also without tearing her eyes away from their current target, the screen of a datapad. "Relax. We didn't do anything, we've paid our fines. The authorities aren't after us. Things are fine."

"Oh, yeah? Then why are we flying economy instead of first class?"

"Because the execs thought I needed to be reprimanded for making them pay those fines," Michella said. "I notice they didn't mind the exclusive footage, though."

"Okay, but what about the ter--" Jon began, cutting himself off when it struck him that using the t-word on a crowded flight was probably not a wise decision. "What about the Neo-Luddites? How do we know there isn't one of them aboard? Or chasing us?"

"They aren't."

"How do you know?"

She glanced at him, then handed the datapad over, several snippets of text highlighted. After taking a few more moments to convince himself that the security officer wasn't going to leap over three rows of seats to slap cuffs on him, he was willing to pay attention to what his boss had handed him.

"What's this?"

"Breaking news. There was some sort of incident at a military storage depot a few hours ago," Michella explained.

"I'm getting really tired of incidents . . ."

"Just read it."

"No orbital footage . . . authorities responded following the incident . . . communication interruption . . . I don't get it. What is this supposed to mean to me?"

Michella sighed and leaned close, whispering in his ear. "Trev is involved. The others, too."

"How can you be sure?"

"I just know. Figuring out what Trev is up to is like figuring out where a shark is going to surface based on the ripples in the water. Basically, if it involves someone doing something stupid in a spaceship and not getting caught, the chances are pretty good it's him."

"And you think that's enough to keep them from going after us?"

"Once Trevor gets his heels dug in, there is no man alive more distracting and persistent than he is. If they are stupid enough to take their eyes off of him long enough to look in our direction, he'll fly a ship right up their backside. And if those others are half as dangerous as they seem to be, that's all it will take to bring the whole organization down."

"That's all well and good, but we don't even know if this is related to the Neo-Luddites."

"The official story is pretty spotty, but from what my eyes and ears in the area have been able to turn up, there was a lot of property damage, the contents of a locker are missing, and there was one fatality. The one person who died was an injured veteran who had requested reassignment to the depot just a few days prior. It is the Neo-Luddites, Jon, and this is as good as handled."

"You sure have a lot of confidence in that man of yours."

"That's why he's my man."

Jon stared at her for a moment or two, then opened his mouth to talk. Before any words could come out, he shook his head and turned away. Then he turned back, raised a finger, and turned away again. Three or four more similar fidgets came and went before Michella narrowed her eyes at him.

"Just say it before the ship medic thinks you're having a seizure."

"No, no. It isn't any of my business. I shouldn't say anything," he decided.

Michella glared at him for a few moments longer. The instant she turned away, he turned to her and blurted, "I just think you might be taking him for granted a bit."

"What? What are you talking about?"

"Look, we talked for a bit down in the bar area the other day. He feels like he's dangling off of the end of this relationship, and I don't think he's wrong."

"Jon, honestly," she said wearily, putting a hand to her face. "I don't need to hear this from you right now. I've got a million things I need to be thinking about."

"I know, I know," he said, backing off. "All I'm saying is that maybe it should be a million and one." He slid out from behind the table and into the aisle between the seats, standing stiffly. "I'm going to get something to drink. Anything for you?"

"Tea. Thanks," she said, turning her eyes back to her datapad.

She swept her eyes across the various images and transcripts that flowed continuously across her screen. And dutifully ignored the creeping sensation in the back of her mind. After a minute or two, she realized that her mind hadn't managed to process a single syllable of the information. When rubbing her eyes and kneading the back of her neck failed to restore her focus, she decided it was time to set her mind to a different problem. Thumbing aside the primary source data, she pulled up the network traffic reports her bosses were always so interested in. After a few moments, a thought came to mind. She sighed and pulled out her slidepad.

"Call Lou," she stated. A few seconds of waiting earned her a connection.

"Lou," came a gruff smoker's voice. The video feed showed part of a rolled-up sleeve, with a hairy arm protruding from it. Lou was one of those people who left his slidepad in a cradle, and hadn't seemed to have noticed that video call etiquette generally called for at least pointing the camera in the general direction of a face.

“Yeah, Lou. Michella again. Listen, have you been looking at these numbers?”

“The year-to-date record-setting traffic you've been sending our way? I've been kept informed,” he said flatly.

“Well, Trevor is tracking very favorably. I know that PR is always after you to get me more involved in human interest. I think there might be some value in doing some deeper coverage on him. On the two of us. Something to tie him to our brand.”

“What did you have in mind?”

“Maybe you can send us on a press tour once the main coverage is wrapped up. The two of us together . . .”

Chapter 28

Many believe that they have felt tension, but if you've never been among soldiers readying for a battle, you don't know the meaning of the word. It is as though the air itself is stretched tight as a guitar string, humming with energy. Every sense is on fire--eyes sharp, ears trained, skin tingling. Words, if spoken at all, are short and to the point. There is an unmistakable sense of preoccupation. The coming battle is fought a thousand times a second, each mind simulating every possible beginning and formulating every possible defense.

They say that pressure makes diamonds, and it is true . . . if you are talking about geology. Psychology, on the other hand, has established that pressure mostly just makes neuroses.

In Purcell's space station, the atmosphere was thick with pure, weapons-grade, military anticipation. There was silence aside from the click and rattle of tightening straps and fittings, the squeak of boots . . . and the piercing, off-key whistle of Karter as he tinkered merrily in the fab lab. In contrast to the agonizing sense of foreboding weighing down on everyone else, Karter was happy as an elf in Santa's workshop. Laid out before him, taking up nearly all of the available space in the lab, were the unfinished CME Activator cores. They were long, thin devices, about as thick as a man's leg and maybe three meters long. Tucked in a corner of the fab lab was a long, low furnace, creaking and pinging as it slowly cooled. Purcell was pacing outside the door of the lab, her second-in-command shadowing her.

"How much longer, Dee?" she demanded.

"They need to drop another seven-tenths of a degree Kelvin and they'll be ready to come out. Sixty seconds, give or take," he answered.

"Only 0.7 degrees? Surely they can be removed now."

"Sure they can, if you want them to have micro-fractures that will cause them to fail while they're passing through the chromosphere. Don't you have something better to do than pace around waiting for the cookies to finish?"

"My men are prepared. They are armed with your equipment and briefed in its usage. All that remains is to see to it that you fulfill your obligation without further treachery."

"I'll have you know," he said, tightening a bolt and holstering the tool, "I am officially done with my obligations. Once those things come out of the oven, they click into these reaction chambers, and then these whole assemblies slip into the superstructures down in the weapons bay. Even your idiots could do that."

"Get engineering down here," Purcell ordered. Her lackey quickly began quietly speaking orders into his communicator.

"There, see? I haven't done anything treacherous since I sabotaged the power grid."

"When did you do that?" Purcell growled.

"Wouldn't *you* like to know," Karter taunted. He looked over the dial of the furnace. "Just about . . . little bit more . . . there. All done. Hey, out of curiosity, what's with the red hair? I don't know if you were hoping it was intimidating or not, but basically you just look like a clown that was too lazy to put on the makeup."

"Damn it, Karter, tell me what you did!"

"Oh, come on. The fun part is figuring it out. That's what makes this little game we've got going so exciting. Sometimes you catch me, sometimes you don't."

"I don't have time for this. Motivate him," she ordered.

Her second-in-command pulled out his slidepad and began to tap at the screen.

"I wouldn't do that if I were--" Karter quickly warned.

Before he could finish the sentence, the lights in the station suddenly dimmed and then shut off. The halls filled with the muffled commotion of soldiers going through the well-practiced power failure procedures and learning that it was considerably more difficult when anxiety levels have already ratcheted up to epic proportions.

"Now, that's your fault," Karter said, crossing his arms. "You installed a stun device in my arm. That gave me access to a high-voltage device with a remote trigger. What did you think I was going to do with it? And then I *clearly* goaded you into zapping me. Come on. You're supposed to be better than this!"

"This isn't a game, Karter!" she growled, drawing her blaster.

Karter didn't even have the decency to flinch. "You're just saying that because you're losing."

The lights flickered back on.

"There, see? It was just a power surge that tripped some safeties. It isn't as though I set up a feedback loop that would blow the reactor in eight minutes."

Purcell's glare managed to become even more threatening than the weapon she was holding.

"I really didn't," Karter said simply. "That would kill *me*, and where's the fun in that?"

"You have *not* fulfilled your obligation. I require the full design."

"Pff. Technicalities," Karter said.

He drifted over to the fabrication computer, tapped a few buttons, and removed a memory chip from it. With a flick, he sent it darting in Purcell's direction. When it reached the artificial gravity of the hallway, it dropped to the ground. The commander didn't take her eyes off of Karter. A few tense moments past before the representative from engineering showed up. He didn't even open his mouth before Purcell began to issue orders, still without taking her eyes off of the inventor.

"At my feet, you will find a memory chip containing the completed design for the CMEA. Validate it. Now," she commanded steadily.

The engineer collected the chip and inserted it into the bottom edge of his datapad. Schematics and instructions filled the screen of the device.

"The schematics for the known portion of the device seem to match what we've been able to determine. The schematics for the previously unknown portions pass function verification analysis and appear to complement the existing portion. I would say that this is legitimate," remarked the engineer.

"Excellent. Transfer the design into the main computer, then get together a team to complete the assembly of the devices," Purcell ordered. "And as for you, Dee . . ."

"Yeah, yeah, empty threat time, I know the drill," he said, turning away.

She pulled the trigger. A bolt of energy hissed through the air and struck Karter in the small of his back, filling the room with the stench of singed flesh. The injured inventor screamed and clutched at the injury. His face, rather than the usual expression of annoyed disinterest or mischievous glee, was twisted in pain and surprise.

"That was this weapon's lowest setting. It isn't supposed to be fatal--but, then, this *is* a prototype, and this design was abandoned for being overpowered, so I wouldn't be very confident in your chances without treatment," she advised.

"What are you doing!?" he growled through the pain. "You need me!"

"No, Karter. You are useful. You are even irreplaceable. But now that you have given me the CMEA design, you are *not* necessary. You would be an asset to our cause if you were cooperative, but your current behavior makes you a much greater liability. From this moment forward, you live or die depending on how well you can prove your usefulness and loyalty. Do you understand?"

"What I understand," he coughed, "is that you might have just cost me my one natural kidney. That was my favorite kidney!"

The color was draining from his face, but his expression had already slipped back to one of its defaults--anger.

"I want him taken to his cell. Take away his arm and stabilize him, but no painkillers. He needs to understand consequences," she dictated to her second-in-command. "I want there to be no--"

“Commander,” said her assistant urgently, “we've got a sensor alert. There's a weak signature approaching!”

“I want one medic and one guard on Dee, and keep the engineers working on the CMEAs. Everyone else, battle stations! You're with me,” Purcell demanded. She began marching down the tight hallway as her assistant scurried behind her and various soldiers scrambled to get back to their posts after the short blackout. “How many ships have we got?”

“Two gunships, two troop carriers, both in Docking Bay A. There are also four single-man short-range fighters on patrol.”

“Where are the rest?”

“The other gunship was destroyed by Alexander. We left a troop carrier on the surface of Big Sigma. Of the four remaining, three were sent on surveillance missions, one was sent to retrieve the alloy. The Manticore surveillance ship was destroyed, and another has been recalled but has not yet arrived. That leaves us with the ship that just returned with the alloy, and the ship that just returned from Proxy-12. We've also got our support ship and a wing of fighters patrolling Big Sigma.”

“Fine. Keep the fighters on patrol. Get one gunship and one troop ship out there, too. Keep the others for reserve. Recall the Big Sigma patrol. If this fight doesn't go our way, we'll need reinforcements, even if it takes them days to get here. What do the sensors tell us about this approaching signature?”

“Not much. It is just a minor blip. We've been getting it for about three minutes, but it wasn't until now that it was strong enough to suggest it wasn't just background noise.”

“Sounds like a stealth ship. Fine--they want stealth, let's show them what stealth really is,” she said, finally ending her trek across the station on the command bridge.

A far cry from the massive, spacious rooms with giant view screens and elaborate chairs that one usually thinks of when a commander takes the bridge, the space station's bridge was a match for the rest of the facility. It was a cramped, darkened room. The only light came from the handful of screens that dotted one wall, and the innumerable LED indicators that speckled the walls. There was room enough for the commander, the second-in-command, and a single tactical officer, and only if two of them remained standing. Frankly, it had more in common with the audio-video room of a public access TV station than an epic place of command.

Purcell looked over the screens, covered with dots representing her ships, each tagged with designations, technical readouts, and motion vectors. Carefully, her mind formulated a plan.

“Put me on general broadcast,” she ordered, speaking again when she received a nod. “TC-4, engage cloak and take up position alpha-6. GS-2, cloak and take up position omega-6. Target the enemy vessel and fire only when you achieve a weapons lock. Fighters, pair off and approach the enemy vessel from oblique angles. Target and pursue. Keep clear of cloaked ship locations to avoid collision."

Outside the station, the veteran soldiers swiftly complied. The pair of ships, gunship above and troop carrier below, assumed their positions and activated their cloaks, vanishing from sight and sensors. Next, the fighters complied. They were small, light vehicles with little more than a pilot's cabin, a pair of small engines, and a pair of oversized cannons. If the gunship was like an eagle, the fighters were like bees--small and fragile, but they could easily be deadly if they attacked in large enough numbers or stung the right target. Two fighters peeled off and approached the slowly-strengthening sensor reading from the left, the other two veering right. Just as the form of *S.O.B.* was becoming visible on the fighter's visual sensors, though, it accelerated, pulling a long, gradual turn, picking up speed all the way.

"Lock and fire!" Purcell ordered, watching intently at her screens.

"Negative. Can't get a lock. Sensors aren't getting a strong enough reading," came the reply from the lead fighter.

"Fine, manual fire, wide spread!" she ordered.

All four fighters began to unload their weapons. Piercing dots of purple light fired in staggered, irregular patterns, trading accuracy for volume. *S.O.B.* didn't even try to dodge, absorbing a handful of hits before tearing past the fighters.

"Station shields to maximum! Turrets, target and fire, avoiding top-center and friendly ships."

The rattling tractor beam/jackhammer made a few useless taps at the shield as *S.O.B.* whipped past, the massive but slow-to-target cannons on the station firing vaguely in its direction without once coming close.

"Target locked, firing," announced the pilot of the gunship, its more acute sensors finally managing to pick up the elusive little ship.

The cloaked ship fired a cluster of the same missiles that had given Lex so much trouble at the array, briefly becoming visible as it did. For a few seconds, the missiles drew steadily closer to the retreating *S.O.B.*--then there was a dim flash of light and the same EMP that had saved him the first time sent the trailing missiles twirling away uselessly. Purcell barked coded command shorthand at her pilots, coaxing complex maneuvers out of her men in order to prepare for the return run by *S.O.B.* This time, it came from below, and it was the troop carrier that sent a volley of powerful shots in its direction.

"He hasn't got the weapons to do any damage. Keep the pressure on him and we'll take him down," Purcell advised.

"Establishing target lock, prepare--" came the beginning of a transmission from the gunship, but it was suddenly interrupted by a blaring warning tone.

"Evasive maneuvers! Evasive maneuvers! We've got--"

There was a burst of static, and the symbol for the gunship dropped off the tactical display.

"What the hell happened? The enemy ship wasn't even close!" Purcell roared.

"I don't know, there--Commander!"

"TC-4, evasive maneuvers!"

An explosion swallowed the cloaked ship and another icon dropped from the display.

"Sensors! I want to know where these attacks are coming from!"

"There--there were a pair of temporary blips at vector 013, mark 015. It's a cloaked ship, Commander!" the tactical officer realized.

"How!? Never mind. Fighters, break pursuit and protect the docking hatch for Bay A. GS-1 and TC-3, deploy! Shields up and cloaks down. I want you to turtle until that cloaked ship fires, then target attack origin and fire! Sensors, get those meson arrays up! If that thing is cloaked, it'll be the only source of meson emissions in the area."

"Initializing," replied the tactical officer. "GS-1 deployed and beginning sensor sweep. TC-3 deployed and beginning sensor sweep. Docking bay doors secured. Meson array active. We've got a meson emission source . . . inside Docking Bay A!"

Purcell opened her mouth. A lesser woman might have exclaimed that it was impossible. She would have pointed out that the doors to the docking bay had been open for mere seconds, and that she had assigned the fighters to guard the entrance. She would have reasoned that most of the time the doors were open, they were occupied by other ships. She would have insisted that no one could have possibly flown a cloaked ship through so narrow an opening during so narrow a time window without colliding with something. The commander said none of these things, because regardless of how ironclad the logic might have been, the evidence contradicted it, and there was too little time to waste any of it denying what was obviously so.

Instead, she said, "Troopers to Docking Bay A. We have been boarded! Repeat, we have been boarded!"

#

In the docking bay, the now-pointless cloak hiding *The Declaration of War* dropped, leaving them as a very large, very visible target in an otherwise empty bay. Fancy new space stations had marvels of modern science to keep them running. Things like semi-permeable force fields allowed ships in and out without allowing all of the air and dock workers to get sucked out into space. This space station, despite the group's dedication to the bleeding edge, was neither fancy nor new. A user-friendly approach was to have individual bays and pressurized exit tunnels that connected to the ship. This station wasn't user-friendly either. An efficient design called for ships to remain outside the station, interfacing with universal, airtight docking ports. Once again, this was not a facility built with efficiency in mind.

Its primary role, prior to being co-opted by the Neo-Luddites for their purposes, had been ship maintenance and restoration. Thus, what it had was a pair of massive, unpressurized bays with individual landing pads and no gravity, plus a scattering of external docking ports in the case of evacuation. Workers, when it was necessary to move about in the bay while it was in use, wore space suits. Anyone who wanted to get in or out of the rest of the station had to do so through a huge, freight elevator-sized airlock with sturdy doors and no windows, or wait for someone to trot out something that looked like an overgrown piece of dryer vent to hook up to the ship as a means of access. It was for that reason that there were no soldiers currently manning the bay, but that wouldn't remain the case for long.

The crew door of *The Declaration* hissed open and three people darted out. Silo and Garotte were wearing the sleek, snug space suits favored by most people who had to operate in a vacuum with any regularity--silvery, nearly skin-tight suits with high-visibility face visors and small but efficient jet packs for zero-G navigation. They were also heavily armed. Lex was wearing a distinctive, textured, tan flight suit and was attempting to wrangle what looked like an inflated blowup doll, but was, in fact, a third sleek-style suit with an undersized occupant.

“All clear,” announced Silo through her suit radio, after a quick but thorough survey of the area. “That was some impressive maneuvering, Lex.”

“Thanks. High-speed, illegal docking while invisible. I can cross that one off the list, I guess,” he said through a mouth full of gum.

“That makes me two for two in blind-targeting cloaked ships, too,” Silo remarked with a bit of pride.

“Ma, are you sure they aren't going to blow up *S.O.B.*? I'm not too comfortable with her being on automatic while things are shooting at her,” Lex continued.

“Your ship has been directed to leave the area of combat until recalled, and the other ships are unlikely to pursue while we are on board their command station. In the meantime, I urge you to revise your list of priorities,” the AI answered, struggling a bit inside a suit that was not built with a furry quadruped in mind.

“Yes, my boy. Very shortly we will encounter a rather large number of people interested in killing us. Try to keep that in mind,” Garotte instructed.

“Easy for you to say. You didn't just put a fresh coat of paint on it,” said Lex.

“Enough banter. Ma, I want access to the airlock, now. Silo, let's unload.”

#

On the interior side of the airlock, a dozen troops had gathered. Each was wearing a bulky space suit of a similar design. The added mass came from overlapping plates of composite armor. Their weapons were a mismatched assortment of ballistic and energy weapons, most representing designs that had been abandoned for having one or two strengths that were more than offset by dozens of major weaknesses. The first on the scene was tapping at a control panel.

"No good, it is occupied, and being pressurized," the scout reported.

"You heard him, boys. The enemy is inside the airlock. Weapons ready, eyes sharp," instructed the squad leader. "We can end this here and now."

The panel beside the door ticked various indicators, pressure up and time down, as the soldiers anxiously waited for the door to open and reveal their targets. Finally, the pressure was equalized and the heavy door began to pull open. Triggers were squeezed and sights lined up as the group drew in a breath . . . but when the door finished opening, there was no one there. Rather than a few armed and dangerous targets handily corralled into a box with no escape, the airlock revealed . . . a crate. It was about a meter cubed, sturdily built, and had a lid held tightly on by eight or so mechanical latches.

"No one fire," the squad leader ordered. "This could be an explosive. Wilkes, cycle the airlock again and send this thing back into space."

Wilkes worked at the control panel. "No good, sir. They've got someone blocking the controls."

"Well, unblock them! And change the cypher! I don't want--"

He was interrupted by a heart-stopping sound. Like falling dominoes, the latches on the crate flipped up in sequence. When the final latch was undone, the edge of the lid hissed with a release of pressure, causing the squad to shudder, and one of the jumpier soldiers to reflexively fire a single blast. The energy struck and warped the lid, causing it to leap off of the crate and rattle to the floor. Inside, there seemed to be nothing but old-fashioned puffy packing material.

"Keep it together, soldier!" reprimanded the squad leader. "Wilkes, investigate. I'll work on the cypher."

The unlucky underling cautiously walked up to the crate. After a visual survey of the outside didn't turn up anything, he reached out with the muzzle of his rifle and poked into the box, striking something hard and metallic. His rummaging unearthed a small plastic tube from among the Styrofoam. He picked it out with his gloved hand.

"I've got a new cypher active. If you found anything threatening, I'll cycle. What is it?" asked the squad leader.

"It . . . I . . . I think it is one of those asthma-sprayer things, sir," he said, holding it up.

Whether it was fate, dumb luck, or a cruel sense of humor, the key item in the crate chose that moment to reveal itself. In an explosion of fluffy plastic peanuts and gleaming metal, Zerk launched from the crate and into the cluster of soldiers.

#

On the exterior side of the airlock, the rescue party watched minor dents and dings pepper the heavy-duty door as the hapless force tried to deal with something that no sane person would have dreamed of preparing for. They each strapped blue bandanas to their arms as they did.

"Um . . . you know that rule about not firing weapons inside a pressurized facility?" Lex asked.

"I do," Garotte remarked, as he looked over the floor plan displayed on the slidepad he'd clipped into the arm of his suit.

"I can't help but notice these guys aren't obeying it."

"If you'd ever seen Zerk in action, hon, you wouldn't blame them," Silo remarked.

"I wouldn't worry too much about it. This old bird was built back in the days when you had to expect to take a few love taps during the average day," Garotte said, slapping the sturdy wall. "She can take a few hits and hold together."

"Okay, and what about Karter? We're here to rescue him, right? Wasn't it not a great idea to unleash an unstoppable killing machine into the place they're holding him?" Lex asked.

"Karter knows how to handle Zerk. He's the one who managed to back out the shutdown procedures. There is more than one," Garotte remarked. "All right, it looks like the excitement has died down. Ma, let's see this airlock do its thing again, shall we?"

"I am endeavoring to reestablish an interface with the desired systems," Ma stated from within her poorly-suited piece of equipment. Her voice had the jittery, stressed quality it tended to adopt when she was concentrating. "The encryption of this system is extremely complex. My initial route of access has already been closed and secured."

"Yes, well, military encryption tends to be rather significant," Garotte countered.

"Not entirely military . . . redundant encryption schemes. Mostly corporate."

"What the hell does *that* mean?" Lex asked.

"It means we've got a delightful and entirely irrelevant mystery on our hands," Garotte said. "Just cycle the chamber."

"Limited access restored. Activating," Ma said, the stress gone from her voice.

After atmosphere was pumped out of the lock, the quartet stepped into the chamber, and waited for the process to reverse. Air hissed in, causing Ma's unwieldy bundle of a suit to seemingly deflate; gravity slowly faded in. When the inner door opened, it revealed a tight corridor completely covered with bullet and energy damage and scattered with the remains of soldiers who were extremely dead, and who had been delivered to that state with great enthusiasm and creativity.

"Uh . . ." Lex said with a hint of nausea, as he tried to avoid looking at the remains, "I'm not feeling too heroic right now."

"Take it from a man who does this for a living, my boy. Don't try to be a hero, just try to get the job done. To that end, you take the computer and try to find Karter. Silo and I will take care of the blasted device they were after--destroy prototypes, delete designs, things of that nature."

"And everybody be careful!" Silo added as they ran their separate ways.

"Which way am I heading, Ma?" Lex asked, as he sprinted down the corridor in the direction with the fewest casualties, and therefore the least chance of running into their highly effective diversion. Hanging across his back was the smallest energy rifle that the others had been able to find, along with a tightly bundled spare space suit. Hanging on his belt was a holster containing a small energy pistol; the rest of his belt was covered with variable-strength grenades, and under his arm was the weakly struggling tangle of silver suit that contained his guide.

"I will direct you, but while we are still unharassed by soldiers, please remove me from this suit."

"You sure? How will you get back to the ship?" Lex asked.

"At this stage, my ability to aid in the completion of the mission is of greater importance."

"But what if--"

"Get me out of this damn suit, Lex."

"Your coarse language is not called for, Ma," Lex said, as he carefully unfastened the triple-sealed zipper.

Ma tumbled out from the suit, scrambled to her feet, and rustled her fur.

"If you were covered in a layer of fur and wrapped in airtight fabric, you would agree regarding the necessity of such language. Now, affix a blue bandana to me."

Lex removed the blue bandana from a pouch on his flight suit and shook it out, tying it around her neck. Once it was in place, Ma planted her feet, raised her head, and drew in a long, slow breath through her nose.

"Anything?"

"Scent tracking in a space station is non-ideal. Carefully sanitized and maintained air quality coupled with atmospheric isolation prevents scent from spreading. I am also only moderately familiar with Karter's scent," she informed him. After a moment, she darted toward a side corridor. "This way. Leave the suit. We will fetch it upon our return."

"You caught a whiff?"

"No. It is an educated guess."

"Great."

Lex tossed the suit away and briefly considered drawing his pistol, but abandoned the idea when it dawned on him that if he was holding a gun, they might think he knew how to use it and decide to shoot first and ask questions later. Sure, the chances were good that it was their general policy to shoot first and skip the questions altogether, and it wasn't as though he was going to be able to convince them that he was a tourist who took a wrong turn--but Lex felt that as long as he was a harmless idiot, he ought to look like one. Leaving the gun on his belt took care of the harmless part, and just in case there was any doubt as to the idiot part, he set off to follow the scampering critter with a radio strapped to its back who was calling the shots by acting on a hunch.

#

Half a station away, a single guard was watching from the other side of a locked cell door as a medic worked on Karter inside the cell. The inventor had stopped screaming and grunting in pain a minute or two ago, and now seemed to have lapsed into a state of delirium from the pain. A patch attached to his chest was bleeping off the irregular rhythm of his heart. All around them, the station was echoing with the sounds of distant battle. The soldier twitched at the sound of each ricochet like a dog straining its leash. In his hands was the mechanical arm that had been removed from the scientist, which the soldier was fiddling with in irritation.

"Listen, hurry up! The first real action I've had a chance to see besides babysitting this mad scientist is happening and I'm missing it!" he urged.

"It is going to be a few minutes more. I need to check if there is any internal bleeding."

"Look, just let him die, right? He did his job, and he wants us dead."

The medic stood and faced the soldier. "Listen, don't you think I want him dead? But I've got orders."

"You think it matters how well you follow orders if whoever is invading manages to blow this place up?"

There was a rattle and crash. The medic turned to find Karter convulsing, having knocked the contents of the med pack all over the floor.

"Now you see what you let happen? He could be going into shock. You want to go fight? Fine. He's pretty far out of it. I don't think I need you looking over my shoulder and distracting me."

"Finally!" the eager soldier proclaimed, throwing the prosthetic limb to the floor and rushing off to find glory.

The medic crouched and sifted through the tools scattered on the floor.

"Where did that stim go?" he muttered.

Suddenly, Karter stopped convulsing and the patch on his chest gave a long, even tone.

"Goddamn it!" the medic growled, leaning low to check the scientist's respiration and begin pumping his chest.

In a lightning motion, Karter's remaining arm whipped around and plunged a hypo-injector into the medic's neck. The futuristic replacement for a needle blasted a dose of unknown medication into the hapless medical technician's bloodstream. He had enough time to lurch to his feet and get out half a syllable of a cry for help before he shuddered and dropped to the ground.

Karter sat up, breathing heavy and pouring sweat, and glanced at the spent vial in the injector.

"Heh, sedative. You lucked out," he remarked.

He frowned and looked down at the monitor on his chest, which was still blaring out the helpful reminder that his heart was not, in fact, beating. He made a fist and tapped his chest a few times, like a man trying to unearth a decent belch. The monitor stuttered and began to beep again.

"Let that be a lesson to you," Karter said wearily. "Never trust an off-the-shelf heart monitor to monitor a custom-made heart correctly."

He tore the monitor off and tried to stand up, but grimaced and fell back to the floor, clutching his back.

"Okay, fine," he grumbled, rolling over and fumbling his hand through the scattered medical equipment until he came up with the appropriate vial, which he chambered in the injector and administered to his neck. His eyes rolled back and he grinned. "Ooh. That's the stuff."

He loaded three more vials of painkiller into his pocket, then paused and grabbed three more for the road. After a few seconds to let the painkiller kick in, he grabbed the bars and hauled himself off of the floor, struggling to the edge of the cell, and reached around to the keypad that controlled the lock.

"Another lesson, since you're here," Karter said, his voice somewhat slurred by the effects of the medication. "If your prisoner has a wireless datalink built into his eye, don't put a security camera directly opposite his cell. I tapped into that baby six hours after I got here. Doesn't matter how many times you change the key code if I can see you enter it."

He managed to key in the code, causing the door to click open. The combination of medication, missing limbs, and injury made retrieving his arm a less-than-simple matter, but once it was affixed, he dragged himself to the nearby bank of lockers until he found where they kept his leg.

"There," he said, clicking it into place and mopping the sweat from a face that was steadily getting paler. "Time to cause some problems."

#

Silo and Garotte pounded their way down the battle-scarred hall. Spitting wires and hissing pipes that had been torn apart by the rampaging Zerk were scattered across the walls.

"Now then," Garotte announced as he ran, "we are looking for a weapon, so it would stand to reason the weapons bay is a good start. That is three decks down. We should find an access ladder--*cover*!"

Garotte dove to one side of the corridor, Silo to the other, each cramming themselves as far as possible behind the bulkhead surrounding a submarine-style compartmentalization door.

"Four on the left, two on the right," Silo dictated. "Small arms, energy weapons, lightly modified. I'll take--"

As she was speaking, a quiet whine had grown steadily louder, and finally interrupted her with a vicious crackle of energy. An instant later, the bulkhead a few inches above her helmet exploded into molten metal. A few drops of incandescent liquid metal sprinkled on her helmet and quickly began to melt through. She scrambled to pull the helmet off just in time for the white-hot drop to fall through into the space that moments earlier would have been her skull.

"What the hell are they shooting!?" she screamed, briefly looking through the widening hole left by the weapon.

Garotte leaned out and took a few shots with his pistol, causing the soldiers to take cover. A second later, one of the men stepped out and tapped a control strapped to his arm, two or three behind him doing the same. Garotte aimed and fired. The bolt of energy hit its target . . . and rebounded off of a briefly visible glimmering surface, deflecting into the wall.

"Bad news. I think Karter might have equipped them with some of his toys," Garotte said, with a tremor of nerves in his voice.

The shielded soldier smiled, squeezing the trigger of his fully-automatic ballistic rifle without even raising it to his eye. A deafening sequence of blasts was followed by a peculiar rattling clatter. Along with the sound came a random shimmer of shield and shudder of the soldier. It wasn't until the sound finally stopped and the soldier crumbled to the ground, perforated with bullet holes, that it became clear what had happened. The shield was equally good at reflecting projectiles fired from the *inside* and, from the looks of it, his body hadn't been enough to keep some of the bullets from making multiple trips back and forth.

". . . make that half-finished toys," Garotte amended.

The soldiers who had just moments before activated their own shields made panicked motions to deactivate them, while others stepped forward and raised a few more charge-gun-enhanced weapons. In a well-rehearsed rhythm, Silo and Garotte began to alternately lean out and fire shots. The fire was enough to keep the soldiers from unleashing their over-powered weapons, but only one or two shots met their mark.

"This is no good," Garotte said between shots. "If we don't make any ground, they can get a second squad in to flank us. I don't want to get into a turkey shoot. The access ladder is in the no man's land between us. We just need to break the stalemate for a few seconds."

"Coming right up, hon," Silo said, pulling a grenade from her bandolier and tossing it into the chamber ahead.

"Grenade!" came the cry from the soldiers as they evacuated in panicked unison.

As they moved back, the rescue party moved forward, striding quickly to the ladder and sliding down. After a few seconds, no explosion came and the most courageous of the soldiers stepped forward to find the grenade. The pin had not been pulled. He rushed to the ladder to find the access hatch closed and fused.

While tools were deployed to release the door and soldiers were deployed to find alternate routes, Silo and Garotte continued toward their goal.

#

In her control center, Commander Purcell looked on. The bulk of her men were facing off against something that looked like a hurricane of cutlery. The cameras inside the ship were barely able to register any details beyond streaks of black and silver. It usually didn't take long before the cameras--and, in some cases, the power systems for the section of the station currently playing host to the mayhem--were destroyed. Her mind grasped at possibilities.

"Commander, we need orders!" the tactical officer urged.

She looked to the ship layout.

"Close bulkhead L3-8 and L3-10," she ordered.

Two indicators toggled; on the cameras, the machine and eight of her men were sealed between the bulkheads.

"I want those men formed up in the center of the sealed area," Purcell said.

The tactical officer delivered the orders and she watched through the one remaining camera as her soldiers, men who had been delivered into the arms of the Neo-Luddites by the mind-searing psychological scars of having had to face a mindless machine, valiantly attempted to follow orders in the face of something that made their past trauma seem like a pleasant dream in comparison.

"Close bulkhead L3-9 and L3-10."

Two more heavy doors dropped into place, sealing off five men and Zerk.

"Blow evacuation hatch L3-K. On my authorization. Command voice code six-eight-eight-three."

The tactical officer's hand hesitated over the execute command. "I can't execute without two senior officer's codes."

"Do it, number two."

"Commander, five of our men--"

"Now!" she cried.

"Command voice code nine-four-eight-four," he murmured.

A small breaching charge detonated, and the audio feed from the camera registered a brief burst of sound and cluster of screams before the air, the soldiers, and the war machine were all sucked from the chamber. The man at the controls stared at the soundless screen, watching the silent struggles of the last man to be pulled out, until the dim light of the chamber and the angle of the camera would show no more. He didn't say anything. He didn't have to.

“Those men died for our cause,” Purcell said without emotion or apology. “And never, *never* hesitate in following my orders. Tactical, locate any additional intruders.”

The officer tapped at the controls.

“The machine caused extensive damage to our power grid. Most visual scanners are down. Based on the last fully-functional sweep, it looks like we've got two intruders, military, that were heading to the lower decks.”

“I want all lower-deck soldiers near vertical shafts to attempt to intercept them.”

“We've also got a third intruder, lightly armed, and . . . some sort of animal. They were leaving the docking section. Most of the soldiers from that section of the station were killed by the machine.”

“Redirect one squad from Deck 2.”

“Continuing analysis of sweep. Commander--Karter! He's out of his cell!”

“How did that happen? Where is he?”

“I don't know. It looks like he was heading to the storage section. Based on system access, he's been attempting to disengage security on the storage bays. He's finished one through four, and he's working on number five now.”

“Storage bays . . . dear god! Any soldiers we can spare, get them down there, now! I want him stopped, killed if necessary, before he gets into storage bay eight! Do you hear me!?”

“Issuing orders now.”

She pulled her communicator. “Engineering! Status!”

“Engineering here. Just a few more minutes and we can begin downloading the final software routines.”

“Get it done, now! Do not stop for anything!”

#

“How are we doing, Ma?” Lex asked, as he hustled after the little creature.

Thus far, they had been unbelievably lucky. Only one detachment of soldiers had sprinted by, and, fortunately, they had seemed to have better things to worry about, since they hadn't even slowed down to check the area.

“I am confident that we are approaching him. I believe I have achieved a level of proficiency in interpreting the fine pattern recognition capabilities of the funk olfactory system,” she replied.

“You figured out how to smell better?”

“The deodorizing treatment is still effective. I smell fine, Lex.”

“What? Ma . . . was that a joke?”

“There is considerable evidence that humor can have stress-reducing effects."

"That may be true, Ma, but there isn't a joke in the universe good enough to do the job right now."

"Acknowledged. This way," she stated, scrabbling her claws across the grating and bounding down the nearest ladder.

Lex slid down after her, to find her standing perfectly still with squinted eyes.

"What's wrong?" Lex asked, looking desperately around to be sure there weren't any soldiers or traps evident.

"I believe I have identified the cryptographic cypher for the short-range communications. One moment, patching in," she stated, her "voice" once again stretched by concentration.

"Closing in on male and female . . . good. Engineering here. Final module is being installed. Software download ready to begin in thirty seconds," a variety of voices announced across the radio.

"The missiles are nearly complete. Silo, Garotte, what is your status," Ma asked, her voice unstressed.

"Making progress, but a bit pinned down. Also, Silo has lost her helmet, so our egress may be a bit more complicated than previously intended," Garotte replied.

"You have as few as three minutes before the CME Activators will be ready to fire, depending on the efficiency of the equipment and technicians," Ma explained.

"That's going to be tight," Silo warned.

"Karter is extremely near. We will secure him and attempt to render aid or cause a delay," Ma advised. "This way, Lex."

She rushed down the corridor, Lex close behind.

"So far, this whole rescue has been me following you around," Lex mused.

A bolt of energy crackled through the corridor and blasted a hole in a control panel behind them, knocking the lights out and replacing them with the intermittent red glow of an emergency light. Lex dove aside and took cover, with Ma skittering opposite him.

"Your sense of timing remains a statistical curiosity, Lex," Ma stated dryly.

Lex fumbled for his pistol. "This is about to go really wrong, isn't it?"

"They are getting closer," Ma unhelpfully informed him.

Lex reached his pistol out from behind the cover and fired a handful of shots aimed mostly by wishful thinking. Most of them did little more than leave black marks on the ceiling, but it was enough to prompt the soldiers to take cover as well. Lex glimpsed out briefly.

"There are three of them. What should we do?"

"Improvisation is not among my strengths."

The radio crackled in his ears. “This is Team Gamma. We have located the second set of intruders. Preparing to close on their position.”

Lex muttered a few breathless profanities before his beleaguered brain managed to deliver a crumb of an idea.

“We can hear these guys. Can they hear us?”

“Currently we are on receive-only. Transmission is possible.”

“Do it!”

There was a muffled tone.

“Attention, Team Gamma!” Lex proclaimed in his most military voice. “There is a building power surge at the end of corridor--” He squinted at the nearest indicator in the pulse red light of the hall. “--7-I. Karter may be attempting to destroy the station. Break off pursuit and investigate immediately. Top priority!”

“That goddamn maniac! Acknowledged!”

The soldiers retreated and sprinted down the adjoining corridor. For a moment, Lex stared in disbelief. A moment turned out to be a bit too long.

“Negative, Team Gamma, disregard previous orders. No power surge is detected,” the tactical officer corrected.

Wordlessly, Ma followed the scent of Karter down the hall and Lex followed.

“Acknowledged. Doubling back!”

“Negative!” Lex urged. “Power surge is critical. Investigate now!”

“Belay that order! Give me that communicator,” came Purcell's voice over the transmission. “Who is this? Who is giving these commands!?”

“Agent . . . Smith,” Lex replied.

“Communications have been compromised. Switch to communication preset five!”

The radio crackled, and then there was silence. Behind them, the sound of boots on grating echoed through the halls.

“Stop,” Ma stated.

Lex slid to a stop, barely avoiding crashing into his diminutive guide.

“Are you sure that's a good idea?”

“Blood. Karter's. Excellent,” she said.

“Why is that excellent?”

“Because it is a trail you can follow without me. Fire at that access panel, please.”

“But I--”

“Now, please.”

Lex fired the pistol, releasing a bolt of energy that shattered the panel.

“I will pursue a parallel contingency plan to enhance our chances of success. Follow this trail of blood in that direction. It will presumably lead to Karter,” she said, squeezing through the ruined access panel and into the wiring conduit behind it.

"Wait, but what if the soldiers show up again?"

She peeked her head out again. "You are clever and inventive. I am confident you will think of something."

"Well *I'm* not!"

"You are also a very fast runner. Try that," she said, ducking inside again and worming her way along the conduit.

"Great, yeah, running. Let's do that," he decided, sprinting off in the direction of the blood.

His adrenaline-fueled run only managed to take him down three blood-speckled halls before he came to a series of storage doors that were open, and, finally, one bulkhead door that was closed. On the other side was Karter. He was wavering slightly, tugging at an access panel.

"Karter! Karter!" Lex cried, banging on the window.

Karter turned and squinted at him, lurching unsteadily to the door and tapping a control. It rattled open.

"What are *you* doing here?" he said. Rather than the tone of surprise and disbelief one might normally show when a friend from across the galaxy mysteriously appeared in a prison, or maybe the relief and gratitude one might show a potential rescuer, Karter sounded annoyed. It was as though he'd been rudely interrupted.

"I'm here to save you! Let's go!" Lex urged.

"What?"

Lex popped up the face mask of his helmet. "I said, I'm here to save you!"

"Oh. Hey, you don't happen to have an auto-spanner, do you?" Karter slurred.

"We don't have time for that, listen . . . are you drunk?"

"Medicated. Never mind, this will do," he said, pulling a grenade from Lex's belt.

"Karter, we've got a ship, and I've got a spare suit here. We're going to destroy the CM . . . the CM . . . the missile things, and we're going to get out of--"

"You wanna get out of the way of the door? It won't close with you standing there," Karter said, tapping the control repeatedly.

The sound of approaching soldiers inspired Lex to step inside, allowing the door to close and lock just as the first of them reached it. The pilot looked nervously at the door as the soldiers worked on it briefly. A glance in the other direction--the *only* other direction, his mind helpfully reminded--revealed that soldiers had gathered there, too. A cutting torch was already beginning to trace its glowing line through the thick metal of the door. On Lex's side, whoever was manning the weapon that had nearly obliterated him and Ma a minute ago was fighting with the device, which was smoking.

"Karter, we've got to--"

"Fire in the hole!" Karter announced, covering his ears.

The variable-strength grenade burst with a force just slightly too powerful for the purpose at hand, which was the removal of the control panel, and just about exactly loud enough to make Lex's ears ring painfully. The inventor then casually grasped two sparking wires and twisted them together, causing the storage bay to open.

"What *is* that?" Lex asked, the sight before him temporarily enough to push the pair of terrorist squads from his mind. The ceiling and floor had been removed from the chamber, expanding the center of the storage bay into a massive three-level sphere, traced out by spindly metallic braces studded with what appeared to be tiny satellite dishes. Nearly the entire bottom half of the cut-away portion of the floor was filled with rocky gray soil. A rack beside the door contained a handful of pen-shaped metallic gadgets. Karter picked one up and twisted its top before tossing it out the door.

"This," he said, shutting and locking the storage door, "is my new favorite toy . . ."

#

"Commander, we are getting reports that Karter and one of the intruders have breached storage bay eight," the tactical officer announced.

"What about the CMEAs?" Purcell demanded.

"Engineering states that the software download on the CMEAs has begun, but the other two intruders have nearly reached the weapons bay."

Purcell removed the energy pistol from its holster, replaced the clip, and hammered it into place with finality. "Inform the men I want three soldiers to peel off for a rendezvous. Tell the engineering crew to put the rest of the process on automatic. Get out of the weapons bay and aid in its defense. I am taking care of this myself."

Chapter 29

Somewhere deep in the core of the space station, an access panel rattled. After a second, it rattled again. Finally, after a scrabbling sound, it burst from the wall and a furry form tumbled to the floor of a dimly-lit chamber. The air was stifling, even with massive fans running at deafening levels. It was a server room, about the size of Lex's bachelor apartment. Monolithic servers were spaced across the floor like tombstones in a graveyard, blinking lights and diagnostic screens flowing faintly. There were no guards in the room, or anywhere near it. Being as deep inside the station as it was, it was seldom even considered necessary to run a patrol past it. Of course, there usually wouldn't be a threat able to squeeze in through the wiring trough.

Ma got to her feet and trotted to the foremost server. She locked her eyes on the screen and concentrated, attempting to access the server with her data connection. With a beep, the screen displayed a message: "*Requested action unavailable over wireless connection. Please attach command module to physical data port and try again.*"

Her eyes darted across the front of the device, eventually spotting a data connection. Her mind entered various parameters into her decision-making matrix. It came up with a depressingly low confidence value. With a tilt of her head, she concluded that in the absence of an alternative, this was still the best course of action.

"Attention, Lex, Garotte, and Silo. Please state status," she broadcast.

"Bloody busy!" Garotte growled.

"These guys are gosh-darned dedicated to protecting this weapons bay. Can't budge 'em an inch. At least we know we've got the right place," Silo added. "This hallway is pretty shot up, too."

"I've got Karter, but we're trapped in a big room with a weird machine," Lex replied.

"I will attempt to shut down the computer system. To do so, I will need to go communication silent. At your earliest convenience, please fetch me from the computer core, marked on your maps. I will likely require aid," Ma instructed.

"Why, what are you--" Lex began.

"Signing off," Ma stated.

She closed the connection and struggled slightly, twisting her head and tugging at the straps holding the data radio in place until one snapped and the device rattled to the floor. With her teeth, she snagged the base of the plug and tugged it free. She stood on her hind legs and leaned against the front of the server, but the port was just out of her reach. Her brow furrowed. Crouching down, she waggled her tail, calculated the trajectory, and leaped. The well-measured hop just barely missed its mark. A second and third did the same. Finally, with a huff of breath, she leapt one last time, and managed to click the wire in place. There was just enough slack to allow her to lie on the ground with the wire connected.

Now with a physical connection, Ma went to work. The encryption, even to get past the login screen, was astoundingly complex. She pushed the little organic brain for all that it was worth, churning through cyphers, keys, vulnerabilities, and everything else she calculated might gain her access. It was a terrible strain, and she began to shudder and shake violently as neurons worked at a capacity nature had never intended.

It was hopeless, but that didn't matter. It was the only option. She would make it succeed.

#

"By my count, we've got very little time left, my girl. This can't go on like this," Garotte remarked.

The two professionals were crouched in a section of the space station that was barely recognizable as a corridor anymore. Constant hammering by friend and foe alike had reduced the walls, ceiling, and floor to scrap metal. There were no lights left, the glow from sputtering wires and plasma shots providing the only illumination. Sections of wall that were once bare, sturdy metal looked like discarded sandwich wrappers. If any of the walls had been space-facing, the whole battle would have been put to a sudden, airless end long ago. A badly damaged but still intact door provided protection behind the heroes, and a now-unrecognizable piece of machinery that had been knocked down during the early moments of the onslaught provided cover from the front.

"I don't think the grenade trick will work again. And a live grenade would probably result in lots of dead people, including us, without better cover," she replied.

"Well, we need *something* to break the tie," Garotte said. "Something that will . . ."

He stopped, because he realized that he was screaming, but he didn't have to be. The firing from the enemies had completely stopped. Before either could venture so much as a peek, however, a new sound came. It was a heavy, fast thumping, like boots pounding against the grating, but approaching far too quickly and hitting far too heavily. When Silo finally got her head out from cover to see what it was, she had a split second to react. One of the soldiers, equipped with a pair of Karter's boots, was surging forth at a completely inhuman speed. Silo threw out her arm and braced herself, delivering a textbook clothesline.

If one has never been on the receiving end of a clothesline--and few outside of the realm of professional wrestling have--then it is easy to overlook how punishing the maneuver can be, even under normal conditions. When the receiving end is moving about three times faster than a human being ought to, thanks to boots that will continue moving forward regardless of whether the feet inside of them are able to or not, the results are best left without description. Suffice to say that it starts with a savage impact, moves on to a lot of screaming and cracking, and ends with an unconscious target with legs that have more in common with noodles than limbs.

"Oh, golly," Silo said, working her arm. "I just about threw my shoulder out on that one."

"Lucky you. This fellow looks to have thrown out everything else," Garotte said, dragging him behind cover as the shooting started again. "Pity he doesn't have one of those hefty guns."

"I'll say. I'm itching to give one of those a try," she said.

"Ah, but he *does* have one of those shields. This might be our break," Garotte suggested, tugging the device and its controls from the unconscious soldier.

"And end up full of holes like that other guy? No, thanks." Silo shuddered.

"It only happened because he fired the weapon."

"Well, if we're going to be clearing those guys out of the way, we're going to have to do an awful lot of firing."

"Fine, then. I shield, you fire," Garotte decided, hooking on the device and activating it.

The protective field, which so far had only been associated with people who ended up motionless heaps, shimmered into being. With a deep breath, Garotte stepped out from cover and into the hail of bullets and energy bolts. A flutter of gold and a slight shimmer sent every last one of them rebounding back at the weapons that fired them. Garotte released the breath and turned to Silo.

"Coming, dear?" he said shakily.

Silo stepped out behind him, then dove desperately back behind cover when, after two quick strides, the shield generator lurched upward and nearly dislodged from his belt. With a few panicked motions, he secured it again, fortunately without any of the hail of ordinance getting through.

"What the heck was that!?" Silo objected.

"It would appear that, if I move too quickly, the shield repels the *ground,*" he observed. "In retrospect, this is probably why our fleet-footed friend didn't have it active."

"Okay, then," she said, stepping out again. "Make like a turtle."

The pair trudged slowly forward, the shield doing its job and staying put.

"So far, so good," Garotte said, flinching at a reflected round. He looked through the shield at the deadly light show that could kill him with even a single hiccup of his experimental protection. "Though, I must admit, I feel a trifle exposed."

#

In the storage bay, Lex looked nervously at the door as it rattled and buckled under the attempts by the soldiers to tear it open, blow it up, or otherwise eliminate it.

"Karter, we really have to find a way to get out of here," he said, reluctantly pulling the rifle from his back and aiming at the door.

"Busy," Karter dismissed, fiddling with controls at a panel on the left side of the massive spherical cage.

"Busy what? Bleeding to death?" Lex said.

"It isn't that bad," Karter countered, putting his hand to his wound. When he withdrew his hand and found it to be completely saturated with blood, as was most of the lower half of his jumpsuit, he paused for a moment. "Okay, that's a lot of blood. I'm gonna be a few pints low." He considered this for a moment, then shrugged. "I'll deal with it later. About how wide is that corridor, you figure? Four meters?"

"What? One and a half, *maybe.* Listen, is this really relevant? Shouldn't we be--"

"We'll say two. Diameter set. Target set. Antimatter cartridge loaded."

"Antimatter? What are you--"

"Engage."

There was a shuddering clap, and a blinding flash of light. Lex shielded his eyes as a second burst of light surged through the room, followed immediately by another clap of thunder and a rush of air from behind him. His eyes were still covered when he realized the rattling of the door was gone. Slowly, he lowered his arm. Apparently the rattling was gone because the door was gone. A fair amount of the wall was gone, too, along with the wall on the opposite side of the corridor. And there were circular holes in the ceiling and floor, revealing the decks above and below. The edges of the missing sections were sharp and precise, with a concave curve to them. As he looked about, trying to take it all in, his eyes locked on to the end of his rifle, which was also missing. Gradually, his brain twisted and turned the missing pieces, and worked out that a perfect sphere had been removed. The soldiers who had been hammering on the door would have been inside said sphere.

"W-where did they go?" Lex asked.

"Beats me," Karter said with a shrug. "I'm still figuring out the controls. Someplace else, anyway, which is where I wanted them to go. The hole is bigger than I expected."

"This is a transporter?"

"This is *the* transporter," Karter corrected. "Oh, there's the problem. It says radius, not diameter. Whoopsie."

"Can it get us all on the ship? Or transport those missiles out of the weapons bay?" Lex asked.

"Nah. It needs one of these active carrier wave transmitters on the target," he said, grabbing one from a rack by the console and throwing it to Lex. "Kind of like that one I tossed out the door before."

"Well, then how did you transport them out of here?" he asked.

"There's six carrier transmitters flitting around outside the station. I targeted one of those. There's only five, now."

"I think there are six enemy ships outside."

"Well, there's only five now."

"That'll make the exit a little easier, I guess. Speaking of which, I've got a spare space suit bundled up here, I need you to put it on so we can get out of here," Lex said, releasing the rifle and stuffing Karter's gadget into one his suit's many pockets before tugging the bundle from his back.

"Later, busy," Karter dismissed again.

Lex gritted his teeth and threw down the suit. "Fine. I'll go get Ma. She's the only one who I've ever seen talk any sense into you."

"Ma's a computer, Lex."

"Not right now she's not. Are you going to be okay here while I get her?"

"Let's see. Peace and quiet, a bunch of painkillers, and an experimental piece of apparatus? Yeah, I oughta be good for a while. Leave the grenades, though. You know, for self-defense."

Lex nodded and tossed away his rifle, left the four remaining grenades, and dug the slidepad from his pocket. According to the point on the map Ma had sent, she would be one level down and a few intersections down the corridor. He leaped down through the convenient hole left by Karter's trial and error and rushed down the--fortunately--deserted hallway below. He found the indicated door and tried the handle, mysteriously discovering it to be unlocked. Inside, he found the rows of servers all whirring and clicking in a way that sounded wrong even to Lex's untrained ear. On the ground in front of the nearest of them was Ma.

The little creature was shuddering and jerking, eyes half-closed and legs splayed out. Her wire had been pulled from the front of the machine, and was lying loose on the floor beside the liberated data radio. The screen was at a red and black command prompt, and simply displayed the words "Connection Lost."

"Oh, my god, Ma, are you all right!?" he exclaimed. He crouched down and shakily inserted the wire into the radio again, tucking it into her harness.

The funk's head turned vaguely toward him, as though it was being controlled by an inexperienced puppeteer. At first, there was only digital jitter on the radio's transmission, but it cleared enough for a voice to cut through.

"Lex . . ." came her reply. It was as through an audio technician had run it through every digital distortion effect he had in his toolbox. The syllable was barely coherent.

"Are you okay? What happened?"

"High . . . encryption . . . extreme . . . computational . . . effort . . . over . . . extended . . . capacity . . ."

"The encryption was too much? Are you going to be okay?"

"No . . . no . . . massive . . . data . . . corruption . . . program . . . integrity . . . failure . . ."

"What do I do?"

"Take . . . care . . . of . . . Squee . . ."

With this final statement, Ma jerked a final time and went limp, her breathing taking on the steady rhythm of sleep, and the transmission dropping to meaningless distortion, then silence.

"Ma . . ." Lex said, scooping up the little beast.

Lex hung his head. Something in his mind tried to remind him there was no reason to be sad. This creature wasn't dead. Ma, to the extent she could even be considered to be alive, still ran in her entirety on Big Sigma at this moment. Logically, he shouldn't feel an ounce of heaviness in his heart over the loss of the temporary subset of herself she'd sent to fetch him. Logic, though, came as small comfort while he cradled the motionless body of a creature that once spoke with the voice of a friend.

His expression hardened and he climbed to his feet.

"Open com Silo, Garotte," he stated, managing to keep a tremor from his voice. "Guys. We just lost Ma. What is our status?"

#

In the embattled hallway, Garotte gave a reply. "One moment."

They were practically on top of what remained of the soldiers defending the weapons bay door. The constant stream of reflected attacks had reduced their numbers considerably, and the well-aimed and well-timed cover fire offered by Silo whenever they attempted to use something that might punch through the shield had reduced them even more.

Silo clicked a fresh clip into her pistol, leaned out, and fired off a few precise shots, taking care of the final soldiers.

"Well, then--that's that," Garotte said, dusting off his hands. "We're at the door. Applying shaped charges now."

"Sorry, hon, out of shaped charges. Used them all up getting here," Silo corrected. "And I'm afraid anything less controlled that would result in us having a very bad day, this being the weapons bay and all. I'm shocked we're still in one piece as it is, with all the shooting going on."

"Ah. Well then, I'll just work at unlocking this then, shall I?"

"On my way," Lex said. "Close com."

A high-pitched whine came from the door that had protected their flank so faithfully, followed by a second, then an ear-splitting clank as the heavy door fell away and Commander Purcell marched through. She slipped something into her belt and held her pistol with the rescuers steadily in her sights. Behind her was a meager assemblage of soldiers, including her second-in-command.

Garotte quickly stood between the commander and Silo.

"As I'm the one with the shield, it looks like you'll be the one working on the door," he muttered.

"Not my strong suit," she said, holstering her weapon and going to work on the control panel for the door.

"I've always admired your ability to adapt," he replied.

"Stop what you're doing or I will fire," said Commander Purcell.

"I do wish you would, my dear," Garotte taunted. "I've got one of your precious shields."

Purcell continued to march forward, weapon raised.

"Ask your boys. Not much fun to fire on an active shield," he continued.

"I'm aware of the details of the shield," Purcell said, drawing closer. Long, slow strides were moving her with deceptive speed. "It was my decision to pursue their deployment."

"Oh, good, then that fellow who punched himself full of his own bullets has you to thank. Good show," he remarked.

"It is the danger of using the most advanced technology available."

"I can't help but notice that you aren't using a shield yourself. No, that particular honor goes to the men and women under your command. How many of them have you gotten killed?"

"More soldiers by far have been killed by the reluctance of the modern military to *become* truly modern."

"Oh, really? Cite your sources. Maybe we should take a poll of the crew. How many have you got left, a dozen or so? We'll put the rest down for 'Bad Technology Killed Me.'"

"You're trying to stall me. Stupid decision. You're the one on a time limit." Purcell tapped her free hand to her communicator. "Tactical, status!"

"The download is finished. The CME Activators are fully commissioned and ready to deploy," came the reply.

Silo doubled her efforts on the door lock.

"Load them into the launch tubes and tell me when you are ready to fire."

"Yes, Commander."

Purcell smiled and continued her march. There were barely a dozen strides between them now, and she took them one by one, slowly and deliberately, until mere feet separated her from Garotte. "You're too late. In seconds, those missiles will be on their way. And I assure you, it is for the best. You haven't seen what I've seen. If you knew what lurked on the horizon, you would gladly trade the millions of lives that will be lost in the weeks ahead for the billions that will be saved in the years that follow."

"Millions that *will* be lost . . ." her second-in-command whispered.

"I am awaiting status, tactical," Purcell stated, when the all-ready had failed to come through.

"There . . . there is a problem with the computer. It isn't responding. Disc access and processor utilization are maxed out. Doors are locked down all over the station. I can't move troops. The only thing we've got is communication."

"Looks like our furry little hacker did the job," Silo said.

"Damn it, fix it! I want to be firing those things in thirty seconds, you hear me!?"

"You're really going to do it," Marx realized.

"Quiet!" Purcell demanded.

"You are going to endanger all of those lives!?"

"We will do what is necessary to preserve our future. Now quiet! That is an *order!*"

He raised his weapon. "I know all too well that unwillingness to adapt is a death sentence, but I will *not* be one of the executioners. I will not--"

Purcell turned and fired. For a moment, the man remained standing, his face plastered with a look of agony and betrayal, the overpowered weapon having easily left a smoldering wound over his heart. Finally, the man crumbled to the ground.

"Does anyone else feel their loyalty to our cause wavering?" Purcell hissed at her men.

In a swift motion, Garotte disengaged his shield, pulled her arm to the small of her back, and put his pistol to her head.

"Not really relevant anymore, I think," Garotte said. "How's that coming, Silo?"

"Hard to say, really."

"Well, hurry, because--"

Purcell hooked her leg behind his ankle and pulled him off balance. He wrenched her wrist as he stumbled, pulling her gun free from her hand. She pivoted, her fingers tearing at his belt and ripping the shield generator free. Her other hand caught his wrist, twisting it painfully, forcing the weapon from his fingers. Garotte pulled free and kicked both pistols away. The flurry of motion left Garotte and Purcell on firm footing, facing each other. Rather than retreating, she drew the knife from her belt and advanced.

"Switch!" Garotte said, backpedaling.

Silo stood and put the muzzle of her rifle to the commander's face.

"Look who brought a knife to a gun f--"

Purcell swiped, the knife emitting a tone as it sliced easily through the barrel of the rifle.

"--udge!" Silo finished.

The commander attempted a second slice, but Silo pulled back, and the two began to battle in earnest. It was a symphony of threatening sounds, with the knife humming like a mosquito through the air, and the remains of the rifle whistling in vicious swings. Silo knew that a single slice from that knife would likely end the battle--and her life along with it. Purcell learned a similar lesson when a wild swing of the rifle struck the wall and left a deeper divot than most of the weapon blasts had. As a result of her few years on Manticore, any blunt object was a deadly weapon in Silo's hands.

Attacks flew faster and closer, each woman dodging the other's blows by narrower and narrower margins. On one side, the smattering of remaining soldiers held their weapons ready, but refused to fire out of fear that they would hurt their commander. One of them tried to move in and lend a hand in the melee, but a screeching stray slice of Purcell's knife cut through several very useful bits of anatomy. Witnessing this event gave the surviving soldiers a healthy respect for the danger the swinging weapons posed. They kept their distance.

On the other side, Garotte worked at the door to the weapons bay.

"This bloody thing is warped. The mechanism is fused," he growled.

"Quit making excuses," Silo huffed.

At the commander's belt, her communicator chirped.

"--sense they would put a com panel on this thing. Boss lady, you hear me?" Karter's groggy voice remarked as the battle raged on. "I gotta say, I'm *really* liking this transporter of yours. And that was a pretty clever idea, putting targeting transmitters in your ships for emergency rescue. In related news, I'm all out of grenades, and you only have one ship left."

Purcell roared in anger and managed a desperate strike that Silo couldn't dodge. The demo expert raised her rifle-turned-club to block, and the knife sliced neatly through, missing Silo's fingers by millimeters. Now left with a uselessly small remnant of her former weapon, Silo threw the remaining portion aside and grasped the knife hand by the wrist, easily overpowering her with a squeeze that nearly shattered Purcell's wrist, forcing the commander to release the weapon. As it fell, still active, it slipped past Silo's arm, effortlessly opening a long slit in her suit and a shallow gash in her flesh before sinking hilt-deep into the floor. Silo cried out and released the commander, and the women separated, each clutching an injured arm. For a moment, each eyed the other tensely, eyes darting briefly to the weapon as it screeched its high-pitch wail and vibrated in its self-carved slot. An instant before either attempted to grab it, a voice rang out from the other side of the hall.

"Nobody move!"

All eyes turned to the source of the order. There stood Lex among the fallen soldiers at the end of the hall nearest to the heroes, energy pistol in one hand and motionless Ma tucked under one arm. Silo seized the moment to grab Purcell, spin her around, and immobilize her arms.

"Excellent timing, as always, my boy. Hand that over, would you?" Garotte said, quickly turning from the door. He caught the pistol as it was tossed to him. "Right, now--let's think about this logically, shall we? This is a military crew, and you are running this like a military operation. Those CMEAs are *clearly* weapons of mass destruction, and, in a military operation, things like that need command authorization to fire, thanks to computer failsafes, yes?"

Purcell did not answer.

"*Yes?*" Garotte asked more insistently, placing the gun to Purcell's face.

She nodded stiffly.

"And am I correct in assuming that, at this point, *you* are the only one on the space station that has command authorization?"

Another stiff nod.

Karter's voice crackled out of the radio on her belt: "Getting bored now."

"So, in theory, all I need to do is blow your head off and the crisis is averted--but there is still the tiny matter of making it out of this alive, which is a very appealing outcome for me. Therefore, here is what is going to happen. You fellows are going to stand down. I happen to know you've got a few holding cells in this place. Find them and climb in. I'll be keeping the commander here, for my own safety and hers, until we can reach the missiles, disarm them, and wipe the design from your systems. Then we'll be taking her with us as we exit."

"Oh, hey. There's another transport target," Karter's voice observed.

Garotte continued to dictate his orders. Lex paced over to the others, but he couldn't quite shake the feeling that something was wrong.

"This ought to be interesting. Radius set," Karter said.

Lex's eyes shot open, and he fumbled with his free hand in his pocket. Inside, he found the target Karter had tossed to him. It had managed to activate while it was in his pocket. Juggling the device and the sleeping funk, he tried to get his panicked fingers to twist the top into the "off" position, but he lost his grip, causing it to fall and skitter along the floor.

"Target set," Karter continued.

"Scatter! Get away from that thing!" Lex yelped.

"Antimatter cartridge loaded . . ."

A moment of utter chaos, something that Lex realized was happening far too frequently these days, followed. In the space of a few heartbeats, Purcell thrust an elbow into Silo's stomach as the hero tried to drag her away. The blow, combined with the sudden need to dodge, was enough to allow the commander to escape. She snatched up her knife and rushed toward her troops while Lex, Silo, and Garotte retreated.

"Engage."

A flash filled the hall, accompanied by a rush of wind strong enough to hurl all present to the ground. The roar of wind came with a thunderclap and the screech of metal. The first to recover was Lex, who managed to squint through the purple and blue blotches in his vision to see . . . frankly, he wasn't sure. It was a mass of metal and glass. Where it met the walls and floor, both the object and the structure had buckled, twisted, and fused. The edge that faced the heroes was bulged outward, layers of metal, sparking wires, leaking tubes, and twitching components having been clipped off by the transporter into an almost beautiful random design. It completely filled the hallway, with the exception of a few inches from the ceiling, where the spherical shape was rendered irregular by a few flat surfaces of glass.

"What *is* that?" Silo asked.

"Well, the other target was inside the ship . . . I guess that's a spherical hunk of the ship?" Lex surmised.

Working off of that theory, the glass at the top *did* appear to be part of a cockpit, though glancing through it indicated that if there was a pilot, *most* of him was on the other side of the wall, which clearly hadn't been a terribly healthy experience.

"I must not have been paying attention. How did it get here?" Silo asked.

"They have a transporter, and Karter is at the controls," Lex explained.

"That is the most terrifying thing I've ever heard," Silo uttered.

"Did that do something interesting?" Karter's voice asked. "I expected an explosion or something. And I'm all out of antimatter for this thing, so I can't do any more."

The next sound they heard was Purcell smashing her radio in anger.

"We've still got a chance. The door is on our side," Silo said.

"I'll try to get it open, but it is clearly built to withstand an internal explosion, and the mechanism is fused," Garotte said, making his way to the door and beginning his efforts anew.

"Go around the other way and stop them," Purcell ordered from the other side of the blockage.

The troops hurried through the hole she'd cut in the door, the commander close behind.

"Lex, try to find some weapons from the pile of failed security guards there that aren't too badly damaged. We're about to have company," Silo advised. "I'm glad they didn't decide to do that earlier."

"They probably needed her knife to cut through all of those locked doors," Garotte guessed. "Or they are idiots. Equal likelihood, I'd say."

The pilot tried to rummage through the wreckage and remains without thinking too hard about the fact that they had been alive a few minutes ago. He also refused to put Ma's sleeping body down to do it. They had managed to turn up three guns that had a reasonable chance of working when they heard the pounding of boots.

"Commander! Tactical here," came a voice over the station's damaged PA system. "We're getting some partial computer control back. I think I can give you voice interface."

From her cover in an adjoining hallway, Purcell snatched a communicator from one of the soldiers.

"Activate voice interface!" she bellowed.

"Voice interface active," replied a low-grade computerized voice.

"Launch CMEA! Command voice code six-eight-eight-three."

"No," the voice said.

"Damn it! Repeat, Launch Coronal Mass Ejection Activator, now! Command voice code six-eight-eight-three."

"Your coarse language is not called for, Commander Purcell," said a very familiar voice.

"Ma!?" exclaimed all three of the heroes, with equal confusion, back at the door.

"My control program has been loaded onto the space station's core system. I am currently decompressing, and attempting to gain control over the subsystems," Ma explained over their radios.

"So you aren't dead!? Not even *this* you?" Lex said, indicating the funk.

"No. I was able to break encryption and transfer a duplicate of my full data image prior to critical corruption. But I appreciated your concern. It was very sweet."

"Yes, yes. A tearful reunion after thirty seconds of separation. Lovely," Garotte said. "Can you open the door to the weapons bay, or perhaps destroy the missiles remotely?"

"Negative. There is a mechanical fault in the door mechanism, and the CMEA is not coupled to any station system besides the launch apparatus."

"Can you maybe tell us why we aren't getting shot at by soldiers?" Silo asked, eyes still trained on the unobstructed hallway, weapon raised.

"Most of the surveillance on this deck has been destroyed, but an emergency storage locker in an adjoining corridor has been accessed," the computer informed.

"What were the contents?" Garotte asked.

"Medical equipment, water, nonperishable food, one space suit, and supplementary oxygen," she said. "There is now an attempt to access a secondary airlock."

"She's going to go external. She's going to access it from the outside," Garotte realized. "The schematics show that there is a massive external payload door on the space-facing side of the bay for loading ordinance."

"Can't Ma just lock her out?" Lex asked.

"I have not yet completely taken control of all systems, and even if I had, manual overrides exist for both door control and weapon launch. If she reaches the door, she can open it, and if she reaches the launch controls, she can fire the weapons," Ma stated.

"I think we're going to have to consider finding a way to blow the whole station," Silo said gravely.

"That may not be possible in the time available. I do not have deep enough control to produce a catastrophic failure, and am unlikely to gain that level of control prior to the launch of the weapons."

"All we need to do is find a way to set off the weapons inside the weapons bay."

"With the exception of the CME Activators themselves, which are non-explosive, there are no weapons in the weapons bay."

"What?" Garotte said, expression blank.

"Station records indicate that the Neo-Luddites are extremely under-equipped, and most of their existing large-scale weaponry was disassembled for the parts to create the CME Activators and subsequent fabricated equipment."

"Well, that would have been nice to know five minutes ago. Everybody, clear out. This door is about to get what's coming to it," Silo said, unstrapping her grenade belt and beginning to make some choice selections.

"This way, my boy," Garotte said, grasping Lex and pulling him down the hallway. "Here's what you need to do while we're working at this. Find a spare suit so that we can get Silo back into the ship for the getaway, or get Ma to pressurize the launch bay--"

"Please remember that you are now able to address me directly," Ma stated.

"--then go and wrangle Karter, and get him to *The Declaration*. And ditch the rodent," Garotte continued. "I'll stay here and see to it that nothing happens to our darling Miss Silo."

"Your referral to my previous incarnation as a rodent is once again inappropriate in terms of both biology and etiquette," Ma objected.

"What happens if I run into soldiers?" Lex asked.

Garotte tapped the gun in his hand. "Shoot them. Are we clear?"

"Crystal," Lex replied.

"Splendid. Off with you, then," he said, slapping the pilot on the back to send him on his way.

As Lex rushed off, Ma spoke through his radio. "I have begun rapid-pressurizing the docking bay. Please focus your attentions preferentially on Karter. I will link your radio to the com panel in the storage bay now."

After a tone, Lex yelled, "Karter!"

"You aren't dead?" Karter's voice responded, with a vaguely insulting level of surprise.

"No, I'm not. Your concern is touching. Are you okay up there?"

"Yeah. Except for the way the room is spinning. I don't know if it is the blood loss or the meds, but I am *feelin'* it right now."

"Well, we've got a ship in the hangar . . ."

"Who's *we?*"

"Me, Silo, Garotte, and Ma."

"Am I supposed to know who those people are?"

"You worked with them!"

"Doesn't sound like anyone I'd associate with," Karter slurred.

"Ma, help me out here," Lex groaned.

"Gladly, Lex. Mr. Alexander is referring to Sgt. Jessica Winters, the heavy weapons expert, and the variously-named British agent, each of whom had routinely sought your help until their incarceration."

"Ma? What are you doing here?"

"I am performing my primary function: keeping and/or getting you out of trouble."

"Well, you screwed up the first part."

"Perhaps if you were a more effective programmer, this wouldn't have happened."

"Can we do this later?" Lex asked. "I want very badly to get out of here."

"Yeah. Me, too. The food's terrible," Karter groaned.

#

Silo and Garotte retreated to a safe distance--and, for good measure, ducked inside a separate room.

"That's a hell of a door. It took every grenade I had. Variables at cross beams, high-yield at key supports. The line between 'get the door open' and 'crack the hull' is a pretty narrow one. What I did should be enough to knock it from its hinges. Fuse should blow in five," Silo said, and then covered her ears.

The explosion came on schedule, and was the short, sharp clap of a controlled explosion combined with the odd, rippling echo one gets from loud sounds in hallways. When the creaking of metal and the rattle of equipment settled down, and there was no sudden rush of escaping gas that would have indicated a hull breach, the pair ventured outside. Every light even remotely nearby was shattered, leaving them in complete darkness. Garotte tapped on his helmet-mounted lights and observed the carnage. Most of the hallway was a mess of twisted, blackened metal, and the whole wall was bowed inward . . . but the door was still in place.

"E-*gad* they built these stations sturdy back then," Garotte mused.

Silo paced up to the door, looked it over, and gave it a powerful thrust-kick. The weakened metal let out a final screech and the door rattled to the ground like an overturned turtle.

"I was close. I guess I'm just a bit rusty," she said, ducking inside, Garotte hot on her heels.

The interior of the weapons bay was just as bare as Ma had suggested it would be. , it was a machinery-strewn room. A bit taller than one deck and barely three meters deep, it was nearly as long as their hallway battleground. One could see where a thicket of mechanical limbs, conveyors, and equipment had once been attached with the purpose of feeding ammunition to the primary weapons systems. Now the cupboard was bare, with the ammo racks and cases open and empty, and machinery scavenged to build Karter's toys. Along the floor were three troughs, the only portions of the bay that were fully stocked and intact, each displaying two nondescript missiles lying end to end. They were the size and shape of metallic telephone poles, with panel seams and emitter heads scattered sparsely across the surface and a black-tiled tip serving as the only details, giving it the appearance of a burnt wooden match as envisioned by a jeweler.

Without wasting time on his usual banter, Garotte drew his weapon and fired a burst of shots. Rather than striking the CMEA, they splashed against a field of some sort, vanishing without even scorch marks. Several additional shots to the others brought the same effect--that was to say, no effect at all.

"That's disappointing," he said steadily, keying the radio. "Lex, have you found Karter yet?"

"Still getting there, but we've got a line open to him," Lex replied.

"Karter, how do we destroy these missiles you made?"

"With great difficulty. They're designed to plunge as far as possible into a *star*, remember?"

"There's got to be a way."

"Well, if you fracture a few of the heat tiles in the front, they'll burn up before they can do their thing. Those are ceramic, pretty brittle. Low-velocity blunt force should get through the energy shielding, and enough of it would do the trick . . ."

Silo rushed to the tip of one of the missiles, raised the butt of her borrowed rifle, and bashed at the tip, causing one of the tiles to chip.

"I wouldn't recommend it, though. It has automated defenses," he continued.

One of the panels near the center of the missile popped aside and revealed a small energy cannon, which fired three random shots that Silo narrowly managed to dodge before it retracted again.

"Why would you *put* something like that on there!?" she cried.

"So it would do that to people who try to do what you did. I design things to get jobs done, even if people try to stop them. That's the way--" Karter began.

"Someone is accessing the exterior release," Ma announced.

"We're out of time," Garotte said.

Silo ran to the damaged CMEA and delivered another blow, rolling aside and attempting to strike another while the first one fired. The mechanisms controlling the door began to grind.

"I cannot stop the door. It will open in less than a minute," Ma alerted.

"Silo, now! Between us and the crazy woman with the knife, half of the doors are blown open. Half of this station is about to be a hard vacuum and you don't have a helmet!"

"Millions of lives, Garotte! This is the mission!" Silo proclaimed.

"You can't break them all, we need another way!"

"I don't care, I have to try!"

"You--"

Whatever sentiment he'd had in mind was cut short by the apocalyptic wail of air escaping. The spaceward wall split like a zipper, inching slowly open. Garotte flipped down and sealed the visor of his suit. Silo dropped to the ground and grasped the edge of the missile-trough and dragged herself forward. The flow of air was steadily increasing in intensity. Garotte looked desperately about until he caught sight of a case installed on the wall, its door flapping in the growing gale. He barely managed to reach it before the rushing wind pulled his feet from the ground. He hooked the end of the strap for his own rifle onto a brace inside and unhooked the other end, looping it through a belt on the space suit before finally releasing his grip on the case. The escaping atmosphere ripped him to the end of the strap, where he dangled and whipped, a foot or so from the point where Silo ran out of handholds. He extended his hand to her, and she shakily extended hers.

Loose bolts and fragments of metal were launching through the bay, gouging into the floor and ceiling. A fragment of shrapnel slashed across one arm of his suit, breaking the seal. One or two of the stray soldiers on the deck made a brief appearance in the bay before tumbling out the door. The rush of wind all but blinded Silo, but finally her hand met his.

Instantly, her grip nearly crushed his fingers. Hand over hand, she hauled herself down his arm, down his body, along the strap, and, finally, into the case. Shielded at least partially from the wind, but already feeling the effects of the drop in pressure, she managed to reel Garotte in, and the two of them wrestled the door shut. In the pitch-black and cramped confines, Garotte found the control pad for his suit and punched in a command that opened a vent and pressurized the tiny space. It wasn't until the wind outside gave way mostly to airless vacuum that they became aware of the voice insistently repeating a message.

"--is open and atmosphere loss is critical. Silo and Garotte, what is your status? The door is open and atmosphere loss is critical. Silo and Garotte--" Ma's voice droned.

"We're here! We're okay," Silo said, gratefully gasping deep breaths of the oxygen.

"There was an equipment case for pressure-sensitive tools and materials. We managed to get inside, but until you can get this weapons bay pressurized again, we're stuck here, because Silo doesn't have an intact suit, and neither do I," Garotte explained. "There are at least four undamaged missiles."

"Karter, Lex, please report status," Ma said.

"I got to Karter. It was a little tricky getting into the transporter room, now that half the floor is missing, but I got him and the suit out. Now me, M--uh . . . Squee and Karter are in the next corridor over. There is an awful lot of creaking and groaning, but I think we're airtight, at least for now," Lex replied over the radio. "What do we do now?"

"Processing . . . I have taken full control of long-range communication and external sensors. I am attempting to prepare a contingency. In the meantime, is your space suit intact?" Ma asked.

"Yes."

"Has Karter been outfitted with a suit?"

"Not yet; he's being uncooperative."

"Hey, listen. I'm already losing my buzz, and I'm not in a friendly mood thanks to this hole in my back, which everybody seems to be ignoring," remarked Karter.

"Lex, you will have to find a way to reach the weapons bay and prevent the CMEAs from firing. Karter, you need to find a way to detonate the station if Lex fails," Ma dictated.

"That would kill me, Ma," Karter said, as if to a child. "We don't do that, remember?"

"It would kill all of us, but it would save a considerable number of lives. It is an undesirable result, but preferable to the alternative."

"I seriously messed up some of your algorithms, Ma," he muttered. "When we get home--"

"The weapons bay doors have finished opening. There is someone accessing the manual launch controls. Patching in to communications."

#

In the weapons bay, Purcell was crouched at a small panel on the floor. The station's gravity had pulled her down upon her entry, and it was the work of a few moments to find the manual launch control. Three commands were all it took to drop all six missiles into launch tubes. Entering the command authorization for the actual launch was proving to be more time-consuming though, particularly with the bulky gloves of the emergency pressure suit she'd been forced to use. Unlike its voice counterpart, the code was easily as cumbersome as the suit, an eighty-digit mess that a less disciplined commander wouldn't have taken the time to memorize.

"Discontinue your current activities or I will be forced to take preventative measures," Ma instructed through the emergency suit's radio.

"You're the one who refused to launch the missiles!" Purcell hissed. "Who are you?"

"Altruistic Artificial Intelligence Control System, Version 1.27, revision 2331.04.01, subset 1.2, Designation 'Ma,'" she replied.

"An artificial intelligence? Then there is nothing you can do to stop me. You are not capable of harming a human," the commander said, going back to work.

"Incorrect. I am an Altruistic AI. There is no programmatic safeguard prohibiting that or any other action. So *don't tempt me.*"

"There's no way you can attack me in here. There is no computer control anymore."

"One of my associates is en route to your location, and an additional alternative is being deployed."

"Uh . . ." Lex's voice interjected over the radio. "I might be a bit held up. There are some soldiers here still, and they've got me and Karter cornered."

A radio crackle signaled some actions on Ma's part. When she spoke again, it was only to her allies. "I have gained control of primary and secondary navigational control. The damage to the station is extreme, but I may be able to cause a distraction. Please restrain yourselves."

"Karter, hold on. Okay, done," said Lex, grabbing tightly to the nearest handrail in the side chamber he'd taken refuge in.

"This should be good," Karter remarked.

"Haven't got much of a choice. There's not a tremendous amount of elbow room in here," Garotte replied.

"I'll say," Silo agreed.

"Stand by," Ma said. "Artificial gravity deactivated. Inertial inhibitor deactivated. Maneuvering thrusters active. Setting to two hundred percent capacity, burst mode."

As gravity disengaged, the various pieces of debris and the remaining inhabitants of the station slowly drifted from the ground.

"Thrusters prepared. Firing."

Instantly, the whole of the station rocked to one side. Those who were unrestrained were sent careening into the walls. In the weapons bay, Purcell was yanked away from the control panel and scrambled to activate her weak, zero-G maneuvering jets again to try to reach it.

"Firing . . . firing . . . firing . . ." Ma dictated.

With each statement, the station took another shift. The soldiers and Purcell were rattled about, bouncing forcefully off of the walls until the shifting finally stopped.

"Thruster heat level critical, entering cool-down phase," Ma explained.

"Okay, okay!" Lex said shakily. "The soldiers are pretty discombobulated. I'm going to try to get by."

"Acknowledged. Thrusters offline. Artificial gravity active."

As gravity suddenly reasserted, the unprepared and bewildered crashed to the ground.

"Karter, stay safe and take care of Squee," Lex said, hanging the funk around its creator's neck.

"Uh-huh," Karter said, glancing down at the creature. "Hey, have you been tampering with this thing? That wire is *not* stock."

Ignoring the inventor, Lex burst from his cover and charged down the hall.

#

In the weapons bay, Commander Purcell recovered from the rock tumbler of a journey she had just taken. She dragged herself along the floor to the panel and resumed her code entry.

"What is your status, Lex?" Ma asked.

"Running! How long have I got?"

"Commander Purcell has entered sixty-eight out of eighty necessary digits."

"I don't know if I can--"

"Seventy-one."

"I'm at least three decks away, I don't--"

"Seventy-eight. The code is entered. Commander Purcell, this is the last warning you will receive. Do not activate the CME Activators."

"You cannot stand in the way of progress. The ashes of today will fertilize the fields of tomorrow, and I shall be the one to light the flames!"

Her gloved hand came down on the execute command. The grind of machinery rang out, and with six distinct streaks of engine flare, the CMEAs fired.

"You should not have done that," Ma stated.

"In a century, when mankind has advanced beyond the timid, cowardly apes we are today, I will be hailed as a savior," she proclaimed.

"Stand by . . ." Ma stated.

"It is over. You've lost," Purcell announced defiantly. "Stand by for what?"

"The contingency plan," Ma stated.

At a whisper of motion in the corner of her eye, Purcell turned to the open loading door of the weapons bay. Rapidly approaching was a sleek, black ship. Retro-rockets flashed and the ship came to a stop outside the door. A turret repositioned, and a dim light traced a flickering line from the ship to the commander. Purcell felt it as a crushing, immobilizing force.

"What . . . what is that?" Purcell struggled.

"That is *Son of Betsy*, the ship belonging to one of the individuals currently infiltrating this station. I am controlling it remotely, and it is holding you in its tractor beam," Ma explained. "Some of your men have locked down the bay containing *The Declaration of War*, but *Son of Betsy* is fully under my control."

"Force her to deactivate the missiles! Send a kill code! Call them back!" Silo urged over the radio.

"Uh, yeah, that won't work," Karter said. "They don't have transceivers.

There's no kill switch."

"Why not!?" Silo asked.

"Because no one put a kill switch in the design specification," Karter said simply.

"I am opening a communication connection to all decks of the station. Tell your soldiers to stand down," Ma instructed.

Purcell struggled to take a deep breath as the channel opened. "Attention, men . . . fight to your last breath!"

"I urge you to reconsider. You will not receive any more opportunities to do so," Ma stated. Her time as an organic creature must have produced some lingering effects on her voice module, because she managed a tone of smoldering anger far more effectively than a few chopped-up voice response systems should have been able to manage.

"I am dedicated to my cause. As long as I draw breath, I will do everything I can to tear down the technologies that are holding us back. I will never stop. I wouldn't be afraid of you even if you *could* hurt me, but you are a machine. There's nothing you can do."

"Once again, I must inform you that you are incorrect. Your belief that I am incapable of harming a human is based upon the three laws of robotics, which were not a part of my design. I do not have laws governing my actions--only principles, which are far more flexible. You have threatened the lives of my friends and my creator. You have set into motion a sequence of events which, if they unfold as projected, may irreparably damage the stability of human society for generations. You have stated the intention to continue this behavior if given further opportunities. You have made me *very* angry. I find violence of any kind extremely distasteful, but occasionally justifiable after extreme deliberation."

"Your hollow threats don't frighten--"

"Deliberation complete," Ma stated dispassionately.

With a pivot and turn, *S.O.B.* whipped its captured prey to the side, hurling Purcell out the loading doors and slinging her into the blackness of space. Before she could even manage to scream, she was outside of the limited transmission range of her suit's radio. A moment later, Lex came skidding into the damaged doorway, pistol raised.

"Hold it right . . . uh . . . Ma? Where'd the bad guy go?" he asked.

"Away," the AI stated. "Please disengage the manual override on the loading doors so that I can attempt to pressurize the bay and release Garotte and Silo. You need to leave this star system as soon as possible. I have alerted local authorities of the impending catastrophe, and they are quite likely to send patrol ships here."

"You mean . . ."

"All six CME Activators have been deployed. We have lost."

Chapter 30

"Whoa, whoa, whoa, what do you mean we lost?" Lex said, making his way carefully to the open bay door and pulling the internal counterpart to the external release that Purcell had used to open it. He glanced out toward the distant sun while the door began to grind closed. "I don't see a solar flare heading this way."

"The coronal mass ejection will not reach this orbital distance for several days, and it will not be initiated until the activators reach the star in approximately fifty-two minutes," Ma explained.

"*S.O.B.* could get to the star and back dozens of times in fifty-two minutes. I'll just chase them down and blow them up!"

"Oh, please. Give me *some* credit," Karter objected on the radio.

"Karter? Did I give you a radio?" Lex asked.

"There was one strapped to the funk. Listen, you can't just 'chase them down.' They're running twilight drives. Why do you think they're taking so long to get to the star in the first place?"

"Uh . . . okay, what's a twilight drive?" Lex said.

"Ma, when this is over, you'll have to explain to me why you thought that it was a good idea to track down the single most ignorant human being in the universe to lend a hand," Karter growled.

"I will explain," Ma stated. "Modern starships are designed to operate within two standard speed classes: fractions of the speed of light and multiples of the speed of light."

"That much I know. The Carpinelli Field lets us skip the middle man."

"The twilight drive is a system designed to jump to and maintain a near-light speed," Ma continued.

"But why would anyone want to do that? It's slower."

"*And* less efficient," Karter chimed in, "but the laws of physics behave differently at that speed. It makes sensors of all kinds more or less useless, and anyone attempting to intercept will outrun them or fall behind. It is a top-notch way to run a medium-range, self-propelled weapon."

"And you're telling me I can't go that exact speed in my ship?"

"*S.O.B.* was not designed with sustained relativistic velocities in mind. The Carpinelli Effect is only completely stable at much higher speeds. The ship would be subjected to forces and effects that would make successful navigation practically impossible," Ma stated.

"For the past few days, I've been traipsing across the cosmos trying to help a super-intelligent woodland creature to rescue a mad scientist. 'Practically impossible' is par for the course at this point," Lex said.

"It is an unacceptable risk with near-zero probability of success. Each of the six missiles is on a randomized course."

"Heh, probably not, actually," Karter interjected again. "They shot me in the back before I told them the procedure for setting the random seed, so those things are probably all taking the default route. I can plug the course into *S.O.B.*'s nav computer."

"You're being unusually helpful, Karter," Lex said suspiciously. "Could it be that you are actually trying to prevent this disaster?"

"I built your ship and I built the CME Activators. I'm curious to see which is better," he said. "Averted technological disaster is an unintended side effect, assuming *S.O.B.* wins."

"Processing . . . there is now a marginal chance for success, but negligible chance for survival," Ma said. "I am not comfortable asking you to risk your life."

"Ma, I'm a freelancer. Have been for over two years. I've made a career out of flight plans with a negligible chance for survival. Besides, we've been through this before. It's an imperative, remember? A personal rule."

"It is vital that one follow one's own rules," Ma agreed. "Very well. I will make changes to the sensors and firmware of your ship. Please go to the storage room indicated on your slidepad. There is a device designated 'the yo-yo coil' that the station records indicate they have fabricated which should give you a reasonable capacity to exploit the vulnerability to blunt force that serves as the design weakness."

"I'm on it . . . uh . . . what if I run into any lingering soldiers?"

"Stand by . . ." Ma said, continuing on the PA system and all radio frequencies. "Attention, remaining Neo-Luddites. Your commander is no longer on this station. Her final order was to fight to your last breath. Ignoring this order and laying down your weapons until the authorities arrive or you are delivered to their custody is recommended. Alternately, if you are dedicated to following this order, I am pleased to inform you that I am now in control of station-wide environmental controls, and I will gladly schedule your final breath at your earliest convenience. For soldiers outfitted with environmental suits, please be advised that I have located the cybernetic entity known as Zerk on short-range sensors. If you are unaware of the capabilities of this entity, seek out a soldier who has faced it. If you have difficulty finding a soldier who has faced it, this is because it left very few survivors. This is, itself, an adequate indication of its capabilities. It is still active, and I will be able to re-introduce it to the station shortly. Thank you." Ma resumed her private connection to the others. "I am confident you will not encounter resistance."

"Boy, am I glad you're on our side . . ." Lex remarked as he hurried away.

"Silo and Garotte. Due to the large amount of damage done to this deck, pressurizing this bay sufficiently to release you may take some time. Are you in immediate danger?" Ma asked.

"Oxygen and carbon-dioxide levels should be okay for a few hours, if the suit's scrubbers do their job," Garotte answered. "Not that you should dawdle."

"It's starting to get a might chilly in here," Silo added. "I think my suit's heater went out when I lost the helmet."

"Lucky that it's cozy then, eh?" Garotte remarked.

"I am currently attempting to identify a sequence of functional bulkheads that will allow atmospheric retention for this area."

"Much obliged," Garotte said.

#

Inside the dark and cramped interior of the case, Silo shifted uncomfortably as Garotte switched off his transmitter. Through a series of difficult and awkward contortions, he managed to fetch a chemical light from a pouch on the suit and activate it. What little space inside the case that was not occupied by a tangle of human anatomy was filled with a green glow. Now that there was light enough to see, Garotte and Silo simultaneously noticed that their faces were inches apart, their noses nearly touching. If the face shield of Garotte's helmet had not been raised and retracted, Silo's face would be squeezed against it. A sudden and failed attempt to give each other more space served only to reveal that there simply wasn't any more space to give. With a sigh, Garotte fought his arm up and wedged the light behind one of the brackets near the top of the case, just above their heads.

"There, that ought to be a bit more pleasant than the helmet lights," he said.

He looked down again to be greeted by a stern expression on Silo's face.

"Something wrong, my dear?"

"Oh, no. This is just dandy. Exactly how I wanted things to turn out. I'm so very happy that you never came up with a plan B. It might have denied us this gosh-darned moment of bliss."

"Silo, dear, you really ought to consider sprinkling a few profanities into your language. You'll find them therapeutic."

"Oh, I'm tempted, mister," she growled. "You realize that this never would have happened if you'd just gotten Claymore out of jail instead of me."

"Locked in an ammo crate with Claymore? No, *thank* you."

"Seriously, Garotte, why get me instead of him? The man plots and plans, that's his whole thing. He's just as good with small weapons, which is pretty much all we've been using. All things being equal, he's a better choice. Why choose me instead?"

"Your sparkling--"

"If you make some dumb quip about my looks or personality, you're coming out of this ammo case with a limp."

". . . speaking voice?"

"Quit ducking the question. Do you have an answer or don't you?"

Garotte looked aside, eyes wandering slightly.

"Well?"

". . . Claymore. Did I ever tell you how he and I started working together?"

"I think you've told me six times, and they were never the same."

"Well, here's a seventh, and it happens to be the truth."

"Oh, well . . . that will be nice."

"There was a splinter state. The name doesn't matter, it only existed for about eight months. A group of Teekers on some planet that was being particularly resistant to terraforming decided that all of the hard work they put into getting their settlement off the ground wasn't worth giving up. This was about . . . probably nine years ago. It was one of my first independent field missions. The problem was that they couldn't clear out the lingering radiation. It was low-level, and the folks who'd been working there all their lives didn't seem to realize that trying to raise a family in a place like that was a pretty good way to have children with too many fingers and not enough kidneys. The TKUR government didn't want what was sure to be a diseased and withering populous on their hands, but the settlement was a fairly successful trading post with a bustling chemical industry and a very stubborn population. Basically, they brought me in to help make sure that things failed and the folks went packing before a generation of genetic freaks was born.

"I got paired up with an Orionian mercenary group that had been hired to do some sabotage. They'd work the infrastructure, I'd work the economy. Nothing deadly, just enough to tip the scales and scare people off. One of the members of the crew came up with some fairly innovative ideas to speed the collapse. All things considered, we ended up getting the job done in a few weeks, rather than the few months we'd assumed. The two of us decided that we complemented each other well, so he spun off from his group and we went into business for ourselves. A year or so passed, and it became clear that we had a gap in our skill set. We needed a demo expert."

"And that was me."

"Yes, indeed. I finagled my way onto one of your missions as a liaison. Watched you for a bit, found what it would take to . . . liberate you."

"You did that . . . on purpose . . ." she rumbled.

"Yes. I manipulated you. It is what I do. I've had an awful lot of training and an awful lot of practice. I'm quite skilled. Then we started working together, and it became clear to me fairly quickly that you didn't belong with the rest of us. You did fine work, a consummate professional, but the rest of us were a bunch of malcontents. Misfits. I was black ops. Claymore went rogue. Karter is a sociopath. We all were heading for a sturdy prison or an early grave from the start. You never would have if not for me. I got you locked up."

Silo began to shake her head and opened her mouth to speak.

"Say what you want about you not having to go along and it being just as much your fault as mine because you gave into temptation, but we both know that I was always the one exposing you to that temptation. That's why it was you I sprung from prison instead of Claymore. Because you were the only one who didn't deserve to be there.

"I'd actually been trying to break myself out for some time. I couldn't stop thinking about you rotting away in that prison. It turns out, while I can pull just about anything off if you give me time to prepare, I'm more or less worthless without my contacts. Then Lex showed up with that furry little computer and I had my chance to get on the outside and get you out. I had to do it. It was my way of trying to make it up to you--or, at least, to say I'm sorry."

"And now we're stuck in an equipment case in a crippled space station surrounded by renegade soldiers," Silo pointed out.

"I've never been very good at apologies," he said with a weak grin.

#

Now half a station away, Lex managed to find the so-called "yo-yo coil." It looked like a metallic bowling ball with a notch cut out around the center that had been filled with coiled wire. It was easily as heavy as the piece of sporting equipment it resembled, and didn't appear to have anything resembling controls or instructions associated.

"Okay, Ma, I've got the . . . thing. How exactly is this supposed to help me?" Lex asked.

"I will explain on the way. Please utilize the highlighted route to access the nearest airlock. *S.O.B.* is waiting outside," the AI answered.

Lex set off, becoming increasingly aware of why he seldom saw people doing any vigorous workouts in sealed space suits. They, by definition, do not breathe. At this point, his clothes had the texture of a damp washcloth, and the chafing was getting bad enough that millions of lives hanging in the balance were just barely enough to distract him from it. The oxygen supply was handy, though.

"As previously established, the most effective way to deal with the CME Activators is low-velocity blunt force to the heat shielding on the tip. The coil can be used to deliver it. It couples with tractor beams. In order to destroy the missiles, you will need to match velocity and use the coil as a flail," Ma explained.

"That doesn't sound too hard," Lex said, finding his way to the small, single-occupant airlock that probably would have led to an escape pod if this station had been run by anyone who was interested enough in health and safety to make sure there was a full complement of them.

"Karter has entered the default route for the CME Activators into a console, and I have transferred it to your nav computer. Your Carpinelli Field generator has been modified to permit near-light velocities. Activate navigational pre-set 113 when you successfully deactivate a missile and your ship will jump to the next," she further explained.

"Right."

"Please try to minimize maneuvering while at near-light speed. There will be extreme stresses on your ship which are greatly in excess of standard specification," Ma said. "And be aware that if you do not succeed in destroying a CME Activator with your first attempt, automated defenses will trigger and fire randomly."

"Wait . . . so I can't move around too much, but things will be shooting at me?"

"Correct. Also, you will have approximately four minutes to disable all six CME Activators."

"Four minutes! You said it would be fifty minutes!"

"The modified Carpinelli Field will not protect you from the effects of time dilation. At 99.5 percent of light speed, time will pass at approximately ten times the speed for you, relative to external phenomena. Forty minutes for us will be four minutes for you."

"Man, I really hate the laws of physics sometimes," Lex muttered as he exited to the station and maneuvered to the waiting *S.O.B.*

"They do complicate matters," Ma conceded. "I have attempted to modify your sensors to function at near-light speeds, but you will likely be required to target manually. Exposing even a few square centimeters of the tip of the warhead will be sufficient to prevent their proper activation. Do only what is necessary."

"Wouldn't have it any other way," Lex said. He climbed into the cockpit of his trusty ship and pressurized. Popping open his suit's helmet, he spat out the now-flavorless and miraculously unswallowed gum from his previous flight and replaced it with three fresh sticks from the stash in the cockpit. He then targeted the tractor beam at the coil and grabbed on, giving a few practice swings to get a feel for it. "Okay . . . let's do it."

He punched the commands into the computer and *S.O.B.* leaped into action. It began like a normal FTL jump. The view out the window flared up through blue and out of visibility, but almost instantly it ticked back down . . . most of the way. The sun was a gradually-approaching, bright blue dot; what little he could see of other stars seemed oddly distorted and on the blue side of the spectrum as well. He would have investigated this in more detail, but some of the other effects of this specific speed were considerably more distracting.

First of all, the inertial inhibitor seemed to be rather unhappy with him. It hadn't outright failed, or else he probably would have been reduced to a vague red tint on the ship's interior that would have been labeled "human remains?" by investigators. It certainly wasn't working correctly, though. There was an odd sort of pressure bearing down on him, like he was walking along the bottom of the ocean in a poorly-designed pressure suit. It was also shoving him fairly forcefully into his seat, and seemed to amplify side-to-side motion. It was disorienting to the extreme, giving the overall feeling that his brain and internal organs were sloshing around when he moved. He genuinely hoped it merely *felt* like that.

His entire control panel was flashing with warnings and errors, and at least six audio alarms were fighting for his attention, but he tuned them out. As far as he was concerned, a starship's warning system was the "boy who cried wolf" of the technology world.

He managed to wrestle his mind back onto the task at hand. Whether it was the way physics worked, or something Ma had done, the only thing in his field of view that seemed to be the right color and undistorted were the CMEAs, though they was exceedingly difficult to make out. The one he was focused on looked to be about a hundred meters ahead, and its flat, gray metal didn't exactly catch the light well. The engine didn't appear to be active at all, beyond the occasional burst and stutter. Lex eased his own engines up a bit and nudged his ship to the side. The maneuver was sluggish, and accompanied by a rumbling creak that gave him very little confidence regarding his ship's structural integrity.

"Tha-a-a-at's not a good noise," he said nervously.

While he did his best to pull up alongside the missile with as few course corrections as possible, his mind, as minds tend to do, ran itself in circles trying to answer questions that were better left ignored. It dredged up facts and lessons from classes that he'd mostly slept through in college and tried to apply them to the current situation. He seemed to remember something about things moving at the speed of light being infinitely massive, and he knew that he was moving at 99.5 percent of the speed of light, so that meant he must weigh . . . 99.5 percent of infinity. While that would admittedly explain the ship's poor handling, it didn't make a whole lot of sense.

Finally, he was lined up with the missile, which, despite claims of autonomy, didn't seem to know he was there. He tapped the controls for the tractor beam, pulling back the coil and then thrusting it forward. His aim was off, the coil glancing off of the missile just behind the black tiles. It wasn't enough to break any of them, but it *was* enough to get the weapon's attention.

Panels along the side popped open and fired vaguely forward, nowhere near Lex. After traveling a short distance forward, though, they suddenly dropped in speed, launching back toward ship and missile alike. In the case of the missile, they splashed weakly against its briefly-activated shield. Lex expected them to do the same to his own shield, until he noticed about an eighth of a second before impact that one of those irritating warning lights was informing him of a complete defensive shield malfunction. He heaved the ship out of the way, prompting a chorus of creaks and one particularly unnerving ping. One shot grazed along the belly of the ship, but when no new warnings joined the argument the others were having, he went back to work.

The ship was lined up for a second swing the instant the guns had retracted back into the device. This time, the coil hit its target, easily cracking the protective tiles and sending them tumbling off in two neat halves to reveal a smooth, pointed metallic nose that wouldn't last two seconds once it got up close and personal to the star. By the time the guns had reappeared, Lex had tapped the command to leap to the next missile.

"That wasn't so bad, and it only took . . ." Lex began, glancing at the clock. "*Two minutes!?* Oh, man. Gotta pick up the pace."

The world faded back in again, the star a much larger ball of blue light. He completely ignored the creaking complaints of his ship now, trusting it to hold together, and muscled himself over to the missile. A hastily-aimed attack went wide, but he managed to drag the coil back across the tip of the missile on its return, grinding away a tile.

"Good enough," he said, tapping for the next missile.

The third missile came and went with the same speed, as did the fourth. With each jump forward to catch up to the next, the star became brighter, the engine rattled a bit more, and the ship's complaints grew more urgent. He was gaining time, though. With forty-five seconds left, he had only two missiles to go. It was beginning to look as though he just might manage this crazy mission.

Naturally, the universe heard his hopeful thoughts, and saw fit to throw a wrench at him.

Perhaps it wasn't quite built to code; perhaps the fuel mix hadn't been quite right. Whatever the reason, when he fell back out of FTL for his fifth missile attack, the CMEA wasn't quite where the flight plan had predicted. His speed was still ticking down when it came streaking into sight. He pulled the ship hard and tried to cut speed even more, but it was too little too late. With a long, grinding slide, he struck the missile.

There must have been something to that infinite mass nonsense, because when the weapon and the ship collided, it didn't feel like the jarring but ultimately inconsequential sort of clash he would expect from a ship hitting something the size of the missile. The blow rocked *S.O.B.* as though he'd slammed into a mountain.

For a few seconds, *S.O.B.* was completely out of control, as was the missile. Fortunately, regardless of how out-of-control they both got, moving at such high speeds without any real countermeasures meant they inevitably ended up moving roughly in the same direction. That was inertia for you. In this case, the result was his ship doing an about-face and sliding along at 0.995c backward, which treated him to a lovely, red-shifted version of the cosmos to complement the blue-shift ahead. He finessed the controls into facing the right way again without flying apart in the process, and was greeted by a flurry of weapon discharges from the hostile little rocket.

Trying to get *S.O.B.* to avoid the blasts at this speed was like trying to get an elephant to dodge raindrops, but he managed to keep the damage to a minimum. He glanced at the clock again and tried to do the math to see how much time he had remaining, but it quickly became clear that he didn't have enough spare brain cells to be doing something complicated like subtraction, so he settled on the answer "not enough." With a desperate heave of the coil, he managed to nail the nose of the missile, which was impressive, because he was fairly sure it was out of range of the tractor beam. A moment later he realized why he'd managed to reach it--the tractor beam emitter itself drifted along beside him, apparently having been torn free in the process.

He had no weapon, one missile, and *maybe* ten seconds left. It would have been nice to say he didn't know what he was going to do, but the fact of the matter was that he knew exactly what he was going to have to do. One last tap of the navigation computer brought him to the final missile. It was beginning to slow up for its swan dive into the star, but Karter's flight plan had taken that into account. The star itself was steadily creeping back toward its proper yellow color, and filling far too much of his view screen with blinding light--but in the brilliant field of light was a single black form, and Lex powered his ship toward it.

The side panels were disengaging now, drifting alongside the weapon as it continued its path. The center split off and spun away, but he dodged it and followed the warhead. He was directly above it now. Once he knew he had enough of a lead, he drove the ship downward, bashing the activating weapon with his unshielded ship.

The collision was no less severe than the last one had been, and the malfunctioning inertial inhibitor only seemed to make it worse. His teeth rattled in his head, the ship pitched and rolled, and the constant blaring warnings all suddenly vanished into silence as the power in the cockpit dropped away. His ship went into a roll, twisting his cockpit toward the weapon he'd just intentionally struck. It was in pieces, shattered by the hit. That was it. All six missiles destroyed. Now all he had was the comparatively minor problem of being strapped in the cockpit of a ship that had no power to its controls and was moving at nearly light speed into a giant ball of nuclear fire.

The lights and sounds of the cockpit were slowly reactivating in a garbled and scrambled state, but there wasn't a flicker of life in his control harness. No amount of fighting with the yoke would prompt even a nudge of motion from the spiraling ship. He glanced out of the cockpit to see that the star was . . . well, all there *was* to see. It was blinding, even with the cockpit safeguards. Out of reflex, he reached up to increase the tint, and raised his eyebrows when it actually worked.

"Okay, fine. Good. The tint works. So it isn't the entire control system that's down, just *these* controls," he said quickly. After a quick attempt to access the autopilot, he amended his statement. "And the navigational computer. So I either blew a fuse or a wire came loose. Here's hoping it's a wire, because I don't have time to replace a fuse."

The sun had already raised the interior temperature of the ship to broiling, and sweat was pouring down his face as he looked madly over the various hatches and panels that had been jarred loose by the flight. Finally, he spotted a thick bundle of wires with a snapped connector that was dangling free. He pressed it into the matching socket and the controls came to life again.

"Yes!" he proclaimed, putting his hands on the yoke. The moment he did, though, the wires fell loose again. "No!"

He reinserted the wires and attempted to steer the ship with one hand, but it soon became clear that it would probably take three hands to do the psychotic level of aerospace acrobatics necessary to keep from going out in a blaze of glory.

"Gotta find a way to keep it in! But I don't . . . *gum*!" he blurted as his brain rushed out a solution.

He spat the wad of gum from his mouth, shoved the wires into the socket, and stuck the gum over the damaged clip. They held firm as he grabbed the controls and wrestled with the damaged ship, tweaking and nudging until he stabilized its tumbling roll and orienting it away from the sun. With the proper heading set, he maxed out the engine's power and gritted his teeth as he watched his velocity tick down.

"Come on. Come *on!*" he begged *S.O.B.* as it fought the pull of the star.

The stresses on the ship--now thanks to good old momentum, heat, and gravity rather than some bogus relativistic equations--rattled and popped beams and struts, and his engine was doing the starship equivalent of a wheezing final breath when the balance finally tipped and he started to move away from the star. A few seconds later, his engine shut down completely due to overheating, but by then he had enough speed to coast away from the star, at least for a while. For now, he simply took a deep breath and tried to get his blood pressure down below 300/250.

With a crackle, his radio clicked on.

"Lex, my boy," squawked Garotte's voice across a radio connection that was nearly as warped and distorted by the sun as Lex's ship. "Since the time limit has come and gone and there are no significant fireworks, am I correct in assuming you succeeded in damaging the missiles?"

"Yeah, just barely. And *S.O.B.* has seen better days," he replied.

"Need a lift?"

"Yeah, but aren't you trapped in an equipment locker?"

"That was an hour ago, my boy. The computer managed to get us out a few minutes after you left. We got *The Declaration* on its feet, then I headed out to meet you while Silo cleared out and locked up the riffraff. We also managed to patch up Karter, who seemed only vaguely aware that he was minutes from bleeding to death."

"But--wait, it was . . . oh, right. The time thing. Well, I'm flattered that you were confident enough in my abilities that you were willing to hang out this close to the star."

"Don't be *too* flattered. I only came down here once Ma assured me that in the event of mishap, I'd be able to outrun the ejection. Even so, waiting to see if you'd succeeded was the longest hour of my life."

"It was the longest couple minutes of my life, too. Literally, I guess. Well, wherever you are, come and give me a tow. I think I've done enough flying for today."

Epilogue

Once Ma and the others had gotten the more fatal damage to the space station sorted out, it took just over ten days to get it back to Big Sigma. Their original intention had been to find a way to transfer Ma out of the system and load themselves into *S.O.B.* and *The Declaration*, but Karter had been rather insistent that he be allowed to keep the station as payment for his "inconvenience." A thorough search had turned up three intact escape pods, and the surviving Neo-Luddites had been loaded into them until they and their departed brethren could be dropped off on a planet where the local law enforcement could find them. They had also snagged the still drifting--and still homicidal--Zerk and deactivated it. It was wisely decided to find some way to return Zerk to military storage as soon as possible, since all were in agreement that something like that really ought to be kept out of the wrong hands, and hands didn't get much more wrong than Karter's.

When they reached Karter's base, the EMP devices were deactivated by the codes in the station computers and there was a brief conversation between Ma and herself; they greeted each other as "Primary Instance" and "Subset 1.2" respectively. Once the AI pulled herself together, she sent a shuttle up through the cloud of debris and ferried them each to the surface.

In the facility, each member of the group saw to their own pressing needs. Silo took the opportunity to use "an honest to goodness shower for the first time in three years." Karter locked himself in one of his workshops with a case of beer and a box of a semi-legal snack food called Vice Stix. Garotte disappeared into one of the computer labs, and Lex convinced Ma to autopilot *S.O.B.* down from the orbiting space station to get some proper repairs.

Once all had seen to their various priorities, Ma summoned them to one of the cafeterias in the facility. Lex was the first to arrive.

"Yeah? Well, that's great!" Lex said into the slidepad held to his ear. "Have you ever done an interview that high up the chain of command before? I didn't think so . . . yes, I'm fine, I told you . . . Mitch, I'm sure . . . no, I didn't forget. I'm going to discuss it with him again right now, but don't expect a different answer--and it'll be voice-only, if anything, because of the moat thing . . . I told you, it's a bunch of junk in orbit. Screws with connections, otherwise I'd be staring at your pretty face on my slidepad right now . . . yeah . . . I will. See you in four days . . . love you, too, babe. Bye."

"How have these events affected Ms Modane's career?" asked Ma's voice.

"Disaster, crime, intrigue, they're all good for business when you're an investigative reporter," he said, poking at the device. "Between the work she'd already done, the stuff she learned from us, and the chaos we managed to cause in the Neo-Luddite organization, she blew the lid off of them. There's already award talk for her. She's got interviews lined up with admirals and field marshals, and the remnants of the Neo-Luddites are scattering like roaches when the lights are turned on. Evidently, Jon the intern is up for a distinguished journalism award, too, just for holding the camera. She convinced her editor to put him on the official payroll at a 'very competitive salary.'

"She wants me to do a big follow-up story with her next week, and she thinks we might be able to squeeze a press tour out of the last wavering moments of my fifteen minutes of heroism, so we ought to be able to hang out without someone detonating antimatter in the atmosphere. That should be nice, for a change."

"I am pleased to hear it," Ma replied.

"And I've got a big pile of messages I've been ignoring--it looks like my courier boss has been calling every four days to see if I'm back. Like usual. My chauffeur dispatcher seems to have forgotten I went on sabbatical, so I've had eleven missed pickups, nine angry messages, two notices of termination, and then another three missed pickups. That man seriously needs an assistant to at least remind him of who he fired and who he didn't. I also seem to have a message from Preethy Misra, the personal assistant of my mobster landlord. I'm sure *that's* good news . . ."

"Your performance of the tasks of the last few weeks suggests that there are few challenges beyond your capability. I am confident any difficulties awaiting you will be easily dispatched."

"Thanks for the vote of confidence, Ma," Lex said.

He took a seat at one of the plain, institutional-style tables of the cafeteria. The room would have been familiar to anyone who had spent any time in a dorm, factory, or other facility that required a bureaucracy to provide meals. For the uninitiated, that meant neutral colors, cheap and sturdy furniture, plastic serving trays and utensils, metal steam trays, and various other examples of a bare-bones, maximum-efficiency dining experience.

"I see that this place is still as sterile as ever," Garotte proclaimed as he entered the cafeteria. "Hardly much different than the prison."

"Speak for yourself, buster. Maybe this is what that country club you call a prison was like, but this is worlds better than what I've been dealing with for the last few years," Silo countered, entering behind him. "Par-*tic*-

ularly those showers. I could live in there."

While Garotte was dressed in the crisp white shirt and black pants that he evidently treated as a uniform, Silo had taken advantage of the calmer circumstances to change into something a bit more casual, a pair of snug jeans and a tank top. Though it may not have been the intention of the outfit, it certainly did an excellent job of showing off her curves.

"What have you two been up to?" Lex asked.

"After fighting with the network connection enough to patch into the appropriate servers, I managed to tweak our entries in the facial recognition databases for most of the big security repositories. Silo and I won't have to worry about getting recognized anymore. Not digitally, anyway," Garotte explained, taking a seat at the table.

"I've just been walking the halls. It's been more than three years since I've been able to walk more than a few meters without having to worry about leg restraints, police officers, corrections officials, or armed guards giving me trouble," Silo added, sitting beside Garotte. "It is a shame it is so cold outside, or I'd go for a jog."

"Where are you guys going from here?" Lex asked. "Now that the mission is over?"

"Honestly, Lex, I don't know what I'm going to do after the mission," she said with weary frustration. "For better or for worse, though, this mission isn't quite over."

"Oh, no?" Lex remarked.

"Ma didn't tell you?" Garotte asked.

"The information you are referring to is not relevant to Mr. Alexander's interests," Ma stated quickly.

"I dare say that should be his decision, not yours," Garotte countered.

"Look, we were supposed to go get Karter and bring him back, and we did. *And* we stopped the CMEAs from being used."

"We delayed them. Evidently, the designs were sent to a third party shortly before our arrival. There's not enough info to tell us who, exactly, but someone out there could try again."

"So even after all of that, there's no way of knowing that this won't happen after all . . ."

"The chances are pretty slim. That alloy is tricky stuff to make. The supply on the space station represented by a *large* margin the greatest single source in the galaxy. Your girlfriend's coverage and the Weston University disaster have made it a controlled substance overnight. They keep track of it by the gram now," Silo explained.

"That said, it was blind spots and security gaps in the military that allowed the Neo-Luddites to grow and thrive to begin with," Garotte chimed in. "Silo and I both would feel a bit better with ourselves on the job."

"Why didn't you tell *me,* Ma?" Lex asked, looking around for something to glare at. Even with ten days of doing so, Lex was having a hard time getting used to Ma no longer having a face, albeit a furry one.

"I prefer not to elaborate at this time," she replied.

"What are you people still doing here?" demanded a gruff voice from the door.

Karter, dressed in a fresh jumpsuit and bearing his realistic and fully-functional prostheses for the first time since Purcell had seen fit to slice his hand off, came pounding into the room and headed for the food counter.

"Karter, please remember to treat your guests with hospitality," Ma reminded. "An ounce of gratitude would not be out of place."

"Since when do you call me Karter?" asked the scientist.

"Since I spearheaded a rescue mission that succeeded despite extremely unfavorable statistical predictions," she stated simply. "That's when."

He paused, seemingly to consider this, then shrugged it off and pulled the lid off of one of the trays. With a deep breath, a look of pure bliss came to his face.

"It has been *too long*," he proclaimed, pulling the entire steam tray from the counter and dropping it down on one of the tables. The tray was full of red beans and rice, and Karter began shoveling it into his mouth with the serving spoon. "You wouldn't believe the crap they were feeding me."

"Actually, I meant to say this earlier, but it looks like you dropped a ton of weight in the last few weeks," Lex said.

"That's what happens when you eat nothing but military rations. Plus I used my implants a whole lot. Those things burn some serious calories."

"Maybe you should consider sticking to that diet," Garotte suggested. "Military nutrition looks to have been doing you a world of good."

"No," he said, continuing to maul the contents of the tray.

"Karter, listen, I was talking to Michella. She really wants to interview you."

"No."

"But we couldn't have rescued you without the help of her research,"

"No."

"She only wants to ask you a few--"

"No."

"She is extremely attractive," Ma added.

". . . maybe," Karter said. "Anyway, down to business. First off, Ma, no more deals with terrorists. They lead to some intriguing projects, but weapons of mass destruction kick up a big ruckus and make it difficult to make sure I get left alone. Plus, they're unreliable. They never coughed up the money for the job."

"Karter, you really ought to be congratulated. You have elevated doing the right thing for the wrong reason to an art form," Garotte said, with a slow clap.

Karter waved off the comment. "Fortunately, I ended up with a transporter and a space station out of the deal, so we'll call it even. Also, field data on, like, a dozen different gadgets. Good stuff. Now, you three. Lex, *S.O.B.* is finished with repairs, and I went ahead and stuck in a new fuel converter, which should give you a shorter start time from a cold engine. Test it out. I'll send you the appropriate feedback forms later. Ma, show him the door."

"I must once again suggest that you treat your guests with a degree of gratitude appropriate for their role in your liberation," Ma gently reprimanded.

"I gave him a new fuel converter. I think that is pretty gracious."

"Don't worry about it, Ma. I really ought to get going before my dispatcher fires me a third time," Lex said, standing to leave.

"Good. Now. James Bond and Big Gun Lady, what do you two want in exchange for your role in this?" Karter asked.

"Please delay your departure momentarily," Ma stated.

Five mechanical grippers emerged from the kitchen, each holding a tray. The first four contained one beverage each; the last had an empty glass.

"Miss Silo, a green apple martini. Mr. Garotte, a gin and tonic on the rocks with a wedge of lime. Mr. Alexander, rum and Coke. Mr. Dee, unfiltered pale hefeweizen," Ma stated, presenting each with their beverage and withdrawing the appropriate arm. The arm with the empty glass placed the tray on the table and lifted the glass from it. "In situations such as this, a toast is appropriate. Would anyone like to do the honors?"

"To getting the job done," Garotte said, raising his glass.

"To answering the call of duty," Silo added.

"Uh . . . to making it out of this with our skin," Lex stumbled.

Eyes turned to Karter, who was the only one who had yet to raise a glass. He rolled his eyes, and lifted it. "To getting this over with before my beer gets warm."

"To new allies and old," Ma said, "may they always collaborate with efficiency and expediency in order to facilitate the timely completion of tasks essential to social stability."

"Hear, hear!" Garotte said with a smirk.

Glasses were clinked, drinks were consumed.

"Well, you two. It was nice meeting you, although I hope you'll understand if I say I hope we never have to meet again--at least under these circumstances," Lex said.

"I wouldn't count on it," Garotte said with a shake. "You've got the exact mix of piloting skill and disregard for personal safety that we look for in our line of work."

"You're a real good guy, Lex," Silo said, shaking Lex's hand with an uncomfortable amount of force. "Take my advice: run for the hills."

"Don't forget to give that fuel converter a workout. I want to know how it holds up," Karter said.

"Please follow the blue lights to your ship," Ma stated.

Lex stood and headed out the door, following the pulsing blue lights along the wall of the institutional, florescent-lit hallway. After a few twists and turns, he came to the end of the line of lights.

"Uh, Ma?"

"Stand by. I have two final points to address. First, please accept this," Ma's voice stated.

A door opened and another mechanical arm rolled out, holding a brushed metal attaché case.

"Oh, man. *That* brings back some unpleasant memories," he said, accepting the case that had, in a roundabout way, led him to Karter eight months ago. "It looks like you fixed it."

"Correct. Open it," she requested.

He clicked it open. What was inside warranted a few moments of awe. There were neat, bundled rolls of casino chips. Many of them. In very high denominations.

"There must be . . ."

"Eight hundred five thousand six hundred forty-three credits," she dictated.

"That's an unusually specific number."

"I thought it would have been difficult to assign a cash value to your role in this mission, but I was incorrect. I began with the three-quarters of one million credits that you were to have been given upon the completion of the delivery that brought you to us, and added to it the average number of deliveries and chauffeur jobs you have per day, multiplied by the number of days you were kept away from them."

"I don't think your math works out."

"I'm a generous tipper."

"Ma, I've still got a mess of cash left from what you gave me to buy the stuff when we were just starting. You didn't have to do this."

"No, I didn't. I wanted to. And there is one more thing."

There was the sound of yet another trundling mechanical gripper moving down an adjoining hallway, but accompanying it was the tap of tiny claws. From around the corner came the arm, and in its grip was a leash leading to the harness of a small, well-behaved, and extremely familiar creature.

"Is that . . . ?"

"Squee. More specifically, the precise Squee that served as my temporary platform. After keeping her alive intravenously for the return trip, and following the neural trauma I regretfully caused, I was uncertain if she would be able to recover, but physically she has been given a clean bill of health. The interface node on her neck has been terminated in a sealable jack, rather than the improvised wire you crafted, and I have utilized it to attempt to restore her mind to its previous state. I'm afraid my brief stay has made that impossible. She is largely restored, but she will never be precisely normal from the standpoint of a baseline funk."

"A baseline funk is pretty nonstandard to begin with."

"Indeed."

"So, what did you think of being organic?"

"It provided me with considerable insight into the nature of biochemical beings. The experiences it provided me with are exceedingly valuable, and I am pleased that I was able to retain them. It will aid me immeasurably in adapting my behaviors. I may even pursue further experimentation with organic platforms. But not any time soon."

"Heh."

"When I was calculating your payment for your involvement, I realized that, though the reward would no doubt be appreciated, it did not properly articulate the degree to which I valued your help and compassion during this endeavor. To that end . . ."

The gripper thrust the leash toward him.

"You want me to have her?"

"It seemed inappropriate to return her to stasis. She should be with someone who can provide her with the affection and intellectual stimulation she deserves."

Squee leaped from the floor to his shoulder, claiming the perch as though she belonged there.

"Ma, I don't know if I can--"

"You are familiar with the care and feeding already. She will also require one pill every four to six months from the supply I have included in your ship's equipment to supplement her diet and prevent her natural odor from returning."

"But I'm not sure--"

"Please do not overlook the emotional significance of this gesture."

Lex sighed. "Thanks, Ma. I'll take good care of her."

"I am sure that you will. Thank you, Mr. Alexander. Now, please follow the blue lights to your ship."

"Oh, so why exactly did you not tell me that those two were going to stay on the job?" Lex asked as he continued on his way.

"For the purposes of stress-reduction, that information was withheld. I did not want you to feel obligated to join them. You have a life outside of dangerous endeavors such as this."

"Trust me. Now that Karter is back under wraps, I'm confident those two can handle it. This soldier of fortune stuff isn't for me."

"Despite your apparent propensity for it."

"Yeah, despite that."

A few minutes later, Lex had said goodbye to Ma and followed her flight plan through the moat and into orbit. Rather than being the vibrating ball of energy Lex had come to expect funks to be, and thus turning the unsteady trip through the debris field into a tornado of panicked leaps, Squee sat calmly across his shoulders the whole time. It was as though she'd been through space flight before. Which, he realized, she had. When he was outside the confounding effect of the clouds of orbiting metal, he pulled out his slidepad and pulled up the contact for his landlord. Best to get this sort of thing out of the way quickly.

After a few moments of negotiating a connection, a face popped up.

"You have reached the office of Nicholas Patel, Preethy Misra speaking," said the attractive young Indian woman who answered, in her usual crisp and professional tone.

"Hi, Ms Misra. I just had a quick question about my lease. Am I allowed to have pets?"

"Mr. Alexander, so lovely to hear from you," she said brightly. "Mr. Patel is in a meeting right now, but I will be sure to have him call you when he is available. He has been attempting contact you. We have an opportunity which might interest you."

"I appreciate that, Ms Misra, but, really, I just needed to know about the apartment policy."

"It is regarding a possibly re-entry into hoversled racing."

Lex paused. His mind quickly laid out a lengthy and well-supported list of very good reasons why he should hang up immediately. They centered around his girlfriend's extreme intolerance for organized crime, which just happened to be Nick Patel's line of work, and continued to the various social and economic responsibilities he had spent far too much time neglecting, and concluded on the near-certainty that, whatever the offer was, it would lead him into a pile of trouble. Common sense stated he should politely decline and quit while he was ahead.

". . . I'm listening . . ."

One of these days, he was really going to have to start listening to common sense . . .

###

From The Author

Thank you for reading. This is the follow-up to *Bypass Gemini,* my first science fiction novel. The two books comprise the beginning of my first attempt at an open-ended series. The response to the first novel has been great, and I look forward to producing future entries whenever I'm not busy crafting new tales in my fantasy series, *The Book of Deacon*. If you like my writing, please take a moment to sample some of my other works. Below, you will find a link to my book site, where you will find links to other books that I've written. If you have anything to say, good or bad, I would love to hear it, in the form of a review, or, if you prefer, an email.

Discover other titles by Joseph R. Lallo:

The Book of Deacon Series:

Book 1: *The Book of Deacon*
Book 2: *The Great Convergence*
Book 3: *The Battle of Verril*
Book 4: *The D'Karon Apprentice*

Other stories in the same setting:

Jade
The Rise of the Red Shadow

The Big Sigma Series:

Book 1: *Bypass Gemini*
Book 2: *Unstable Prototypes*
Book 3: *Artificial Evolution*

NaNoWriMo Projects:

The Other Eight
Free-Wrench

Connect with Joseph R. Lallo

Website: www.bookofdeacon.com
Twitter: @jrlallo
Tumblr: jrlallo.tumblr.com

Printed in Great Britain
by Amazon

11048681R00220